MY FRIENDS

Call Me Moon

James Morrow Walton

1

Friday, June 6, 1958, Jack typed his "30" and called for a copy person; his explosive article was on its way, five minutes to spare before deadline. The by-line would read, Jack E. Ward, *Senior Investigative Reporter,* New Orleans *States Item.* The article was the headline story for tonight's Saturday Early Edition, to be on the streets by ten p.m. hawked by street vendors calling, "Read all about it!" By early morning, radio and TV would have it, much obliged to Jack. This final segment was the last of three investigating the largest case of misappropriation of funds to occur within one of the most powerful governmental agencies in the city.

The first of the two preceding segments had told of the many sources of income that brought money into the agency coffers. The second reported expenditures, some quite unusual. This final segment revealed the names of recipients of the ill-gained funds, names of people arrested earlier in the day and charged. Jack could never reveal his sources; he did not know them by name, only that the information was factual. He had verified it.

Three other explosive articles in the past year had won awards. Along with the awards had come ire, then threats of vindication. However, the personal impact made on Jack by a horrible police brutality incident had hurt more than the threats. Etched in his mind was a scene so awful that it was unimaginable that persons could inflict such horror on others. Until then, he'd thought he had seen it all. Friends, and especially Adrianna, had seen a noticeable change come over him. It was Adrianna, the love of his life, who always came to mind when the threats came. Was his work also placing her in harm's way? There was no way he could have known that in one week he would tearfully compose one of his final articles as a reporter. Adrianna had definitely been in harm's way.

Jack had first met Adrianna on the tennis courts at Audubon Park. Adrianna and her tennis partner had appeared at the court at the same time Jack and his partner arrived for their regular Saturday time. They had consulted postings to the court bulletin board and had seen that both couples had the same court at the same time. Adrianna had suggested they play doubles.

Jack introduced himself, and Adrianna's ears perked.

"Staff writer for the *SI?*" she asked. Jack bowed. "Adrianna Breaux, Society desk, *News.*" She curtsied. The *News* was the competitor newspaper in town.

They had been a couple ever since. Each had lived in a small apartment in the Garden District, but within months, they moved into an apartment together. It was half a block off St. Charles Avenue, only a few blocks from the park. Nearby were small shops, several bars, and a cute neighborhood restaurant.

A year later, Adrianna was hired by the maven of all New Orleans society, Penny Pebworth, Society Editor for the *States Item.* The job came with the promise that Mrs. Pebworth would mentor Adrianna to be her successor. Eighteen months later, to the day, the promise became fact. During the course of an intimate candlelight dinner at the Gulf Coast home of a nationally known women's advice columnist, Mrs. Pebworth made the announcement. What a way to tell the world.

Jack's day was done; he was anxious to leave the building. Quickly clearing his desk, he plopped on his well-worn felt fedora, a gift from his father, with a "PRESS" card in the band reading, "Property of the *Chicago Tribune.*" At that moment, a young woman tapped on the glass partition separating his cubicle from the hallway. She passed a brown envelope through, and Jack flung it into his IN tray to rest until Monday. But on second glance, he saw a note on the envelope that read, "FROM THE DESK OF: *A. Breaux.*"

He spilled the envelope; a clip held the top sheet to several other pages. There were instructions from Adrianna, plus the comment, "see Jan's notes, there is a story here." She signed with a heart circling her initials. Next was a galley proof of an article, a wedding announcement, to appear in the Sunday Society Section. The headline included the name of a person Jack knew from his youth: Will MacMorogh. Adrianna had underscored several items in red.

The following page held additional notes from articles in the paper's archives; the dates were from twenty-three years prior. Those reported that two persons killed in a plane crash on a mountain in Alabama were the brother and sister-in law of a prominent New Orleans pediatrician, Dr. Beatrice MacMorogh.

Then there was another note, "FROM THE DESK OF: *Jan Plow 6-6-58.*" She had scribbled notes stemming from a conversation with a reporter at the *Birmingham Daily News.* According to that reporter, Mr. Woodall, the weather on July 8, 1936, was clear, and the pilots were high time ex-military. The aircraft was a well-maintained Lockheed owned by a Texas meat packer. Wreckage covered a large area; an eyewitness had seen a flash and then heard a boom. Jan also reported that Mr. Woodall knew of Reverend John Pope; he was a charismatic colored preacher with a large congregation.

Jack stuffed the articles into his already bulging briefcase, trotted to the corner of Canal and St. Charles, and boarded the St. Charles Avenue streetcar. He alighted at the stop nearest his and Adrianna's apartment and crossed the street to the K&B to refresh his supply of gin, vermouth, and olives. According to Adrianna, Friday night was their "night to howl at the moon." Customarily, they had martinis at home, then walked to Justin's, a small neighborhood bar/restaurant with only eight tables. The food was outstanding, the crowd familiar.

Before Adrianna was due home, he stirred martinis and put a platter of cheese and crackers on the coffee table. She arrived, dashed in, and took a sip of her martini before going to change. Dressed in a long cotton skirt and a colorful tee, she slid to the floor alongside Jack, to sift through the accumulated material.

"What do you think?" Adrianna held the galley sheet. "Interesting layout?"

"My first thought: who prepared this?" answered Jack.

Before the words left his mouth, Adrianna replied. "The subject planned and wrote it herself. She is a broadcast reporter for the BBC. The placement idea is mine."

Jack smiled, "You sure that is not a mistake?"

"Not on your life," Adrianna said and pointed to the underlined name of Dr. MacMorogh. "She is a wonderful philanthropist. If you want to draw a crowd to a fundraiser and raise beaucoup bucks, mention her name as guest speaker. The name will pique a lot of interest. I think the article and placement are both epic."

The town in Mississippi, Leeville, which also had a red line, was twenty miles north of where Jack had spent time as a boy, and Will MacMorogh was a boyhood acquaintance.

"You remember me telling you about announcing an entire football game all by myself when I was in high school?" Then he started, *"There's only two minutes on the clock, the score is 28 to 21 and…it looks like Leeville is going to win this…,"* all in the fast-paced, nasal tone of a radio announcer.

Adrianna threw up her hands. "No, no, I have heard it, no more!" Jack acted miffed and dipped his head. She called his attention back to the article and insisted, "There is a *story* in waiting. For instance, take the plane crash; that is why we have guardians named. Will's parents died in that crash. There is no end to what may show up with a little more research." She continued, "The preacher is from an A.M.E. church. Does that indicate it might be a colored church? Moreover, the Louisiana State Attorney General attended. It seems strange the Mrs. resides in London, the Mr. resides on the North Shore, plus," pointing at another underlined item, "looks like this is seven years overdue." Jack agreed. He had the scent; the story had its beginning.

With fresh drinks in go cups and the afterglow of the first martini, the two strolled arm in arm to their favorite Friday night spot, owned by the unflappable Justin. As they turned the corner, there was the sound of a revving engine, and a car raced toward them. Just before hitting the curb, it collided with a garbage can, sending it flying like a missile. Jack pushed Adrianna to the ground as the can passed overhead and into a nearby house. The car screamed away. Several people in the restaurant came out at the sound of the racket, one saying, "Damn fools."

Jack had honed his craft on intuition and it seldom failed. He had a bad feeling.

On Saturday, they did laundry, cleaned house, and ran errands. The housework fell to Jack. His mother had died when he was three, and in a house without a mother, he had learned early on to share chores. He did laundry and dishes and took out trash, while his father took care of the rest, including meals. On weekends, his father attempted cooking; the food was tasty and filling, but not gourmet.

In contrast, Adrianna had grown up in White Castle, Louisiana, the only daughter in a family with five boys. Theirs was a rich Cajun heritage including a penchant for great food. By the time she could stand in a chair and stir a pot, she helped in the kitchen.

Her father was a game warden, her mother a schoolteacher. Raising six children on modest incomes was a chore. The family lived on a small plot outside the city limits and raised chickens, guineas, milk goats, and a cow. Adrianna sold milk, eggs, and butter, and the boys grew a variety of fresh vegetables. Father and boys hunted, fished, and trapped, always bringing home plenty of game.

While Jack got the house in order, Adrianna indulged in her weekend treat, shopping at *Schwegmann's*. She liked strolling aisle-by-aisle, department-by-department, working off a list that always included ingredients for a sumptuous dinner.

If a local team did not have a home game, Jack listened to the radio or watched TV. Regardless, he took notes. After the game, he would write a column to voice his opinion on a variety of things: teams as a whole, coaches, changes in league rules, or whatever else struck his fancy. There was a box in his closet full of these columns.

Tulane was playing at home, so it was baseball, beer, dogs, and cigars. As soon as his chores were complete, he left for the stadium. Adrianna urged him to quit smoking, but he was sure to come home with the smell of tobacco and beer.

Adrianna spent her afternoon patiently stirring a roux, chopping vegetables, and peeling shrimp. The shells she saved to boil with vegetable trimmings for her stock. She packed ice around oysters in the bucket of an old ice cream freezer. A couple dozen would be appetizers. Rich gumbo with shrimp, crab, and oysters would be the entrée. Brownies with a good port would be dessert.

Tulane won, and Jack came home elated and starved. While he showered to rid himself of the cigar smell, Adrianna stirred a sauce with a selection of condiments and shucked the oysters. From the freezer came two frosted glasses, into which Jack poured Dixie 45s. Over the next hour or so, he and Adrianna slowly dined on the oysters and the rich gumbo. Later, outside on the back patio, they enjoyed brownies, the port, and coffee with chicory while they ruminated over how Jack might get an interview with Will MacMorogh.

Sunday had its own routine. Jack woke for his usual 5:30 a.m. nature call, then slipped quietly out to see if the papers had arrived, only to discover that there were none and it was raining. He crawled back into bed and spooned up to Adrianna; she had shed her gown. Jack slept only in pajama bottoms. Adrianna helped pull those down and disentangled them from his big feet. They made love, then snoozed a while longer.

Later, hearing a thump on the front stoop, Adrianna dashed to the door, pulling on her robe as she went. Jack started coffee. Adrianna placed the paper on the coffee table and stood back, admiring the front page of her Society Section. "Unorthodox, but an attention getter. Everyone should be pleased."

The phone rang as she spoke, and as soon as the receiver left the cradle, Jack could hear Mrs. Pebworth on the other end. "Adrianna, you did it; I did not believe you when you told me. It is marvelous."

Jan Plow, a staff writer in Adrianna's department, called next. She apologized for the Sunday call and explained why she was in the office. The MacMorogh article continued to pique her curiosity, so much so that she was in the office on her own time. Digging back through the archives, she had found more. There was an account of William MacMorogh III being MIA during the Korean War. Another piece confirmed his escape; yet another reported him in a US Navy hospital in San Diego. Most recently, there was an account of his buying a dredge ship to use at the Port of Gulfport, Mississippi.

Jack and Adrianna pored over the papers for another hour until Jack stood, rubbing his belly. Adrianna looked up. "Me too, let's go."

Due to the rain, they drove. The Camellia Grill was packed. After a short wait, they sat at the counter, joining some of the regulars. Jack spotted a well-known face across the way, Captain Joe McNamara of the New Orleans Police Department. He was the "go to man" if one needed something handled. That included private citizens and cops. For some, it might be nothing more than a speeding ticket, for others problems much more serious. Capt. Joe had been around for years. He had worked under a number of chiefs, several mayors, police commissioners, and other city officials. They were well aware that that he knew where the skeletons were, literally. Jack had befriended him during his earliest months on the paper.

Capt. Joe and his companion, whom Jack did not recognize, finished their meal first. Jack followed with his eyes as they departed. At the door, Capt. Joe turned, pointed a finger toward him, and then held his hand to an ear, like a phone. Jack got the message.

After completing their meal, however, Jack and Adrianna found the captain still at the curb talking. Spotting Jack, he called out, "Wait Up." He strolled over and shook hands, and Jack introduced Adrianna. They exchanged pleasantries before the captain politely asked Adrianna if she would mind if he had a word with Jack.

"Surely not," she smiled and stepped out of earshot.

The captain placed a hand on Jack's shoulder. "Jack, I've known you several years now, always admired your work. You and I've not always agreed, but you've always been fair. I am glad I've this opportunity to clue you in on something. There is a rumor that you and the paper may be in danger. I can't consider it only a rumor. Surely, you must know you frequently step on toes. I'm not sure you always know how many. Tomorrow, I'm going to advise the paper to tuck you away for a few days, let us get to the bottom of this. I'm reasonably sure where the threat is coming from. We can handle it in a day or two. Believe me."

Jack said, "I appreciate your concern, but you know better than anybody that this is not my first threat."

"I know, and I've known about others in the past, and they were of little concern. Jack, listen to me," and the captain paused a moment. "This one is real."

Jack drove home in silence, thinking about the previous night's incident. Adrianna was always curious when Jack got quiet but knew he would come around to talking to her in time. Back at the apartment, Jack sat on the sofa going over the papers. He read a few minutes, Adrianna puttered in the kitchen. She could tell by his countenance that even though the paper was in front of him, he was not reading. He was in deep thought.

She sat on the edge of the sofa and took the paper from him, folded it, and put it on the coffee table. "Jack, what's wrong? I am not talking about what the police captain said to you. You have been different for at least a month. Can you tell me?"

He sighed deeply, pulled her to him, and settled back into the cushions. The story he told was not about the captain's message or the threats. It was about the police brutality he had witnessed. Jack had been first on the scene of a gruesome discovery. The torture of two individuals was horrendous; it was inconceivable that humans could inflict such things on one another. Capt. Joe had asked Jack at the time to play it down. He promised he would see justice was done; he did and did it well. Jack had made sure the public knew, but they did not know it all. The whole story would have had catastrophic results, but only Jack and a few policemen knew.

When he was done, Adrianna pulled him close. "Oh my God, how have you lived with that?"

"It has not been easy. Maybe it will help now that it's off my chest. I know this: I am tired of the police beat and all that it represents. It is affecting me, and I am concerned that it affects you. I have given a lot of thought to asking for another assignment. What do you think?"

It did not take long for her to answer. "Jack, what about a sabbatical? What if there is a story surrounding William MacMorogh ? The timing would be perfect. We can manage. We are frugal; we work most of the time anyway. Why don't you sleep on it?"

Before turning in for the night, she asked, "What are your plans for tomorrow?"

His main objective was to make an appointment with MacMorogh, his old acquaintance. He wanted to do so before he left the apartment in the morning. She kissed him and left him on the sofa, mulling over what they had discussed.

Adrianna had been thinking ahead. She knew there was something else Jack could do; was it time to address it? She went into the bedroom, and closed the door quietly. She hesitated a moment or two to be sure; she did not hear Jack stir. She went to the closet where he kept his things and carefully pulled down the box in which he stored his columns. She selected a few at random.

Sleep would not come. Jack tossed and turned all night, considering her suggestion. By morning, he agreed. As he shaved, he asked the man in the mirror if he was making a mistake, and the man replied, "No." He discussed it once more, concern showed on his brow, his eyes tired from the restless night. Then, he informed her of his decision.

2

Monday

Adrianna did not own a car and managed quite well with public transportation. On the rare occasions she needed a car, Jack's was always available. She asked if she might take it, since she planned to leave early.

She arrived at the meeting early and spoke around the table to the others present, Bill Pullen, the news editor, and Jack's superior, Mac Brown, city editor. Huddled in the front of the room with Bob Bomar, the managing editor, was the man she and Jack had seen at the Camellia Grill with the police captain. After she sat, Bomar rapped on a glass for attention. First, he wanted to introduce Mr. Pat Crutchfield, corporate attorney for the paper. When the attorney made eye contact with Adrianna, he raised his hand toward her.

Then Bomar asked that they go once around the room for updates from each page editor. After that, he spoke again. "From time to time, we get threats because of what we do. I want to emphasize how important it is that you report all threats, regardless of how real you might consider one to be. I have asked Mr. Crutchfield to come here this morning in case you have questions." He paused for response; there was none. "If not, let's go put out a paper."

He then called out, "Bill, you stay a minute; Miss Breaux, you also, please."

After everyone was out, he turned to Adrianna, "Miss Breaux, first off, great section yesterday, many compliments. Now, I know this is of a personal nature, but I have good reason to ask. What is your relationship with Jack Ward?"

She knew that the attorney must have mentioned seeing them together, and she knew not to lie. "We share an apartment together."

"You are close friends and share an apartment. Is there more?"

Adrianna fumed. She was polite, but firm, "We are more than close friends. What we share is not your business."

Bomar was quick to respond. She was correct, and he wanted to apologize for implying that it might be otherwise. However, there was reason to be concerned for her safety. He said, "I am sure Jack has shared this with you, the fact that the paper has received a threat against both the paper and Jack. They suggest we get him off the street for a few days, and we will. We often do trade-outs with advertisers and take goods or services in lieu of money. We have such a policy with the Roosevelt Hotel and have arranged with them for a suite for you for several days. It is available now, and we suggest you move in today."

At this, the lid blew off. "Jack has not mentioned one word to me about a threat, nor has he mentioned moving to the hotel. Now you tell me I should go home to pack and move today. That is incredible!" She was close to screaming.

Bomar said, "We have not yet told Jack about the hotel, and if I had known you were unaware of the threat, believe me, Miss Breaux, I would not have sprung it on you."

With that, Adrianna threw up her hands, "I have to go. I have work to do. Wait until I get my hands on Jack!" She stormed out of the room, but not before she plopped the packet of Jack's columns in front of Bill Pullen.

Bomar spoke to Pullen. "Find Jack."

Pullen replied, "He is out making appointments. He plans to be in after lunch. Think I should alert Security?" They both laughed.

Adrianna did not slow down in the hall. She raced to her phone to call their apartment and there was no answer. She had the number of the office Jack planned to visit, so she called there and identified herself before she asked if Jack had dropped by or called.

The receptionist replied that he had, but at that point, she was the only one in the office. He was to call back. Adrianna, now cool enough to be civil, politely requested the receptionist to have Jack return her call. But she had appointments all day, and she heard nothing from him.

Jack did not leave the apartment that morning until he had successfully made his appointment, but it did not come easy. He was sure that his clever means of introduction was what had saved him. It did require a favor, however. As soon as he was off the phone, he raced to radio station WWL and his friend Dom Doucette. He needed to make a tape and several copies. It cost a quart of good Scotch, but the investment would come back tenfold.

It was noon before he finished with the taping session, so he joined Dom Doucette and a sports announcer for lunch. During lunch, he remembered to turn on his pager. He had ten messages: six to call Adrianna, three to call Bill Pullen, and one from his answering service.

He first called Pullen, who informed him that he was in impending danger and should come to his office immediately. Jack assured him that he was on the way. The second call was to Adrianna's office only to find she was on assignment. Fifteen minutes later, Jack sat in front of his boss. Bill Pullen reiterated the morning meeting with Adrianna and apologized for the *faux pas*. They then discussed the arrangements with the Roosevelt Hotel. Jack objected, but agreed to take advantage of it. Foremost in his mind was concern for Adrianna.

Pullen gave instructions as to whom Jack should contact at the hotel. The person expected them that evening. Hotel records would not show them as guests. The paper would cover the room and all incidental expenses. As their discussion ended, Jack decided to inform Pullen of his decision to take leave. Under the current circumstances, it was sure to look like he was running away. He chose his words carefully.

"Bill, I think you know me well enough to know that what I would prefer to say would be, screw the bastards, nobody can scare me away from my job!"

Bill smiled, "That is exactly what I told Bomar."

"Then I feel safe in knowing that you will not think I am running away." Jack paused. "I want to take a sabbatical for a period of time, perhaps six months."

Bill's forehead wrinkled. He slowly leaned back in his chair, sighed heavily, and let his arms droop to the side of his chair. It took several moments for him to regain his composure.

"Jack, are you ill? If so, we'll support you in any way possible. What can I do to help you?" Pullen was deeply concerned.

Jack told him the reasons. Primarily, he was tired of swimming in crime, the very cesspool of the city. He was not the same person he had been when he had arrived seven years earlier. He needed a breather.

Pullen continued to frown. "I'll discuss it with Bomar. What's your time frame? What kind of notice will you give?"

Jack replied that he had just given notice; the time frame was flexible. He felt two weeks hence for a departure date was fair. Pullen asked if he knew what a void he would leave and once more, asked him to reconsider. Then he excused him with a handshake, patted him on the back, and said, "Please sleep on it!"

In his cubicle, Jack sat down, dropped his arms to the side of his chair and sighed in relief. Now all he had to do was face Adrianna. He hesitated a few minutes to get his thoughts together before buzzing her office. He tried to talk, but she butted in, "I have been waiting for you to call. I am ready to leave the building; can you meet me at the car?" She did not wait for an answer. At the car, she leaned her head across hands that firmly gripped the steering wheel. She turned toward Jack when he crawled in on the passenger side.

"I am sorry, I—" he tried to say.

Adrianna interrupted, "This has not been one of my better days Jack. You have sorely disappointed me, and I am hurt. Just don't say anything. Let's get home, pack, and move into the damn hotel." With that, they drove silently to the apartment.

Both packed what they felt they would need for a few days. Jack was careful not to ask questions or make suggestions while he gathered his belongings. When he looked into the living room, Adrianna sat on the sofa, hands folded in front of her, her bags at the door. He gathered his; she followed to the car with hers. They made another silent trip to the Roosevelt.

The luxury of the suite was some relief. There were flowers and a bucket with iced champagne on the wet bar. The small refrigerator under the bar held two quarts of gin, a bottle of vermouth, olives, and pickled onions. Bill Pullen and Bob Bomar had signed a card with the flowers.

Adrianna unpacked, stowed away her things, and came out in jeans and a tee. Jack mixed martinis and handed her one. She took it and said, "I saved you room in the closet and one drawer in the dresser."

Jack smiled inwardly and said to himself, "Thank God for small favors." To her he said, "Thank you."

"Jack we are both stressed out. Let's not talk about this right now. I am afraid of what I might say and someday regret."

He smiled, "Again, thank you."

They sipped their drinks and silently watched the local evening news.

When the national news was over, she said, "So tell me about your day."

"You first." he said. She related a summary of the meeting with the women at the DAR, what a bore, how disorganized. She covered another staff thing before she turned her hand to him.

"Well, I have an appointment for tomorrow morning with Will MacMorogh."

She expressed her pleasure, "Great, how' d you manage that?"

Jack held his martini glass to his mouth like a microphone and said, "The score is 28 to 21 only three minutes to play, it looks like Leeville —"

"Come on Jack," pleaded Adrianna.

"That's how I got an appointment to see him."

"What?"

"That's right, when he answered the phone, I started right in, the whole last two minutes of the game right down to the two-point conversion. He began laughing about thirty seconds after I started, but he let me finish before asking me who the heck I was."

Jack explained the rest. "I told him and confirmed that I worked for the paper. Then I discussed the article that had appeared in the paper and mentioned that his name reminded me of the historic game. Will asked specifically if I was the Jack E. Ward who did the investigative things in the paper. When I confirmed that, he said he was glad I called, glad I remembered him, and thanks. He was ready to hang up."

"That is when I went into my selling mode. I told him about our review of the article and the fact that we thought there might be a great human interest story. He was hesitant, but finally said that if I would make a tape of that thing about the game, he would see me for a few minutes. The appointment is in the morning, ten o'clock in his office."

"There's one other thing." Jack hesitated. "I told Pullen I wanted to take a six month sabbatical."

She frowned, "What did he say?"

"He was shocked, thought I might be ill. I gave my reasons and said that there was no reconsidering. He will present my request to Bomar and I should hear in a day or two."

Adrianna was silent for a long time before she spoke again. "I've got a busy day tomorrow with meetings, plus I am short two staff persons. You have a big day ahead. Let's order room service—greasy hamburgers with fries and a six pack—then get to bed early."

3

William MacMorogh

Jack got off the elevator on the ninth floor at William MacMorogh's building and faced large double doors. "Suite 900" appeared in gold letters on a glass panel over the doors. On a vertical glass panel to the left, gold lettering announced "Charles Chacherie, Attorney-at-Law." Below that panel, another read, "New Orleans Office, State Attorney General." On a similar panel to the right of the doors, gold lettering stated, "Chacherie and Son Companies." There was no mention of MacMorogh. Jack looked to the left, toward doors on that side of the hall. Over one was a stainless placard with the number "901" in black.

At the door, Jack knocked lightly and turned the knob. The door opened, and a petite woman, well-dressed, probably mid-fifties, greeted him. She stood in front of a beautifully carved antique desk with a matching credenza. With a warm smile, the woman said, "I am Mimi; you must be Mr. Ward. Will is expecting you but he is across the hall for a moment." She offered seating but he declined and remained standing as he took in the office.

Above the credenza was one of several large black and white photos in like frames. One was of a World War I Jenny. Two people in caps and goggles waved from the cockpits. Clearly, the picture was from another aircraft looking down on the Jenny. The other pictures included a weathered barn with an antique Ford tractor parked nearby and an old country store with colored children sitting on the front steps with soda pops in hand. Then there was a picture of City Livery, a building Jack remembered being in New Cotswold.

At one end of the reception area was a closed door and Jack assumed it to be another office. To the left of Mimi's desk was an open door and he could see another beautifully decorated office.

The reception area door opened, two men entered, and Jack recognized Charles Chacherie. He wore an expensive linen suit and white shirt with the collar and tie undone. He came toward Jack, his hand out to shake. "I am Charles Chacherie. I recognize you as Jack E. Ward. How are you?" They shook hands, and Mr. Chacherie turned to the other man.

"Will MacMorogh," the man offered. "It is my pleasure, Jack," he said and extended his hand.

Mr. Chacherie said, "I heard you were here and wanted to congratulate you on your work. I have heard a rumor and if it is so, I want to offer my support. Do you know Sammy D'Antoni, our special investigator?"

"I've met him, but haven't seen him in a while," replied Jack. Sammy had been a detective lieutenant at NOPD when chosen to be a special investigator for the attorney general. He and Chacherie had been at Tulane together, Jack had known him at NOPD. He held him in high regard and the feeling was mutual.

With that, Chacherie said, "I will send his card back across the hall to Mimi. Get it from her before you leave. He might be of some help, and by the way, call me if you get tired of that rag you work with... I am serious."

Will's appearance was a surprise. Jack knew that the man's age had to be within a year or so of his own, however, his close-cropped hair was white. His nose was off center, and when he turned his head, Jack discerned a pink scar under the hair from his left temple over his ear. His blue eyes had a depth you saw in men much older.

He wore freshly starched khaki trousers and a white cotton shirt in a coarse weave, with two button-down pockets. Over the right, in blue stitching, was printed, "Will." Over the left was a mono-grammed "MacMoCorp." A buckle with a *Caterpillar* logo clasped his belt. The belt held a case for sunglasses. His shoes were high-top jodhpurs in rich English leather.

Mimi ushered the two into Will's office. It had a corner view of Canal Street, looking across the French Quarter. Will motioned Jack to a low table with four leather chairs. In the middle of the table sat a silver service, and next to it, a tray covered with a white cloth.

Will poured coffee, then said, "When I told Chas you were coming in today, he said he was eager to meet you. Seems you have established a fine reputation as a journalist. I know he is impressed. Interestingly enough, my aunt said the same thing when I told her you were coming in."

Jack expressed his appreciation for the compliments, then drew a small package from his jacket pocket. He handed it across to Will. "Five tapes, one original, and four copies, all professionally done by a friend of mine at WWL."

Will said he had tried to place Jack from school days but guessed that because Jack was in Leeville, they'd never had the opportunity to meet. Jack said he had only known Will as a player on the opposing team. He also stated that he had only lived in Leeville that one year. His Dad was with the newspaper there and after that year, they had moved on.

Jack had come to the meeting fearful that it would be short and quick. He felt better that Will did not seem in a rush to get him out of the way. He was even more relieved when Will took the time to tell him about the last time he had gone in for a haircut at Mr. Upton's barbershop in New Cotswold. He'd had to relive the game with some old codgers in the shop.

Mimi tapped on the door and excused the interruption, but she said she had a call from the boat, and it was rather important. Jack attempted to excuse himself while Will made his call. Will shook his head and told him not to leave. After the call was completed, they got back to the business at hand. "Now, about the human interest story you talked about," Will said. "What gave you that idea?"

Jack again mentioned the article that had appeared in the Sunday paper. Dr. MacMorogh's name had drawn their attention and prompted them to research their archives. He briefly touched on each thing that had been found before presenting the article from the previous Sunday edition of the paper. "Last," and Jack had to laugh, "this one." He handed over a clipping of the article.

Will grinned, "Yes, I am well aware of that one."

"As I see it," Jack said, "you were orphaned at an early age, raised by guardians, went on to be a Korean War hero. Now you are on the board of a very large corporation and beginning a new chapter in your life. That has the making of a good story."

Will frowned. "First, let me say in no uncertain terms, I am no hero. I went to war and did my job. I ended up being a guest of the North Koreans for two years. However," and he paused, "I came back under my own power. The guys that came back in boxes, they are the true heroes."

Then he followed with, "In our family, we prefer to keep a low profile. I will explain part of the reason." He went to his desk to retrieve a well-worn magazine and passed it to Jack. On the cover of *Dixie Business Gazette* was a picture of General William MacMorogh with his two stars. Under the picture were written these words: "Is This the Richest Man in the Deep South?" Will asked, "Tell me how that cover strikes you."

Jack gave some thought before answering. "It would be easy to get a negative impression. My first thought is that the general is rich because of his rank. However, I do know that generals do not make fortunes off military pay; there has to be more. I would want to know, how did he get rich?"

Will smiled. "A large percentage of the people who saw this cover had your first thought. It sent the wrong message; it was negative. Many never went past the cover. Fact is, the author wanted to tell the story of a dedicated soldier who fought in World War I. A man so dedicated to his country that he walked away from a huge financial empire to serve his country a second time in World War II.

"The article itself was not intended to be damaging. However, it did not overlook the fact that my grandfather did benefit from his military life, especially contacts he made in Washington. That negative response followed him for several years and made him anti-press. He will tell you that who we are, what we do, is nobody's damn business. He has never sought out publicity and prefers that the family follow suit."

Jack felt he had struck out.

Will then questioned Jack about his career. Had he worked outside the newspaper? Did he have further ambitions in journalism? He pointed out that he had heard from Chas Chacherie that Jack had the tenacity of a bulldog when it came to research. He would not turn loose until he shook it to pieces.

Jack told Will that he had done some freelance things during his university days. A documentary on black pilots during World War II intrigued him; he met some great men. He lost his mother at three and knew little of his ancestors, so he had done a thorough search and come up with a good family history. "And of course," Jack said, "like every other journalist, there is a book out there somewhere."

"The history is very interesting," Will said. "It is something my aunt has insisted upon, a history of our family and company. She has even worked on it sporadically herself. But we know little about my great-grandfather, Seamus MacMorogh, other than the fact that he is entombed standing upright in the old cemetery in New Cotswold. Where he came from, who our ancestors were prior to him, is only speculation."

He took a sip of coffee. "As for my grandfather, he and my grandmother have lived one heck of a productive life. However, they only share bits and pieces as they see fit. What we would like to know is how we came from Seamus to here." He held up the magazine again and thumped the cover. Jack looked again into the eyes of the man on the cover. Then he looked into those same eyes in Will.

Will said, "My aunt would like to meet with us tomorrow morning. She is friends with the lady who was society editor at your paper. Also, she knows the young lady who replaced her. However, she is only familiar with you by name and reputation. She thinks it important that she meet you. She has authority from the rest of our family to commission someone to develop our history and the family-owned company Seamus founded. My aunt would like for us to discuss with you the possibility of your being that person."

Jack could not have been more surprised. He hesitated, frowning, a finger to his temple as his eyes focused on the wall behind Will's desk. "I will need to think about that. It sounds intriguing, and it is something I would enjoy. However, there are things I have to consider. I will certainly do that and look forward to talking more tomorrow."

"I am pleased that you will at least consider it. We will give you more details of what we expect. You might think about how and when you might be able to do it." With that, a time was set, and both men rose to bid each other farewell.

Jack could not wait to get to a pay phone to call Adrianna. Connected, she immediately said, "Jack, I 'm too busy to talk right now. Talk to me later." She hung up quickly; not a good sign. Next, he called Bill Pullen, but Bill had not talked to Bob Bomar. Since Jack had another thought in mind and nothing else on his agenda, he went back to the Roosevelt.

Back in the room, he set up his typewriter and created a workspace overlooking Canal Street, but there was no way he could keep his mind off his visit with Will. He tuned in on the baseball game, and now he could think better. At about four o'clock, he poured mixed nuts from a can into a crystal dish on the coffee table. The martinis were mixed and in the refrigerator. He was uncomfortable with the tension between him and Adrianna. A little before five, he unlocked the door to the suite and when he heard the door swing open, he jumped up, all smiles, to greet her.

"Why was the door unlocked? You are absolutely impossible!" she shouted.

She walked past him and into the bedroom and closed the door. He could hear drawers opening and slamming, as she muttered something he could not decipher. He poured drinks and waited.

Finally, she came out dressed in shorts with a sleeveless blouse and with her hair tied on top of her head; she had removed her makeup. She was gorgeous. Ever since that first day they met at the tennis courts, Jack had felt he was damn lucky. She was tall enough that his six-one frame was not too much. Her black hair, blue eyes, and that cute little Cajun accent had charmed him.

She took a martini and took a sip. "Well?"

"You mean my meeting with Will?" he asked.

"What else?"

Jack decided a little fibbing would not hurt. "Well, during our meeting he asked me if I had a family and if I was married. I told him about you. He said that he and Dr. Bea had talked about me last night. She was familiar with me only by my by-line. She told Will that the people she knew well at the paper were Miss Penny, before she retired, and the darling girl that took her place. He said I must be a lucky fellow. Of course I agreed."

"You are lucky. You are damn lucky I am not out of here. Don't be pressing your luck, like leaving the doors unlocked!"

Then he covered the meeting, taking his time to relate the details. He had a plan and needed her opinion. He knew he was qualified, but this project definitely would require a lot of research, more than he could possibly do during or after regular working hours. He already knew enough about the family to confirm that there was definitely a *story*. The problem was time.

Adrianna said, "Interesting how things that are supposed to happen come together so easily. You have already given notice of your leave. What else do you need?"

4

Wednesday

When Jack went to work at the paper, he had fully expected to be working the Sports Desk. His thoughts were of polo shirts, jeans, ball caps, and sweaters. However, that did not come about. Instead, he got the police beat. His mentor, a crabby old veteran, wore corduroys, dress shirts with collar buttons missing, neckties with year-old mustard stains, and an old sport coat with leather patches at the elbows.

Jack was disappointed in the police beat from the beginning, and he confessed to his father that he had made a mistake. His father, a seasoned newsman himself, gave him good advice. "Belly up to it. You can do it. What you want will come in time." His father had also told him to make the best of it by getting to know the best detectives, the best cops on the beats, and the best of the desk sergeants. They were his bread and butter. Then one other piece of advice: dress to stand out in a crowd. Make it easy for the cops to recognize you.

He'd had twenty-three dollars in his pocket and was rooming at the YMCA. With his first paycheck, he went to Sears and Roebuck and bought three pairs of khaki work pants, three matching shirts, and a pair of bright red wide suspenders. He bought high-top work shoes with leather strings and black rubber soles, because of the sloppy, wet streets of the city. His hat was an old brown fedora: the one with the "PRESS" card in the brim that said "Property of the *Chicago Tribune*." That had become his uniform. Those clothes and his red hair, freckles, and lanky, slightly stooped six-one frame did stand out. That was how he had dressed for the last seven years.

On Wednesday morning, disregarding the threat, he strolled across the street from the Roosevelt to the building on Carondolet. No one would take a second look at him; he was traveling incognito. He wore a pair of gray slacks, a black sport coat, and a white shirt with a red, blue, and black striped tie. His penny loafers were in a high shine. Anybody looking for Jack E. Ward would not even waste a second glance.

The door to Will's office was not open when he entered the reception area. Mimi stood to greet him. "You look handsome this morning," she said and added in a whisper, "Dr. Bea is in with Will. They told me to see you in when you arrived." She stepped to the door, tapped, "Mr. Ward is here," then stepped aside so Jack could enter.

Will stepped forward to shake Will's hand and turned toward his aunt.

"Aunt Bea, meet Jack Ward."

Jack had seen her picture numerous times but had not met her in person. She was tall and pretty and stood ramrod straight. Sunlight turned her red hair to gold. She had on lightweight, pleated front, gabardine trousers, with a white blouse and the obligatory white lab coat, with a stethoscope in a pocket.

She nodded and with a smile, said, "Hello Jack. I feel I already know you. I have heard a lot about you from a secret admirer."

Jack looked at her and laughingly said, "I wish that person would come forward. It would be nice to know I have at least one admirer,"

Dr. Bea smiled. "A little clue: she owns a Bentley and adores your girlfriend."   Jack grinned, "Miss Penny."

Will motioned Jack to sit. They were at the low round table with the high back chairs. Dr. Bea had papers open on the table, which she folded and stuck in the purse at her side. She then cut right to the chase. "Will tells me that you might consider taking on our history project. We are anxious to hear what you have to say."

Jack looked first at Will and then turned to her. "I have made a decision. If given the opportunity, yes, I would like to do the project for you. Not to be presumptuous, I have already requested six months leave of absence for another reason," he explained. "I am becoming calloused as an individual. In the beginning, every day on the police beat brought a surprise. There were murders over a nickel candy bar, the rape of babies, kidnappings, gang fights, wife beatings, police brutality, and corruption. Each new day would present another example of how inhumane people can be to one another. Now there are no more surprises, just expectations. Each day I can only look forward to one more day swimming in the cesspool of crime in the city. I need a break."

Will asked, "What kind of time frame are we looking at? When do you plan to start your leave?"

Jack hesitated to mention it, but decided it would be best to discuss the threat. He covered it as briefly as possible, but he did include the fact that he was living in seclusion. He also said that he felt responsible to a degree, and even though he had given two weeks' notice, he would not leave the paper in the lurch. The positive side was that he thought he would have time to begin working on the project immediately. What he would need most would be direction from them.

Will and Dr. Bea shared smiles, and then Will turned his hand to Dr. Bea in a motion for her to continue.

"Last night I told Will that I thought it would be impossible for you to do this for us. Since it will not be for publication, I did not think the paper would be interested. I could not see how you would have time otherwise. However, we did come to a favorable conclusion, just in case. I have the authority to finalize an agreement with you, if you are interested in our terms." Over the next hour, Dr. Bea gave him a lot to think about, plenty to work with.

She said that all direction would come from her. Foremost, she wanted it clear that his would not be a published piece. It would be printed and bound, and copies would be made, but they would not be for sale. The entire family would be involved in development. To save confusion, she would be the primary in giving direction. In addition, she had done a lot herself, and in her office closet she had four document boxes of her research. The boxes included numerous notes, letters, and various legal documents collected over the years.

Dr. Bea said, "Now, remuneration." She paused for a moment. "We have discussed commissions and how else you might be paid. We did not consider the fact that you might take leave. That fact changes the landscape." She directed her attention to Will. "Will, I am going to take the liberty of a little different proposal. I believe everyone will agree with what I suggest." Will told her that he was sure they would and smiled.

"Last evening, we agreed to offer you a fifty thousand dollar commission for the project. That would be over and above expenses incurred.

If you are no longer receiving remuneration from the paper, I will offer you the same amount you currently make monthly. That, of course, would be over and above the commission. There is one other thing. Will tells me you came here looking for a story. First, we want a precise history for our use. If you develop a story out of this, it is yours."

Jack was flabbergasted. He honestly had not considered remuneration, and this was far more than he would have dreamed. Holding a poker face was impossible. He grinned broadly, "You are quite generous, and I could not possibly turn that down."

Dr. Bea rose. "I am so pleased. I have to go now. I will leave it to Will to cover some other things." She reached across to shake Jack's hand and walked swiftly out. Jack thought he heard her say to Mimi, "Mission accomplished." There were additional directions Jack did not overhear. Meanwhile, Will suggested a rest room and refreshment break.

Back at the table, Will covered much more: a legal contract, confidentiality agreements, remuneration, and expense documentation. He restated the importance that the history was his prime project. If a story came out of it, it was Jack's for the telling.

Next, Will had a concern about workspace. Where did Jack plan to work? Jack told him he'd work at the hotel until such time as he and Adrianna could go back to the apartment. But Will had another suggestion. What about the extra office in this suite? He would be close to all of the material Dr. Bea had accumulated, and Mimi could do light secretarial work if needed. "After all," Will said. "You could not be any safer than across the hall from the attorney general's law offices."

Will then laid out his own plans. Beginning the following week, he would be out of town for two weeks, perhaps longer. Thursday he would be in New Cotswold and would formulate plans with the other family members. Maybe they could meet again on Friday to lay out a schedule. Jack could get on with the project in Will's absence. Will called Mimi in to inform her that Jack would use the office, and Mimi did not hide the fact that she was pleased.

It was near noon, their discussion over for the day and Jack was free to go. Will was leaving to visit the boat in Gulfport. He was going by helicopter and invited Jack, but Jack passed. Even if he had wanted to take the helicopter ride, which he definitely did not, he was too eager to deliver exciting news to Adrianna. *Wow*! What would she say about this? There would be enough money to think about buying a small house, maybe a fixer upper shotgun somewhere in the Garden District. Or maybe even a ring. But on second thought…that might need more consideration.

He called Adrianna's office from the pay phones in the lobby. She was on an assignment, not expected back until late afternoon. Jack was disappointed; he was dying to tell her and hear the squeal of joy. So instead, he went back across the street to the Roosevelt and their home away from home, to begin preparing a plan of action. Down deep, he knew it was impossible to leave here until the threat was behind them. He wrestled with that.

At four o'clock, he lay down for a nap, but not before locking the dead bolt on the suite door and hooking the safety chain. He slept until a quarter to five. Adrianna should be home soon. Time for martinis, and he'd better lay out the hotel menu. Tonight was going to be a special night.

It was. Adrianna rushed in, all excited about her afternoon with women from the Crewe of Rex, the preeminent Carnival Crewe in the city. She had a schedule that would fill a book: parties, balls, soirees to New York for designer clothes. She was not getting an exclusive, but she was going to cover it all herself and would be the only editor accompanying the group. It was six months until Carnival, and already things were buzzing. After spilling that important news nonstop, and ready for a second martini, Adrianna took a breath to ask Jack, "So what about your day?"

"Oh same old same old, got a commission offer to do the history project for the MacMoroghs. I am little disappointed; only fifty grand, but they will pay me the same salary I now make for six months. Other than that, not much."

Adrianna looked at him and smiled, "Jack, you jerk, you are just trying to top my coup with the ladies of the Crewe of Rex." He said nothing, but just grinned. Then the squeal erupted. "You are telling me the truth aren't you? Lord, thank-you for such great favors!" She looking upward and crossed herself. "Jack, we need to start going back to church. I miss it, and this streak of good fortune is not just luck."

It was a great evening until almost two a.m. They talked nonstop about everything from houses to trips to rest and relaxation to entire new careers, and yes, even about marriage. One of these days.

5

Thursday

Jack made coffee, then went to the door to pick up the daily papers. He looked both ways up and down the hall as he did so. Adrianna was up; he took her coffee. She had laid out her favorite skirt and sweater outfit and a new pair of leather pumps to match. Their good fortune had given her a new outlook.

An exciting day helping Miss Penny celebrate her birthday was in store. Adrianna and the others had purchased small gifts; Miss Penny would be delighted. Adrianna asked Jack if it would be safe to take the car, since four were traveling together with purses and packages. Jack felt it would be; the car was secure at the hotel, and it should be safe at the paper. He suggested that she park in a very visible place at the hotel where Miss Penny lived. Adrianna took the car keys from Jack's dresser, came out holding them up, and leaned over to peck his cheek.

Jack made a call to Bill Pullen to let him know he was on his pager or at the suite. No one else knew where he was. Then he immediately went to work on the notes he had gotten from Will the day before. He was satisfied with this as a beginning. He made one more call, and as he was talking to the other person, his pager beeped.

It was Pullen. "Jack, call me now, urgent."

Jack returned the call. Pullen was breathless, "Jack, where is your car?"

"Adrianna took it, should be in the garage, why?"

Pullen screamed *"Garage!"* at someone else. Then he told Jack to get over to the paper. There might be a problem.

Jack looked at the clock: 11:39 a.m. *Oh my God*. He could only think the worst—sabotaging his car. Adrianna was taking it out for lunch. He burst out the door of the suite, pounded on the down button for an elevator. After what seemed like an eternity, one stopped. The doors had barely begun to open when Jack reached both hands inside to try to open them more quickly. Two men on the elevator jumped against the back wall as the wild man jumped on. Jack hit the G button. The elevator stopped on three. Jack immediately pushed the Close Door button, and the elevator moved on down.

One of the men on the elevator said, "Hey, I was getting off there!"

Jack was down tying his sneakers and said as he stood, "I wasn't." At the ground floor, he bounded off and turned left down the long hall in the Roosevelt to the street doors.

He exited on St. Charles, turned right, then ran at full speed across the street to the end of the block, where he turned left and raced toward the paper. From behind, he heard sirens. An ambulance blasted by, followed by a fire engine, then two police cars. Red lights flashed at the garage entrance. Jack, out of breath, raced into the garage and spotted Bill Pullen milling around, looking in all directions. Police were doing the same. Jack spotted his car three quarters of the way down the length of the garage. The deck lid was open. Adrianna and two other women were placing packages inside.

Jack screamed *"Adrianna!"* at the top of his lungs. An idling fire engine started moving in the same direction that Jack ran. Firemen with extinguishers bounded off the truck.

Jack stumbled on a speed bump, almost falling as he raced toward his car, screaming Adrianna's name. She moved to the car door, and the other two women stood by the passenger doors. Then the lights from the engine and Jack's screaming got their attention. Adrianna looked up, just as she was about to open the door. Again, Jack screamed, *"Do not touch the car! Get away from the car!"*

Adrianna froze. Jack got close enough to reach out, literally lifting her off her feet. He carried her between the two cars parked in front of his. Two firefighters grabbed the other women and did the same. They guided them toward the rear exit of the garage. On the street, people filed out of the building.

Bill Pullen came trotting down the sidewalk toward them. He explained what had happened. He had gotten a call from the NOPD, telling him that they had information that there might be an attempt to set off a bomb in Jack's car. His relief was obvious. "Thank God." He had tears in his eyes.

Adrianna put her arm around Jan Plow, who had her hands over her face and was crying. Jack tried to console them. "Look, I'll get you a cab, go on out and have a nice lunch and try to put this behind you." They shook their heads in unison.

Adrianna gathered the others. "I will call Miss Penny. We can do this another time."

Bill Pullen, who was still within earshot, spoke up. "It will be awhile before we can go back into the building. Go home."

Jack was huddled with police officers when a NOPD bomb squad truck arrived, pulling a cylindrical blast chamber. With the building emptied, they went to work. Jack and the others waited across the street while police dispersed onlookers.

Jack looked toward the end of the block where Adrianna stood with her arm still around Jan Plow. In retrospect, he should have gone with them, but he was too anxious to get back inside the building. It took an hour for the bomb squad to find the device and another to disarm and remove it. Experts would examine every facet of the bomb. FBI and members of the ATF were now on the scene.

A tow truck removed Jack's car to a police compound, where technicians would microscopically examine it. They would photograph, fingerprint, and vacuum for any particles that might give them a clue. Several days would pass before Jack would see the car again.

It was a puzzle: how anyone could have gotten into the garage, place the bomb, and leave without anyone seeing. Where was Security all this time? He was upset and wondered if somebody inside the building was helping? Of even more concern, were police department individuals involved? The security service for the paper was a local firm with a good reputation, but they did hire off duty police.

People slowly went back into the building, but not before in-house security thoroughly searched every inch. As soon as he was back in, Jack made his way to the Security Office. A detective informed him that the device had had enough dynamite to blow a hole in the roof of the garage. That roof was the pressroom floor.

The Security Office was inside, just to the left of the door to the parking garage. It was medium sized, with three walls of glass giving security personnel an unobstructed view of the garage as well as of all doors. The solid wall held screens displaying a view from every security camera in the building. There were twenty-four of those. Two men, their backs to the door, were scanning the screens with the security chief, a retired detective by the name of Roscoe. The other two men Jack knew well: Lieutenant Bridges and Detective Sergeant Wade, NOPD, both top-notch men.

Jack stepped through the door. Roscoe turned to the others. "Here he is now. We can ask him?"

"Ask me what you need to ask me, because believe me, I've questions of my own." Jack's irritation was obvious.

Roscoe looked at Jack, shaking his head. "We're trying to put it together Jack. You have every reason to be upset, but hold on a minute; look what we have here." Roscoe described what they presently knew. At 8:56 that morning, a small Chevrolet truck with a utility box drove in through the entrance, preceded down to the middle of the garage, and stopped. A big man with a ball cap pulled tight on his head trotted to the office. Officer Green stepped out to greet him.

The man was nervous; his hands trembled as he glanced back at the truck and then at his funny watch. Speaking was difficult; he had to refer to a note he held in his hand. He said that they had come to change a battery in a customer's car. He had directions as well as a license number.

At the same moment, Security got a call about a fire on the loading dock. Everyone, including Officer Green, took off running. That left one officer alone at her desk inside the office. The phone rang incessantly as people saw the loading dock smoke. The lone officer was oblivious to anything else going on and certainly wasn't concentrating on the truck.

Jack said, "I did not call anyone about the damn car. You should 've called me." Then he stopped short. Even if they had, he would not have been immediately available. Roscoe agreed that it was inexcusable, but he wanted to carry on. He brought their attention back to the security cameras. Two cameras were down for repair, their screens off. Security noticed the other two blacked out after the fire commotion was over.

Roscoe pointed to the top left screen. It was set to 8:56 a.m. That screen pointed to the entrance door. A Chevrolet truck with a small cargo body rolled in and continued past. He pointed to the camera in the third screen: it showed the rear of the truck as it rolled down and stopped by Jack's car. It was possible to see the fellow running up to talk to Green. When he was halfway back to where Jack's car sat, the screen went black. It was 8:57. After they discovered that screen to be out, they reviewed the other. It had gone out at the same time, 8:57.

Roscoe said, "So now, let's look back at the first screen." The truck, including the windshield, was filthy. It was impossible to determine the number of passengers, much less to identify anyone. The truck went by the second camera and toward the garage with the side windows obscured. At the third camera, which was adjacent to Jack's car, the door swung open, a figure with a cardboard box over his head jumped out, and the screen went black. Roscoe directed their attention to the other screen. Same thing, man bails out with a cardboard box on his head and bingo, out goes that camera. Both were spray-painted.

They rolled the tape again and Jack was the first to speak. "No license plate, and it looks like there is a small air-condition unit on top of the cargo box."

Detective Sgt. Wade pointed out that due to the black and white of the security film, they could assume that the truck could be white or aluminum in color. They agreed that the cargo box was about six by eight by six feet. A side view of the cargo box showed fading but with an area that was shiny clean. Perhaps a logo had been there. The other side, front, and rear had the same shiny areas. The watchers continued rerunning the tapes, commenting as they went, each making different observations.

It took a while, then all of a sudden, Jack said, "Stop it right there!" Then he asked, "What do you see?"

One of the detectives said, "Same thing we been seeing."

Then Jack said, "Look at the wheel covers. In contrast to the rest of the truck, they are sparkling clean. Then look at the picture we have here. What do you see?"

Roscoe said it first. "The right rear wheel cover is missing."

Jack said, "Back the tape to the first scene or two." They did, and Sgt. Wade was the first to comment. "I'll be damned; the rear wheel cover is on. That means the cover is somewhere here in the garage."

An immediate search took place. They engaged as many people as possible to look under every car in the garage and found nothing. But the wheel cover had to be there. Then someone said, "Not unless they knew they lost it and retrieved it." That was a discouraging thought.

Jack said, "That's enough for me. Something about that truck keeps tugging. I think I have seen it or one similar. I keep seeing something printed where there appears to have been emblems. I just cannot pull it up."

Jack went up to his cubicle, tried Adrianna's extension, and got no response. Several people came over with one comment or another. His mind was racing; he knew he needed to get to work. The bomb incident had created excitement all over downtown. Emergency equipment rushing to the scene had snarled traffic for blocks. It was all that was on local radio and TV. Finally, the editors made a decision: the *TP* had to put out a special evening edition. Jack had another deadline.

He sat hunched over his typewriter. When the necessary words came to him, his eyes filled with tears at the thought of how horrible it might have been. He began to write what would be one of his last pieces as an investigative reporter on the police beat. It was about the fact that a bomb planted in his car, with the power to bring down the building, was, by the grace of God, discovered. He praised the NOPD; their fast response to an anonymous tip was what had saved the day. When he was through, he typed his "30" and hand-carried the piece to Bill Pullen.

Bill asked Jack how he was doing and told him to rent a car for as long as needed and to use the paper's credit card. He then suggested that Jack go back to the hotel. Jack turned his head away from Pullen, half mumbling, "If I was on the street, I could run those assholes down."

Pullen looked at Jack with a stern expression. "I 'm not even going to ask you to repeat what I think I just heard. Go to the hotel and calm down!"

On the way back to the hotel, Jack stopped in the Pearl Oyster Bar for a foot-long Peacemaker, fries, and two draft beers. Afterward, he stopped at the car rental agency in the hotel lobby and rented a new black '58 Ford Thunderbird. "Might as well go first class," he muttered to himself.

In the suite, he went into the bathroom, splashed cold water on his face. He looked in the mirror and saw a tramp. He had not shaved since the day before; his T-shirt was yellow under the armpits. He was looking into red-rimmed and bloodshot eyes.

At the window, he looked out on Canal Street at the rush hour traffic. How could it already be 4:30? Adrianna would be in soon; she would not approve of what he was thinking and would raise holy hell. He grabbed a windbreaker and a cap, then went to the bar and scribbled on a napkin, "I am running an errand or two. Love you, J."

Jack knew that the emblems on the truck body had to do with something in the food or drink line, something that needed heat or refrigeration. He based that idea on the unit atop the cargo box. He tried to associate the food or drink idea with places offering snacks, gas stations, bars, bus stations, or the like. He began at one of his old police beat bars in the edge of the Quarter. He sat at the bar, with no recognition by the bartender or anyone else. He sipped a beer, listened. Only bar talk, no comment about the bomb scare.

He moved to a similar joint a block away. Again, he sat at the bar, scanning available snack items. Chips, peanuts, pickles, pickled pig ears, and an assortment of smokes and gum stood out. The third spot was much the same. He ordered another beer. Then there was a hard slap on his back. A plainclothes cop he knew laughed, "If I had been through what you have today, damn if beer would be strong enough."

Jacked grinned, "I 'm just paving the way." They laughed; the cop strolled back to his table. It was visible in the bar mirror. Jack saw all heads turn his way; the cop had told them who he was. He had obviously been there long enough. He went to the rest room, and when he left, it was through a rear door to an alley.

Over on Rampart, there was a corner grocery at a busy intersection where streetcar routes converged. It was busy with people grabbing small snacks, cold drinks, or cans of beer in individual paper sacks to sneak onto the bus. He parked one stop down the block and trotted back. Looking through the racks of hundreds of snack items, he saw nothing. He got two beers in sacks. His eyes roamed as he was paying the attendant. And then, there it was, on the counter beside the cash register: a small glass case about a foot high and a foot wide. On two rows of shelves inside sat small, half-moon packages. The case had a light bulb for heat.

"Give me one of those also," he pointed to the glass case.

"Beef or pork?" the clerk asked.

"One of each." He handed the clerk his money. Sure enough, across the package was a logo, the same shape as the blank space on the truck. It was a red stripe centered with a large circle. Inside the circle, a caricature of "Gabby." On one side of the caricature was written, "Natchitoches Meat Pies," with "Hot from the Oven" on the other. Printed above the caricature was the name, "Gabby," and below, "Since 1928." On the back of the package was a listing of the ingredients. Below that, the company name, address, and the phone number in Natchitoches, Louisiana.

There was a phone booth outside but too many people stood around, so Jack drove to a service station with another phone booth. It was 8:45 p.m., maybe too late to reach anyone at Gabby's. Using his telephone credit card, Jack called the number. After twenty rings, and as he was about to hang up, someone answered, "Gabby's." Jack explained who he was and gave the reason he was calling. Had the company recently sold off any of its trucks?

He was talking to Charlie, who made pies on the night shift. He told Jack to hold on. Finally, another person came on the line, "Yeah?" Jack went through it all again.

The other party knew that they had sold six trucks some time back. It would be best to call back the next day and talk to Mrs. Gabby; she was usually in the office before rush hour. There was nothing else to do but wait until morning.

It was now almost ten o'clock. He rushed back to the hotel, knowing that if Adrianna was still up, he was in for a royal ass chewing. He stuck his key in the door of the suite and turned the knob. The chain opened just to the length of the security chain on the door inside.

"Who is it?"

"Me," Jack replied.

The chain slipped off as Adrianna stepped back. He was right; the fangs were out.

"Where have you been? Don't tell me. I can smell it on you! You are half plastered. You've been running your so-called traps haven't you? You are the biggest fool. I've called your pager every fifteen minutes the last five hours. Oh, I know you probably had it turned off. I can only thank God that he takes care of little babies and fools like you." All spoken rapidly in one breath.

Jack should have stood there and let her run out of steam. But he was dirty and tired, and he said the wrong thing. *"That's it, enough!"*

He was going to say more, but it was as if she had been shot out of a cannon. She flew out of the parlor and into the bedroom, and the door slammed, rattling pictures on the wall. There was no mistake about the click of the lock.

Jack knocked. "I 'm sorry."

There was no response. That night, he lay awake for a long time, sorry that he had exploded. He had been remiss in not checking back with Adrianna. At 5:30 a.m., his bladder alarm woke him, and he went into the bathroom that connected the two bedrooms. There was light under Adrianna's door. He started to knock, but decided not, and went back to bed for another half hour. He dressed as he had the previous day, in nice slacks and a white shirt with buttoned-down collar. At 7:00 a.m., he picked up the phone in the bedroom and placed a call to Gabby's, hoping to catch Mrs. Gabby before the rush hour. Luckily, she answered. He went again through his reason for calling. She confirmed that they did have six trucks for sale several months back. Five sold but unfortunately, one was stolen.

When Jack asked if she could tell him who had bought the trucks, she told him she would look up the information and then call him back. There was no way until after noon. Jack tried to emphasize the urgency, but she apologized; it was impossible. From now until past the noon hour, there would be a steady line at the counter. She took his pager number and promised to call ASAP.

A few moments later, he stood at the wet bar making coffee, when he glanced toward the suite door and noticed two suitcases, one with a raincoat lying across it. Then Adrianna stepped into the room.

"What's this?" Jack nodded toward the bags.

"Can I talk now, or have you had enough?"

Jack tried to apologize, but she would have nothing of it. "I talked to Bob Bomar yesterday afternoon," she said. "I asked for a week's vacation. He agreed that it might be best. I 'm going to White Castle after work today."

"How are you going? Don't you want me to drive you?" Jack asked.

"No, I 'll take the bus." She was emphatic.

"I know you are mad. It's my fault. I am sorry, but I do have a lead on the truck. I will know later in the day. Right now I have to go to my session with William." Jack was polite and spoke in a calm, quiet voice.

The phone rang, the car from the paper was there for Adrianna. "Good luck, Jack." She got her two bags.

At the door, Jack said," Please, I want to at least help you with the bags."

She shook her head. "I can do it."

6

Carole Anne MacMorogh

Jack was at William's office early. Mimi greeted him warmly, anxious to hear what had happened the day before. "Are you OK?" she asked.

"Fine, thanks, just thankful no one was killed."

Before he or Mimi could say anything else, the door opened. A nice looking man came in; he was about five-foot-nine, with broad shoulders and dark hair graying a little at the temples. He had on summer weight wool slacks, a silk, semi-turtleneck shirt, and a seersucker coat with a black stripe. A black silk hanky adorned the pocket. His tasseled alligator loafers were in high shine. It took Jack a moment, and then he recognized the man: Sammy D'Antoni.

The man first greeted Mimi, then came at Jack with his hand out to shake. "You may not remember me. I'm Sammy D'Antoni."

"Sure, sure, I remember. It's nice to see you again." Jack smiled.

"Anything new since yesterday?" he asked. "The AG may end up involved in this thing, as you know. At this point, I am staying out of it. He wants me to keep an eye out for you, though. I thought I might ask if there is anything I can do for you."

"There is. I was going to call on you later this morning." Jack invited Sammy into his office and closed the door. "This is something that took place last night, and I haven't had a chance to talk to the NOPD." Jack went on to tell him about the six trucks. "When I get the information from Mrs. Gabby, I want to verify the location of the purchased trucks. If she has the VIN on all of them, maybe we can eliminate the ones that cannot possibly be in this area."

"Then you haven't talked to the NOPD this morning at all?"

Jack shook his head. "No."

"I visited with one of the FBI agents a few minutes ago. NOPD plans to run the surveillance camera tapes on the news this evening. I think it's a mistake," said Sammy.

"They can't do that!" Jack said angrily. "Something kept coming to mind last night. I am reasonably sure I saw that truck or one similar when I was researching a piece about the Flood Control District. I want to look for it and if they run those tapes on that truck, it will disappear."

"My thoughts exactly!" exclaimed Sammy. "My bet is, it may already be gone. It would be great if the truck was sold to someone locally. It might be easier to trace."

Jack said, "How can we stall this TV thing?"

"Don't worry, I'll get it done. When the AG talks, they will listen. Are you going to give the information on the trucks to NOPD when you get it?"

Jack was hesitant to respond. Sammy said, "Problem?"

"I actually wonder if you could get that done. I have concerns." Jack said.

"About the police?"

"Not them, totally; I am not sure I even trust the security in our own building."

Sammy's response was a surprise. "I think your caution is justified. Get the info to me. I can run it down in no time."

"Thanks, I'll do it."

After Sammy left, Mimi came to Jack's door. "Carole Anne MacMorogh is in the office for a while; do you have time to meet her?" Jack was happy to have the opportunity.

She walked through the door, flipping through a message pad.

She stuck her hand out as if she might have been taking lessons from Chas Chacherie across the hall. "Dr. Carole Anne MacMorogh," she said in a strong voice. "You must be Jack."

Jack assured her that he was and asked her if she would prefer to use her own office if it would be more comfortable. She was OK, only had an hour, and would like to visit if he had time. Carole Anne MacMorogh and Will were brother and sister, beyond doubt. Where he was handsome, she was striking , pretty in a different sort of way and something else grabbed you: the eyes. They cinched it.

She took a seat in his visitor chair, leaned it back on two legs, and placed a foot against his desk. She was dressed in scrubs and explained that she was taking some time before returning to the hospital. She was anxious to get on Jack's schedule so she could plan around it. Jack assured her that it was not his schedule; he would work at her convenience.

She got right to it. She explained at first that she had some real concerns about the project and felt he should know about those concerns. When their parents had died, she was twelve, twice the age of Willie. They were fortunate to have the finest two people in the world to be their guardians and she would be forever indebted to both.

"However," she said, "I have a very strong feeling that I got at the time. I felt I was responsible for Willie. If we had not had our relatives, what would have happened to us? What would happen if something happened to them? So I took it upon myself to always keep him foremost in my mind. With that said, I hope you will understand my biggest concern at the moment. Surely, the loss of our parents had a huge impact on all of us. Our grandparents lost a cherished son and daughter-in-law, and Aunt Bea and Uncle Jonathan lost their brother who was, without a doubt, on the brink of becoming a great man."

At that point, she reached out toward Jack with her right hand for emphasis. "Poor Will has suffered one thing after another, most of his adult life. Not only has he suffered physically and mentally, he is on an outcast list in a town full of damn rednecks that have no idea what he has done for them. Because of our company and the strength of it, we are responsible for putting food on the tables in about thirty-five percent of the homes. Yet today, almost seven years later, Will is an outcast in the eyes of many because of a dastardly rumor. I do not want him hurt any further! If this project ends up further embarrassing our family or Will, I will bust my booty to see that it comes to a halt."

With that, she stuck her hand out, thanked Jack for his time, and was gone. This was going to be an interesting venture, for sure.

A short time later, Will appeared at the door. Jack was still pondering Carole Anne's comments and fervor. He greeted Will and waved him in. Will sat in the same chair where his sister had sat earlier, and he leaned back and propped one foot against the desk, just as she had.

A crooked smile broke, "So, you've met Carole Anne?"

Jack grinned and said, "Very striking, a charming young lady."

"You writer fellows really have a way with words." Will laughed. "Carole Anne is a charming lady, and I do love her dearly, but she can get rather intense." Will looked off into the distance, contemplating his next words. "Let me tell you about my sister."

In Will's opinion, Carole Anne had been practicing medicine since she was a child, with dolls, frogs, bugs, dogs, cats, you name it. She was born to be a doctor. She had been in awe of Aunt Bea's presence and stayed in her shadow much of the time. She did not annoy, did not ask many questions, and spoke only if Aunt Bea spoke to her. It was only natural that when their parents were traveling, she spent her time with Aunt Bea and her live-in housekeeper, Rose. Rose was a great nanny.

Will pointed out that Carole Anne had very little social life. Her boyfriend, also a doctor, was as devoted to his practice as she was to hers. They spent time together when possible and seemed to care a great deal about each other; maybe someday, something would come of it. Then Will expressed his real concern. "She has every reason to question not only my ability, but my devotion when it comes to the company. She sees the company as grandfather sees it. She has a strong feeling of responsibility to take care of our people. She would not blame me if at some point I said the people could all go to hell."

"My feeling is not entirely different from hers. I feel just as strong a responsibility as she does, except to the company as its own entity. I would not do anything to let it down. There have been several times during my life that Carole Anne felt she was the only one capable or available to take over the reins someday. Seeing no others on the way, she made a vow to learn as much as she could. She has studied the company in depth, everything it does, all the people, and all that it encompasses. If it came to a point where it was necessary, she would quit medicine and devote the rest of her life to company management."

"My sister has seen me at my worst and still considers me to be fragile and vulnerable. As you learn more about me, you will understand why. So if she gets protective of me, try to understand her. Underneath it all, though—I think it would be devastating to her to have to live up to her vow—quit medicine and go to the company. Medicine is her passion. She probably will never surpass what Aunt Bea has accomplished. I will tell you this, however. If anyone could do that, it would be Carole Anne." Jack could see the love and devotion Will had for his sister and admired him for it.

7

Will suggested they go into his office; it was more comfortable, and he would be close to his phone. Maybe they could talk a little more about his life. Jack had a tape recorder and note pads. He asked Will if he had made any notes. Will pointed to his head and said, "It is all right here." Jack looked a little skeptical.

"I can see where you might be hesitant to rely on my memory, and I understand. My case is a little different, however. Let me relate something to you." Will began to talk. Jack did not attempt to interrupt with comment or questions.

When Will was finished, Jack just sat in silence, clearly in thought. Finally, he said, "I am deeply moved." There was a lot more to learn about Will.

Will also sat silently, reflecting for a moment on his last comments. Then, "Shall we continue?" He began to tell Jack about those earliest days, the time before their parents died. Jack found it hard to believe that one could remember so much about one's life. Going back as far as Will did and still remembering the season, the weather, the moods of the people involved, the enormity of the particular situation, was hard to comprehend. However, Jack now knew the reason.

Will's life began with his earliest recollections. He was "Willie" in those days. His grandfather did not spend much time with him, and Willie was thrilled with the time when he did. Even at three and a half, he liked adventure. One incident in particular took place on a bright spring day at a small fishing pond on the airfield property. He and his grandfather were sitting on the dock, Willie learning to fish. He had his hook baited with a big worm. His grandfather did it perfectly, including spitting on the worm for good luck. He showed Willie how far his cork float should be from the hook. Next, his grandfather showed him where to place the line to be in the best position for a fish. The only thing to do then was to sit quietly, be patient.

Patience was not one of Willie's virtues. His hook had been in the water less than half a minute. It was time to check his worm so decided he needed another. He picked out a new one from the bait box, spit on it, and put it back in the water. He chattered the whole time, talking to the worm. Once he had the hook back in the water, nothing happened immediately so it was time to move the worm. He reasoned that if the fish were not going to come to his worm, he would help the worm look for fish.

In his restlessness, he got up to replace his worm again. This time, he kicked over the worm box, and half the worms fell through the cracks in the dock. Now his grandfather lost *his* patience. He stood, took Willie by the seat of his pants, and pitched him as far out in the pond as he could. Willie was startled beyond belief. It was not until he was back at the dock and out of the water that Willie realized he had learned to swim. However, fighting was on his mind, all he wanted to do was kick his grandfather's shins.

In another story, Willie's father was chief of staff for United States Senator Scoggins. His mother was in charge of the senator's home office. When the Senate was in session, both her husband and the senator were gone. She was constantly on the phone or in face-to-face meetings with constituents, determined to get word to the senator, so in the evenings, she sometimes spent an hour or so on the phone with her husband or with the senator. Most mornings, she was slow to arise, but not Willie.

One morning before his mother arose, he decided to go visit his Uncle Jonathan, Winston, and Aunt Tilda. He slipped quietly out the back door, then through the hedgerow in the backyard and down the alley behind. It was only a few steps to the corner where he could cross the street. Once across, he would be in the back of the large livery building where Uncle Jonathan lived and worked.

Willie was dressed in pajamas; his play dog was along for protection. Uncle Jonathan was busy preparing the shop for opening. He saw his nephew and let out a big, "Hey, Willie!" He was happy to see the boy, but surprised that he was out roaming alone at such an early hour. Uncle Jonathan took him home, where he got a good scolding. The next morning, it was the same routine all over again. Jonathan took him home, he got a light slap on the fanny, and his mother went back to bed. He helped himself to juice and entertained himself until she finally got up. The third time he went visiting, Aunt Tilda took charge.

Matilda Jackson and Winston Jackson, a colored couple, were married while they were both at Tugaloo College. He was going to be a schoolteacher, and so was she. By the time graduation came, Winston's grandfather, Putman Dishman, needed help in the black-smith shop owned by the MacMorogh family. Put's family was one of the first colored families that Seamus MacMorogh had brought to town in the early days. Put begged his grandson Winston to come work with him. Tilda took a teaching job in the colored school until their daughter was born; she then quit to tend to her child. They lived in one of the apartments that adjoined the blacksmith shop in the City Livery building.

Years later, during the worst of the Great Depression, the MacMorogh family came back to live in New Cotswold. Jonathan was a teenager then, but the whole family had to work; he went to work at the blacksmith shop. In time, he moved into the other apart-ment in the City Livery building. To him, Matilda became Aunt Tilda.

So that third morning, when Willie appeared, Jonathan told him to climb aboard. But Aunt Tilda told Jonathan to let her take care of it this time. She took Willie into her apartment and sat him on the counter by the kitchen sink. She took a bath cloth and soap, cleaned his face and hands, wet and combed his hair, and hugged him as tightly as she could. Still today, Will could feel the warmth of her breast against him.

Next, she got a big book from another room, laid it flat on a din-ing chair, sat Will on it, and pulled the chair to the same table where she would serve breakfast to Winston and Uncle Jonathan. After he'd eaten a big breakfast of biscuits, fatback, and eggs, Aunt Tilda wiped his hands good. Afterward, Uncle Jonathan took him home to his sleeping mother.

When the Senate was not in session, Willie's father came home to the district office. Home life settled, and meals and bedtime were regular. When Willie was old enough to play in the neighborhood, he had juice and cereal for breakfast at home and then took off. Little did his parents know he was going straight to Aunt Tilda's kitchen for a breakfast like the one a man should eat.

There was a morning, however, when he opened the kitchen door at Aunt Tilda's, and there in his chair sat a little colored boy. Aunt Tilda was at the stove when she heard the screen door open. Before she could turn around to make introductions, Willie said, "You are in my chair!" Then came a quick response, "No I ain't."

A tug of war ensued. Aunt Tilda interceded with a game of "eenie, meaney, miney, moe, catch a tiger by the toe." First, she let Willie win the chair; it was his, after all. Then John Pope got the first sausage, and by the time she distributed eggs, molasses, and coffee, the two were giggling. That was the beginning of a lifelong friendship.

John Pope's mother was a school teacher like her mother had been. John Pope was already reading little books, knew "*Jesus Loves Me*" without any help, and could count to twenty. Realizing that Willie was behind, Aunt Tilda started working with him. Jonathan saw what was going on and helped. He would send Willie for twenty nails, five bolts, or whatever, in order to get him to practice his numbers. Jonathan started teaching him words that he should always recognize, like "stop," "slow," "fire," and such. Before long, Willie was catching up to John Pope

Every morning when Willie came to the shop, he had a job. There was a cold drink box outside the front door for the use of customers. A cigar box sat on top of the drink box for the customer to pay a nickel and a penny. The nickel was for the drink; the penny was a bottle deposit. The iceman came by early each morning to place a large block of ice in the box. Uncle Jonathan used an ice pick to chip the ice into smaller pieces. Next, he filled the box with Coca-Cola, RC Cola, Nehi Big Red, Nehi Big Orange, and sometimes Grapette, Willie's favorite. Willie's job was to pick up the empty bottles often left scattered around by the customers. A bottle rack was in place for that purpose, but not always used. Willie soon learned to put the bottles into the proper cases. In so doing, he discovered that the town where Coca-Cola was bottled was on the bottom of the bottle. Soon he was learning even more names, like "Tupelo," "Jackson," "Newton," and even "Hattiesburg." He was sure to get ahead of John Pope with that one.

Something else he found out: people did not always come back for their penny deposit. That meant more money for the shop. It did not take Willie long to discover that he could go around the court square and find more bottles left behind. He could take those and retrieve the penny deposit for himself. He began taking his wagon, especially on Saturday, and sometimes he made as much as thirty cents. Occasionally, if he saw someone almost through with their drink, he would simply stand by them until they were finished and then take the bottle from their hand. The first Saturday John Pope came to visit, Willie let him in on the bottle business. It made it even more fun trying to see who could outdo the other. But then a problem arose.

Early on Saturday mornings, a man called Moon always came to the shop. Uncle Jonathan would go to the back of the building and let the man drive his big Lincoln inside the structure. Moon parked in one of the stalls where they put cows and horses on auction days, and there, the man's car was not visible. All day long, he sat back there, selling something. It took a while for Willie and John Pope to realize that the man was selling moonshine whiskey.

Then came the most memorable Saturday morning of all. The man called Moon drove up in front of the shop and went inside. Willie and John Pope were outside, tending the empty bottles. Willie looked up, and hanging out of the window on the passenger side of the big Lincoln was a little red-haired girl with fat cheeks and arms. She also had a mouth full of protruding teeth, all looking like they wanted to escape.

When she smiled, the dimples in her cheeks and her sparkling eyes made Willie blush. He said to her, "You sure are *purdy*." With that, John Pope fell down on the ground, laughing. When he got up, he started mocking Willie, teasing him with, "You sho' are *purdy*. You sho' are *purdy*." The little girl slid down in the car and out of sight.

The man called Moon came out, got in his car, and pulled it into the space inside the building .The little girl stayed with him all day long playing or napping.

The following Saturday, they were back: the man called Moon and the fat little red-haired girl. That day, however, Aunt Tilda found out about the little girl. She would have none of it. She chewed on Winston and Uncle Jonathan unmercifully; called them both fools. Then she had a conversation with the man called Moon.

After a while, she came outside where the boys were taking care of their bottle business. She invited them in for refreshments, something they never turned down. Inside her kitchen, they found the little red-haired girl already sitting at the table with lemonade and cookies, and they met Letitia Mullens. John Pope wanted to know, "What kinda' name's that?"

Tish, as her daddy called her, joined the bottle collection business. That began a lifelong friendship between her and both boys. There was a problem, however; she seemed to think she had management capabilities. Willie and John Pope thought they were doing just fine without her. She had a certain way to place the bottles. Then she did not want even a drop left in the bottles, such silly stuff as that. She won.

The town, as usual, was full with people on Saturdays; a carnival atmosphere existed. The blacksmith shop was busy, with a line of men with wagons waiting for shoeing or repairs. On the courthouse lawn, Indian women set up their wares of baskets and colorful dresses. Some farmers brought watermelons and other vegetables for sale.

The earliest people to arrive claimed the shady spots under the sparse magnolia trees. One of these groups was the Butterfield boys, a rough, ignorant bunch. They were all brothers who lived in shacks down by the river. The river often flooded, and they made their living selling homebrew and noodling for catfish.

Willie, Letitia, and John Pope left the shop, pulling Willie's wagon. Often Willie would ride in the wagon and John Pope would pull, or vice versa. This particular morning, Willie pulled, John Pope rode, and Letitia pushed. When they got to a spot on the sidewalk opposite where the Butterfield boys sat eating watermelon, there was trouble.

The oldest Butterfield, seeing Willie pulling and Letitia pushing while a colored boy rode, felt that this was too much. He got up from where he hunkered, grabbed the wagon tongue out of Willie's hand, and then pulled it straight up, spilling John Pope headfirst onto the concrete. Next, he grabbed Willie by the front of his overalls and shook him. He had his dirty, tobacco stained beard in the boy's face when he said in a loud, fierce voice, "Don't you know better'n to be ridin' a little nigger like he was a prince?"

Willie remembered Letitia's fat little legs churning as fast as they could, her arms tucked into her sides. She was running toward the shop calling, "Daddy!"

Jonathan, the first to see her, grabbed her up as she raced through the door. She was crying now, but able to tell Jonathan what was happening. He broke into a run. Winston laid his hammer down, but just stood. Jonathan would have to handle this alone.

When he got to the scene, the oldest Butterfield still had Willie by the shirt, shaking him and cursing. John Pope was crying and rubbing a bloody spot on his head. The other brothers were laughing, until one saw Jonathan. That brother stood, clutching the knife he'd been using to eat watermelon. Jonathan grabbed the brother who had been shaking Willie but had now turned him loose, and threw him against the trunk of a magnolia tree.

The one with the knife came at Jonathan. He made one thrust; Jonathan stepped aside and grabbed his arm. Willie heard it snap. The brother under the tree got up and ran at Jonathan with his head down, like a mad bull. When he was close enough, Jonathan grabbed the hair of the man's head and smashed his face against his knee. Jonathan turned around to see Moon with a pistol barrel in the mouth of the third brother. But then the marshal showed up, and things calmed down.

Winston calmly walked up, took John Pope by the hand, and walked away. The fire in his eyes burned deeply into several people who had stood around doing nothing to interfere. Aunt Tilda sat the children down after she had gotten all three of their faces washed and had put a patch on John Pope's head. She talked to them about what the man had said. She also told them they had a lot more to learn. How true that was.

Will talked on for another hour, taking Jack up to the point of the crash and his parents' death. "That enough to get you started?" Jack agreed that it was. He was still amazed at what Will had related in the beginning. Now he had gone for another length of time, as if he were reading right from a script. They kicked around another thought or two, before calling it a day.

Jack went back into his office to start transcribing the earlier session. He was pleased; he could make this work, and that was an exciting thought. He had forgotten all about his appointment with Wildlife and Fisheries. He called to apologize and to see if he could make it later that day. He was invited him to come at two o'clock.

Leaning against the windowsill, he stared into space, trying to force his mind to bring up where he thought he had seen that truck. At 1:15, his pager buzzed. It was a message to call Mrs. Gabby.

She apologized for not getting back sooner. "You got a pen?" she asked. First, she gave him the information on the trucks: which ones had sold, along with the name, address, phone, date of sale, mileage on vehicle, VIN, color, and license number at the time of sale. Then she told him about the stolen truck. After five trucks sold, they were not trying as hard to sell the last one. They even used it some more and whoever used it last parked it on the lot next to the building. It could have been a week before anyone noticed it was gone. They reported it stolen but she had all of the information on it also, except for a buyer. Jack took his information across the hall to Sammy's office.

"Got it already?" Sammy said. Jack nodded and passed on his notes. Sammy summoned a secretary and gave her instructions, then said, "Today please, this is rather urgent." Then he asked, "So what is your next step?"

"I 'm late for an appointment at Wildlife and Fisheries. When I leave there, I'm going to look for the truck." Jack said.

"Are you asking NOPD for help?

"No. "

"You sure you are not sticking your neck out, given the fact that whoever tried the bomb yesterday failed? Don't try to act like a lone cowboy on this."

Jack replied, "I think I will start by revisiting two or three companies out on the river road. That's where my subconscious is leading me."

"You know you will be out of this parish and away from the NOPD for protection. You should not be going alone on this." Sammy shook his head to indicate disapproval.

"I haven't given that a thought. All I want to do is see if I see the truck or something that triggers a positive association. If that happens and I need help, suppose I give you a call for assistance."

"Great, take another of my cards. The number is the AG switchboard. They can locate me in minutes, day or night. Also, give me a description of your car and license number," Sammy said.

"That's easy enough. Here are the keys to my rental car, with everything on there, 1958 Ford Thunderbird, black, VIN, and license number." Sammy copied the information, then slipped the note into his shirt pocket.

Jack rose, expressed his appreciation, and then left for his appointment at the Wildlife and Fisheries Department. They were well prepared. In less than an hour, he had all the information he needed, plus some very enthusiastic support for his offshore project.

It was still two hours until dark. Jack stopped by the suite, slipped on jeans, one of his khaki work shirts, and a cap. From the refrigerator he took two bottles of beer and slipped them into a paper sack along with two packages of peanut butter crackers.

He tried Adrianna's phone once more, the receptionist on her floor said she had left for the day. As he was hanging up the phone, he heard a key slip into the lock on the suite door. It startled him, and he wrapped his hand around the neck of one of the beer bottles. The door opened, two suitcases slid in followed by Adrianna herself. She looked at him standing at the wet bar with his hand down inside a paper sack. She threw back her head to toss her hair out of her eyes. "I decided not to go."

Jack nodded, "OK."

"Are you headed somewhere?" she asked.

"Yep."

"Mind if I ask where?"

"To look for that truck. I told you I have a lead." He did not smile. She said nothing for a minute. Jack expected another outburst.

"May I go along?" she finally asked.

"Sure, but maybe you should change clothes," he said as she started to the bedroom. "And bring a jacket; it may get cooler after dark."

In less than five minutes, she was back in the room. "I'll unpack later."

Jack picked up the sack and made sure he had his keys, wallet, money, and pad. In the car, both were silent for a while before Adrianna spoke up. "Tell me how you got onto this truck." Jack told her in detail, beginning with everything that had happened from the time he'd started looking for the logo that could have been on the truck until his latest conversation with Sammy D'Antoni.

Traffic on Friday night, headed toward the Huey Long Bridge, was a nightmare. Jack took Airline to Clearview Pkwy, then south toward the access to the bridge. Instead of crossing, they turned right onto the road that ran along the river levee. It was a rough area with boarded up buildings, a few distressed businesses with advertisements for tire repair, tamales, and used auto parts, and sleazy beer joints.

Soon they arrived in a less populated area. Jack slowed at a gasoline distributor business. He saw some above ground tanks, and a truck sat near a metal building. Once white, it now was rust and gray stain. A sign on a personnel door read, "OFFICE." A loading dock attached to the building held another sign, which read, "LUBRICANTS." Still another, hanging askew, read, "NO SMOKING." The business did not look operational.

Jack turned the car around and drove slowly back by the building. He explained that when he was doing his original investigation, the company was supposedly delivering far more fuel than could have come out of that facility. Back then, he had found an employee on the premises. The man had confirmed this to be the only location of the business. Thinking he would get nowhere, Jack had asked the employee for the phone number or the address of the owner. Surprisingly, the man had scribbled both on a piece of paper.

Jack had gone to Lutcher, Louisiana, where he'd found the owner's house. It was a new, large, plantation style home with two Cadillac sedans snuggled close to a new Ford truck parked in the driveway. Behind the house stood a new metal barn, and in front of the barn, on a triple axle trailer, sat a shrimp boat. A white fence welded from old drill stems surrounded the property. Above the gate, scrolled in iron, "Chateau Dubois." Mr. Dubois owned the gas and oil distribution business. Jack had called him, requesting an interview. Mr. Dubois had declined.

They turned around to continue further out the river road. Within a mile, they came to another place of business on the opposite side of the highway, a retail tire center. It, too, was not of an adequate size to be doing the volume it was doing with the Flood District. Jack had gotten all the information he could on the owner, but had not gotten a home address. The phone number he had was not a working number.

He had contacted a person at the area tire distribution center. After quite a bit of coaxing, the man had relinquished the information Jack needed, that the store was almost out of business. Purchases from the manufacturer were minimal. Only a fraction of their sales actually came from the distributor. Perhaps there was another source, perhaps an illegal one. Jack had also found that the owner owned a home that overlooked the water in Bay St. Louis, Mississippi. Not cheap property.

Suddenly, Jack saw in his rearview mirror a rapidly approaching car with red lights flashing. "I wasn't speeding," he griped. He pulled to the shoulder. The officer in the car focused a powerful spotlight through the back glass of the rented Thunderbird. Two officers got out, and each came to opposite sides of the vehicle. Jack lowered his window.

The officer on his side spoke first. "License, please." Jack reached for his wallet and asked, "What's the problem?" The officer looked at the license and then addressed Adrianna. "Out of the car please, Ma'am."

Jack said, "Hey, what is this?"

Adrianna did as instructed. The officer on her side told her to stand in place.

The officer on Jack's side said in a low voice, "You OK, Mr. Ward?"

"Sure," Jack said, still puzzled. "What's going on?"

"Investigator D'Antoni with the AG's office has us keeping an eye out for you. According to him, you are supposed to be traveling alone."

Jack started laughing. "She is my girlfriend. I 'm OK."

"Just thought you might have been kidnapped," the officer said. "Let 'er go, Rex," he said to his partner.

The partner opened the door for Adrianna and tipped his hat politely. "Sorry for the intrusion."

The officer standing next to Jack's window said, "I am Officer Meador; my partner is Sergeant Ray. We 'll be in the vicinity until D'Antoni tells us otherwise. Will you call him when you are leaving the area, so he can cut us loose?"

"Sure," Jack assured him, "and thanks."

They pulled back onto the road and continued on the way. "What was that all about?" Adrianna asked.

"They thought you might have kidnapped me and had me at gunpoint."

"There are times I feel like pointing a gun and pulling the trigger," she replied.

Dusk settled in. It was dark when they approached a side road. Jack slowed. The road ran north off the river road. It was familiar. About one hundred yards down that road stood an older building with a new glass showroom. Behind the building, a board fence about eight feet high surrounded a large area. Two large chain link gates guarding the fenced area stood open. On a fascia across the front of the building was printed the name of the business, "VELMA's EQUIPMENT CO." Smaller print below read, "Heavy Equipment Rental, Used Trucks, Tractors, Parts & Accessories."

Jack's chest tightened. He braked to make a quick turn onto the road, and drove slowly past the business. The showroom lights were on, indicating that the business might still be open; one lone man leaned at a counter. Jack was sure that this was the place, and he was determined to look inside that fence. He drove past, maybe a half mile, and found a place to turn around. Then he stopped the car and said to Adrianna, "I want to look in the yard in back of that building. Here's the plan. You drive, and I'll get down in back. Drive alongside the building far enough toward the gate for that person at the counter not to see the driver's side of the car. You get out; I will roll out onto the ground, then sneak along the side of the building to get through that gate. While I do that, I want you to go inside and engage the man in conversation for a few minutes, just long enough for me to look around."

"Jack, you are nuts, what am I going to say to him?" she asked.

"Tell him you and your husband are looking for a small tractor for your farm."

"But I do not have a husband, much less a farm," she laughed.

"Fake it 'til you make it," he said.

As they approached the property Jack said, "I wish I had a flashlight." Adrianna dug in her purse and held up her house keys.

A tiny flashlight dangled from the ring. She did what Jack asked, driving in, parking, and stepping out, starting to walk toward the building entrance. Jack rolled onto the ground. In a crouch, he ran into the shadows alongside the building, then stepped through the gate. Inside the yard, at the back of the building, he looked right and left. Down the right, toward the end of the building, light shone from a large overhead door. He could hear the sound of an impact wrench.

An assortment of dismantled vehicles sat along the fence facing Jack but no little truck. As his eyes grew more acclimated to the dark, he spotted something at the back corner of the fence. There was a large dark shape. He realized that it was a tarp pulled over a mound of something. He could make out what appeared to be the hood of a vehicle facing outward, and then maybe a large square like a box, with a bulge on top. There were heavy truck tires on the tarp, probably to keep it secure in the wind. The tarp and tires further disguised what was underneath. That's it, Jack thought to himself. Again, he looked all around, especially toward the overhead door where he saw light. He hung to the fence on his side until he got to the end, then darted across to the tarp covered object. Other vehicles stood on both sides, so it was hard to wedge in between.

He managed to get on his hands and knees before crawling under the tarp on the driver's side of the vehicle. He was sure he had hit pay dirt. That was, until he got the tarp up and realized that the truck was not a light color but was red. Struggling to half stand under the tarp, he managed to get a door open far enough to read the serial number on the doorjamb. It was dusty and filmed over with red overspray. Jack spit on his fingers to clear the VIN. With the key chain light, he was able read the number. Hot damn! It was the same number he had on the card in his hand. The truck was freshly painted; he could smell it. He shined the light into the cab of the truck. Just visible was a cardboard box.

Suddenly, he heard the loud thunder of an un-muffled engine start up at the other end of the property, his heart pounded. The engine revved to full throttle, and tires screamed as rubber burned. In seconds, another scream of rubber, as the vehicle skidded to a stop right in front of where he was crouched. He did not move. Then the same loud thunder of the engine, and again rubber burned. The smoke from the rubber drifted under the tarp as the thundering vehicle raced back to the other end of the lot. "Thank-you, Lord," Jack muttered to himself. "Since you've come this far, can you hang with me just another minute or two?"

He then dropped back to his knees and wedged himself further back past the truck door. With his feet against the open door, he managed to open it wider. It was impossible to get his whole body in, but he wanted that box. He reached an arm across the seat, stretching as far as he could. He was able to grab onto a flap of the box, and he pulled it toward him. Here again, he could not get the box through the narrow opening.

By now, sweat was stinging his eyes. He was strictly going by feel. He managed to get the light between his teeth, and by squeezing his other arm in, he ripped the bottom flaps loose from the box, flattening the box and dragging it outside. He handled it as much as possible on the inside of the box, where there would be less probability of smearing any prints. Gasping for air, he managed to get himself and the folded box out from under the tarp. He stood still for a few seconds, casting a careful eye toward the overhead door, in the direction of which he could now hear the idling engine. Just a few more seconds was all he needed. Still under the tarp, he worked his way around the back of the truck on his hands and knees, going far enough to lie on his side and pull himself to a point where he could see the right rear wheel of the truck. No wheel cover.

He followed the same path he had taken getting to the truck, in order to get back to the rented Thunderbird. Peering over the side, he could see Adrianna standing near the front door, still talking to the man inside. She turned toward the door; the man stepped past her and opened it for her. Oh crap, thought Jack, he is going to walk her to the car. Again, his heart started thumping. But the two of them got to the corner of the building, where they stopped. Adrianna leaned toward the man and kissed him on the cheek, "You have been so nice; we'll see you tomorrow." With that, she turned and trotted to the car, leaving the man standing there. The man turned, went back inside, locked the front door, then started dousing lights.

Adrianna came around the front of the car where Jack knelt behind the door. "Quick, open the door," he said. As soon as she did, he dived inside. She got in and started the car. "I found the truck. Can you believe it; it is sitting there under a tarp." He was almost screaming with joy. As they drove off the lot, a loaded pickup, sagging on its springs, turned into the driveway. The "VELMA'S" company logo was on the door.

A soon as they got to a place to stop, Jack got out and took the wheel. "We have to get to a phone and call D'Antoni. I have to get this box to him."

"What's the deal with the box?" Adrianna asked.

"The surveillance tapes show two persons getting out of the truck with cardboard boxes over their heads. They hid their faces while they sprayed the surveillance cameras. This may be one of the boxes used. It was in the truck," Jack said excitedly. "And besides that, a wheel cover is missing."

When he was done, she said, "I think you will like my tractor. It has a backhoe, whatever that means. I do not particularly care for the color. The man said my model only comes in orange. Can you believe that?"

"You did a great job, darling. I could not have pulled this off without you!"

She reached across and took his hand. "We are a pretty good team, aren't we?"

"The best," he answered. Neither said more about the spat the night before. "Let's find a phone. I'll call Sammy D'Antoni, see what he suggests we do now."

The phone was at a place selling hot boudin. While Jack called Sammy, Adrianna bought two large rings of the sausage.

Sammy was elated at Jack's find. "Tell you what," he said. "Stay right where you are. I will call a couple of state troopers in the area to come to you. Hand over what you have to them, I'll get it to the FBI, and we will go from there."

"I think I met your troopers," laughed Jack. He told Sammy about their stopping him. Within minutes, Adrianna spotted flashing red lights coming at them from the west. The troopers pulled in, and the driver got out and greeted them again. Jack handed over what he had.

Once again, they had missed their usual Friday night get together with the gang at Justin's. Both agreed that even though the others might all still be there, they themselves were tired. They went to the hotel, showered, cracked open cold Dixie 45s, and ate boudin with saltines.

8

Early on Monday morning, Jack headed straight to his workspace then went across the hall, where Sammy was already at work. He motioned Jack back to his office.

Sammy said, "It's too early to know if we have any prints that are worth anything. Unless we find matches on your car or prints of somebody with a known record, we may not have any reason to go in to look at the truck. You were not there legally. At this point, we do not have a leg to stand on." Jack pondered that, and agreed that they would just have to wait.

When he got back across the hall, Mimi was in. and someone was on the phone in the office that Dr. Bea and Will's sister Carol Anne used. Mimi asked about his weekend, and they chitchatted a moment before Dr. Bea stepped to the door of her office. She, too, expressed her concern. He gave both her and Mimi a synopsis.

Dr. Bea invited Jack into her office, closed the door, and motioned him to sit across from her desk. She said, "I am concerned about your safety. If you need a place to hide out, let me know. I might have just the place."

Jack thanked her and said he thought it would be over in a few days. For now, he felt safe. The failed attempt had given him more courage. Then he asked about establishing a schedule of convenient times to meet with her.

She explained how she and Carole Anne alternated weekends, covering the office and making patient rounds. The one who worked took off the following Monday. On her Mondays, she usually came into the office to take care of anything pertaining to the company. She would like to meet with him also on those days. She could spare a few minutes that day, in fact, if he had time.

She had a list of people he should talk with, and she now handed the list across.

Dr. Beatrice MacMorogh,	N.O.
Dr. Carole Anne MacMorogh	"
William MacMorogh, III	"
Mrs. Anne MacMorogh	New Cotswold
Jonathan MacMorogh	"
Winston Jackson	"
Matilda Jackson	"
Maureen Mullens	"
Gen. William MacMorogh, Sr	"
Maudie Lee Jackson	Mobile
Rev. John Pope	Birmingham
Charles Chacherie	N.O.
Mrs. Grace Abernathy	Jackson

Jack said that he would put people and places in chronological order later. His main objective was starting interviews with everyone to get as much information as possible before he started his own research. He had also constructed a flow chart that would show other persons recommended by the persons on the original list.

Dr. Bea said, "Most of what I learned about Seamus I learned from a wonderful woman by the name of Maudie Lee Jackson. Her name is on the list I made. She is someone you must go visit, and I suggest that you visit her soon. Not that she is in poor health. Quite the contrary; she is ninety-three years old, fit as a fiddle, brighter than most people her age, and a sports fanatic. She lives in a house next door to her caretaker in Mobile. I first met her by accident right after I got out of med school. I loved visiting with her. I try to see her a couple of times a year, and we chat on the phone every month or so. She is a delight."

Dr. Bea continued, "When you decide to go, and you must, let me know. I will make all the arrangements, with the exception of buying her a quart of Old Crow. I will let you take care of that. Remember, a quart, not a fifth."

"Also," she said. "I suggest that you talk to all the people that were in that article you read." Jack acknowledged that he had already listed those.

"We are not ones to talk about ourselves, so you will probably learn more about each of us based on the perspective of others," Dr. Bea laughed. "And that may make for some interesting reading!"

Then she told Jack about the four boxes of documents she had collected over the years. One was full of things she had gotten from Grandmother Mollie and had never gone through. The information might very well hold some important keys. They went to the closet, and she gave Jack a brief chronology of each box. There were individual packets that at one time had been in chronological order. Also, in the beginning, she had tried to separate the many pieces of paper according to whether they pertained to personal or business, but she'd given up with that along the way. Finally, in fact, had given up on the project altogether.

One last note: Mimi kept the key to the closet in the safe. She would give it to him when needed. They agreed to meet again on her next scheduled Monday in the office.

Jack planned to work in his office the rest of the day. However, at mid-morning, his pager summoned him. It was Bill Pullen; the NOPD was in his office, something had come up, and could Jack come over?

When Jack got there, Detective Lt. Bridges and Detective Sgt. Wade greeted him. By the looks on their faces, it was apparent that they were not happy. Right away, the discussion went to Jack's Friday evening excursion, the discovery of the truck, and the prints on the box. "Why did we have to get it third hand, since it had passed from D'Antoni to the FBI and then to us, when you knew damn well it was our case? We might have someone in jail by now."

Jack decided to eat crow rather than fire back at them. He begged off, pleading fear and excitement when he found the truck. He knew he should have contacted them, even though he was out of their jurisdiction at the time. They bought little of it and told him so.

Lt. Bridges said with a smirk, "Now, unlike you, we have something to share, and we are ready to move on it." What he shared was, "The day of the bomb scare, the man who ran the sweeping machine to clean the garage made a discovery. Lo and behold, he found a wheel cover near one of the speed bumps. It was an aftermarket cover, but of the same size wheel used on the Chevrolet truck. The best part, it has a bright slick finish, with finger prints and palm prints all over it. And…" Lt. Bridges left Jack hanging.

Taking his time, he finally said, "The prints belong to a Wilford Wasserman, ANA Goofy. His last known address is with his mother. He has a prior, boosted a billfold from a taxi where he worked. Got thirty in parish jail."

"Next…," and Bridges paused, dragging Jack along again. "Guess who his attorney was? Well, would you believe, Mike Messina, board member of the Orleans Parish Flood Control District? Same folks you have succeeded in nailing to the cross."

Jack responded, "Do you really think there is a connection? I know there are some bad actors on the board, but not that bad."

"Best thing we can do is to find Wasserman," Lt. Bridges said. "We had to chase his mother down, and we found her selling tickets at the Gretna Ferry. She hasn't seen Wilford in weeks. She sent us to his stepsister. Same thing; she has no idea where he might be."

Now he just sat silent. Jack waited. Finally, "If we find him," Bridges said, "he will run all this through your friend D'Antoni. I am sure he will keep you abreast." No sooner did he have it out of his mouth than Jack's pager sounded. "Call Sammy!" They all heard the message.

Jack smiled. "Maybe he read your minds, and I can get it right now." He dialed Sammy's office, and the receptionist announced his call. Sammy asked for Jack's whereabouts. Jack told him, but could not tell him who else was present. Sammy went on to tell Jack what Jack had, moments before, already heard from Lt. Bridges. Jack made notes.

When Jack got off the phone, Lt. Bridges said, "Well?"

Jack said, "Oh, that call from Sammy? We are meeting at his brother's sandwich shop for lunch, and then maybe we'll go for a beer or two, shoot a little pool."

Lt. Bridges had watched Jack while he was on the phone. He knew Jack had jotted down the same information he himself divulged earlier. He said, "Jack, am I the only one that ever calls you an asshole?"

Jack smiled, "Surely you jest."

Lt. Bridges said, "We will keep you informed, old buddy."

As they parted, Jack said, "By the way, I guess Messina does not know where Wasserman is?"

Lt. Bridges looked at Sgt. Wade, and both faces turned red.

Jack said, "I may be an asshole, but I am a smart one."

That evening, after describing the discussion with Dr. Bea in Will's office, Jack told Adrianna about the whole day, including the information about the wheel cover discovery and the possibility of a lead on the bombers.

He also told her about the woman Dr. Bea wanted him to visit in Mobile. He suggested that they drive over to Biloxi after work on Friday. On Saturday, he would go over to visit with the woman in Mobile, and Adrianna could read and soak up sun on the beach. Soaking up sun and eating at their favorite Gulf Coast restaurant got a thumbs up from Adrianna.

Jack contacted Dr. Bea the next morning and by late afternoon, Mimi had instructions for him. The meeting with Maudie Lee Jackson in Mobile was set for Saturday at 2:00 PM. Dr. Bea gave general directions, and Mimi provided a Mobile map. For the next two days, Jack worked like a Trojan, juggling work he needed to do for the paper and getting as much done as possible on the MacMorogh project.

On Thursday, his pager was beeping before he could get out of bed. Call Lt. Bridges, Urgent. As soon as Jack had him on the line, Lt. Bridges started talking, and fast. He reiterated to Jack what he currently knew. They had contacted Mike Messina. Wasserman's mother was married at one time to Mike Messina's father, but after Mike had been born. His contact with Marie was limited, but he had taken an interest in Wilford simply out of concern for the welfare of the boy. In Messina's words, Wilford, for a lack of a better word, was *slow*. He verified that he had represented him when he'd stolen the wallet in the cab. Since that time, he felt that he'd been successful in helping him not only to find work but to stay out of trouble as well.

Then Lt. Bridges said, "Wasserman is working at the place you found the truck! Messina is going to go with us to interview him. We will stay in touch. And by the way, Jack, thanks."

9

Jack and Adrianna left on Friday for the Mississippi Gulf Coast. They checked in at a motel right on the beach, lounged in a shaded cabana, and drank cold beer. That night, they went to a dinner club show with a great comedian. The next morning, Jack made the short drive to Mobile alone, leaving Adrianna to sunbathe, read, and catch up on her sleep.

He found the address for Maudie Lee with no problem, thanks to Mimi. The house was in a predominately colored section of the city. It was upscale, all brick. At one time, the neighborhood had been all white, but it was slowly transforming into colored. It was still well kept and held a lot of charm.

Maudie Lee's house sat on a corner lot, where the front faced a busy street. A detached garage at the back of the house connected with a breezeway. The garage faced the side street. The yard was well maintained, clipped, and edged with care. Jack parked on the side and walked in the street around to the front of the house rather than crossing the yard.

Leading from the street to the front door was a brick walk laid in a herringbone design. A colorful array of zinnias grew on each side of the walk. On both sides of the front steps, blue hydrangeas had been planted, and azaleas lined the front of the house, rounding the left corner and following the porch.

As he reached the front steps, a voice within called out that the screen door was unlatched. "Come on in!" Stepping onto the front porch, he heard a greeting from a big white, cane back rocker. Maudie Lee. She was dressed in all white linen, starched to perfection. Black beads, with a matching cross, hung at her neck. Her white hair, fixed in a bun at the back of her head, had mother-of-pearl combs holding it in place.

Even though her face was lined, Jack saw that she must have been gorgeous when she was young. She held out her hand for him to take. He did and introduced himself. She said she had been looking forward to his visit since Beatrice called.

A woman quietly stepped through the open front door of the house. She placed a large pitcher of lemonade with two iced crystal glasses on a table between Maudie Lee and a chair similar to hers. This was Reba. She was introduced by Maudie Lee as her companion, caretaker, and watchdog. Reba exclaimed that Maudie Lee indeed needed watching at times. They all laughed.

Maudie Lee told Reba she could go on back to her TV, as she and Jack would be visiting for a spell. Reba left the porch for a moment, but came back with an unopened pack of Lucky Strikes and a gold cigarette lighter.

After Reba left, Jack reached into his briefcase to take out the quart of Old Crow that he'd purchased that morning. Maudie cut her eyes cautiously to the door, then with both hands, motioned for Jack to pass her the bottle. She quickly stuffed it into the large sewing bag to the left of her chair and immediately covered it with crochet work. She whispered her thanks across to Jack. "She watches me like a hawk," she said as she shook her head from side to side and patted the arm of the chair.

They chatted a bit about the weather, the times, and baseball before she took a long, deep breath, and then told Jack she was well aware of what the MacMorogh family was attempting. She was only too happy to give what history she could. To begin with, she said she was probably the most expert on Seamus MacMorogh, William's father. She was quick to point out that the "William" she referred to was the first William, the one now referred to as "the General." After that, she gave a heavy, "Humph."

For one solid hour, Maudie Lee talked, sometimes with great animation, sometimes laughing out loud at things that, to her, were funny. Exactly at the end of the hour, Reba appeared, walked over to Maudie Lee's chair, took her cane from across the arms of the chair, and helped her stand. Once on her feet, she stood as erect and tall as she probably had been when she was a young woman. Reba walked behind her as they departed the front porch without explanation.

A few minutes passed before they returned in the same fashion. Reba stood beside her chair as Maudie Lee easily seated herself. She then explained that she took powders every hour on the hour. It would not be polite to do so in front of company. She also explained the cigarettes. She had quit smoking thirty years back, but thought about it every day or two. If there were some right at hand, she did not seem to want one as badly as if none were readily available.

The next hour went as the first. Only once did Maudie Lee thumb through some very well-worn postcard sized notes. In addition, she had a photo or two of things of interest. She thought that maybe Jack might take them with him for copying. However, she did want them back. Then Reba appeared as before, and they made their trip and returned. This time, Reba replenished the lemonade.

During the third hour, Maudie Lee stopped halfway. She told Jack that she was about through. For the most part, she had covered the life of the MacMoroghs from the time she first knew of Seamus until the time that he built a house in Memphis. Before that, she had visited a lot with Seamus's wife, Mollie; they were dear friends and stayed in contact. She suggested several other people, still living, that Jack should visit. Most lived in and around New Cotswold. Some were white, others colored. She had made a list.

Jack referred to his notes to talk about several other people they had not mentioned. Jack confirmed that she was a Dishman, daughter of the first Dishmans Seamus had brought to town. Who was the Mr. Jackson that she had married? She had met him at Tougaloo College and married him there, during her first year at school. Seamus took a liking to Mr. Jackson and got him a job as a conductor on the railroad. Eventually he was head conductor and trained all the rest.

She mentioned her son, Winston Jackson, but only in passing. Jack asked her to tell him more about him. She sat without answering for a long time before she answered. "You should visit with him. He is a fine man, a very fine man. As you folks go along with this story, maybe Beatrice will have some say as to what all goes in it."

Reba appeared again. Maudie Lee got up, but this time she stuck out her hand and expressed her delight in having visited with Jack. She also suggested that maybe they might meet again sometime. Call her if need be. Without another word, she went into the house.

Jack walked slowly to his car, then started once to go back, but decided he should be content to have what he had. He could already write a book on what Maudie Lee had told him about Seamus. It was strange, though, that when he had mentioned Winston, it had turned off the spigot.

Back with Adrianna, Jack could not wait to tell her about the afternoon. At dinner, it was the same, all he could talk about, what Maudie Lee had said, how she'd said it, the inflections she made in her speech. He wished that he could have spent more time with her.

On Sunday morning on the way home, Adrianna was driving; Jack was thumbing through his notes. He was in high spirits. He was confident that he had enough for the book. That evening, back in their suite, Jack started checking his answering service for messages, and there was a string: Bomar at the paper, Lt. Bridges, Mike Messina. He would return calls early on Monday. He prioritized them before going to bed.

On Monday, Jack called Lt. Bridges first, suggesting that they get together in an hour. Next he spoke with Bill Pullen, who questioned what was going on and whether Jack had heard from the NOPD. Finally, Mike Messina. Jack decided to wait on that one. At the station, he was met not only by Lt. Bridges and Sgt. Wade but by Capt. Joe as well. They were smiling and shook hands all around. "Have we a tale to tell you!" stated Lt. Bridges.

They had interviewed Wasserman, and yes, the poor fellow was slow. In the beginning of the interview, they showed him the wheel cover. When asked if he recognized it, he was thrilled to death. It belonged to his truck. Further questioning about his whereabouts at 9:30 a.m. on the day of the bomb confused them all. He could not tell them where he was at that particular time. He only knew he was on the road going to Mississippi; how could he know exactly where he was at 9:30 a.m.? That was when they asked questions of Wasserman's supervisor, a Mr. Moore. He confirmed Wasserman's whereabouts. There was confusion again when they asked to see the truck. Wasserman did not know where it was. It took a long time and a lot of patience before Messina was able to get more of the story. Wasserman was not yet through paying for the truck. The person he'd bought the truck from worked there at Velma's also. He was the one who had painted it red, but the man had left town and taken the truck with him.

They called Mr. Moore again for help, and he verified the story. The man and his brother had skipped town. From that point, Lt. Bridges boastfully told how he and his team had diligently gone to work and traced the people down in Idaho. As far as the truck, it was along the highway, abandoned in Louisiana with two flat tires. When they got it back to the city, they found more prints and struck it rich. One of the prints was from a known bomb expert with ties to the Biloxi Mafia. Some arrests were made, and others were pending. They saved the story for Jack to report.

Jack had one other call, to Mike Messina. The man was relieved to hear from him, and told Jack it was important that they get together as soon as possible. Could they meet for a drink? It was almost five, and Jack was anxious to meet Adrianna. After all, he had good news: they could move back to their apartment and get his car back. There was going to be a celebration that evening. Jack tried to postpone Messina, but the man was insistent. Jack feared that this was about the Flood Control District piece. He did not care to discuss it.

Finally, after more insistence, he agreed. It would have to be quick and at the Sazerac Bar in the Roosevelt. That was perfect; Messina was no more than fifteen minutes away. When Messina arrived, he insisted that they sit at the bar. The bartender came for their order, and Messina ordered a beer, Jack a martini. When the bartender brought the drinks, he placed a cardboard beer coaster under the beer and a nice napkin under the martini. After he left, Messina reached into his pocket, took out another beer coaster, and switched it with the napkin under Jack's drink.

An odd conversation ensued, mostly from Messina's side. He was glad that Jack's final exposé had revealed the fact that he, Messina, was not involved with any of the wrongdoing. Lastly, Messina told Jack not to be surprised at anything that might happen. He got up to leave and said, "Thanks, for your service to the community; I hope I can consider you a friend. By the way, do not leave that coaster behind." Jack took it, turned it over, and read: "You are looking in the wrong place; follow the money. In, out, and back."

Jack sat back down. He just stared at Messina. "You?" he asked.

Months before, there had been an identical coaster, but it had been anonymous. It had triggered Jack's investigation. Three more, with clues, had arrived in envelopes with no return address. Jack, all the while, was suspicious that they had come from an Assistant DA involved in the investigation. And no one else but Jack knew about the coasters.

The last item under Jack's by-line had included this statement: "The arrest of Walter LaLonde and his imposed resignation from the Orleans Parish Flood Control District Board leaves little doubt that Mike Messina is now the front-runner in the forthcoming election for City Councilman.

The following morning, Jack went to work with some anxiety. He had not received a response to his request for leave. He did not want to resign, but if that was what it took, he was prepared to do so. He met this time with Pullen in Bomar's office. After they sat down, Bomar got right to it. Jack's proposal to take leave was acceptable, but they had a request. Would Jack consider a weekly column while he was on leave, and when he returned, would he go on the sports desk? He was elated. "Yes to both questions. When can I start my leave?"

"Now," smiled Bomar. "Go, before we change our minds. You know that you are temporarily leaving quite a void here. One more thing: do not go putting any ideas in your girlfriend's mind."

10

On the first day of his leave, Jack stopped in at the paper to collect a few things. The place was the same beehive of activity. There was excitement that someone outside the newspaper business would not understand. The prospect of something about to break, and knowing that he could be in the middle, had kept his adrenalin flowing for seven years. He knew that he had gotten sick of crime reporting, had even called it a cesspool, but…was this something he really could walk away from, even for just six months?

Mimi was all smiles when he arrived at his new office. She had the latest paper open to the article with his by-line; she was a real fan. That afternoon, Jack made a work plan with tentative dates for different plateaus aimed toward a completion date. Afterward, he transcribed his interview with Maudie Lee. That section of the history was well underway.

The following day, he dug into the first document box handed over by Dr. Bea. It did not take long to realize that he was finding material way over his head. There were financial records, contracts, lawsuits, bank records, stacks of things he did not recognize. That evening, he confessed his consternation to Adrianna. The documents held the key to the company history. He needed help deciphering and cataloging the material.

She reminded Jack about Jan Plow. Jan had come to work as a copywriter at the paper, and for the first few weeks, she had not seemed to fit in. She was quiet; Jack said mousey. She was morose and kept to herself. However, she did her work better than any of the other staff. She was a complete surprise; the more work and responsibility she got, the more originality she exhibited.

Later, Adrianna found out something else about Jan, quite by accident. After the bomb scare, Jan was more upset than the others were. She fell back into her quiet state and had less enthusiasm.

Adrianna, in an attempt to get her back on track, asked if she might drop by Jan's apartment one evening. It was a small one bedroom in a nice house on Canal St. Surprisingly, Jan had a baby grand piano. There were stacks of music on every shelf, and on one shelf rested a picture of Jan and a young man. A diploma revealed that Jan had a degree in business administration.

Adrianna questioned her about her music and the grand piano. All Jan said was, "I grew up singing and playing piano. My mother taught music, and my father loved singing in a gospel quartet. I am the pianist in the family." Meanwhile, when it came to the business degree, she had earned it from Peabody College and had hoped to work as a CPA. Upon graduation, she had taken a job in an accounting firm in her hometown. But soon came a need to go somewhere else; she needed to be away from her parents and her old neighborhood. New Orleans was the new place, and Adrianna knew the rest.

Jack contacted Jan to discuss the project and to have her look at the material in the document boxes; she was thrilled. The next evening, Jack signed a "check out" slip for Mimi and brought the material home. Jan came over for hamburgers. The three of them sat on the living room floor and ate the hamburgers off the coffee table before digging into the boxes. After they were finished with their meal, Jan and Jack went to work. Along the way, Jan made a few comments, mostly consisting of remarks such as, "Oh, my goodness."

At eleven, she stood and excused herself to go to the bathroom. She padded back in her stocking feet and exclaimed, "I do not have a lot of professional experience, but what I see here is enough material for me to reconstruct the early days of Seamus' business empire."

Jack was ecstatic. Would she be willing to do it for a satisfactory hourly wage? Would she agree to sign a Statement of Confidentiality? Jan clasped her hands together with an enthusiastic, "Oh yes, how exciting!"

Seamus MacMorogh: Family Patriarch

Thus began the chronicling of the Seamus years. Jan worked after hours and weekends. She touched base frequently, always with new and exciting revelations. Many evenings, she and Jack worked off the coffee table while Adrianna cooked and kept the coffee pot going. The MacMorogh history was coming together.

There was nothing factual about the ancestry of the MacMorogh family prior to Seamus. There was a monument to him in the Old Church Graveyard in New Cotswold where his body stood today. His tomb was above ground and held an upright casket, because it was his desire to look out over his vast holdings forever.

He was possibly the son of either Elijah or Elisha MacMorogh. They might have been twins and had lived in the Tennessee, Georgia, and Alabama regions during the Civil War. There were documents showing purchases of spirits from either Elijah or Elisha MacMorogh or both, and purchases by both armies. Confusion over the spelling of the names could also mean that Elijah or Elisha were one and the same. Whether they arrived in the states through the original colonies or through Canada was not certain. However, the Georgia, Alabama, connection leaned toward entry through the colonies.

Seamus arrived in the general area of New Cotswold around 1866 or 1867. The war had decimated the town, and much of the surrounding farmland was fallow. Some cities were only memories of what they once were. Settlements that had been on the brink of becoming viable communities had all but disappeared. Land was cheap, but there was little money.

Some of the same land went to the Choctaw Indians in the Treaty of Dancing Rabbit in 1831. As result of the treaty, some Indians went to a new reservation on the new frontier of Oklahoma. An alternative 640 acres of land went to those who wished to remain. Some of those few succeeded in farming or in other occupations. Others eventually sold or simply left the land and moved on to Oklahoma.

Means of transportation were poor. Army wagons or horse drawn cannons made deep ruts, and the roads were impassable. This was surely the case in Cool Springs, the name first given to the settlement. The Choctaws befriended the earliest settlers, taught them their ways, and established a bartering system.

Long before the war, settlers made a viable settlement. They founded New Cotswold in1833, and the name changed from Cool Springs. Like many other settlements, some essential businesses and services were established. There were a three saloons, a livery, a hotel, a mercantile store, a small school, two churches, a doctor, a barber/dentist, one bank, a land office, and a town hall. Outside of farming, the lumber mill was the number one employer. The owner of the millworks hid it during the war, but not well enough; enemy soldiers had destroyed it.

There was a plan for a railroad. Surveying was complete and some rights-of-way purchased. That rail line would have run north to an existing line in Tupelo. That line joined another to Memphis. More important for the lumber mill would have been a line that would connect to one at Mobile Alabama; it ran east and west.

How Seamus knew of the area was unclear. What was clear was that he knew as much about the area as the people who were among the earliest settlers. He did not simply stumble upon the town; it was his planned destination. He claimed no allegiance to either side during the war, nor did he ever indicate that he'd fought for either side. This led some to believe he might have come out of Canada. When asked about his background, he would reply, "Let's put the past behind us and go forth in diligent pursuit of good health and prosperity." He volunteered nothing else.

Another fact that puzzled the community: he arrived with an apparently bottomless purse. His first stop was at the one and only bank in town. No one knew the source of the money, but some believed it to be from the whiskey trade. Whiskey making was an old Irish and Scottish tradition. The land the Irish found, traveling into the Appalachians west of Pennsylvania, was ideal for whiskey. If that was the source of his money, it could have meant he was from a family of earlier settlers in that area.

It was no surprise to many that his first venture would indeed be whiskey making. Since most of the settlement relied on farming, the prospect of growing crops like corn was exciting; it could be consumed in short time. Corn converted to alcohol did not require immediate shipping and would last forever.

In the beginning, Seamus purchased large sections of land. The land offered acre upon acre of rich soil laid down by flooding of the nearby rivers, the Pearl and Big Black. Further west lay the Mississippi Alluvial Plain offering more fertile land deposited year by year from floodwaters of the Mississippi River. The land in the east gave way to higher ridges, some with outcroppings of limestone. On much of the land, Seamus found a variety of timbers including cedar, pine, oak, walnut, beau d'arc, and willow.

For his whiskey making, the oak would provide barrels for stowing and shipping. The pine and beau d'arc would fuel the stills. The numerous springs provided pure cool water; the farmland provided the corn. The other timbers offered substantial building material for future development. There was a definite need of another sawmill.

Copper for the stills came from Memphis, Seamus' last stop before arriving in New Cotswold. While he waited for notification that the copper was at the rail station in Jackson, he went about learning more about the community. He spent many days and evenings on the gallery of his rented house, talking to leaders of the settlement about the future. Seamus' enthusiasm spread among some who saw the opportunity for more rapid recovery. He offered financial aid to bolster the enthusiasm. His relationship was welcome because he *listened to* their vision before he shared his.

Many colored free men came to town of their own accord, and if not, Seamus imported them. They were accepted, but they lived in their quarter on the other side of the creek that divided the town. They had had little input or acknowledgement prior to Seamus arriving.

Just as he quietly arrived, Seamus then disappeared, causing some concern. But he did return, this time with a new wagon and a load of copper sheets. He solicited the help of Irish in the town who knew the business, and soon he was making whiskey. His purchases of locally grown corn improved the small economy. There was a small market for the whiskey in the area, but not enough to support his vision. As soon as he had a couple of wagonloads, Seamus set out to peddle his product. Soon he was sending shipments to Vicksburg for transport on steamboats to markets in Natchez, Port Gibson, and on to New Orleans. The whiskey making operations bolstered his already deep pockets.

Seamus was sociable, but he made no close friends. His coming and going without notification was unsettling. However, he always returned with a new idea from wherever he might have been. Most often, he returned with a small band of craftsmen with skills that Seamus foresaw being necessary for future ventures.

A plan was in his mind for rebuilding the town, but he did not want to set forth without community input. He needed all the support he could get for his long-range vision. Evenings spent on his gallery often ended in disagreements. Some of his ideas were not as popular as he wished. But eventually, there was mutual agreement on what the town might become. Retail establishments that would attract trade from others in the area, including from the Indians, were important. New public buildings, schools, churches, courthouses, a hospital, and a jail were absolute necessities. These they platted in likely spots on a map. There was much discussion about a railroad.

To many who offered suggestions, theirs was only a dream. For Seamus, it was a plan for action. He immediately went to work. Shortly after his last meeting with the others, he withdrew a large amount of money from the bank and disappeared for several weeks. Many feared he was disappointed that the long discussions brought forth little action. Maybe he was more ambitious than they were and had moved on, taking his money with him.

But again, as quietly as he left, he returned. Following in his wake were several heavy wagons. Along with the wagons came a small band of men and women. The men were trained in the operation of sawmills and lumber equipment. It was their task to put together and operate the first of Seamus' several mills. The mill came in pieces for reassembly on-site.

The first timbers cut in this mill were stacked to cure. After a suitable time for curing, the large timbers were set aside to be used use to construct the City Livery building. The structure would be on a site suggested by the committee and would cover most of an entire city block. Seamus felt a livery was necessary to accommodate travelers who might come speculating in the area.

The east side of the building would parallel an alleyway that would be used to bring merchandise to the existing retail businesses currently facing the old town hall that would someday become the courthouse with its square. The existing businesses included a saloon, the bank, a general mercantile, a barber/dentist, and a land office. The west side of the livery building would parallel a site where a jail was proposed. The front of the livery building would face to the south on a street that would one day be School Street. The rear of the building would open onto another street, yet unnamed.

The Tadlock Lamar family was one of the first families to arrive with the sawmill. Tadlock was a skilled mill operator as well as an excellent carpenter. In his family he boasted four strong boys and two girls. Seamus brought Tadlock to the area, not knowing if he would stay any longer than necessary to set up the sawmill.

To encourage him, he gave him the job of not only designing but also building the livery building. It was Tadlock's desire to do so, but Mrs. Lamar put her foot down. Under no circumstance would she live in a community without a suitable school. School was currently in what had been a cotton warehouse. Besides that, she and her family were living in a temporary camp of sawmill shacks that were not suitable as permanent quarters for raising her family. To appease her, Seamus suggested that Tadlock first build her a house. If there were not enough laborers available in the settlement to build a small schoolhouse at the same time, Seamus himself would go in search of others; the livery could wait. It was agreed, and construction on the Lamar residence began immediately, using the limited amount of local labor available from the whites and a few Indians.

However, Seamus, still eager to get the livery underway, suggested to Tadlock that he approach some of the people in the colored community for help. But that idea was not popular. Meanwhile, white laborers who had lived in the area before the war had left. The town did not offer a large labor pool, and it was definitely a deterrent to progress.

Seamus did not push Tadlock with his idea of using the colored, and instead went into the colored quarter himself. He had visited the quarters on more than one occasion. It was even rumored that he was sleeping with a mulatto girl. That was not true, but he did know one. Her husband was six feet six inches tall, and he was stronger than an ox. Seamus had loaned him seed money, and he was barely making a living farming.

His name was Putnam Dishman, better known as Put. Never before had Seamus asked Put if he had skills besides farming. When Seamus inquired, Put said that farming had been the last thing he thought he would do for a livelihood; he was a blacksmith by trade. He also knew stonework and bricklaying. He had two brothers and a cousin, all with similar skills, with the exception of one called Steamboat. That one worked on a steamboat and was a passable steam engine mechanic. All were still in Georgia.

Without hesitation, Seamus asked how soon Put could have his kinfolks in New Cotswold. The man scratched his head a bit; he would have to talk to his wife about being gone for a couple of weeks. It would take at least that long to go to Georgia, pack up his relatives, and then move them back. In addition, he would probably need two, maybe three wagons, one of them a real sturdy one.

His concern about his wife was that he had plowing to do that could not wait. She would have to agree to do that. Seamus promised he would pay someone else to take care of the plowing. As for the wagons and teams, Seamus suggested that he go along on the trip, using his carriage. When they got to Georgia, Seamus would buy teams and wagons for the trip back. Of course, Put was astounded that this white man was so willing to help. Seamus was by no means trying to take advantage of Put or his family, but he did have a plan for them.

The trip was uneventful until they got to Georgia. It took Put more time than he thought to talk his brothers, cousins, and their families into moving. They considered Mississippi to be halfway around the world. But once he had everything in order, Seamus rounded up the wagons and teams. When he questioned the need for the extra heavy wagon, he was led to a shed where Steamboat stayed. Inside was a complete blacksmith shop plus all the tools, including iron bars and rolls of leather for harness making. Steamboat suggested one other thing. If Seamus was interested, he could show him a complete steam engine and a steam tractor he could buy. It was another grand opportunity in Seamus' eye.

As soon as they were back in New Cotswold, the new families went to work picking lumber from Seamus' mill. They built small houses and settled in the quarter. The new additions to the colored community were welcome, especially since they were Methodists.

The two churches in town had suffered damage during the war, and a new one seemed to be a priority for the womenfolk, many of whom considered Seamus' whiskey making to be unacceptable. For that reason, he totally funded a church. Some said he never entered it himself.

The very first settlers to the area camped out along a creek where Indians before them had camped. The settlement grew along that creek. Life was harsh in those early days, and deaths were frequent. Some of the first burials were in gravesites in the lower land. Caskets from some of those first burials washed up in flooding, so a place on higher ground was designated to be used for a future cemetery, on an open hillside surrounded by giant oaks. On June 1, 1869, almost three years to the day since Seamus had arrived in town, the new church opened its doors. Most of the Irish at that time were Presbyterian, with some from the Anglican Church of England, plus a few Catholics. There were also a few Baptists and Methodists. Seamus asked once what might be the difference. The person he asked replied that Methodists were Baptists who could read.

Since Seamus built the church for the entire community, he suggested that it be a nonsectarian church. Over the years, as the community grew, the definite denominations formed large enough congregations to build their own structures. Even though this was not the first church constructed in the settlement, it became Old Church. It still stood, having been in constant use to this day.

The plans for the livery went through any number of changes. When Seamus returned from Georgia, he found the work to be well underway. Tadlock had taken some liberty in the design, improving it as he did so. Seamus had drawn the plans to include two apartments, one on each side of the building. These would be shotguns, similar to the houses seen in New Orleans. Each had a small front porch facing onto School Street.

Upon entering the apartments, which were identical, one would see a parlor, two bedrooms, a bath, and a kitchen. A small vestibule opened to either the alleyway or the side street or into the interior of the livery barn. The vestibule gave entry to two other bedrooms and a bath. This allowed entry without disturbing the privacy of the front apartment. Overnight travelers who stabled their teams at the livery could use these apartments.

Inside the livery, a blacksmith shop occupied the center section at the front of the building. Large double doors opened to the street. Further inside and to the rear of the structure was an arena for livestock auctions. Surrounding the arena were stalls for stabling animals.

Mrs. Lamar soon became a thorn in Seamus' side. First, she reported that they needed a bell for the schoolhouse. Seamus reminded her that there was need for another teacher or two. She had that taken care of; the circuit preacher had located a young woman with good qualifications. She would arrive by the start of school. With three teachers, the school could offer grades one through twelve.

Seeing the livery almost complete, Seamus was anxious to leave again. This time he hired two other men from the colored quarter. He would drive his carriage; they would follow with the wagons. They trip would last at least ten days. Little did the men know where they were going. As usual, Seamus was private in his affairs.

The hiring of the colored, plus the relocation of three more families to the colored community, did not go unnoticed. Quiet discussions among the local whites grew intense at times, but from these discussions, one conclusion was drawn. Seamus MacMorogh was not going to have a color line. They'd best begin to hire and train colored people themselves.

Seamus and the little group returned with furnishings of a nicer quality than those owned by most of the locals. In his carriage, he brought another surprise: a beautiful woman, a six-year-old girl, and a ten-year-old boy. These were Seamus' wife Laura, daughter Matilda, and son Logan. It had been almost four years since he had lived with them. He moved the family into one of the livery apartments. The accommodations were comfortable, but by no means as grand as the home they owned in New Orleans. Laura would make the best of it, though. Her husband had great plans for the future, and so had she. Meanwhile, the fact that Mrs. MacMorogh had moved from a home in New Orleans offered an ample supply of additional grist for the gossip mill. Seamus was one mysterious character.

Other communities around the area heard of what was happening in New Cotswold. Drummers peddling their wares and other settlers looking for opportunity began to drift in. Most of the original settlement could see that recovery was happening, but to some, not fast enough.

A problem arose between Seamus, Tadlock Lamar, and several others of the group who had worked on the town plan. They expressed their concerns. For instance, the local bank was weak, and the only other bank in the area, a strong one, was twenty miles away in the town of Bluster. That settlement also was nearer the town of Jackson; more people had begun to settle there. Was it possible that priorities set by Seamus and the groups were in fact incorrect?

Tadlock Lamar, for one, had taken cash for most of his work, but he had also taken several acres of property in the midst of what was supposed to become a thriving community. The town was not going to make it if they did not attract more people, more businesses, and more skilled labor. The others were of like opinion.

Seamus shared these discussions with Laura, and she agreed. She had made friends with several women, including Mrs. Lamar. The women were concerned, and that always meant trouble. The same problem that the others saw was going to affect Seamus in the same way. He owned much of the land for miles around. He was friendly with the bank, but was discouraged at the owners' lack of foresight or vision. He needed to own the bank to further control growth.

He revisited his personal priorities. First, he went to all of the people making whiskey in partnership with him. How much more could they produce? That same question was put to the sawmill people, including Tadlock. He also included Put Dishman in his discussions. What everyone needed was a bigger market. If they could not develop it here in New Cotswold, Seamus would go get orders from other markets.

Another problem that they all recognized was the lack of ambition in some of the original settlers. They had developed a minimal trade area in the Bottoms and seemed content. Those that were in the whiskey business with Seamus thrived, but the rest were just barely getting by. The unproductive had become a negative force.

With estimates of additional production in timber and whiskey and with a few wagons that Put could build for sale, Seamus left on a sales trip. He returned days later with orders that would help put more cash into their pockets. He was sure that his next plan would be the salvation of all of them. He would buy the bank and offer stock to the others if they wished.

11

Seamus' action again bolstered the faith of Tadlock Lamar, who had become spokesperson for the rest. They joined in the bank purchase. However, they still had strong concerns with the growth of the neighboring community of Bluster. It was now calling itself a crossroads town, and that was catching on.

Therefore, even though it was going to strain his reserve of cash, Seamus set his next project in motion. It was far in advance of his proposed time schedule. The first thing he did was to have one of his mills start cutting large timbers to a specific length and size. Vat after vat of creosote started arriving by wagon. It did not take long for people to take notice. Finally, one of the townspeople caught on to the idea. Seamus was going to build a railroad. The rumor spread like wild fire.

The rumor, and that was all it was at the time, did what Seamus hoped. More speculators arrived, even investors wanting to be a part of this new opportunity. The closest rail was almost twelve miles away. Connection with that rail line would give the community access to markets no one else in the area yet dreamed of having. New businesses began to arrive, bringing more people to town. Tadlock Lamar took credit for spurring Seamus and was elected town mayor.

The renewed attention to the town did what Seamus needed it to do. His coffers filled; he had new business interests. New bank loans came as result of new deposits. However, it took almost two years before Seamus was convinced enough that his own future was secure and his capital quite adequate to go forward with the railroad.

His earnest efforts to get the rail project underway did not go well. He considered the problem to be an uncooperative attitude by the owners of the existing BK Line. His plan was to connect to it. His earliest conversations with them left him believing that if he would provide the right of way through his property, they would build the track and operate the railroad from Tupelo to New Cotswold. At that time, he owned all of the property to within four miles of their line.

To him, allowing them access along his right-of-way was a fair exchange. After all, he would own the property adjoining the track as well. In the future, the increase in value could be astronomical. But his renewed visits with the line owners proved to be less than satisfactory. A recession was causing some strain on their business. The freight they estimated to be possible out of New Cotswold, including Seamus' lumber shipments, was no longer as lucrative to them as it first appeared. In order for them to allow Seamus to connect to their line, he would have to build the track all the way to their line, furnishing right-of-way, road bed, crossties, rails, and anything else needed to run a train, including water stations. The money was not impossible, but the logistics were.

Most railroads started at one end and built out ahead of themselves, not only creating the rail line but making it possible to haul in all the ties, rails, heavy equipment for digging, and rail cars on which the laborers could eat and sleep. Seamus fretted over this for days. Finally, he confided in Laura that the rail venture was not feasible. He told her the reasons. They talked almost half the night about possible solutions and even talked about the possibility of selling everything they could in New Cotswold except the bank and going back to New Orleans. That was Laura's least desire; she was stunned at the suggestion.

The next morning, she asked Seamus if it was possible to get to the point where "*our* line" would connect with theirs. She stressed the "*our.*" He had been to the other line a number of times; she said she wanted to go. Could they take a carriage to the line the next day? He assured her that they could but warned that the round trip would take two days. Laura arranged for a friend to look after Logan and Matilda. She packed rough clothes for both, along with a picnic basket with food, whiskey, water, coffee pot, coffee, and quilts for sleeping.

Seamus had an idea. Instead of the carriage, he chose a light wagon. They left just at daybreak, but instead of heading out north, he headed south on the three miles to his sawmill. He collected one hundred small strips of wood to use as stakes. He also collected two cans of red paint. With his new supplies, he and Laura headed back toward town. Laura read his mind. She asked about a hammer to drive the stakes. He pulled one out from under the wagon seat, and Laura took the reins. About every half mile or so, Seamus jumped off the wagon and drove a stake, painting the tip red. When they got to the edge of town, he stopped driving stakes until they were through town and back on the wagon trail headed north.

This went on all day, and Laura took notes. They arrived at the BK rail line as dark was approaching. Seamus pitched a tent, built a fire, and took care of the team. Laura poured water and whiskey, then unpacked biscuits and ham for their supper. They turned in for the night, but at about two in the morning, the ground began to shake. Then came the sound of a steam engine puffing away in the distance. As it came around the bend, its bright light turned the trees across the way into day. The two of them waved as the train passed, but neither the engineer nor the fireman saw them.

For a long time after the train passed, they stared down the track until the light on the caboose was just a memory. Next morning, with the wagon loaded, they went back a mile or so to a creek, built a fire, and had coffee and hoe cakes before bathing in the cold water and heading home. While they drove, Seamus talked. Did Laura see the poor logistics of starting their railroad at the sawmill in New Cotswold? To build the railroad the way others were constructed was impossible, in his mind. It was a logistical nightmare. In their case, they would have to transport ties from the mill back to the other line before they could begin. Transporting the ties, especially in bad weather, with wagon trails mired in mud, would be impossible. Next was still the problem of the four miles of property they did not own.

Laura rode along without speaking. When she did, she asked Seamus who owned the property between their land and the other rail line. He did not know. Suppose the owners would have an interest in participating on their line. Suppose the property owners could see the same advantage of having a rail line through their property as Seamus could see. Suppose he could acquire that property. Suppose he was depending on the other line doing too much. Suppose he could do it all by himself.

Seamus' first response was that there was a lot of supposing. Laura kept on. How many sawmills did Seamus own? He held up four fingers and explained that one was the stationary mill in New Cotswold, while three were transportable mills, all run by steam. They moved from timber cutting to timber cutting.

They had gone in and out of timber several times on the journey. At every place, they could cut ties. Why not mark it as a place to take a portable mill and cut ties? That would cut out hauling from New Cotswold. He had not thought of that. The first thing to do was see who owned the other property. Could they buy it? He was enthusiastic about the thought. Laura suggested that he try. By the time they arrived home, he was convinced.

The next day, with a bag of cash hidden in the carriage, he again left New Cotswold, this time with Logan. He was making his way back on the same wagon road where he and Laura had spent the last two days. This time he hoped to get some agreement on the property they needed to complete the line. After four days of searching records in the courthouse at Needville, the closest town to the property, he was able to determine the owners, find them, and make his pitch.

He and Logan returned home, five days after they left, both wild with excitement not only at Seamus' success but also at the times they had had together. They had laughed, talked about Logan's future, had a man-to-man chat, and even shared a sip of whiskey, the first that Logan, now thirteen, had ever tasted. That time with Logan would be the last time the two would enjoy such revelry.

Seamus wasted no time in getting the rail line under way just as Laura had suggested. She did not receive any thanks; nor did she expect any. Seamus knew, however, that her thought process had helped his and had probably saved the line. He would call it the Laura Line.

Once underway, they needed many more men. A short recession resulting in unemployment was to Seamus' advantage. He built temporary housing for the men that moved with the line as it progressed. Once there was enough track laid to hook onto the other line, they made the connection, and Seamus was able to buy a steam shovel, a light steam locomotive, three flat cars to haul rails, and finally an old railroad sleeping car to use for tool storage and kitchen facilities. Seamus spent much of his time overseeing the rail construction; Laura took his place at the bank. Both worked hard most of the time but enjoyed it immensely. Then tragedy struck.

A typhoid epidemic struck the entire southland, and New Cotswold did not escape. Many of the townspeople blamed Seamus. They claimed that the workers brought in to work on the railroad were unclean. They were dumping garbage and defecating in the creek upstream from the town. People exclaimed, "Many of the workers are niggers and chinks, and you know what that means!" Laura herself was fearful, especially being in a town with one "quack" for a doctor.

In addition, she actually feared some of the townspeople themselves. People openly cursed Seamus. Logan received harassment at school. One night when Seamus came home, she presented him with her decision. She was taking Logan and Matilda back to New Orleans. Even though the epidemic was there, and probably worse, it would not be as bad as being in New Cotswold with its limited medical care. She begged Seamus to go along. He agreed that they should go, but not him.

That night, after Logan was in bed, they had another discussion. It might be time to send him off to a better school. He had talked to Seamus on their trip. The boy was determined to go to Princeton, a college he had read about in Presbyterian literature. Laura was astounded. Why had he not discussed this with her before? Seamus barely knew the boy, he was always gone, how could he know what was best? Seamus asked her to discuss it with Logan. They might be able to work it out somehow.

A few days later, using his carriage, Seamus dispatched his family to Vicksburg to board a paddle wheeler to New Orleans. That had been a specific request of Logan because he loved steamboats. Within three months, Laura, Matilda, and Logan were all dead. The first to go had been little Matilda. As soon as Seamus got word, he went to New Orleans, only to find Logan also dead. Laura passed away three days later. Seamus was devastated. He entombed his family, closed his home in New Orleans, and returned to New Cotswold a broken man.

Several months later, with the railroad within a mile of the north side of town, Seamus had a decision to make. The one he made may well have set the tone for the history of the town for many years to come. The most practical thing to do was to follow the lowland near where the creek flowed. To do that meant one of two things. One, he would have to go almost down the middle of the original old town, which had grown in size but not in desirability. Housing there, for the most part, was shanties, while the old saloons and other shops were poorly kept and the dirt streets were in disrepair. Discussion with the people resulted in opposition; they would put up one hell of a fight.

The second option was to run the line on the other side of the creek. That meant not only displacing the colored community, but it would require two bridges. The decision was not easy. Seamus surveyed the property between the Bottoms and the ridgeline of new construction. The line ran through that property.

The people in the Bottoms were inflamed. "They had been banished to the wrong side of the tracks with the niggers." Seamus, heartsick at the loss of his family, had more grief in his life. Much of the community now despised him. Up until that time, there had been only a few minor problems concerning coloreds and whites. The Bottoms people blamed Seamus, "the nigger lover," and took out their frustration on the colored, creating a never ending strife.

With his family gone and himself no longer admired by many of the people, Seamus started roaming the state, looking for other ventures. He spent day upon day in Jackson at the state capital. He made friends with many of the more prominent politicians.

Back in New Cotswold, he lived like a recluse. Before his family died, he had found a location in the woods west of Old Church where he'd planned to build a home. It was remote from the town and well secluded. There he built a magnificent stone and log house, and he named it Laura's Lodge.

Tadlock Lamar had a great deal to do with the design, but Seamus dictated much of it. The heavy, oversized front doors opened into a huge hallway. On either side of the hall, parlors were designed, one a gentlemen's parlor, the other for ladies. There was a large dining room and an equipped kitchen of the size found in a hotel. On the back left corner of the downstairs were servants' quarters.

On the opposite side were the owner's quarters. A wide double stairway led upstairs to six bedrooms, another large parlor, and three baths. Across the entire back was a screened gallery for summer sleeping. Seamus moved there alone.

The railroad had been a wise decision. Others had suffered severely during the panic of 1873. His bank was one of the strongest in the area, but with so much money loaned out, it could have been in jeopardy had there not been a large cash reserve.

The first time Seamus visited with the officials of the BK Line, they met in their offices. He remembered looking like a common laborer after traveling two days on horseback. They visited one other time in his tiny bank. At neither time did they seem to take him seriously.

Now they were asking for a third meeting. This time, he invited them to the lodge and had a fine meal prepared by a cook from town. They drank good whiskey before dining on a delectable game dinner served with the finest in local wines. The men were there to offer to buy his section of railroad. Seamus questioned their motives, but it was his understanding that they were short of funds. They made a fair offer, which he promised to consider, but he had concerns. He would have to think on it.

The following week, he trekked to the capital to visit with legislators whom he had befriended. In so doing, he came upon answers to some of his concerns. Another rail line in Mobile was looking for a direct route to Memphis. The BK could provide that access with their line and the Laura Line. The offer they'd received was a small fortune, but that offer was the result of mistaken information. Possibly, it was information supplied by the BK, claiming Seamus' Laura Line to be part of the BK. The BK did operate on it, but Seamus was the owner.

Seamus had the BK by the short hairs. He found that the Mobile line would have to borrow heavily in order to buy the BK. He approached them and offered up his line plus an abundance of cash. With that, the Mobile line bought BK, and Seamus became a major stockholder and went on the board of directors. The railroad became the basis of the MacMorogh fortune, and to this day, it remains so.

The mental activity involved in the railroad took Seamus' mind off the sorrow he had been enduring. He was beginning to enjoy his new position in railroading. He traveled the country, often by private car. It was a grand new adventure.

Seamus had had housekeeping help from the time he came to town, even in the little two-room houses he had first rented. He was reputed to be hard to please when it came to washing, ironing, and mending. Cleaning was important, but he had little need for food preparation. He chose instead to eat in the saloons, where he could listen and keep is finger on the pulse of the community.

When Laura and the children had arrived, she sought help that could do cooking and tend to the children. She'd often had several house servants. One of the most faithful was Aunt Sally Dishman, the wife of Put. As Aunt Sally's daughters grew, they too worked in the household. Maudie Lee was twelve when she started. Her task was to tend the little girl, whom they called Tilly. Cora Lee also joined the household staff when she was twelve.

Maudie Lee was born in 1868, soon after the Dishman family arrived in New Cotswold. Her mother, the one called Aunt Sally, was twenty-three at the time. Cora Lee was born in 1870. No one knew as much about Laura, Seamus, or their children as the three Dishman women. They would go home dead tired at night, sometimes to be recalled to Mrs. Laura's for another late night chore. If there was complaining, it was under their own roof. It never left there.

After Laura and the children died and Seamus came back from New Orleans totally devastated, he wanted no one in his presence. He fired Aunt Sally, but she never stopped going to the house every day. She cleaned, picked up after him, and tried to get him straightened out, but he would have nothing of it. He kept firing her; she kept coming back. Sometimes she went to his apartment in the livery for days on end, dusted a little, cleaned windows, aired the place out, or whatever she might find needed to be done. Every day during the year, when fresh flowers were available, she kept a vase on the mantel over the fireplace. Seamus never said anything about paying her, and she never asked. There was a nice woman at the bank, named Mrs. Abernathy. She paid Aunt Sally every Friday at noon.

Mrs. Abernathy had more authority than most women of twenty-three, especially in the position she held. She had begun her career with Seamus the day after she graduated from high school and three months after she discovered she was pregnant. The woman who served as assistant to Seamus, Mrs. Fanny Knox, knew her mother, knew her circumstance, and wanted to help. The young woman's first responsibilities were minimal and required little imagination or skill. It was not long, however, until she began creating additional responsibilities and soon got the attention of Seamus. He praised Mrs. Knox for her skill in training the girl so well. That pleased Mrs. Knox, and she began training her in earnest.

When Mrs. Abernathy was twenty-one, Mrs. Knox wanted to retire to take care of her ailing mother. Mrs. Knox requested that Mrs. Abernathy replace her, but not until some discussion took place with Seamus. He thought Mrs. Abernathy was well qualified, but she was going into a responsible position requiring some authority over others, and he questioned her ability to do so because of her youthful appearance. Mrs. Knox took care of that. The next day, Mrs. Abernathy appeared at work with her hair in a tight bun, wearing horn-rimmed glasses, a long skirt, heavy shoes, and no makeup; she looked forty. Seamus laughed and told Mrs. Knox that Mrs. Abernathy could have the job.

Things changed when he moved into Laura's Lodge. He began to overcome his sorrow. New adventures stirred in his mind. He would need a full-time housekeeper. He could offer private quarters and a small salary. He wanted someone to move into Laura's Lodge to be on the premises when he was gone. He also wanted someone to take fiscal responsibility, someone with the ability to shop for, prepare, and elegantly serve fine meals. He wanted a person with the ability to hire, train, and manage additional servants if necessary. No one in town felt up to or wanted the task. It certainly was not something that Aunt Sally wanted, since living outside her household was not an option. Nor did she feel capable of accepting the responsibility.

Mrs. Abernathy suggested that Seamus run an ad in the Jackson paper or, perhaps, in Memphis. She did not suggest that the reason might be to get out of the area where people knew him. She would write a nice ad if he would like and would even handle responses and interviews. He agreed.

Weeks passed with no response. Mrs. Abernathy asked Aunt Sally about sending Maudie Lee out to the house, just to keep it clean. Seamus was seldom there. When he was, he would surely need clothes tended, beds changed, and tidying done. The extra income would help with plans for schooling the girls. Maudie Lee worked there for almost a year before anything different happened. Mrs. Abernathy continued to run ads. No one was interested.

One dreadfully hot August day, a young woman appeared at the bank. She came without an appointment to answer the ad posted in the *Memphis Commercial Appeal.* She introduced herself as Mollie Kathryn O'Ryan. She wore a heavy broadcloth skirt, much too heavy for the August weather. The string of buttons on her long sleeve white shirt went all the way to her neck. It was too hot for a jacket, which rested between the handles on her purse; she clutched it in both hands. She wore low heeled but heavy women's work shoes with thick cotton stockings.

Mrs. Abernathy, at first taken aback by her attire, did not notice that in fact she was quite attractive. Her eyes were green and bright. Her auburn hair, cut in an attractive bob, was shiny and clean. Her nose was thin, just a little pointy but not unattractive. Straight, white teeth gleamed when she smiled. When she did smile, her eyes smiled with her; truly an Irish lass.

How did the young woman come upon the ad was Mrs. Abernathy's first question. Did she live in Memphis?

"No longer, Ma'am," was her response.

"Then where do you live now?" asked Mrs. Abernathy

"I am planning on living here; I have my things stored at the rail station."

Mrs. Abernathy was a little annoyed at the impudence of this woman in thinking she could just have the job by showing up, and she told her so.

Mollie apologized; she had read the qualifications over and over. She was sure she could fulfill every one of them. She was well educated and had tilled the soil, cared for animals, and done load after load of heavy laundry. She had cooked for as many as one hundred at a time. In addition, she had been responsible for bookkeeping on several occasions, knew how to work with a budget, was frugal to a fault, and had never stolen a penny from anyone. Her ability to work with others was without fault until one recent problem. She went on to explain the problem. She had decided to leave the convent, a decision made on her own. She had not been defrocked.

"You were a nun!" exclaimed Mrs. Abernathy. "What brought you to a decision to leave?"

"With my apologies Ma'am, I can no longer live the life of a nun. I made another promise to God, and to do that, I cannot uphold my vows."

"Do you have any kind of reference?" asked Mrs. Abernathy. "How do I know you are telling me the truth?"

With that, Mollie loosened the grip on her purse handle, untied the top, and brought out an envelope and handed it across to Mrs. Abernathy. The woman read the contents of the envelope and read them again. Before finishing the second time, a tear leaked out of the corner of her eye. She tried to wipe it away unnoticed. When she looked up, Mollie also had tears in her eyes. They both sat for a long time.

Finally Mrs. Abernathy spoke. "Mollie, I live alone; you are welcome to spend the night with me. We can have supper and get a good night's sleep. Tomorrow we can go out to the house. We have a young colored girl staying on the premises. Her name is Maudie Lee. She can show you around. You can take a few days to decide if you would like her to stay on working with you. Tonight, I will tell you about your employer."

With that, Mollie smiled and brushed away the tears. "Thank-you, Ma'am."

That evening, after allowing Mollie the opportunity to clean up, Mrs. Abernathy treated them to a nice dinner. After dinner they went into the living room, where Mrs. Abernathy suggested some of her homemade wine. Mollie accepted, and they talked for hours. First, Mrs. Abernathy told Mollie that she was a widow with one child, a son who was currently living with Mrs. Abernathy's parents. Mollie stared in disbelief when she found out that the two had been born only months apart and were the same age.

Then Mrs. Abernathy told how she had come to have a responsible position at the bank. Now she was more involved in other aspects of Seamus' businesses. In short, she was his trusted aid. She revealed most of what she knew about Seamus, how he looked, how old he was, what very little she knew of his heritage, and the fact that he probably was one of the wealthiest men she would ever meet. She related the tragedy of the family, and spoke about several years of depression and what appeared to be a recovery.

Without asking, Mollie began her own story. She was Irish, Catholic from day one. Her family was near starvation. In order for there to be more food to go around, her family had sent her to a convent at age thirteen. At the convent, she was nothing more than an indentured servant. That accounted for her household experience. The strong desire to become a nun had come as she grew older. She got the attention of the mother superior, was educated, and took her vows.

She got the opportunity to go from Ireland to Canada to work in a convent and held several responsible positions. She taught, kept records, planned details for the Mother Superior, and was a model nun. The rest Mr. Abernathy knew from the letter.

12

The next morning, Mrs. Abernathy got a coach driver who served the bank to drive for them. They went first to collect Mollie Kathryn's baggage from the rail station. One modest trunk held her total life's possessions.

The noise of the horse and carriage inside the covered bridge alerted Maudie Lee. Before Mrs. Abernathy and Mollie could alight, she ran to the front screen door to unlatch it. She was barefoot, but wore a very pretty, freshly ironed cotton dress. She had not tied the sash in the back, and it appeared to Mrs. Abernathy that she had just gotten up. The truth was that she had just had a soda bath after an early morning blackberry picking. She spoke to Mrs. Abernathy, smiled at Mollie, and then nodded to the carriage driver.

After introducing Mollie to Maudie Lee, Mrs. Abernathy suggested that they sit in the parlor. Maudie Lee had known that one day, a person would arrive to take full responsibility for the lodge. Mrs. Abernathy told her that this was the lady. She was going to be the full-time house manager they had discussed. She went on further to tell her that she expected her to co-operate fully with Miss Mollie and to help her to settle in the house.

While she had been talking, Mrs. Abernathy paid close attention to Maudie Lee. She could not believe the change in her. She remembered the girl being tall, shy, and a little clumsy. She had ducked her head and pulled her lips tight over her teeth when someone spoke to her. Now she sat erect with ankles crossed in front of her and her skirt smooth over her pretty legs, not the least bit shy, and with diction unusual with the colored.

Now was the time to broach the subject of Maudie Lee's continued employment. She would be under the supervision of Miss Mollie. Her wage would continue as it had been. She could still stay in the room she occupied if it met with Miss Mollie's approval. If she felt more comfortable moving back home with her parents, that would be acceptable also.

Mrs. Abernathy did not expect her response. Maudie Lee said that she would be forever grateful for the kindness shown by Mrs. Abernathy, since she had been her direct supervisor. However, she had been dreading having to tell her that after the end of the month, which was still three weeks away, she would no longer be living in the area; she would be going to Tougaloo College in Jackson.

She was the first Dishman to graduate twelve grades. Now she was going to be the first to graduate college. Her eyes sparkled with enthusiasm. She would someday come back to New Cotswold to teach school.

It took only a day or two for Mollie and Maudie Lee to become pals. Maudie Lee prepared a list, seven pages long, written in beautiful cursive. It included everything she could think of for the person coming to take responsibility for the lodge.

The first thing Maudie Lee did each morning after making coffee was to go to a calendar tacked on the back of the pantry door. There she carefully studied the calendar, then made an "X" in that day. Mollie glanced at it once. There was a red "X" on the 17th, but black ones for the rest of the days from the first onward. On the twenty-first was a blue "X." Written under that was one word, "returns." Mollie asked no questions.

However, Maudie Lee did ask many, one question after another. As with a small child, some of the responses prompted yet another question. Where did Mollie grow up? Why had she become a nun? When had she stopped liking men? Mollie answered some questions with the wave of a hand and a smile. Maudie Lee learned soon enough: subject closed.

Coincidentally, Seamus returned from his travels on the same day that the blue

"X" appeared. Several days before, Maudie Lee had suggested that they give everything another thorough cleaning, pick flowers and vegetables from the gardens, clean chimneys on all oil lamps, fill lamps with fresh oil, trim wicks, air all the rooms, sweep the house, and then mop. Her list was a foot long. Mr. Seamus would arrive on Saturday.

Mrs. Abernathy had a carriage waiting at the station the day Seamus arrived. His first stop was the bank and her office upstairs above it.

"And you hired this woman without even allowing me the opportunity to visit with her first!" exclaimed Seamus when Mrs. Abernathy told him about Mollie.

"Actually, I did as you asked. I hired someone whom *I thought* would be suitable. You said nothing about the hiring to be upon your approval. I have made it quite clear with Miss O'Ryan that if you found her intolerable, or she found you so, which is the most likely case, she is welcome to stay with me in my house until she can find other employment."

To this, Seamus replied, "Mrs. Abernathy, does it ever occur to you that you are in my employ, not me in yours, and that I can fire you at will?'

"Yes sir, it does, and when I think of that, I consider the fact that you then would have no friends at all!" she snapped back.

Seamus arose from his chair, plopped his hat heavily on his head, and replied, "Let's go meet this person." They exchanged few words during the short ride to the lodge.

Upon his arrival, Maudie Lee stood quietly in the background as Mrs. Abernathy introduced Mollie Kathryn to Seamus. He greeted her courteously. She bowed slightly. He nodded and spoke to Maudie Lee without feeling, as would be expected of a gentleman speaking to a servant. Maudie Lee helped the carriage driver remove Seamus' things from the carriage while the others went into the parlor. After seeing that Seamus' bag was unpacked and things neatly hung, Maudie Lee retired to the kitchen.

Mrs. Abernathy did most of the talking as she briefly covered the responsibilities she had explained in the beginning. She then asked Seamus if he had anything to add. He did not. His plan was to go back into town to his office. He wanted to meet with some people for supper at the hotel. Tomorrow they could have further discussions.

Maudie Lee and Mollie went about their evening chores, fed the barn animals and chickens, milked the cow, pumped more water into the horse troughs, and then went inside. Maudie Lee showed Mollie how she placed a fresh can of tobacco, clean pipes, and a bottle of whiskey with a tumbler on a table next to Seamus' large leather chair in the men's parlor.

If she heard his carriage come through the covered bridge, she would quickly light the lamp. If he had not arrived home by ten, it was not necessary to leave that lamp lit. Instead, she was to leave a smaller lamp burning on the hall table. She must always follow this nightly ritual.

Then the two of them had leftovers from dinner for their supper. Maudie Lee explained that Seamus seldom ate supper at home, choosing instead to have a few drinks and a meal at the hotel or saloon. If the weather permitted, he usually went across the street to the quarters he still had in the livery. There he sat on the front porch and visited with local businessmen who might pass by.

That evening, he was not back by ten, and Maudie Lee lit the small lamp; she and Mollie each retired to their rooms. Sometime during the night, Mollie was sure she heard a floorboard squeak. She became alert and then was sure that she heard muffled conversation.

Maudie Lee was up earlier than usual, with coffee made by the time Mollie got up. Seamus called for coffee; Maudie Lee put a cup, saucer, spoon, sugar, and rich cream on a silver tray, then nodded toward his room, signaling Mollie that she should serve it. She knocked lightly on his door; he beckoned her in and thanked her as she placed the tray on a small desk near his bed.

While Mollie served the coffee, Maudie Lee ran to the henhouse for fresh eggs. As soon as she returned, she stirred dough for biscuits. After sticking the biscuits in the oven, she took a smoked slab of pork belly wrapped in cheesecloth from the cupboard, cut thick slices, and began frying it. A pitcher of molasses along with salt, pepper, and fresh butter went on the dining table.

When Seamus appeared at the kitchen door, he greeted them both pleasantly, then went to his chair. After he sat, Mollie poured fresh coffee, then at Maudie Lee's instruction, served breakfast.

After breakfast, Seamus summoned Mollie to the front porch where he sat, smoking his pipe. He was staring out at the mile long field across the road. He wanted to talk about the fact that Maudie Lee would no longer be there after the end of the month. Apparently, Mrs. Abernathy had told him prior to their coming to the house yesterday. There sure was no discussion during their introductions.

Seamus suggested that Mollie solicit additional help as soon as possible. His idea was that it might be good to get a man and wife. It might be best to have a man to handle heavier work. Mollie said she would try to do that, and Seamus then left for the day. The remaining days before the end of the month went along about the same as that first day, and the nights as well. Mollie felt sure she could hear quiet voices during the night.

Seamus sat with Mollie almost every morning for a few minutes of additional instruction. She had access to charge accounts at most of the stores in town worthy of his business. Anything she needed for the house, she was to purchase on credit and turn a copy of the bills in to Mrs. Abernathy each Friday. Mrs. Abernathy would make payment no later than Saturdays at noon. Another morning, he suggested to Mollie that she feel free to take Sunday as a day of rest. She could have use of the horses and a buggy if she chose to attend church or to visit anyone during the day. On one of the final days before Maudie Lee left, Seamus suggested that Mollie visit with Mrs. Abernathy about an adequate gift to present to Maudie Lee. Then Maudie Lee was gone.

Seamus's habits usually were predictable, but there was an evening when he came home early and found Mollie having her supper at the table in the kitchen. Mollie apologized; she did not know he would be home in time to eat. He asked what she was having. She told him fried chicken left from a whole chicken she had fried at noon. There was more in the oven, if she could serve him? He told her to keep her seat and went to the oven and took two pieces from it along with two sticks of corn bread. He then took the lid off a pot on the stove and got a large serving of butter beans. Before he sat at the table with her, he got a cup for tea. He ate quietly, and after supper, he slipped on a sweater and went to sit on the front porch.

Mollie cleaned the kitchen and prepared for the following morning's breakfast. Seamus had not suggested that she join him. When she was through with the kitchen chores, she too got a sweater and went out to sit in one of the rockers on the porch. He did not say much, other than that it was a nice evening. Perhaps she should prepare evening meals for him more often. He would offer up some suggestions. Soon he bid her good night before tuning in.

Mollie and Mrs. Abernathy bonded almost immediately. The time that Mollie spent with her was most enjoyable, and she looked forward to their visits. She had her regular Friday accounting meeting, and Mrs. Abernathy had gotten her to attend the Methodist church with her. After Sunday worship services, they ate lunch at the hotel. These times gave Mollie an opportunity to get Mrs. Abernathy's opinion on how well she was doing. Did she ever get any comments, good or bad, from Seamus? As time went on, it also gave Mollie an opportunity to express her own feelings.

One Friday, Mrs. Abernathy asked how things were going. Mollie responded by clasping her hands together and saying, "Oh, he is learning to talk! Only a word or two at a time, mind you, but I bet he will be talking in complete sentences before you know it." Mrs. Abernathy had a great laugh over not only the comment but also the animation with which Mollie had expressed herself. She was happy.

Seamus left on one of his mysterious trips, to be gone for a week. During that time, Mollie went into town with the buggy to restock the pantry and do some other shopping for the house. With her first paycheck, she bought a used sewing machine, some material in a nice print, thread and buttons, and just for fun, a ribbon that matched the material. She spent most of the week sewing and delighted herself with her work. Seamus pleased her when he made a nice comment about the dress upon his return.

Seamus too had visits with Mrs. Abernathy. He expressed his satisfactory feelings, but did comment that he felt Mollie had a bit of temper. At times, she also had a sharp tongue. Mrs. Abernathy knew not to press him for further comment.

When he saw that she was not going to make any kind of statement, he said, "She has adopted a damn cat." Mrs. Abernathy just smiled. He paused a moment before he stood and said, "A little too much of you is rubbing off on her, Mrs. Abernathy. Perhaps you should consider spending less time with her." He stalked out.

It was approaching Christmas time. Mollie was pleased at the thought that she might see Maudie Lee when she came home for Christmas break. Luckily, she ran into Maudie's mother while doing her marketing. When asked about Maudie, her mother stated quite sadly that Maudie Lee would be staying at school during the holiday break. She had taken a part-time job during the holidays, needing the money, and would not be coming home.

The Sunday before Christmas, Mrs. Abernathy informed Mollie that Seamus would be out of town for Christmas. Was she aware of that? It was not a surprise to Mollie. On several occasions, she had asked him if she might help prepare for Christmas, and he had said no. She asked if she might do some decorating. There were things in the storage room that might look nice. He told her to suit herself.

Mollie was disappointed at his response, since it had seemed lately that the two had developed a closer relationship. Mrs. Abernathy even commented one Friday that the charges at the market for food seemed to be higher than usual. Mollie then told her about the fact that Seamus seemed to enjoy her cooking, especially desserts. He was eating at home several nights each week.

When Mrs. Abernathy informed Mollie that Seamus would be out of town, she also asked her to her house for Christmas Eve and Christmas Day. During the afternoon on Christmas Day, both of them were lying across Mrs. Abernathy's bed, chatting away, as usual. Then Mrs. Abernathy said something that Mollie herself had felt for several weeks. She mentioned that Seamus seemed like his mind was miles away. It was, and they should be accustomed to it, but now it was as if he was in much deeper thought, at times morose. Mrs. Abernathy related the way he had been just after the death of his family. Her feeling was that something very sad was going on his life. She wondered if he was ill.

Her concern was short-lived. Seamus returned by train on New Year's afternoon. Before he went to the lodge, he asked his carriage driver to take him by Mrs. Abernathy's house. He was not surprised to find both her and Mollie there. He had brought belated Christmas gifts for both. For Mrs. Abernathy, a beautiful watch to wear as a necklace. It had a small circle of rubies. For Mollie, a beautiful cameo. They had refreshments, fruitcake, and herbed tea, which Mrs. Abernathy knew he loved. When he was ready to depart, Mollie, who was in the buggy, suggested that he ride with her. He dismissed his driver, allowing him to go back to the livery.

When they got to the lodge, he seemed well pleased with the Christmas decorations. He even asked Mollie if they could stay up a few days before taking them down. It was getting on toward evening, and Seamus suggested a toddy. While Mollie got out his favorite decanter and tumbler, he made a fire in the fireplace. They sat for a long time. He seemed more relaxed than she had seen in several weeks. He was even cheerful with his few comments. After a while, he said, "Mollie Kathryn." He usually just called her Mollie. "Are you happy here?"

"Very," she replied.

"Then why haven't you hired additional staff as I asked you to do?"

Mollie was startled; things had seemed so pleasant, and now she was going to get a scolding. She thought for only for a moment, then replied, "One of the things on my list of responsibilities was to take fiscal responsibility. In my opinion, that means being careful with money and not spending unwisely. I am able to take care of everything alone. My chores keep me quite busy. If I had help, I might become extremely bored."

"That is good enough reason," he replied. "However, I do not want you to continue doing as much as you do. I would like to see you more in a position of hostess of the lodge. I hear very nice things about you from the businesses on the square. They say you light the whole square when you are in town shopping."

He continued, "I was in Jackson during Christmas and met with some of my friends in the legislature. I plan to support a young Indian man who is going to run for the United States Congress. I want to have some guests here at the lodge to raise support for him. There may be two or three different groups. I would like to have nice meals. The lodge needs to be in grand shape. I will be inviting man and wife." Then Seamus paused for a while. "That means the ladies need to be made welcome. You need to be a good hostess and make sure everyone is being entertained. Will you do that for me?"

Mollie was thrilled beyond words. "Certainly, I will!"

"Then get to work on hiring more servants. I left a list of what I think we need in the way of help." With that, he got up to go to bed. "One other thing: the first group will be coming three weekends from now. Get Mrs. Abernathy to introduce you to that one called Imogene, the colored girl; she makes most of the ladies' clothes in town. She can help you with some dresses if you need them."

Mollie could not wait to tell Mrs. Abernathy. She made a beeline for town after Seamus left for work. Her first stop was the livery. She visited with Put Dishman first, about servants. Would he make some recommendations? Would he ask Aunt Sally for her recommendations also?

The first campaign dinner at Laura Lodge included ten of the wealthiest and most influential Republicans on Seamus' list. The plan was for all of the couples, including the governor and his wife, to stay at the hotel. All arrived on Seamus' private rail car that he had sent to Jackson for the group. Carriages sent to the hotel arrived at the lodge shortly before time for cocktails. Cocktail service began at six p.m.; dinner followed at eight. Afterward, the men retired to the men's parlor, and the ladies to theirs. Mollie had arranged locally for a harpist and a pianist to entertain the ladies.

Seamus had requested preparation of a large bone-in roast beef on a spit outside, along with young quail for those who preferred something lighter. The waiters served pies and cakes after dinner with rich coffee or tea. There was not a hitch in preparation or in serving. Mollie had assembled six servants to help with serving inside the house, while four cooked on pits outside. All wore white jackets, black pants or skirts, and white gloves.

The evening ended, and Seamus stood with Mollie as the guests boarded their carriages to leave. The governor thanked Seamus while Mollie and the governor's wife walked to the waiting carriages, arms around each other's waists. The governor's wife declared that she had never been so pleasantly entertained; she was sure the governor agreed.

After all had boarded their carriages and the last lantern went across the covered bridge, Mollie immediately went inside to supervise the staff. They put dishes away, and the silver went back into the respective chests. In the dining room, Mollie smoothed a curtain here, straightened a chair there, and picked a piece of lint from a chest. She went room to room, touching, aligning pictures, generally putting things back in perfect order. She went into the kitchen, complimented the staff, and then stepped out into the yard where the men were dousing the fire pits. She again praised their good work.

Back inside the house, she thought that Seamus must have retired for the evening. She doused the lamps in the men's parlor and then went to the small lamp on the table by the front door and was about to douse it, when Seamus called out.

"Leave that lamp, please." He was on the front porch smoking his pipe. She opened the screen door and looked out. He sat on a settee rather than on his usual rocker. When she stuck her head out, he asked her to sit for a moment. She sat down beside him on the settee, something that she had not done before.

"I have never been so pleased in my life," he said. "Never before have I heard such nice compliments from both men and women. I think you really made a hit with the governor's wife. Thank-you for such a splendid evening!"

Mollie smiled, "I rather enjoyed it, and, yes, it was very nice. Nice for me because it pleased you."

"Mollie Kathryn." Seamus had that faraway stare. "I loved my wife and my children more than you can ever believe. Not a day goes by that I do not think about them. Not a day goes by that I do not blame myself for sending them to their deaths."

"Oh, Mr. MacMorogh," she said, ever so sadly. She had never called him Seamus or even Mr. Seamus, as was the custom of the help. Then she shuddered at the horrible thought that she often had about her own life. She lightly touched her eyes, hoping he did not notice the tears.

Seamus went on, "I put them on a paddle wheeler in Vicksburg, knowing full well they were going to the wrong place. The typhoid hit epidemic proportions. We had it here, but we had clean water. The open sewage here was nothing like New Orleans. Laura persisted; she feared being in town with one or two quacks, as she called them. I listened to her and gave in. I was too busy; I had a railroad to build."

He paused for a while and then put down his pipe. "I promised myself that I would never again put myself in such a position of loving and losing so much." He had both hands flat on his knees, and his head slightly tilted toward her. "I want you to know that I care a great deal for you. I only wish that I were a young man again. I would break that promise I made to myself."

With that, Mollie reached over with both her hands and wrapped them around one of his. "Do you think that I have not had similar feelings for you? And you are not too old a man."

Then she released his hand, put her hand on his cheek, and turned his head toward her. "How old would you think you are if you did not know?"

He thought about it for a minute or so. Smiling he said, "About half of what I really am."

"Good; now we are the same age!" Mollie said, laughing.

He put his arm around her, and they sat for a long, long time. Mollie did not know how to say what she had to say next, but she felt she must.

"Seamus, you know that I was a nun from age thirteen to twenty-two, almost ten years. That does not mean that I am a virgin." Then she got up to leave. "Good night," she whispered. "I will leave the lamp burning."

After cleaning her face, she put on her nightgown and slowly combed out her hair. It was quite a long time before she heard the front door close and heard his footsteps to his quarters and the closing of his door. She lay thinking about what she was getting ready to do. Tiptoeing as she went, she moved to his door and ever so slowly turned the knob; the door squeaked slightly as it opened. She got to the bed, pulled back the covers, and gently lay down beside him. He stirred and then rolled over to put his arms around her. She never slept in her quarters again.

13

Mrs. Abernathy said nothing to either of them, but over the past several months, she could tell that something was going on between them. It was Seamus who said something first that stirred her curiosity. "Would you make an appointment for me with Judge Madden in Jackson? Try to make it on Thursday or Friday. If he is available, then also make one on either the same day or Friday with Dr. Calhoun."

"You feeling bad, Seamus?' was Mrs. Abernathy's response.

"No just my regular physical. Need to see how strong my heart is," he replied.

"Why don't you get him to check the temperature of your heart and see if it is still cold?"

"Someday, Mrs. Abernathy, someday."

He got up to leave. "Visit some with Mollie Kathryn today, would you please? Maybe you two could have dinner together at the hotel."

Mrs. Abernathy was puzzled. It took two hours to get her work caught up. She called for the bank carriage, directing the driver to make straight away to the lodge. Mollie was on the front porch, giving directions to one of the help. Two big wagons full of lumber were on the side of the house. A small structure was under construction behind the house. It was near the barn and was to house a husband and wife to watch over the lodge. Mollie greeted her with a big smile.

Mrs. Abernathy could not wait. "What in the world is going on? Seamus instructed me to visit with you *today*. He also asked me to make an appointment for him with his doctor and Judge Madden."

"He wanted me to tell you," said Mollie. "The doctor appointment is to make sure he can make babies. The appointment with the Judge is to set a time to marry us." Mrs. Abernathy screamed so loud one of the workers dropped what he was doing and ran around to the front of the house.

Judge John K. Madden married Seamus MacMorogh and Mollie Kathryn O'Ryan in his chambers. Ten months later, William MacMorogh was born. They soon settled into a routine of being husband, wife, and parents. However, Seamus was not the settling type when it came to activity outside the home. New Cotswold did not offer enough excitement or discovery of newfound opportunities. He had built a strong regional empire in banking, land, and lumber. The railroad investment had made him a fortune, not to mention giving him national notoriety.

In addition, probably due to the loss of his first family, Seamus felt the need to be closer to professionals in areas that might best suit his own needs as well as those of Mollie and the baby. As a toddler, the baby was already revealing his hunger for knowledge. Not only did he want to touch everything he saw, but he wanted to look under it, over it, and inside it. Someday he would need better opportunities for education than what New Cotswold offered.

The opportunity to travel called for nothing more than to get on a train. Because of Seamus' railroad affiliation, they traveled by private rail car. Seamus, for his own interest, decided that there were three cities offering the opportunity he sought. They were New Orleans,

Memphis, or Jackson, Mississippi. Great things were happening in all three; they even had gas lighting. Using telegraph to dispatch trains was common, and now, a fellow named Bell and his associate had developed a means of transmitting the voice over lines. There were steam powered tractors and trains in this country, and from Europe came reports of steam cars. After his experience hauling tons of ice from Jackson to New Cotswold, Seamus began investigating ice plants. Tadlock Lamar and Sons had orders to build one in New Cotswold.

Seamus took Mollie to the three cities he had in mind. They took their time, thoroughly touring the three; only then did he pose the question. Would she consider having a second home in one of the three? And if so, which one? Mollie wasted no time in answering, "Memphis."

She loved the bluffs that overlooked the river, the paddle wheelers moving up and down, the far off steam whistles. In addition, she liked the close proximity of New Cotswold, now only a few hours away by rail. Seamus chose an architect and erected a house on one of the highest bluffs overlooking the river. It was more house than any small family needed, but it would better serve Seamus' desire to entertain. He wanted to gather 'round entrepreneurs, adventurers, and others looking for opportunity. Finished in 1900, the house was the perfect venue. The view, the gardens, the furnishings, and most of all the warm hospitality of the owners awed visitors to their home. As long as a guest could get along with a very active William, several dogs, plus a cat or two, the guest would be fine.

Seamus bought his first car in 1904, a Stanley Steamer. That car went direct to New Cotswold to be under the care of Steamboat Dishman, now head of maintenance for all of the equipment owned by the company. The next two cars were matching 1904 Ford Model T Touring cars. Seamus bought them directly from Henry Ford on one of his trips to secure freight business from the inventor.

Mollie learned to drive before Seamus did. He preferred to ride in the back seat, with a chauffeur doing the driving. A sight to behold was that of an older man, flowing white hair blowing in the breeze, trying to hold his hat with one hand and his seat with the other. Mollie would be dressed out in proper attire for driving: a bonnet that tied around her neck, goggles, and a long white driving coat.

Meanwhile, William stood behind her, giving advice on the proper mixture of spark and throttle and how to operate the foot pedals.

William had figured the thing out with no trouble. Unbeknownst to anyone other than the chauffeur, he had actually been the first in the family to drive the car. William also was the first to dismantle the engine, much to the surprise of the chauffeur, who found it totally apart one morning when he went to fetch it. William had his own ideas of how to make the car faster.

Mollie might have preferred to spend more time in New Cotswold, but gave in to Seamus' wishes to enroll William in Memphis schools. Mollie knew better than to disagree. Once William was in school, though, her days became a bore. She enjoyed doing the parties for Seamus and his business associates. She was an excellent hostess, but down deep, was no socialite. She busied herself in charitable organizations, raised money, and became known as the "go to" person for financial help.

Seamus spent most of every week in New Cotswold and would come home on Thursday nights for long weekends in Memphis. When in New Cotswold, he stayed at Laura's Lodge. In the evenings, he could be seen smoking his pipe on the front veranda, staring out at the land before him. During the summer, the whole family spent two months there. Mollie loved every minute and made the best of each of them. She and Mrs. Abernathy visited almost daily. She attended the Methodist Church on Sundays, bringing William for both Sunday school and church. Seamus stayed home.

On one visit into town, she ran into her old friend, Maudie Lee; they had lost contact soon after the young woman had left for college. Maudie Lee had kept her vision in sight and was now teaching in the colored school. And there was something else that Mollie had not been aware of: Maudie Lee had married in her first year at Tougaloo. The lad with her, who looked to be only a year or so older than William, was her son, Winston Jackson. Mr. Jackson, her husband, worked as chief conductor on the railroad. Mr. MacMorogh had helped him get the job.

During that summer, Seamus took William with him everywhere he went during the day. He taught him as much as he could about the things they saw and the people they encountered. Seamus often talked of William's future role in the company.

On one such day, they met with Put Dishman, who was now the boss of City Livery. That business was now more a machine shop than blacksmith shop. A small foundry operated there and cast manhole covers, fireplugs, and other cast parts sold to growing cities all around the area. Put contributed greatly to the success of that business; he earned accordingly.

Winston was the grandson of Put Dishman and worked right along with him. William visited with him at length. The lucky boy spent each day working with his grandfather, building things and experimenting with different metals, and he knew how to weld. Put and Seamus agreed that William could stay with them the rest of the day. Seamus let him return the next day and then the next. The final day of the week, Put paid William a small wage. He was elated when he got home that night and could not wait to tell his mother what all he and Winston had done. He was filthy dirty and had a smashed finger. But that did not matter; he had a new friend, and his friend was coming to visit in Memphis someday.

Before the two months was over, though, an incident occurred that made a huge impression on William. He was at the big sawmill with Seamus. Most of the laborers were colored. Something happened that caused a log to topple from a loaded wagon. The log rolled toward a white supervisor, who was able to jump over it and escape injury.

The ill-tempered supervisor pulled the colored driver off the wagon and was close to beating him unconscious. Several other whites stood by and did not step in. Seamus, seeing what was happening, stepped into the fray and pulled the white supervisor up and off the beaten driver.

After some discussion about the accident and after determining that it was just that, an accident, he told the supervisor to go to the paymaster and draw his pay. Another man standing around seemed annoyed with Seamus' action and told him so. He also went to join the other man at the paymaster desk. With that, the little group broke up, but not without complaining.

That evening, while the family was having dinner, a fire erupted down by the road in front of the covered bridge. The flames immediately turned into a burning cross. It was possible to see the men milling around the fire. Shouts, at first not clear, became quite clear. They were racial slurs that Seamus abhorred. Mollie was petrified.

The colored family living in the servant's house on the property ran into the woods behind the house. Mollie grabbed William by the hand, pulling him behind her and up the stairs. She parked him in a bedroom closet and then ran into another bedroom to retrieve a pistol that she knew Seamus kept hidden there.

She almost fainted at the thought of using the weapon, and slid to the floor. Then she heard Seamus calling for her and the boy. She got up and managed to get to the top of the stairs to tell Seamus they were alright. Seeing that they were safe, Seamus slipped out the back door and into the woods alongside the house. He made his way down to the creek in front of the house. Under cover of the bridge, he crawled to within fifty feet of the men. He recognized them all. The men, feeling they had made their point with the cross, drifted off toward town. Back inside the house, they heard the men in the distance, laughing and cursing in their drunken state. Neither Mollie nor Seamus knew what to say to William when his questions started to fly. They sat back at the table to try to finish dinner as if nothing had happened, but William would have none of it.

Seamus went into the men's parlor and picked up a bottle of whiskey, his pipe, and a lap robe. He asked Mollie and the boy to come sit on the front veranda with him. The fire at the side of the road had burned itself out. No remnant of it would remain by morning; Seamus would see to that. He put his arm around Mollie and the boy under her arm, and then placed the lap over all three of them.

He related the tale of the afternoon fight that William had witnessed. He told Mollie about his impulsive discharge of the white man who had taken things into hand and beat the colored man senseless. The disturbance tonight was no doubt retaliation.

After he completed the account, William raised up to speak. "I do not understand why you did what you did. The white man was the boss. You took up for the 'nigger,'" uttered William in a strong tone. "Everybody knows how stupid most of them are."

Mollie was horrified beyond belief. Seamus stiffened. She had seen him lose his temper on two other occasions; both times were times she did not want to remember.

"Please Seamus," she whispered, "he doesn't know any better." She had tears in her eyes, pleading.

William sat erect at his mother's response. "What's wrong?"

Then Seamus, again in a calm voice, said to her. "Go to bed; we will be alright." She rose slowly, but again looked at Seamus with pleading eyes. She left the veranda, but stood quietly within earshot. What she heard she would never forget.

Seamus pulled a rocker around in front of him and told William to sit. He began by questioning William about where and how he had developed his opinion about colored people. William did not know. It seemed to be something that everybody knew.

"And who do you associate with, who call colored people 'niggers?'" William responded that he heard lots of people use that term, including their own servants. There seemed to be nothing wrong with it.

His father then said, "This time and this time only, I will forgive you for using that term, based on your not knowing better. The next time I hear you utter that word, and I hope I never do, I will spank your little butt so long and so hard that your mother will be rubbing cold lard on it for weeks. Do you understand what I just said?"

Seamus had made the last statement for the benefit of Mollie, whom he knew probably had her ears perked not far away. He had whipped William once before for some deed he could not remember. Mollie had cried for an hour.

William nodded in an affirmative to his father's question.

"Now for your opinion about the stupidity or ignorance of the race," asked Seamus again. "Where does that come from?"

"Well, they do most of the jobs that nobody else does. They live in shacks and do not seem to care. I don't see any of them doing work in offices or in the bank. I do not see any of them being nurses or doctors where we go to get shots. I do not see any of them doing much of anything important." The boy was sincere.

"Do you think the reason is because white people are smarter or better than the colored? Do you think you are better than Winston, who you have been playing and working with at the livery?" Mollie, hearing this, slowly shook her head back and forth. Something about Winston was unusual.

"I guess, by the way you ask that, I better say no," William voiced ever so quietly.

"Someday, I hope you will answer no because it is your own strong opinion rather than out of fear of your father," Seamus said.

"William," and he reached across to hold the boy's hand. *"We* are of Scotch and Irish ancestry. We came to this country because in our homeland, we were the people being treated as colored are being treated here today. People persecuted us because of our religion. We were poor, ignorant, and often starving to death. When we got to this country, we could only get menial jobs. People despised our ancestors. We did not sound the same when we talked. In our own country, our religious belief resulted in persecution. Now here we were in a strange country that seemed to hate us even more because we were Irish.

"Employers ran ads in the newspaper, advertising for employees to come to do the simplest of tasks. At the end of the advertisements were these four letters, in capital letters: INNA. What do you suppose that meant?" William could not answer: he shook his head.

"Those four letters meant that 'Irish Need Not Apply.' Not only were they not wanted for employment, but other people could not stand them. Why do you think that was, William? The Irish were white, just like you are white now."

Seamus went on. "They were afraid of us. They did not know what we might become if we were given opportunity. Because of that fear, we were given no opportunity.

"Now look at us today. We did not get an opportunity in the beginning, but we did not give up, regardless of the way we were treated. We took all of the terrible jobs. Irish men dug ditches. Irish men built that railroad right out there with not much more than picks and shovels. Many *died* doing it. Irish women got no work other than menial house labor. However, we became citizens, we had babies, and we grew in numbers to a point that in many neighborhoods and areas, we were the majority. We could soon outvote other people, simply because there were more of us. We *earned* opportunity, and as time went on, we got recognition. More and more opportunity was afforded us.

"You go to church with your mother, and I know that she sits with you at night, reading stories about people in the Bible. That is good, and you should continue learning all you can about God. I do not go to church, but I do know some things from the Bible, and the most important one of all is that God made each of us. We are all in the same identical bodies. We are just decorated differently, some red, some yellow, some black, some white. And as a result of being different in some way, people are persecuted by others."

William giggled, "Decorated?"

His father continued, "In this country, we have persecuted the Indians; we even ran most of them off the land and took it for ourselves. It did not take long for us Irish to forget that these same Indians sent us money in Ireland because we were starving.

"And now we come to the last thing. Do not ever be afraid to give someone you meet or someone who works for you an opportunity to do the same things you do. That is what all of this was tonight. Men acting out of fear. Fear that the colored will take their jobs or be better than they are.

"You know Putnam Dishman, whom you worked for at the livery?" Seamus asked. "I knew he had skills beyond farming. I gave him an opportunity to use those skills. In the process, he has made our family, and his own, very successful. He has used that success to provide opportunities for others in the colored community."

Then Seamus said, "Your friend Winston's mother is named Maudie Lee. Maudie Lee was shy and probably would have been a housemaid today, but she got an opportunity to go to school. Now today, she teaches in the school.

"You know 'Steamboat,' who takes care of every piece of equipment we own. He, in his own way, has learned about steam, hydraulics, gas power, electricity, metallurgy, and the many other things it takes to be an expert in his field. I gave him the opportunity. Now he is teaching others, colored and white, to take his place.

"I have not been selective in whom I have chosen to lead, only in what I consider to be the ability to lead, black or white. I have gone to great lengths to hire people to do a job *better* than I could do it myself. Think about that.

"As for the men last night, they are fearful of what society is doing and what they are doing to themselves. They will be boasting about it tomorrow. That will be their only reward. You and I and your mother will go about our business as if nothing took place."

He continued on, "Am I forgiving them? No, I have nothing for which to forgive them. Their actions were because they were born not knowing any better and along the way had no one to teach them. There is one thing, however: it is not necessary to continue to abide them. They have shown themselves, and I do not wish to have them around me anymore. If a dog bites you, it is foolish to run after it and stick your hand in its mouth to give it another chance.

"I love you and your mother more than anyone can imagine. I am becoming an old man, and if I do not impart to you the things that I think have made me who I am, I will not be true to you or your mother. Keep this in mind. You are not perfect, nor will you ever be. That same applies to everyone you may now know or will ever know. I forgive you for upsetting me tonight. I only pray that God will do the same for me."

After they went to bed, Mollie sat beside Seamus, combing out her long red hair. "You are mellowing as you grow up."

Seamus said, "Do not count on it."

The next day, only the slightest hint of smoke remained in the low places along the road. Any semblance of the burning cross was gone. It looked like rain in the west. Seamus was trying his own hand at driving the "T." He was sure that when he got to the bank, he would round up a driver.

At the office, he settled comfortably in his big chair before he summoned Mrs. Abernathy. She came in with a questioning look on her face. He stared at her for a few moments and said, "Sit." He told her about the incident the night before, and then gave her a list of names and instructions for talking to their lawyers. He asked one final question. "Are any of those people related to you or do they mean anything to you? What about anyone else that works for us?"

She promised to cross-reference the list and get back to him before noon. After lunch, she came back with a negative report. Three on the list had loans at the bank for their small businesses. All three businesses were in the Bottoms. One other had a mortgage for a small piece of property. The other worked at the new ice plant.

According to Seamus' company attorney, they could pull all loan agreements at any time. They could demand payment in full or collect their collateral. He told Mrs. Abernathy to execute the rights of the bank.

14

Late Summer, 1958

Jack was elated at the progress he was making. He had finalized his portion of the Seamus segment. The next step was to put in final form the information he had gathered to this point from Will. That completed, he would move on to more interviews. He asked Mimi for her assistance in making appointments with Dr. Bea, Carole Anne, and Chas Chacherie.

The work that Jan had undertaken was tedious and time consuming. But it would be a major factor in establishing the foundation for the MacMorogh businesses. It would probably take weeks, so Jack had to be patient. She was taking on a project he himself was not capable of undertaking.

The following day, Jack arrived at the office at about nine in the morning. Mimi was expecting him. After their greeting, she asked, "Do you have time to visit with Mr. Chacherie? He was just here looking for you."

"Absolutely," Jack replied. Mimi called across the hall and made the arrangements.

Chas Chacherie was as gracious as one might expect of a seasoned politician. However, down deep, this was his true nature. He put his arm around Jack's shoulder and ushered him into a massive office. The flooring was actual ship decking from an old schooner. There were several beautiful rugs prominently positioned in the tastefully furnished room. There was nautical memorabilia in glassed cabinets and on shelves covering one entire wall.

The main desk was massive and needed to be. It held stacks upon stacks of neat files. All of the chairs, including the high back chair that Chas apparently used, were upholstered in rich, dark green leather. Against one wall stood a double sized partner's desk with matching chairs on each side.

Chas explained that this was actually his father's desk, but he was allowed to use it when his father was not in—which, now, was most of the time. He pointed to the partner's desk. "That is where we sit when he comes to visit. There is where he goes over the books and gives me pointers." Then he laughed.

They went further on to another office that Chas explained was his law office where he conducted Attorney General Department business when he was in the city. As Jack knew, Chas's chief investigator, Sammy D'Antoni, worked out of there also. Next to the windows, facing out onto the street, was a conversation grouping of wingback chairs in the same matching leather as the rest. Jack and Chas sat there, and a young woman appeared through a side door with a silver service with demitasse cups and saucers. Alongside the coffee and cups was a covered tray with small cornbread muffins with a dribbling of thick honey on each.

Chas was sincerely interested in the project and the progress so far. "You know, I really like what the MacMorogh family is doing. I think it is important to have some history of families, especially where family-owned companies are involved. We need something similar here in our company." Then he emphatically stated, "In writing."

Then the conversation got around to why they were there. Chas had had a meeting cancelled; he could spare an hour or so. He understood that Will wanted him to be included in the project, so this would be a good time. He surprised Jack by telling him that he had only known Will since their military service. He could relate the events of that period, if it would help.

Jack assured Chas that all input helped. "I am actually enjoying getting the different points of view of others about times, incidents, and about each other. Each perception is different."

Chas said, "My years are going to begin where Will and I first met. It will be very interesting to see how his memories of those times compare to mine. I can bet you that he will not tell you the whole story."

Jack, as usual, asked permission to record their discussion. In addition, he ordinarily took notes. But about halfway into the story, Jack stopped taking notes. Chas at several points was near tears. It was all Jack could do to keep his own composure.

After he was through, Chas poured another demitasse of the coffee. Then they sat silently for a long time. Finally, Jack told Chas how much he appreciated the time and then excused himself. He had been blindsided again.

Jack went back across the hall to review what notes he had taken; he then labeled the tape. It was two hours before Adrianna would be coming home, and he was at a loss as what to do during that time. On any other day, he would be only too glad to have a few minutes to catch a nap, but not today. The morning session with Chas Chacherie would not leave him.

He spoke briefly with Mimi about Dr. Bea's schedule, when she might be back in the office, and when they might have another brief session. She was coming into the office the next day. Perhaps Jack could visit with her then. Mimi would make the arrangements if possible.

The next day, after a warm greeting, they got right to business. Dr. Bea had read most of what he had written about Seamus. The first thing she said was, "What in the world possesses you to write this in the style you are writing it in?" Jack was confused until she continued.

"I feel like I am in a history lecture with a charismatic professor who is telling a very interesting story, and I cannot wait to hear more." Jack's sigh of relief had to be obvious. She continued. "To me, history was always my worst subject. I remember that at the end of each chapter was a list of dates, names, and places that would be on the next test. For the life of me, I could see no reason for taking up brain space for such. I really like what you are doing."

Jack laughed and told her that that was what had possessed him to do what he was doing. He felt the same way about history. Then the subject changed to chronology. Where were they? Generally, it was about the time of the crash that had killed her brother. He asked whether she could expound on that.

Dr. Bea said that she had taken Willie back to New Orleans with her immediately after the funeral for her oldest brother and her sister-in-law. Her other brother Jonathan had come along. They had fretted over what was best for the children, and eventually made the decision to send Willie back to New Cotswold to live with Jonathan.

She had given a lot of thought to the time when she had put the two on the train in order to get Willie started in school. Jonathan was going home to a situation that they had not foreseen. Their father and mother were taking the crash and deaths much harder than expected. Their father rarely spoke to anyone. He sat for hours in his office or at home, staring into space or pacing the floor. At times, people in the office would hear him on the rare times he did talk. They usually involved shouting angrily at whoever was on the other end of the phone.

Their mother ordinarily spent several days each month with her sister, tending to the affairs of the large cotton business they owned. She now was spending all her time there. It seemed that neither she nor their father could console each other. It was better that they be apart to handle the tragedy as best as each could.

At one point in her recollection of these times, Dr. Bea said to Jack, "I think that somewhere along the line, you are going to discover something that I later began to suspect about this time that my parents were apart. We'll see." And she said no more about that.

Then she got back to Willie. She said that his grammar school years were the ones she remembered as being the ones where he really found himself. He knew who he was. He had to deal with living with Jonathan, under the same roof with colored people. At that point, Dr. Bea rolled her eyes. In addition, he had to deal with the fact that people considered him an orphan. Willie even asked more than once what an orphan was. *He was not an orphan! He had a family.* He was very positive in his declaration.

This had happened in first grade. When he came home, he related the experience. Jonathan's reply was that he was exactly right. He had more people loving him than most children had. He was special. Then Jonathan asked him who had challenged him.

Willie told him, and Jonathan's response was, "Tomorrow, go to school and casually mention to her that she has garments on her back, and see what happens." The next day, according to Dr. Bea, Willie did just that. When he got home, he told Jonathan about it. The girl went to the teacher, crying and wanting her to get them off her back. Jonathan asked what had happened then. Willie got stood in the corner for teasing the girl.

Dr. Bea leaned her head back, stared at nothing for a moment, and then continued relating the story of the time. Everything was going smoothly. Willie was a happy child, healthy, smart, and as well-adjusted as possible. Then the war came, and the bombing of Pearl Harbor. World War II affected the whole country deeply. The MacMorogh family was no exception.

The older William had many friends and associates in Washington; he had seen this war coming for a long time. He warned the family and the company. In fact, he began to position the company to take advantage of war times.

As soon as war broke out, he brought the family together to tell them that he was going back into the military. He had left the air service as commander of a training unit, and he was going back in to do the same thing. He was a full colonel when he left; he was going back with one star. That is why he is now called the General. He was a West Pointer. His training was to be a soldier. He wanted the memory of him to be as a soldier.

He announced to the heads of the various interests that Miss Annie was taking over as president of the companies. He explained that she had a long history in the business world. With her sister, she had been operating one of the largest cotton businesses in the country, from planting, picking, ginning, compressing, and storing to brokering. She was a tough woman and as far as he was concerned, the employees' easy days were over.

Dr. Bea said, "Then Jonathan and I both had to talk. I was a young doctor surely needed in some capacity. He was a young man with two engineering degrees. He certainly could be an asset to the war effort. However, we had two children. I was not concerned about Carole Anne. She was soon to begin her pre-med studies at Tulane. She had a good home within walking distance of school and had the most wonderful servant in the world to care for her, if need be. Willie, on the other hand, could be a problem. Having him consider going to live with any of the Lamar family was a deep concern. Even though several were great parents, would Willie fit into their families? Unfortunately, the relationship between the MacMoroghs and the Lamar sisters was not that great."

"Jonathan got impatient and felt like he needed to get on with it. He enlisted and was given a report date to be inducted at Camp

Shelby, Mississippi. We discussed the change in Willie's life with as much care as we could. My mother suggested that he come live with her. She was alone and needed a man to be with her. She had two wonderful servants who lived on the premises in their own house. Having Willie in the house would actually be a help to her in her loneliness, since my father was already gone. With her servants caring for Willie's physical needs, he would be no problem".

"We patiently established with Willie what his day might be like. He would go to school, and as soon as school was over in the afternoon, he could report for his job with Winston and could visit Aunt Tilda. That was some consolation. Before time to report for his enlistment, Jonathan moved into the house with Mother and Willie .That made it somewhat easier. In those days, Jonathan got Willie to school. After school, he went to the shop, just as usual."

"When the time came for Jonathan's departure, Willie took it like a little man. It was not all roses, by any means, and it took several days for him to adjust. He went from being the little boy at school who lived in the same house with colored to being the little boy who was driven to school each day by a chauffeur."

15

Will's return from London was a relief; by the time Jack got to the office that morning, a welcome party was underway. Will, Chas Chacherie, and Mimi were all trying to talk at the same time, and Jack joined right in. Finally, Chas put his fingers to his lips and blew like a whistle. "I need to get to work, and I know you folks do." The party was over.

After Chas left and they themselves settled down, Will told Jack that he had a lot of catching up to do, but would like to visit for a few minutes. He had talked to his aunt only briefly, but long enough to know that she was well pleased. He would take some work home in the evening and start reviewing the project also. He then excused himself to get to other more pressing items.

Later in the morning, they got together again. "What would you think about following me around for a day or two?" Will asked. "I want to go to the boat today. Tomorrow, I would like to show you the operations I am responsible for on the North Shore. Then Thursday, I have to be in New Cotswold; I will arrange things there. Perhaps Friday we can get back together here."

Jack had never flown in a helicopter and was not looking forward to the adventure. However, once his stomach caught up with the rest of his body, he was completely comfortable, and there was no doubt that Will was a very competent helicopter pilot.

For four hours, including a worker's lunch of fresh caught redfish in a Cajun sauce, Will showed Jack all over the boat. He explained its function, and then pointed to show Jack the result of the work the dredge was doing. It was sucking up what looked like black mud from the bottom of the Gulf, then pumping it through huge pipes to a point against the concrete seawall. To the right of where Will pointed, Jack could see a beautiful white sand beach. All of that was the result of the dredging.

The trip back was uneventful. At the airport, Will suggested that he pick Jack up the next morning, again at Lakefront Airport. They would fly over the lake and not spend the time it would take going both ways on the causeway bridge.

Jack and Adrianna had spent time on the North Shore, but had no idea what lay off the beaten path. Will had a vehicle parked in a hangar at the airport there. It was a new GMC pickup, white, with two long antennae on the back, similar to those that state troopers had on their cars. Once inside the truck, Will laid out his plan for the day. They would first go by The Point, where Will was now living. Next, they would go to his office and Jack could meet Susie Scott, the business manager for the operation. There he would get an overview of the concrete and aggregate business. Then they would go as far as Slidell to see their other operations, which were about the same, except for product or size. Will would give Jack a little history on the way.

At noon, they met two people who were on Jack's list of contacts. The first was a most interesting fellow. He stepped out of a Cadillac Coupe, on the side of which read the logo, "Ludlow Haulers." This person was Nate Ludlow. When Jack first saw him walking across the restaurant parking lot where they met, his first thought was that the man had to be some kind of life-sized hand puppet. His legs, arms, and head appeared disconnected.

He was about six feet tall, with sandy hair, a sunburned face, and big smile; he was maybe a little older than Will. A severe scar ran from his left eyebrow across his nose and across his right cheek, ending at the bottom of his right jaw. He was dressed similarly to Will, but his uniform was starched khaki, shirt and pants. It reminded Jack of his own uniform. Over the right pocket, his name was stitched in red, and over the left, the company logo. Will introduced him and explained their relationship. Jack would hear more when he spent time with Nate. Moments later, one of the most attractive women Jack had met since meeting Adrianna joined them at their table. He made a mental note that that was what he would tell Adrianna. This was René Stedman-Bates. Before lunch was over, they made definite appointments for follow-up visits. That evening, Jack started two additional tablets, *Nat Ludlow, René Stedman-Bates.*

In the afternoon, they toured the other operations. Jack was impressed with the cleanliness of every piece of equipment, every building, every office, every person. Commenting on this, Will replied that they had never had a major accident. Cleanliness and order played a large role.

They were back at Lakefront Airport by five. They agreed that the two days together had been good for both of them. A bond was forming. Will had given a lot of thought to the visit they should make to New Cotswold. He would clear some of his ideas up and get general agreement while he was there the following day. Perhaps they could go up next week.

When Jack arrived at the office on Friday, Mimi greeted him with a nod toward Will's door. She mouthed quietly, "Phone, Carole

Anne." Jack understood and went into his little office and prepared his desk for work. Shortly after, Will came to his door, tapped, and smiled, "Take line one, Carole Anne. Good luck." He did a thumbs-up and laughed.

When Jack answered, Carole Anne was cordial and said that she understood he was with Will for the morning, but wondered what his afternoon plans were. When Jack told her he was flexible, she invited him out to the house. If he could come at noon, she would have Rose fix "to die for" hamburgers with sweet potato fries. Jack said that with that offer, he could darn well make it.

Jack's concern about the crash that had killed Will's parents seemed especially important if, in fact, there was foul play. So far, he had gotten little from any of the family regarding the crash. Will had related as much as he knew of what happened up until the time of the crash, but much of what he remembered was vague. A visit with Carole Anne might give Jack a better perspective.

She was not as brusque as she had been on her first visit. In fact, she was quite gracious. When she greeted him at the front door, she was barefoot. Her Bermuda shorts were linen, and she had on a matching sleeveless shirt with the tail out. A blue ribbon matching her eyes contained a short ponytail.

Immediately she asked if Jack minded eating out on the patio. It was cool and nice outside, and the back courtyard featured a price-less three-tiered fountain. Lily pads hid goldfish in the pool surrounding it. Numerous potted bromeliads and tropical plants rested beautifully along the walls of the courtyard. Comfortable chairs surrounded a stone table, with cushions that matched the umbrella.

Places were set for three. After admiring the setting and discussing various interesting things about the courtyard, Carole Anne went into the house and returned, helping Rose bring the lunch. No hamburger could have been better. They sat sipping ice tea while Rose cleared the table. She suggested just a little banana pudding to round out the meal. They did not decline.

Carole Anne had read all of the rough drafts that Jack had prepared. She had her share of questions. Interestingly enough, she was quite interested in Seamus. She did ask Jack for clarification on a point or two. Each time, she smiled and asked, "Are you sure about this?" or "Where did you find this?" or "Can we be sure this is fact?" Then she asked one question that made Jack know she wanted the facts to be correct. "Have you been to the tombs of Laura and the children?" she asked at one point.

He should kick his own butt, was his thought. He had not. Their entombment was in a graveyard on Magazine Street. Carole Anne said that she had questioned the period of their death from typhoid fever, because it did not exactly go along with the dates of the big typhoid break of 1878. Therefore, she had gone to the graveyard on Magazine Street. Sure enough, though, there were the tombs, and Jack's date was correct. He would have to heed Will's warning "Good luck" advice; Will had been right.

Jack felt that he knew enough from the other interviews to know how Carole Anne and Will had spent their years before the deaths of their parents. He was concerned about the time of the crash and her recollections, if any. She had very few. She was with Aunt Bea, at the house where they now sat, when the call came. They immediately flew to New Cotswold in Aunt Bea's airplane. Willie was with Jonathan.

Poor Willie was mad about their parents not coming back. It was hard for him to understand. He asked over and over what was going to happen now. There had been no official reading of their parents' wills, but Aunt Bea and Jonathan knew that they were co-guardians. As soon as the funeral service was over, they took the children to a waiting car, then to the airfield and to Aunt Bea's airplane.

There was sure to be a squabble about Willie and her. Aunt Bea had told her a long time later that it would actually have been dangerous for Uncle Jonathan to have to confront any of the Lamar family at the time. If any of them had suggested Nadine and Percival making a good home for the children, he would probably have exploded.

Carole Anne said the intent was to get the both of them settled into Aunt Bea's house before school started. That was still a month off. Her enrollment in a private girl's school was complete. They had hoped that Willie could make friends in the neighborhood and decide to stay in New Orleans. Jonathan stayed with them the entire time. It was important to give both Carole Anne and Willie a sense of parents and a home.

She was conscious of the quiet discussions between Aunt Bea and Uncle Jonathan. Often they sat holding hands, tears in their eyes. She overheard Aunt Bea emphasize to Jonathan one evening that regardless of what they each might prefer, they would try to abide by the wishes of the children.

One week before time for school to start, Aunt Bea took Willie to visit a McDonough School where he would enroll in first grade. She knew the principal well. School was not yet in session, and they took a guided tour.

That evening while they sat around the dinner table, Uncle Jonathan asked Willie with as much enthusiasm as he could muster what he thought of the nice school he had visited. Without hesitation, Willie answered, "Oh, it was OK, but I think I am going to go to first grade with my friends." No one said anything else. Uncle Jonathan got up from the table, and as he walked out the dining room door, he pulled his handkerchief from his pocket to wipe his eyes.

That was on a Tuesday; school would start in New Cotswold on the following Monday. The next afternoon, Aunt Bea, Carole Anne, and Willie went to Maison Blanche, then to D.H. Holmes. Lastly, they went down the street to Tom McCann Shoes to round out Willie's new school wardrobe. He was beaming. On Friday night, Carole Anne and Dr. Bea put two happy boys on the train; Uncle Jonathan and Willie headed home.

Jack then asked, "And what about you?"

"I can't say that I was displaced. Over the years, I had spent almost as much time with my aunt as I had with my parents. I worshiped her; still do. From the time I was a little girl, I knew I wanted to be a physician just like her. Aunt Bea says that when I was born, I grabbed the tending physician's stethoscope and have never turned it loose. I was happy for them to leave me in her care. By the time I was twelve, I was practically living with her full-time. I was deeply concerned about the untimely death of my parents, more for Willie than myself."

The discussion was ending. She was very happy with what she had read so far. Like Will, she did not care to get blindsided. She just had to ask another question or two. Obviously, from Jack's questions, the crash was important. Did he know something they did not?

Jack responded that all he was going by was the old newspaper report that indicated that at one time, foul play could have played a part. No one seemed to know the extent of the investigation that had taken place or if the family had pushed it. Carole Anne said she imagined that her grandfather might be the only one who knew. Though Jack wondered if, in fact, he and Jan Plow were actually the only ones who knew.

Her final question was to inquire where Will was, chronologically, in their discussions. Jack told her the truth; he was not much further along than these earliest years. Then Carole Anne said with sincerity, "It is the later years that cause me some concern. Can he relive those years with no trouble? If he can, then I will feel much better about his future. He certainly seems to have it all together now. Maybe this is what he has been searching for. Maybe this is catharsis."

16

September, 1936: Will begins school

The first day of school was a day to behold. Jonathan put on nice trousers and a clean white shirt. His shoes were even polished. Aunt Tilda wanted to tag along, and it was alright, but Jonathan wanted to make sure that Willie's aunts on the Lamar side of the family knew *he* was taking charge.

They were a half block from the school when Letitia Mullens and her mother drove by in the big Lincoln. Willie took off running and caught up with them as soon as the car stopped. He and Letitia were so happy to see each other, they hugged. Letitia's mother looked at Jonathan and commented on how nice he looked. "First day of school, and you are already running for President of the PTA, how nice." Aunt Tilda overheard this and let out her famed, "Whoop."

The seating arrangement in the classroom was in alphabetical order. Letitia sat directly behind Willie. On the second day, the teacher sent them to separate corners with their backs to the class. They talked entirely too much. As time went on, the problem with the two became very apparent; they were bored silly.

The two children were ahead of the rest of the class; at some point, they probably should skip a grade. They knew their numbers and ABCs, and both could already read at second- or third-grade level. Had the teacher known of the relationship these two had with Miss Tilda, she would have understood. Miss Tilda had been the best teacher in the colored school before she'd quit to care for her family.

School had its other advantages for both. Up until school, they had had little exposure to many children. Neither had attended Sunday school. Letitia lived out in the country where her father made his headquarters as the leading bootlegger in the county. Willie, living in a blacksmith shop under the same roof with colored, had few friends. Most parents did not see the blacksmith shop and mule barn as an attractive playground. Willie's exposure to other children was mostly through cousins or friends of theirs.

Neither had seen some of the exciting new faces before. One was new in town and new to all the other children. Her name was Kacky Kaplan. Her father had come from Jackson to open a new department store in town. It was like none other the town had ever seen. The store had a full line of clothes, shoes, hats, and other things for the entire family. The Kaplan family also operated a huge store in Jackson that reportedly had a moving staircase. Willie doubted that. Kacky was, without reservation, the prettiest girl in the class. Her mother was just as pretty. Someone said the family was Jewish.

Willie's only cousin close to his age was Aunt Jessie's daughter, Patricia. As they grew older, they became close. At one point, she even enticed him to go to Vacation Bible School, and he liked it. At least he liked the crafts and refreshments and the games they played. The Bible stories he heard, like Jonah and the whale, no longer appealed to him. You had to be real young to believe all of that stuff; that was his opinion. John Pope still came to visit with his grandma on weekends, and he and Letitia helped keep the bottle business going. Their ring of friends grew, and often they ended up playing games down at the schoolyard.

Two incidents that occurred in first grade stuck in Willie's mind. In the very first talks regarding doing this project, Will had told Jack how he recollected so much and so accurately. One of these incidents in first grade was a point that he always went back to in his exercise of remembering his life.

It went like this. It was a Friday, and all the children were ready for the weekend to start. However, on this particular Friday, most of the class came dressed in better clothes than usual. As soon as the bell rang to dismiss classes, Letitia flew out of the room and ran through the door so hard that it crashed against the outside wall. Willie was right behind her; she was crying. Her mother was leaning against the big Lincoln, chatting with another woman, when she saw Letitia running toward her.

What Will remembered the most was that Mrs. Mullens, in her nice clean dress, dropped to her knees right in the dirt of the playground. Letitia ran into her mother's arms and just boohooed. Willie stood close by. Her mother looked at him questionably. He shrugged his shoulders. Finally, as Mrs. Mullens gently stroked her daughter's head, she got the answer. Kacky Kaplan was having a birthday party, and she did not get an invitation because her daddy sold whiskey. Willie did not get one either; he lived with colored people.

Willie said to Letitia, "Even when you are crying, you sure are purdy." With that, she clenched her fists and came after him screaming, "Shut up, shut up, shut up!" Mrs. Mullens hugged Letitia tighter and told her that she should not get mad at Willie when he said that to her. "What he really might be saying is that he loves you." Then she said to her, "When he says you are so pretty, say to him, I love you too."

No one said much about the incident when Willie was around. Mrs. Mullens did stop by the blacksmith shop and talk to Jonathan that same afternoon. Many years later, Will heard that his grandmother had gone to visit Mrs. Kaplan the next afternoon. She told her very politely that she should consider the fact there were more people selling whiskey and more people sharing the same roof with colored than there were Jews in the area. Interestingly enough, Mrs. Kaplan ended up being the favorite mother of all the children. As they all grew older and had parties or dances, Mrs. Kaplan usually chaperoned. They had a swimming pool at their house; it was the center of summer activity for many of the kids. Very few of the teenage boys would have learned to dance, had it not been for her. Willie learned the reason after he was in college.

Will told Jack that that was the first time he had ever considered that living with Uncle Jonathan in the livery with Aunt Tilda and Winston was unusual in the least. It made a lasting impression. He realized that similar conversations he had heard from some of the Lamar sisters implied their dislike of the situation. He could tell by their tone of voice that they had a distaste for Jonathan. Now he knew part of the reason.

One other incident in the lower grades stuck out. It was the first time Letitia's daddy had his picture in the paper. The picture was of Moon standing in handcuffs alongside a stack of gallon jugs of moonshine. The Sheriff had confiscated them the day before in a raid on one of his moonshine operations. The sheriff was using an ax to break open cases of shine.

Letitia was the fourth person to enter the classroom that morning. As she passed by the teachers' desk, she saw the newspaper neatly folded so that the picture was prominent. There was no way she could miss it. Three other pupils sat in the back corner of the room. Of the three, one was Alan Curry, the sissy in the class. Letitia looked back at them with no expression. Alan turned red as a beet.

Letitia sat at her desk and began to cry. Other pupils filed into the room. Some saw the picture and immediately looked at her with her head on the desk. When Willie came in, he saw her head down, and before he sat, he asked her what was wrong. She shook her head.

The teacher, Mrs. Monroe, realized what it was at a glance and simply put her book down over the picture. At recess, Will still could not get anything out of Letitia. She went directly to the water fountain and stood. Then the time came. Alan came to the fountain and dared not look at Letitia. When he had his mouth down on the spigot, Letitia hit him on the back of the head so hard that the force knocked his mouth down on the fountainhead.

Alan's head flew up as he spit blood and teeth into the basin. Mrs. Monroe was the schoolyard monitor that morning. She simply turned her head away. The vice principal investigated the incident. No action took place. Alan went through the rest of the school year with two teeth missing.

17

Early Fall, 1958

On Monday, Jack was up early, eager to get to the airport. Will had spent the weekend at home at The Point and flew back across the lake to get Jack. As soon as Jack was aboard, Will explained that the plane was a partnership between him and Nate Ludlow.

Neither of them individually needed a twin engine airplane, but having it together made sense. The plane was an Aero Commander 560. It would safely carry six people plus luggage. It cruised at over two hundred miles per hour. They would be in New Cotswold in slightly over an hour.

After they were out of Lakefront traffic and at cruising altitude, Will switched on the intercom. Always the tour guide, he pointed out things of interest on the way. Mostly it was one sand pit or gravel pit after another, or it was a huge acreage of timber the company leased or owned outright.

Will's plan was to tour Jack around, show him some places he wanted him to see. Afterward, he would introduce him to Uncle Jonathan. From there, Jack was to make his own plan. He did not want anyone to be uncomfortable talking to him. In fact, Will planned to be as discreet as possible when they toured the town.

Approaching the small airfield, Will used the plane's radio to announce his presence, in case any other aircraft were in the immediate area. It was unlikely, but Will took no chance. The wind was out of the south, so they flew north over the town and did a slow one hundred and eighty degree turn to line up with the runway. Approaching the field, Jack could see a long grass runway ahead. To the right of the runway were several World War II Quonset hut hangars, then a cute house with picket fence, a carriage house with five doors, and finally the back of a very large, white two-story house.

Gardens, vegetable and flower, a hot house, and a swimming pool were in the rear of the large house. A white picket fence surrounded the backyard, the same fence that was around the house that Jack surmised to be servants' quarters. There was a pergola over a gate in the picket fence. Under the pergola, a woman stood waiting.

Will did not taxi up to the gate but stopped at a fuel pump in front of the third hangar. A gray Ford pickup sat there, with a note under the windshield. Will laughed and told Jack that they were getting the royal treatment; the pickup was their ride for the day. They unloaded Jack's baggage and drove to the gate. Jack was about to meet Miss Annie, Will's grandmother.

She was an unforgettable character; just how unforgettable, Jack was to find out. Will told her his plans and promised to give her a hug before he left. She informed him that his grandfather was in Alaska, fishing for a week. "Thank my Lord for small favors." They both laughed.

Will asked Jack to drive. He said that the old truck would go unnoticed. They could tour discreetly around town. He then gave Jack directions out the front gate and to the right, heading away from town. They were on School Road. A couple of miles down the road, he pointed at a store at the intersection of School with another road. Will told Jack to pull into the parking lot at the store.

They sat in the truck, which did have air-conditioning, and with the truck idling, Will said, "This is Nap Marrs' store. He is a colored man, third generation owner of the store and a good friend of the family. His clientele is mostly colored, except for the few white people who know he sells the best meat in the county. His butcher ages beef to perfection. Go in sometime; introduce yourself. He will probably buy you a cold drink. If he is not busy, he will talk your ear off. He is a good source of information."

He pointed down the road that ran perpendicular to School Road. That was Nap Road. "Drive down about two hundred yards and you will see a driveway. Stop there." When they got to the spot, Will pointed to the simple iron gate. There was an entry pad on a post to enter a code to get in. "That long drive you see curves 'round to a house with grounds like a country club. There is a small bass pond in back. I know for a fact that there are fish that will weigh ten to twelve pounds. That is Uncle Winston and Aunt Tilda Jackson's house."

"You mean Maudie Lee's son?" Jack asked.

"You've met Maudie Lee?" Will questioned.

Jack acknowledged that he had, but said no more.

Will said in a quiet voice, "Remember this place well; we will visit it again later." He then instructed Jack to go back to School Road and drive on west, a mile or so. They came to a white house on the left. Directly across the road, a small driveway went to a steel gate. Will jumped out of the truck, opened the gate, and waved Jack through. They drove about thirty yards up to a small cabin still in weather-beaten board and batten siding. There was a cute front porch and a tin roof. Bright red paint trimmed the front screen door. The same red trim had been painted around the windows.

"Get out and come in," Will said. "I will show you my 'rehab center.'" Inside, there were only four rooms. One was a sitting room with an old leather chair, a sofa, and a small table and desk. Books lined one wall. A door from that room opened to the kitchen. There were modern appliances, and the few cupboards had screen doors. Will opened a door to a small pantry. It was completely full of staples, including at least three dozen bottles of premium whiskey and wine.

The house was a true dogtrot, and across the wide hall were two more rooms. There was one neatly furnished bedroom. It looked as if someone might be living there. Books lined one whole wall there also. Adjoining that room was a large room that served as a combination bath and closet. Will took Jack out the back door and onto another screened porch. It had several cane back rockers. Across the yard was a small barn with a fenced paddock; there was also an old smoke house.

"This was a tenant shack almost in ruin when I started working on it. It took me almost a year to get it to this point. Of course, I was drunk for that year, so I did not work real fast." Then he laughed, "I will tell you about that sometime. "

Back in the truck, Jack asked Will if he could go to a place where he wanted to begin his own tour. Without any direction, Jack drove to the courthouse, turned right, and continued to a point about five miles from town. He recognized what he was looking for and made a U-turn, crossed the highway, and parked under a shade tree. He kept the truck running and the air-conditioning on. They just sat there silently. Will said nothing, and Jack was off in another world.

After a few moments, Jack asked Will to lower his window. "Listen carefully; you can hear activity out on those fields. There are horses walking at a slow pace, low conversation, I even think I see men walking behind some horses, women in colorful dresses behind them. A few small children are skipping along." Will frowned, but Jack continued.

"They are Choctaw Indians. They are leaving; look at the heavy laden wagons. They decided not to stay. They had an opportunity to take six hundred and forty acres of land or go to a reservation in Oklahoma. Those decided to leave."

Jack turned to Will. "In my mind, I see it as plain as day. Maudie Lee described it in detail, just as her mother described it to her. She told me to come to this exact point, and I could see it like her mother had envisioned it. I do." They drove on back toward town and came upon an area that was far from what one would want the entrance to their town to be. On each side of the street were small businesses, in low, flat-topped buildings, many with boarded windows. Some had been painted in bright colors, now faded. Others were in the original clapboard siding or plain cement block. Trash was blowing along the street. Sand and dirt lingered on the pavement, deposited there by muddy tires that had come along in the last rain, regardless of how long that might have been.

Jack spoke. "This is the Quarters. The first people living on both sides of this creek were Indians. Then as the Indians left, the colored ended up here." Crossing the creek, Jack said, "And this is the Bottoms. It is predominantly white; some of the earliest settlers lived here. Some descendants still do."

As they approached the railroad, Jack said, "This railroad started out twenty miles long. It went north from your sawmill. Seamus named this the 'Laura Line.' He made a mistake running this rail line here and later came to realize it. It might have changed this town forever." Will made no comment.

When they reached the courthouse, Jack took a left, back onto School Street, then slowed past an alley and stopped in front of a building with a modern fascia. The sign across the front said, "City Livery." Underneath that, in bold block lettering, "Foundry and Machine Works," and underneath that, "Since 1868." Jack said, "And that is the original blacksmith shop. 'Put' Dishman was the blacksmith and wagon builder. There were two apartments in that building, one along each side."

Will smiled, "The one on the right is still there, and the one on the left has been converted to Winston Jackson's private offices. That is where I lived for the major part of my childhood and young adulthood. Seamus lived there a great deal of his life too."

Jack continued his tour. "The school should be down on the left. It probably is a lot different now. Seamus built it in order to keep Tadlock Lamar and his family in town. Tadlock's wife took charge of getting the school built. Tadlock was your great grandfather on your mother's side."

Jack amazed Will with his knowledge of the city as he went about pointing out things he had learned about from Maudie Lee. Jack drove on past the modern school building which now stood where he thought the old one had been. He was right. They drove another hundred yards down a slight grade.

Will instructed him to pull over and stop. "Look at what you see next to the creek." Jack looked and then exclaimed, "That is the original school house!" Originally, it sat on a sandstone foundation that eventually collapsed. Now it sat on a brick foundation and served as the school library. A large house stood on the other side of the stream. Will explained that it was a more recent boarding house for the teachers. Mrs. Farmer had operated one on the other side of the street.

Then Jack turned around and went back toward the town square. When he got to the street alongside the City Livery building, he turned left. Jack pointed out what used to be the jail.

Will spoke up. "Okay, let me show you a couple of things. At the next corner, turn right." That took them directly behind the City Livery structure. At the next corner, Will told Jack to turn left and pointed out a Sinclair service station on the northeast corner. After they turned, Will suggested that they stop midway down the block in front of the post office. He pointed across the street to two small brick bungalows.

The one on the left, Will and Carole Anne still owned. Now it was a gift shop. The one on the right had been the Mississippi offices of Senator Scoggins. Will's mother had been in charge of that office, and his father, William, Jr., was chief of staff for Senator Scoggins' Washington office. When Senate was not in session, they had all worked out of that small building. Will made sure that Jack could see the proximity of the house his parents owned to the building that housed City Livery. That was why it had been easy for him as a child to go visit Uncle Jonathan.

He then instructed Jack to drive further on north. Four miles out of town, they came to a beautifully landscaped property with lots of tall pines and lush plantings. It was shady and cool. They came to a gate, and Will instructed Jack to drive past. He pointed through the gates and down a long drive lined with pines.

There was no structure visible. This was now MacMoCorp headquarters. Will had more he wanted to show Jack before they went in, but these were the main offices, plus another very large foundry and a machinery test facility. The facility was only visible from the air.

They turned around and headed back to town. Will looked at his watch and asked Jack if it was too soon for a hamburger. The best ones in Mississippi were just ahead. At Will's direction, Jack turned in at the Toot'n Tell'em. It was a U-shaped property with a canopy completely covering the perimeter. A small building stood in the center, which housed the kitchen and a small lunch counter. Service outside was by carhop. Some vehicles sat under the canopy front first, while others backed in. Will explained that if you wanted to see, you backed your car in. Otherwise, drive straight in.

Will recommended the cheeseburger with fried green tomatoes on the side. Sweet ice tea was a must. After they made their decision, Will told Jack to flash his lights. When the carhops saw it, one would come out to take their order. Jack did so, and through the rearview mirror, he saw a young woman roller-skating toward their truck. In the mirror, she was kind of cute, maybe five eight on skates, with a long ponytail.

She glided up to the window and said, "Hey ya'll, watsit gonna' be today?" Close up, it was apparent that the mirror had been kind to her. She was still attractive, but her facial odometer showed plenty of miles, maybe hard ones. Jack gave her the order and she skated away. Will went on talking about kids who gathered here and the times he would come out with Letitia Mullens, sip wine out of paper cups, and watch the continual stream of kids driving past.

When the carhop returned with the food order, she carefully put a tray in the window. She crooked her head a bit, stuck her head closer to the window, and said across to Will, "Hey there, Sugah, ain't seen you in a long time. Where you stayin' now?"

Will replied, "Oh, here and there."

She said, "Must be mostly theah, shuah ain't seen you heah. Doan be gone so long next time." Will pulled out his wallet and handed Jack two twenty dollar bills. The amount was more than enough for the food and a generous tip.

Will ate slowly, seeming to enjoy reminiscing. After he was through chewing, he said, "That girl's name is Holly Porterfield. She and some other girls here had a bad experience several years ago. All of them have had problems as a result. But hers were not the worst." That was all he said, but Jack made a mental note. That evening he wrote the name "Holly Porterfield" in his notes.

On the way back into town, Will continued to give directions. At Church Street, which Jack recognized again from Maudie Lee's description, Will directed them to the right. Here, Jack commented again, "Up ahead on the right, about a mile, we will come to Old Church. Seamus is in a tomb there, standing up, facing to the west. He built that Church to appease the women in town who thought he was moving too quickly to build whiskey stills and livery stables. The story goes, he was never inside the church."

Will laughed, "Sounds like Uncle Jonathan took after him." He made no further explanation.

They stopped at the church and got out. Jack stood for a long time by Seamus' tomb and followed his gaze over the land. Back in the car, Will told Jack to drive about one half mile further and pull into a gate there. Jack now realized that the airfield where they had landed was to his left. It stretched a mile from School Road to Church Road.

Once again, Will was out, big key ring in hand, ready for gate duty. Back in the truck, he cautioned Jack to drive slowly. The covered bridge ahead had some loose boards; the bridge rattled like thunder as they passed through. A large stone and log structure stood straight ahead.

"Laura's Lodge," said Jack.

Will questioned, "How much time did you spend with Maudie Lee?"

"Not enough." He was already thinking about visiting her again.

Even though he knew a lot about what they were going to see inside, Jack let Will tell him. They stepped up to the screen door, and Will told him to turn around. There was a panoramic view of the whole valley, the airfield, and Will's grandfather's estate.

Inside the vast welcoming hall, Will pointed out the ladies' parlor on the left and the gentlemen's parlor on the right. Both had pocket doors. The ones to the ladies' parlor stood open, while the gentlemen's parlor doors stood shut. Will explained. "That room has not been opened since my parents died. I'll tell you more about that later."

They went past steps that led to the upstairs and into rooms on the left, which had at one time been servants' quarters. Then the rooms on the right, which were the owner's quarters. Not much had changed. Lighting and plumbing was new; the furnishings were very old, but beautifully oiled and kept. Upstairs were the guest rooms and the sleeping porch. One of the rooms at the front of the house was now a nice office. There was rich leather seating, an ornate desk, and one complete wall for books, and a beautiful tapestry hung from one wall. The view from the large window, like the one from the porch, was outstanding. In the kitchen, Will opened a door to the back screened porch. It looked toward the barn and a servant's house close by. It was exactly as Maudie Lee had described it.

Laid out on a cupboard were several packages including a covered dish. Will opened them. There was fresh cooked bread, fresh picked corn, beefsteak tomatoes, and lemon meringue pie. Will laughed, "Grandma cannot stand to have me left alone to do my own thing. Her help has brought all of this. I have some T-bones in the refrigerator. If it is OK with you, we'll grill the steaks for dinner and spend the night here tonight. After that, you can stay here for the nights you are in town alone, or you can use my rehab center or stay at the hotel. It is your choice.

"I would imagine you will want to spend more time here; however, you might enjoy staying at the other places to get a feel. The hotel is nice, with good food in the dining room, and it can be interesting at night. Upstairs is a private club, and you are already a member. You can get a drink there. Also, and I caution you, lots of gossip gets started there, and of course lots ends up there." Jack was delighted with the arrangements. Will was a great host.

Will looked at his watch, "We are on schedule, so let's go out to the offices. I want to at least introduce you to Uncle Jonathan and some others today. If we have time, we will also stop by and meet Winston Jackson at his office. If not, we'll get that done in the morning before I leave."

Will drove. They got to the gate at the corporate offices, and he rolled down the window on the truck. A guard, a colored fellow in a crisp blue uniform, frowned as he stepped to the window. Apparently a little startled, he said, "Oh my goodness, Mr. Will, I thought it was Miss Annie! She knows you driving her truck?"

Will laughed. "She knows, Adam. I have a guest, permanent pass please, Mr. Jack E. Ward." The guard answered very professionally, "Yes, sir." He handed the badge in and leaned into the window. "Welcome, sir, we happy you here." With that, they drove on down the curving drive.

The main facility came into view. Astonishing as it was, what caught Jack's eye was a very impressive building in a field to the left. A sign read, "New Cotswold Regional Fire Department." Will described the fire department and how it worked. "Uncle Jonathan has been Fire Chief of the Volunteer Fire Department in town for years. Living in the livery building as he did for many years, he was the volunteer closest to the one and only fire truck. The original old truck was in a shed, under the water tower. If there was a fire, whoever discovered it dialed zero to get the telephone operator to report the fire and the quadrant of the city where the fire was. The operator then keyed a buzzer attached to a siren on top of the water tower. If she keyed in one signal, the siren wailed one time. She would wait a few seconds and then repeat it. It meant the fire would be in quadrant one of the city, and so on. Volunteers would rush to that area. The town being as small as it is, it was not hard to find the fire.

"Over the years, however, volunteerism has not been at its best, nor has money for equipment. Often the quadrant of the city where the fire occurred drew fewer responses than it might have in another quadrant. Volunteers in the other quadrants retaliated. On occasion, houses burned to the ground because of racism or class structure. We established this privately owned fire department, and we train all the people and furnish all the equipment. We also serve other counties if need be. We charge nothing."

In the reception area were a number of comfortable chairs, several tables with lamps, and a rack of reading material. The reception desk itself was a horseshoe of stainless steel. Behind the desk sat a very attractive woman, probably in her fifties. A plaque on her desk read "Mrs. Abernathy."

Will introduced her to Jack, and Jack's jaw dropped. His puzzled look caught Mrs. Abernathy's eye, and she laughed, "I am her daughter-in-law. But you are too young to have known her. How do you know about Granny Abernathy?"

"I heard about her through Dr. Bea and Maudie Lee," Jack responded. "Certainly Maudie Lee would have told me if she still was working." Mrs. Abernathy smiled before she replied, "She still would be if we would let her, but she is up in years and a little frail."

Jack's excitement was obvious. "She is still alive? Where does she live?"

"She's in a Catholic Retirement home in Jackson. Miss Mollie set that all up for her before she went back to Scotland. She has a paid for home and nursing care 'til the day she dies, bless Miss Mollie's soul."

Jack inquired, "May I visit her? I feel like I know her already. Do you think it's possible I might see her on Friday?" Will stood by while

Mrs. Abernathy made arrangements, gave Jack the address, and told him whom to call when he was ready to go to see her mother-in-law. He was pleased but could not understand why Maudie Lee, after her long history of Seamus, had not told him that the elder Mrs. Abernathy was still alive.

This had really been a day. Jack felt he should start another tablet, even though he had not contacted the woman. It was *Mrs. Abernathy.*

A young woman came to the reception area, and Will stepped over to her. They both turned their backs to Jack and Mrs. Abernathy and talked quietly for a few moments. Will then turned to Jack to tell him he had some rather urgent business to attend to and that he had to excuse himself for a short time. However, Jonathan was expecting him and would be up in a moment to get him.

Uncle Jonathan was more than what Jack had expected. He had felt sure, from other discussions, that Jonathan was a large man, but Jack had not imagined him as this big. He was not any taller than Jack, but was wide across the shoulders, with a thick chest and big arms and hands. Jack could see that years of slinging a blacksmith hammer had had their effect.

Jonathan had on suit pants, a white shirt and conservative tie, and black leather suspenders. He directed Jack to his office. It was not until they were walking down the hall that Jack noticed the limp. He looked down at Jonathan's feet and noticed that the man wore finely polished, high-top work shoes. The right one was about a size twelve, and the left more like an eighteen and loosely tied.

Seated in the office, Jack noticed three pretty model fire engines. He commented on those and on the fire department building he had seen as they were arriving. Jonathan told Jack that his hobby was fighting fires, then laughed. He said that if there was not at least one fire a week, he would go set one somewhere. Jack asked him to tell him a little more about himself.

Jonathan's response was, "I will let other people tell you about me. Momma for example, she will wear you out, talking about all of us. Since you are here to get as much of the history of the company as possible, let's talk about it."

Jonathan and the rest of the family had moved from Memphis back to New Cotswold during the Depression. His grandfather,

Seamus, was alive but doing poorly in health and in business. The company was unraveling. William, Jonathan's father, was a West Pointer serving in the Army Air Corp with every intention of being a career officer. He saw action during the First World War and loved every minute. He was reluctant to move the family to New Cotswold. He had met Miss Annie in Memphis before they had married, and her family lived there. Moving to New Cotswold was not desirable.

But Grandmother Mollie was insistent. She could not hold things together. William had not been on great terms with Seamus for a long time. It was like pouring gas on fire when he returned. The company was in shambles, and Seamus a wreck. They were far from broke, but Seamus was determined that they were on the way to the poor house, and he seemed determined to lead the way.

The bank was the main concern, with millions of dollars on loans and people who could not pay. Runs on banks were common. William assessed the situation, and he and Mollie made a decision that caused Seamus to go berserk. William had his father forcibly removed from the bank and sent to the house in Memphis. William and his family moved into the lodge.

One by one, William and Mollie met with every loan customer at the bank. Most of them, when called to the bank, came ready to turn over the keys to their house or businesses. Instead, they found William and Mollie seated in Seamus's old office, loan files at hand and hopeful proposals to make. William explained their plan to each customer. The bank was far from going under, and their customers came first. They asked each one how much money they could continue to pay toward their notes. It did not matter to William, as long as it was just *something*. In many cases, it was no more than a dozen eggs a week.

If they would commit *anything* at all, William would let them ride until times got better. All interest charges would stop, and anything a customer could pay would go toward principal. Word soon spread. There was only one run on the bank: fortunately, everyone got their money. But many others were convinced and did keep their money in the bank. William and Mollie saved the bank.

The mills were close to closing, and there William also brought things under control. He would not shut the mills as long as every employee cooperated. First, they would start by reducing everyone's hours, but they would lay no one off. If that did not work, they would have to sacrifice more. They managed to save the mills and did not shut down.

"Furthermore, "Jonathan said, "Our family sacrificed as well. We were down to one car. I went to work every day after school and on Saturday, working for Winston's father, Put Dishman. Winston and I worked side by side at the livery. Mother took a job at the bank. Beatrice took in sewing and worked part-time at the hospital. William, Jr., was ready for college, but he waited a year to earn money and drove a lumber truck at the mill."

Jonathan paused a minute and got them both a Coca-Cola from a refrigerator in his cloakroom. When he sat back down, Jack said, "I know a lot about Seamus, but very little about your dad. What you have told me is a great help. My opinion at this point is that Seamus developed quite an empire, and your father saved it from ruin."

"Very true, but a lot more has been accomplished since. We will get to that in time. Speaking of time, I have to leave in about ten minutes to go to a meeting in town. Sorry I cannot eat with you people tonight; maybe we can get together again before you leave. By the way, what are your plans for this week?"

Jack told him he planned to stay in town through Thursday and on Friday would drive back to New Orleans. He would visit with Mrs. Abernathy in Jackson on the way. He would return to New Cotswold the following week.

Jonathan said, "Glad you will be staying around a few days. I will get in touch for the next visit."

Will finished his work and was in the reception area when Jack returned. They bid Mrs. Abernathy good-night and left for the lodge. After unloading luggage, Will showed Jack to a room upstairs. He explained that if it got too hot, Jack should go out onto the sleeping porch. Usually there was a great breeze.

While Jack unpacked, he could hear Will stirring around in the kitchen and then heard the clink of glasses. Will called up, "Did you bring swim trunks?" Jack replied that he had not. "Not a problem," Will said. "I have extras. Come to the top of the stairs and I'll throw you a pair. We have to go take a dip before we start cooking."

Jack found Will with towels laid out and a small bar set up on the kitchen counter. "I hope you will have a drink with me. Pour yourself a heavy one, and we will take them to the creek."

Jack barely noticed the swimming hole when they crossed through the covered bridge. A big oak stood at the water's edge, with some roots showing. A huge rope hung from a low limb. Will dared Jack to swing out on the rope, and Jack accepted the challenge. Will took their drinks to the other side of the pool, set the drinks on a rock at water's edge, and jumped in. Jack did not hit the water well, before he screamed out, "Ohhh, wow, this is cold!" Will was standing in the water at the edge of the pool. His own lips were blue, and he had chill bumps all over, but he was laughing all the while.

"See why I suggested we bring a strong drink?" He handed Jack his. "It gets bearable in a few minutes." He reminisced about the time he had sat on the side of the creek while his dad and Uncle Jonathan built the dam to capture the water for the pool. He had been here often to go skinny-dipping.

They stayed in the water until the whiskey was gone. On the way back to the house was the first time Jack had noticed the long scar along Will's left leg; other scars on his shoulder appeared to be bullet wounds.

Will got a fire going in a fifty-five gallon barrel made into a cooker. Both fixed another drink. Together they shucked the corn and removed all the silks. Jack sliced tomatoes while they sat on stools at the kitchen counter.

Will inquired as to Jack's visit with Jonathan. Jack confirmed his pleasure as well his astonishment; Jonathan was not what he had expected. Will's only comment was, "You know that I scarcely knew my parents. I remember little about them. I have always looked up to Uncle Jonathan as my dad, and a great one too."

After shucking the corn, Will slathered the cobs with soft butter, then salt, pepper, and a little chili powder. Next, he pulled the shucks around the corn and tied them securely with twine. They would go on the fire with the steaks. There was time for one more "toddy" before Will started cooking. They sat on the back doorsteps until the steaks were done.

They ate at the kitchen counter, saying little. Will finished first, plugged in a coffee pot, and took a bottle of coffee liqueur down from a cabinet. They each took coffee, with a shot of the liqueur, to the front porch. A cool breeze blew across the valley. It was a great evening. After a period of solitude, Will asked Jack if they could talk for a while. First, however, he would like to call home. Jack could do the same; he could use the phone in the office upstairs. Will talked a long time, apparently to more than one person. There was a lot of laughter on his end.

Seated again on the porch with another cup of coffee and liqueur, Will started first by asking Jack about his own mother and father. Jack told him about his mother having a heart problem and her death when he was three. He had inherited a murmur, which kept him out of contact sports as well as the military. He wanted to follow in his father's footsteps and be a war correspondent in the signal corps, but that would never come to pass.

His father was his hero. They had struggled along together, though mostly it was his father. He was always chasing that next journalistic dream, and worked for several papers while Jack was growing up. His father had not shown much interest in women while Jack was still at home. His father was now city editor at the leading newspaper in Jackson.

Jack told Will that one of the saddest days in his life had been the day his father took him out to the highway to hitchhike a ride to New Orleans for the job at the paper. He said that as he drove away, he got tears in his eyes, not so much for himself but for the fact that his father was going to be alone. Thankfully, he found a nice lady, whom Jack adored, and the two were happily married.

Then Will began to tell more of his own story. It was midnight when they stopped. Both yawned a time or two and decided to call it an evening. But Jack did not go to bed before reviewing his notes and beginning several new tablets. The book was well underway in his mind.

Early the next morning, Will had Jack up early to deliver him to the livery to meet Winston Jackson. After a brief introduction, he was off. He told Jack that the car he would be using while working on the project was in the back of the building, and they would touch base later in the week.

Winston's appearance was a surprise. He was probably five ten and a hundred and eighty pounds, with wide shoulders and big arms and hands. What surprised Jack most was his coloring: he was lighter than any colored man Jack had seen outside New Orleans. He had a bald pallet, with a rim of salt-and-pepper hair over the ears. He wore an expensive summer weight suit with necktie loose at the collar, rimless glasses, and alligator shoes. He asked Jack to step into his office before they took a tour. Winston sat at his desk, and Jack in a guest chair.

Winston slowly took off his glasses and took his time cleaning them to perfection before he looked Jack firmly in the eye. He spoke in a serious tone, "Who do you think you are, bribing my momma to talk with a quart of Old Crow?" It took Jack by surprise, and he stammered a bit to answer.

Winston could not go through with it, and he started laughing. "I believe I had you there for a moment." Jack agreed. Winston went on about his mother's phone call alerting him that Jack was coming to visit. "She thought that you were a very nice man and hopes you will come again. She is a card, that one," he said. Next, he covered the plan for the day. He would be with Jack until eleven sharp. At that time, he had to deliver Jack to Miss Annie for lunch and conversation, until two. Afterward, Jack would be back with Jonathan for the rest of the day. Winston said, "You got your work cut out for you today; Miss Annie alone will wear you out."

Before they took a tour of the facility, Jack told Winston that he had not pictured him or Jonathan as they appeared today. In his mind, he had a picture based on Maudie Lee's description. He expected two men in bib overalls and leather aprons, pounding hot iron bars on anvils. With that, Winston took him over to his wall of fame. Many of the pictures were of family, the old livery barn, and the blacksmith shop. Many customer pictures were there and sure enough, he and Jonathan looked just as Maudie Lee had described. Jack asked if he might borrow some of the pictures to make copies later. Winston agreed, but also told him that Miss Annie probably would bury him with material.

Looking at the pictures, Jack saw that Jonathan, even when young, had been an ox of a man. He had a big head of shaggy hair, black horn-rimmed glasses, and a two-day growth of beard. In many pictures, he clenched a cigar between his teeth. Jack commented on

Jonathan's appearance. Winston told him that he was glad that fighting fires had become the man's hobby. "Used to be, his hobby was beating the tar out of anybody who would fight him."

They took a brief tour of the plant, with hard hats and safety glasses. Winston covered it quite well. It was obviously refurbished, but neat and clean, like facilities Jack had seen elsewhere. The facility was still a functioning machine shop with a forge; most of the work was to make prototypes of things they would manufacture at the main plant. In short, this was a lab and was Winston's baby. Before going back to Winston's office, they stopped at a point in the center of the big open area of the building. Winston explained how the building was originally constructed, the changes that had been made over the years, and the future for the facility.

They sat in a corner of Winston's office at a large circular table with rocking chairs. Winston began by first asking Jack if had made plans for tomorrow. When Jack answered that he had not, Winston told him his plan. At lunchtime on Wednesday, most of the businesses in town closed for the afternoon. He would like Jack to come out to his house for lunch and to meet Miss Tilda, and then the three of them could fish in Winston's private lake. If they caught anything, then Jack could stay for supper too.

"Now," Winston said, "as I understand it, you are doing a history of the company. In my opinion, most of that is a history of the family. Since Miss Tilda and I are William's age, we probably can contribute quite a bit."

Jack agreed and was thrilled with the reception. For some reason, maybe it was Maudie Lee's reaction when he asked her about Winston, he had felt that his relationship with Winston might be uncomfortable. It was far from it.

Winston's story

Winston related what he could remember, and it began with Seamus. According to him, Seamus took Miss Mollie as his second wife a year or so after the death of his first wife and kids. After William was born, they moved the family to Memphis. William was born a year and a half after Winston. They schooled him in Memphis, but in the summers, they would come back to New Cotswold, often for the whole summer. Seamus brought William to the livery to work one morning, and Winston's grandfather, Put Dishman, put William to work with Winston.

Since Winston was the oldest, he was the boss man. They were not capable of doing much, but Grandpa Put kept them busy. That was how the two became close. When he was older, William went to boarding school. Winston felt that the family might have sent him there to get rid of him. It seemed like no time at all before both boys graduated from high school and went their own ways. They kept in touch, but with both going to college and on to careers, they saw little of each other until after Miss Mollie begged William to return to help. Had she not, he would have stayed away. William and Seamus did not see eye to eye on much of anything, and he reluctantly returned for his mother's sake.

Winston knew things were bad because of the Depression, but he'd had no knowledge of the whole picture. His grandpa had cut out all help, and it was just him and Winston. By then, William had three children. Miss Tilda and Winston had one girl. William moved his family into the lodge house, which was a real step down from the house in Memphis. The whole family went to work: Miss Annie, the girl Beatrice, and William, Jr.

Winston did not have a great opinion of William, and he chuckled when he recalled it. "Big dumb ass Jonathan came to work with me and Grandpa. He was high school age, and oldest of the three. You could look at him and tell he was the school dunce." Then Winston told of the change in him. "However, Jonathan was meant to be a blacksmith. He took to it like a duck to water. Within a year, he was walking around with his head up and a bit of self-esteem."

When Winston and William's children got to college age, Winston's daughter went to Tougaloo, where Winston and Miss Tilda had gone. She got her teaching certificate and a husband about the same time. The only grandchild Winston and Tilda had was a boy, John Pope.

Beatrice went off to Newcomb first. She was the only girl, and she had skipped two grades in school. The story of her achievements was well-known. William, Jr. was good-looking, smart as a whip, and the apple of his father's eye. Money was tight, and when time came for Jonathan to go to college, he held back; three of them in college would be a strain on the family. When things got better, Jonathan enrolled at Mississippi State without even discussing it with his father. He hitched a ride there and registered for classes. That first year, he did not come home until Christmas. In the summers, he came back to work at the blacksmith shop with Winston and Grandpa Put. It became very apparent that he had a passion for learning. He was a lot smarter than anyone had suspected. He ended up with a double major, Mechanical and Aeronautical Engineering.

Winston graduated with a degree in education. Put needed him at the shop, so rather than taking a teaching job, he came home to help. Times had changed. Horseshoe work and blacksmithing were becoming a thing of the past, but they still accounted for a lot of the work. Put had started doing some machine shop work along with the blacksmithing, but times were still hard.

When Jonathan graduated, he returned also. "It was not an opportune time to have an engineer on staff," lamented Winston with his eyes wide open for emphasis. "Jonathan knew that his work was not going to be with a white shirt and slide rule. He worked right alongside Grandpa and me, doing whatever needed to be done. Many Saturdays we shoed more horses and beat out more bent plows than anything else. However, Jonathan had more on his mind. He had a dream. What you see today is a result of his labor and his intellect. Not mine, and not all William's either."

With that, their time was up; Jack had an appointment with Miss Annie. He left with a great admiration for Winston and his gracious manner. He was excited about the next day. He wanted to hear more.

18

Miss Annie's story

Miss Annie was waiting at the back gate. She ushered Jack in, introduced him to her cook, and handed him a Bloody Mary. "I do not think it is too early, do you?" she chirped. She loved her house and had reason to enjoy showing it off. Various *objets d'art* stood out, and she was pleased that Jack recognized some of the artists.

A tiny poodle named "Hardly" came rushing in and leaped into Miss Annie's lap. She explained the name. Her cook had said, when Miss Annie brought the dog home as a puppy, that it was *hardly* a dog at all. The name stuck.

They adjourned into her parlor; she sat Jack in a chair so close she could almost reach out and touch him. She kept eye contact all of the time that they talked. He did not know if she was hard of hearing or looking into his eyes for truth.

"Tell me first," she said. "How did you and Beatrice get together to do this thing?" Jack told her, and she smiled. "It is something I think needed to be done long before now. Thank-you."

"Next," she said, "how do you think Will is, I mean his mental state? Is he happy, is he content as he seems?" Jack told her that he had only known him about three weeks, and that as best as he could tell, Will was quite happy. She nodded as if that was exactly her assessment. Jack pondered her comment; he had a lot more to find out about Will.

Miss Annie reminded him that they only had a couple of hours, so what would he like to discuss? Jack explained that he was trying to keep things in chronological order and would like to hear as much as possible about her husband. He also stated that he understood that it was not going to be easy finding out much about him. She agreed that that was true, but said that she would tell him what she believed would give him a very good analysis of the man.

Placed next to her chair was a stack of albums, each three inches thick, filled with pictures. Nothing was worse than having to sit while someone went picture by picture, telling you all about each one. Jack was not thrilled at the prospect. But it did not turn out so badly, after all.

She grabbed the top album and turned to a marked page to show Jack a picture of William, the West Point cadet. He was a handsome man. Miss Annie told Jack about the Christmas they had met. She was in the train station in St. Louis, waiting to go to her home in Memphis for the holidays. She was a college student at Stephens. Jack smiled and told her that he had gone to Mizzou. Both schools were in the same city.

She was sitting on a bench in the train station, and the train was terribly late. She looked up and saw this handsome man in uniform coming toward her. She shook all over a little bit, to let Jack know how handsome she thought he was. She told Jack she had been Maid of Cotton her first year in college and was pretty darn good-looking herself. William walked right past without even cutting an eye toward her. She followed him with her eyes, and all of a sudden, he wheeled around, came back, and sat down right beside her.

Miss Annie said that he had this big grin on his face and said, "Are you married?" Of course, she had answered, "No!" Then he said, "Would you like to be?" She started to get up to leave. Then he put his arm out for her to stay. "You don't have to decide right away, but at least give me a chance." He was as serious as he could be.

"Eight hours later, when the train finally pulled out, I had found out all about him. He had heard of my family; I had heard of his. We were both on our way to Memphis, and we talked and talked. By the time the trip was over, I knew him better than boys I had dated for a year or more. My parents were at the station to pick me up. His father sent a chauffeur to fetch him. We arranged to get together while we were both home for Christmas. The following June, just a week after he graduated the academy and I had my diploma, we were married."

"Four years later, I had three babies under four years old and a husband who had just reenlisted to be a part of the US Army Air

Service, flying all over the sky in aeroplanes. My parents were beside themselves. Seamus admitted he had raised a fool. But Mollie thought William could do no wrong. Then the fool goes off to France to fight in World War I. I had been living back in Memphis close to my parents most of my married life."

The story she told Jack was a lot like what Maudie Lee remembered.

William had made colonel and went to an air training command. The family was barely settling down to a normal life, when Seamus got ill and despondent. The Depression was at its worst, the company was in trouble, and Mollie was in trouble: she begged William for help. William went to her aid, saw the terrible situation, and realized how desperate the situation was. He resigned his commission and moved the family to New Cotswold. It was extremely hard on all of them. They all had to go to work. But Miss Annie was sincere when she admitted that these were probably the best years of the family. They were, at last, all one family living under the same roof.

William was never one to sit still, however. As things got better, he started trying to see how he could grow the company to an even higher level. Seamus died and left a vast estate. Many people were recipients. Luckily, the stock in the company, the railroad, and several other smaller ventures went solely to William and Mollie. That left one small problem. The bulk of Seamus' cash and insurance benefits went to the rest of the beneficiaries. The Dishman family got some, Maudie Lee got some, Winston got some, and several others who had been loyal to Seamus over the years got some. With this cash drain, William had to be frugal and extremely careful how he invested. He needed immediate cash flow. Over the years, it was probably a blessing that he had nothing to squander. It had made him a much better manager.

William continued something that Seamus had done quite well. He created indebtedness among many politicians. All one had to do was ask, and William would provide money or endorsement. In time, his name as a supporter of a candidate could get a person elected. On top of that, he had no great party affiliation, nor did race or sex make any difference. If he thought someone was well qualified for a position, he helped.

That fact had some implications, especially as the race issue grew more heated in the South. William was just as much an enemy to some as he was a benevolent friend to others. One of his strongest friends and allies was State Senator Scoggins. The senator's home was in New Cotswold, and he kept a home office there.

William, Jr. got his law degree, passed the bar, and moved back to New Cotswold to practice. He married Noreen Lamar, his childhood sweetheart during college. Carole Anne was born ten months later. The Lamar sisters had to eat crow. They thought she had had to be pregnant when they'd gotten married.

Six years later, after they moved back, William III (Willie) was born. In a short time, William, Jr. caught the eye of Senator Scoggins. The senator did not have much trouble convincing William Jr. to go to Washington as his chief of staff. He hired Noreen to manage the home district office.

The MacMorogh companies were beginning to see some recovery from the Depression. Annie was able to spend more time at home. William, Jr. had a promising career, Beatrice had completed med school, and Jonathan was back at home from college. He jumped into the machine shop business with both feet.

As soon as Miss Annie finished that sentence, she glanced briefly to the doorway; her cook stood there. Miss Annie made the slightest nod, and the cook announced, "Lunch is served, Miss Annie."

The lunch was delightful. Jack could have been at Commander's Palace in New Orleans. The first course was a cup of turtle soup with a thimble of cognac served alongside. If it pleased the diner to give the soup a little more kick, the cognac was just right. Next, a salad of artichoke hearts with fresh lettuce from the garden. A covered basket with a selection of small rolls and cornbread sat on the table. The entree was a brace of roasted quail, and the wine a choice Chardonnay. Key lime pie served with coffee rounded out the luncheon.

After lunch, Miss Annie continued her commentary. Her husband was never content. He wanted more, and more. He had a close relationship with Senator Scoggins; it opened otherwise impossible doors. When the senator knew he was terminally ill, William, Sr. was the first to know. The senator made an astounding proposal. He wanted to resign his Senate seat before the next election, fourteen months away. His suggestion was that William, Sr. convince the governor to appoint William, Jr. to his seat. It would then give William, Jr. the opportunity to run as the incumbent in the next election.

That would take some manipulation. William knew that as soon as the governor found out about the senator, he would want to appoint someone, maybe even himself. The lieutenant governor was, in Miss Annie's opinion, "a rabid little son of a bitch" who would stop at nothing to support the governor and his decision. *Miss Annie minced no words!* Doing so would give him the governor's seat, meaning that he, too, could run as the incumbent in the next gubernatorial election. William had his work cut for him.

The first thing he did was approach Governor Ainsworth. He told him what his desire was before the governor had an opportunity to voice his own. The governor thought it over for a short while and rejected William's plan. He did, indeed, prefer to appoint himself and give Lt. Governor Hawkins a chance at the governor's seat.

William got tough. He reminded Ainsworth that it was he, William MacMorogh, who had put him in office to begin with. If the governor did not go along with his own plan to have William, Jr. appointed, he would see to it that when the unexpired term of Senator Scoggins was over, that would be the last time Ainsworth would see Washington, D.C. On the other hand, if he went along with the plan to appoint William, Jr., William would guarantee him another term as governor. Furthermore, he had plans for William, Jr. past the Senate seat. He would throw his full support to the governor at that time if he still wanted to represent the state in the Senate.

Governor Ainsworth confided in Lieutenant Governor Hawkins. He laid out his plan to appoint William, Jr. Understandably, Lieutenant Governor Hawkins was livid, but not as livid as his wife was. She was from a very wealthy Mississippi Delta family. They had thrown a lot of money toward getting Ainsworth elected. Getting her husband elected lieutenant governor along *with* him had cost another bundle. "William MacMorogh was not," in her own words "goin' to screw over us!"

The senator, with William, Sr. doing all of the planning, called a meeting in New Cotswold. Included were the most influential constituents in his district. They reserved the entire hotel for the meeting guests. The meeting itself, however, would be held at Laura's Lodge.

The men's parlor was cleared of most all furniture, and a huge conference table in the form of a horseshoe took its place.

On Wednesday, prior to the weekend of the meeting, Senator Scoggins and William, Jr. flew to New Cotswold from Washington on a private airplane provided by a meat packing company; that company had benefited well during Senator Scoggins' terms in office. The airplane was a twin engine Lockheed. It landed in New Cotswold, dropped off the senator and William, Jr., then continued on to Gulfport, Mississippi. It would return on Friday afternoon for the return flight to Washington that same night.

William planned well. Senator Scoggins would make public his early retirement due to ill health. Governor Ainsworth would speak briefly and express his decision to appoint William, Jr. to take the unexpired term. In addition, William, put together a plan for the election that would take place at the expiration of the term. Most of the attendees would hoorah his efforts. To further galvanize the decision to appoint William, Jr., the elder William had gone so far as to have an array of campaign literature, buttons, pennants, and large signs printed. He already had a campaign finance committee in place.

Several small groups assembled for preliminary meetings at the hotel. Rumor got to William that the meeting at Laura's Lodge might not go as smoothly as anticipated. Lieutenant Governor Hawkins had an invitation to the lodge, and not his wife. But she was demanding to be present; she wanted to make a statement. Someone took Hawkins aside and told him in no uncertain terms that if his wife came to the meeting, he could kiss his own ass good-bye! He left prior to the meeting, with his wife kicking and screaming. *Once again, Miss Annie minced no words.*

The meeting began on Friday with breakfast in the hotel dining room. William welcomed everybody and handed out the day's agenda. The meeting should be over by noon, so everyone could get home before dark. William, Jr. introduced the Rev. John Milwee, an Episcopal priest and friend of the family, who blessed the meal. Afterward, a caravan of cars departed for Laura's Lodge.

"That night…" Miss Annie paused, put her hand to her mouth, and shook her head. She could say no more.

As if on cue, the same servant who had signaled that lunch was ready came to the door. Miss Annie nodded slightly, and the servant said, "Baxter is ready with the car, Ma'am."

Miss Annie turned to Jack. She was in a different, lighthearted mood when she spoke. "I have had the same beauty shop appointment at the same place, with the same woman, at the same time, on the same day for thirty years. Do you believe that she will be mad if I show up a minute late? I must run. We are going to visit a lot more, aren't we? I have not told you anything about my girls." Miss Annie departed, leaving Jack to thank the cook for a wonderful meal.

The visit with Miss Annie was far more productive than anticipated. She was a delight to talk with and one of the most gracious women he had ever encountered. In addition, she was brilliant and apparently had an important role in the company. Jack expressed this to Jonathan when they were back together that afternoon.

Jonathan smiled and agreed. He further stated that she seldom mentioned the company that her family owned and continued to operate under the guidance of her and one other sister. They dealt primarily in cotton. Not only did they own large acreages in Mississippi and Arkansas, but they also ginned, compressed, and stored cotton for other farmers. They were fortunate in being able to surround themselves with loyal, dedicated leadership. Through them, they maintained control.

MacMoCorp

Jonathan was anxious to continue showing Jack more about the MacMorogh operations. He planned an extensive tour of the facility and grounds. He laid out a white lab coat and suggested that Jack bring it along; they would need it later. The tour began with the front offices of the facility. In all, Jack estimated there to be fifty people, most of them in one large room with partitions. Several private offices, all with glass fronts, lined one side of the room. William. had an aversion to people being out of sight.

They stepped outside the back door and met a young colored man dressed in white shirt and tie. He was as an intern currently enrolled in a co-op training program available at several colleges and universities supported by the company.

Students in their junior year could opt to stretch their senior year into a two-year program whereby they went to school for a semester and worked at the company for a semester, alternating until they graduated. This delayed graduation by several months, but it ensured the student an opportunity for employment with the company. The program had a ninety-six percent success rate.

The young man drove a four-seat Cushman Truckster, a vehicle useful for transportation inside large facilities. The tour took an hour. Acting as guide, the young man did most of the talking. A couple of times, Jack looked over at Jonathan after a certain lengthy presentation or details about a specific area, and Jonathan winked. He was beaming with his pride. The young man spoke with knowledge about the facility, pointing out various forges, stamping machines, and welders and explaining their usage on the line.

Out the back door of that facility and across a rail spur was the manufacturing area. It turned out five heavy machines weekly; they would go somewhere in the world to work in the lumber industry. The remaining facility was another surprise. Hidden behind a large grove of pine trees all planted in perfectly straight rows were the proving grounds. Here many different pieces of equipment in various stages of completion went through testing. What these pieces of equipment were, as yet, remained a secret.

Jack commented on the entire complex being immaculately clean and orderly. Jonathan surprised him with his assessment. There was a time when they could not make that statement. During the war years, when his father was back in the service, Miss Annie was not only in charge, but she ruled with an iron hand. The cleanliness and order had come from her and not from the fact that William was a military man. Surely, because of the military experience, it was easier to conform with and continue after his return.

Jonathan said, "Let me tell you a bit about this facility being here at this location and another reason that our family has gotten a lot of negative criticism." The need to expand had been imminent, and there had been no space for further growth in town. They had approached the city and county for help in locating an area in close proximity to their lumber mills. They had given the city and county an opportunity to help with the location. In return, they asked for tax abatements. Both entities balked in spite of the fact that the MacMorogh Group currently employed over two hundred people.

The General also balked. The location where they were sitting at that moment was only four miles from New Cotswold but in the adjoining county. It was still convenient for the workers. The adjoining county welcomed them with open arms and offered them large incentives, and the company took them. New Cotswold officials were devastated. They had not killed the golden goose but had caused it to roost elsewhere.

In addition, the labor requirement for the new facility jumped by fifty per cent. Many of the white laborers who could have filled the jobs cut off their noses to spite their faces. They refused to work for the MacMorogh Group because of its decision to move across the county line. In so doing, they caused the ratio of colored to white to rise to about sixty to forty. The prosperity of the colored community grew, which caused further anguish among some of the bigots. Forty percent of the total payroll of the area came from the company, and the colored benefited the most.

Jonathan then wanted to chat about his mother a bit. Jack would learn more about her and enough to recognize that she was the binding force that held the family together, and thus the company. Jack had to chuckle to himself. Was Jonathan talking about the same woman who was afraid to piss off her hairdresser?

It was almost five. Jack was exhausted, and he was happy that Jonathan did not suggest cocktails or dinner. He was ready to go get a drink and mull over the day. The first thing Jack did when he got to the lodge was to call Adrianna. Gosh, he missed her. They talked for an hour, both pausing long enough to get a fresh drink. Jack had been contemplating something, and he planted the seed. How would Adrianna feel about spending a few days with him in New Cotswold? Adrianna agreed, and they would talk more when he got home on Friday.

After Jack hung up, he bolstered his drink again and walked down to the creek. The sun was beginning to sink. The water in the pool was like a mirror, nothing stirred, and there was no sound except that from a far off train. As he sat looking into the pool, a lone leaf dropped from above and did a slow pirouette to the surface. As it touched down, it sent a ring of small signals out over the pool. Jack watched as the last one made it to the bank.

19

Jonathan: As told by Winston and Tilda Jackson

On Wednesday morning, Jack worked on the notes from the day before. He was well pleased with the cooperation he was getting. At the appointed time, he met Winston at his office. Winston gave instructions, and Jack followed in his own car to the house. They turned in the drive and crossed a new concrete bridge leading to iron gates. Winston punched a code on a key pad, and the gates quietly opened. He motioned Jack to follow. The driveway circled to the right, and a beautiful white house came into view. It was of an old farmhouse design, with screened porches all around, chimneys at each end, and a row of hydrangeas across the front. At each corner post, blooming wisteria crawled to roof level. To the right of the house, set back about twenty yards, was a barn of the same exterior material as the house, board and batten. It gleamed white also. The barn doors were oversized and closed.

Winston drove his truck almost to the barn and signaled Jack to park alongside. As soon as Winston got out, an Irish setter came bolting from behind the barn to greet them. "We are going to have to walk back around to the front of the house. Miss Tilda would be hoppin' mad if I brought you through the back door."

Sure enough, as the two rounded the front corner of the house, the front screen door came open, and Miss Tilda called out, "You better not be comin' in that back door, Winston Jackson!" Miss Tilda had darker skin than Winston and for her age, was a pretty woman. She had on a freshly starched pair of bib overalls with a colorful apron tied 'round. "I already have my fishing clothes on," she exclaimed.

Winston introduced Jack. She knew why he was in town, but had to tease him a little. "You that white boy been bribing poor old women into a bunch of gossip with liquor?" She winked at Winston. Jack smiled back and pretended to retreat. Miss Tilda grabbed his hand and pulled him toward the front door.

"Come on in, you two, and let's have a glass of tea. My dinner is not quite ready, and I need to find out more about you before I am sure I want to feed you." She directed the remark to Jack. She reached out and hugged him. "Welcome. Winston says you are a nice boy. Now sit, and I will get us some tea."

Jack had had only coffee and a roll for breakfast, and the smell emanating from the kitchen was almost more than he could bare. They sat in white rockers with ruffled lavender cushions. The design on the cushions matched the wisteria vine growing at the corners of the house. Miss Tilda returned with tea; she had sugar and lemon slices on the side.

Winston sat back in the chair. "Go ahead, Miss Tilda, tell Jack about your house." So she got started. The exterior was identical to that of the house she had grown up in as a youngster. She had reconfigured the house to suit the needs of her and Mr. Jackson. She would take him on a tour after lunch. That was a blessing to Jack; the smells were getting to him.

Miss Tilda served lunch in the dining room, along with a young colored girl named Agnes. Agnes was a church member's daughter, three months pregnant. Her mother had passed several years earlier. Her father had kicked her out of the house, so Miss Tilda was seeing after her. The lunch was a sumptuous chicken salad, light but ample, with hot rolls and peach ice cream for dessert.

The small lake was in view from the back porch. A gravel path led to it. Winston excused himself to change clothes and returned with a big straw hat for Jack. Miss Tilda already had her big floppy hat. "Used to be my church hat," she explained. She also had slipped on one of Winston's long sleeve shirts. Winston had all the tackle necessary. Jack could choose between several rods with reels and a number of different artificial baits. Miss Tilda took a cane pole, with a red and white bobber and a can of worms. She looked at the fancy equipment Winston offered up and scoffed. "Humph."

Within an hour, Winston said they had caught enough. They had three big bass for supper and a nice mess of little perch that they would deep freeze until there was enough to have a big fish fry for the church. Miss Tilda objected, "We gonna' need two more big ones," she said and rolled her eyes at Winston. He caught the eye action and said, laughing, "You don't have to tell me, Jonathan and June are coming for supper. Well that's good, let's snag another one or two." He coached Jack about the choice spots to cast. Jack caught another beauty, not a prize, but four pounds at least.

Back at the house, Miss Tilda directed them out to the cook-house. It was a twenty-five foot square tabernacle, screened, with a full kitchen in the center. Tables with upended chairs were stacked against one wall. They could easily feed a crowd. There was an arrangement of wicker chairs with good cushions and a small table by each chair. The young girl came out with a pitcher of lemonade and a tray of sugar cookies. Miss Tilda complimented the girl, "My, you do make good cookies, child, I am going to keep you." The girl smiled timidly and thanked her.

Once the girl was out of earshot, Miss Tilda said, "Now let's talk about the history of the MacMorogh family and the company. Since Mr. Jackson and I had a large part in raising both Jonathan and Willie, I think we are very good sources of information."

Winston smiled before he spoke, "But I can tell you, Miss Tilda did most of the raising; I did a lot of the discipline. She does not hold much back."

Jack said he wanted to know more about Jonathan, since he had been reluctant to talk about himself. Winston had already told him a lot, but he knew there was more. Winston was the first to talk, and occasionally Miss Tilda would interject something, but for the most part, she waited her turn.

After Jonathan had come back with the twin degrees, he moved right into the second apartment in the livery. Winston and Miss Tilda lived in the first. Jonathan did not impose on either of them. He got his own breakfast, worked alongside Winston until lunch, and would go fix himself a sandwich or more likely eat sardines and crackers or some cheese and fruit for lunch. At night, he usually walked to the café around the corner.

The jail was just across the street from the back door of their apartment. Miss Tilda had a contract with the county to prepare meals for the prisoners. Times were harder then, and she was happy to do it. The small income helped. She fixed three meals a day, and it was not just bread and water jail food. Her philosophy was, criminals are God's children too, and they got to eat.

She kept insisting that Jonathan eat with her and Mr. Jackson. It was foolish, him doing what he was doing, and besides, she did not think he ate well. After some coaxing, he began to take most of his meals with them, but he insisted on contributing more than an ample amount of money to help with the food. In addition, he furnished a little sip of whiskey occasionally.

Jonathan was a loner but not necessarily by choice. Not having spent much of his childhood or school years in New Cotswold, he had few friends his age, and what few there were had a limited amount of education. Jonathan was not one for idle conversation or gossip. He found a few friends in the volunteer fire department, but that was usually limited to an illegal beer or drink of whiskey after fighting a grass fire.

Then one of the nicest things in the world happened. A young doctor came to town, Doctor Rubin Cohen, a Jew boy about the same size and stature as Jonathan. He was a complete stranger. He had no one but patients and nurses to befriend at the little county-owned hospital. Late one night, the doctor had car trouble on the way out in the country to deliver a baby. Who should come along but Jonathan. He stopped, put the doctor in his own old truck, and went along with him to deliver the baby. It was not an easy birth, and it took several hours. Jonathan ended up helping. The two bonded that evening and continued to be best friends.

The doctor was sociable, and he did like young nurses. It was not long before he had a girlfriend. He talked Jonathan into double dating with him a time or two, but poor old Jonathan begged off. He was just too shy around the girls. Now, the funny part. Miss June, who Jack would meet that evening, started out being the doctor's girlfriend. She came to town to nurse in the little clinic.

Doctor Rubin was more or less taking over the practice of an older doctor, and he did the hiring. He hired Miss June because she was a big girl and pretty. As time went on, he moved her into an apartment across from the hospital. Then one thing led to another. The clinic caught fire and burned to the ground, leaving the town without a hospital. The MacMorogh family owned the hotel across from the livery. A man and wife team was running it poorly, and Jonathan had been tempted to run them off several times. The morning after the fire at the clinic, Jonathan went to the hotel and asked the manager to show him how many reservations they currently had.

There were not so many that Jonathan could not make other arrangements for them at Mrs. Farmer's boarding house. She was more than happy to accommodate them, since it was summer, school was out, and she had few guests. Winter was her busy part of the year. Jonathan fired the manager and his wife and opened the doors of the hotel to Dr. Rubin to use as a temporary hospital. Miss June moved in at the same time. It took the county three years to get around to raising enough money to build a new clinic, due in part to the fact that the MacMorogh family rented the county the hotel for one dollar a year.

Dr. Rubin was fickle and took interest in another girl, but still dated Miss June on and off. Being so close, Jonathan would sometimes go across the street to the hospital after supper. He would sit on the front porch and visit with Miss June. It was not like asking her for a date. To him, he was simply visiting a neighbor. Not for long though; he took a real liking to her. He did not want to offend his friend, so he just came right out and asked the doctor was he still interested in Miss June. Of course Dr. Rubin wanted to know why, and Jonathan told him he liked her too.

Miss Tilda slowed talking for a minute and rolled her eyes like she was getting ready to deliver a bombshell. "Dr. Rubin told Jonathan if he wanted her, she was his. All he wanted was a case of moonshine from that no account bootlegger friend of his; then she would be all his. Jonathan never tells that story in mixed company, for fear Miss June will hear that he got her for a fifty-dollar case of 'shine." They all laughed at the story, more at the way Miss Tilda told it than anything.

"After the new hospital was finished, the MacMorogh family refurbished the hotel building, updated the kitchen and some of the rooms, and opened it back up as a hotel. They did not have a manager and put out advertisements for the position. Surprisingly, Miss June asked if she might apply. She has been there ever since, and she and Jonathan have been an item ever since." Miss Tilda smiled as if finishing a fairy tale.

Winston joined in again. "The city lawman was the town marshal. The county had a sheriff. That was all they could afford. Any deputies either of them might need had to come from volunteers. Jonathan, big and strong as he was, was always willing to help. The marshal would knock on his door all hours of the night."

"He would go out to the car and ride on the running board of the marshal's old beat up Buick car. The red light would be flashing, the siren wailing, and there would be Jonathan standing on the running board, hanging on to the side of the car. Sometime his pajama shirt would still be on and flapping in the wind. When they got to a fight or wherever they were going, Jonathan would jump off the car and be in the midst of it before the marshal could get his butt out of the car. Jonathan was especially a lot of help in the Quarter. The colored knew Jonathan through us. They trusted him to be fair and not come in the Quarter cursing and swinging axe handles at whoever they saw."

Miss Tilda chimed in. "Usually what would happen would be the minute they saw it was Jonathan with the marshal, the fighters would back apart. Both would be trying to tell Jonathan their side of the story at the same time. Jonathan would run the bystanders off, and then he would hold court. Most of the time he made them shake hands and go their separate ways. I heard that story too many times," she said.

Miss Tilda then excused herself to see about some things in the kitchen and suggested that Winston take Jack out to see his barn. It was good to stretch. The barn was a surprise. Winston opened one of the carriage doors, and only then did Jack realize the depth of the building. It was a huge facility. Once all the lights came on, it was obvious that this was more a museum than a barn. On display were antique carriages, cars, trucks, tractors, and other farm equipment. Much of the equipment was steam driven. Winston told Jack about his uncle, "Steamboat." The man had come to the area with Winston's grandfather. Jack remembered hearing about that time from Miss Maudie Lee.

While they were touring the barn and looking at all the things in it, Winston asked Jack how much time he planned to spend in New Cotswold. Jack explained about his leave of absence at the paper and the fact that he would like to get over the research well before that time was up. His plan had not been to spend a lot of time here once he had all the interviews he needed. Winston then turned to him and told him that there was a lot that he would like to provide in the way of family information. However, presently, it would be mostly anecdotes about the various members of the family. That was unless Jack asked him any specific questions simply for verification.

Winston also alerted Jack. "Miss Tilda has a very special place in her heart for both Jonathan and especially Willie. She has every right. As time goes by and you keep getting information, you will see that Miss Tilda sees Willie to be as much her baby as our own daughter or our grandson, John Pope.

"Miss Tilda has loved that boy through all the things he has been through. She and I have stood by him when nobody else would. I am hoping this history you are doing will, in some way, bring out the truth about him. He is more than just a war hero!"

Jack was puzzled. They strolled on slowly, talking and chatting about one thing or another. Miss Tilda called from the back door that it was time for them to freshen up before company got there. When she opened the back door, she was all cleaned up, with a print dress on and some bright ribbon in her hair. She ushered Jack down the hall, handed him a fresh towel and washcloth, and pointed to a bathroom he could use. She knew he might be hot from all that fishing and talking.

To Winston she said, "Go get yourself cleaned up, Mr. Jackson. Look how pretty and nice I look. You know Jonathan and Miss June will look like shiny new pennies."

And she was right. They arrived at about six. Jack was amazed how tidy and neat a big man could look if he worked at it. Miss June was as starched and fresh as Miss Tilda who, spry as a much younger woman, was out in the yard greeting them before they could make it up the path to the back door. They all hugged each other. It was not hard to tell these were close friends.

They made introductions. Jack was not surprised. His assessment of what June would look like was right on. She was tall, big boned, and very attractive in an outdoorsy way. Her smile lit up her whole face, and her eyes smiled with her. Jack thought to himself, "This lady is a perfect match for big Jonathan."

Winston had the ceiling fans cooling the back porch and had set up a bar with an iced down bucket of beer, wine, and three kinds of liquor. After they all fixed a drink, the young girl came out with a special treat, fried perch tails and a dipping sauce. Jack had not tasted this specialty before. The tails were as crispy as a potato chip, with a touch of seasoning like that used by Adrianna.

Winston fixed Jack and Jonathan another drink, then asked them to join him in the cookhouse to fry the fish. They were planning to eat off TV trays, right on the back porch. There was thunder off in the distance, and a nice breeze was blowing. It was a pleasant evening.

After a dinner of fried bass filets, hush puppies, fried green tomatoes, and a green salad, there was chocolate cake and ice cream. While the women took care of the kitchen, Winston offered cigars. He lit his pipe, and when Miss Tilda came back, she lit up a tiny little pipe herself.

The evening chat, which went well into the night, began with them asking Jack all about his family, his girlfriend Adrianna, and his years at the paper. They were sincere in their interest in his life, his schooling, and his father. With each answer, Miss Tilda would nod her approval. In time, the discussion got back around to the project. He confirmed his appreciation for information gathered thus far. He confessed that it was more than he had expected, and said that he could see that it was the tip of the iceberg. They all seemed to agree and urged him to ask questions.

Even though Jack had gotten a lot of information from Will, it was interesting to hear the accounts from a different point of view—for instance, Miss Tilda and her account of Willie's early trips to the livery building. She wanted to tell about Willie, her baby, and the point where she realized that she, Jonathan, and Mr. Jackson were destined to raise him. She picked up her version during the time prior to the air crash that took the lives of his parents.

Willie was three, maybe four years old. The house that William, Jr. and Noreen lived in was across the street from the back corner of the livery building. Miss Tilda was in her kitchen finishing the biscuits and frying up a mess of sausage. Jonathan and Winston were out in the shop, getting things ready to start the day. She heard Jonathan say real loud, "Look who's here!" There stood little Willie, still in his pajamas, and barefoot. Jonathan picked him up and brought him inside. Poor child still had sleep in his eyes; saliva had dried on his cheek. His hair was a mess. Miss Tilda went about cleaning him up a bit, took him to pee pee, and asked him did his mama know he was gone. He told her his mama was still asleep. After Miss Tilda gave him some juice, Jonathan said he better get him home. His mama would be in a panic if she discovered him missing.

He took Willie by the hand and walked back across the street, down the alley, and through his backyard to the house. The back door stood open. Jonathan called out for Noreen. She didn't answer. He called again, louder. Still no answer. He put Willie down, and he ran down the hall to the bedroom. Out stepped Noreen, still in her nightgown. Jonathan told her that Willie had come to the shop. He was afraid she would be concerned if she could not find him. She said she must have overslept, and she'd had no idea he was gone. Then she fussed at the child as if he was supposed to know better. Jonathan was mad, but he said nothing. He felt sorry for her in a way; his brother was in Washington most of the time. With that and having to keep her house as well as the senator's office going, she had a lot of responsibility and little help.

Two days later, it happened again. This time, Willie said he was hungry. Miss Tilda took him into the bathroom, helped him get his little pajamas off, and gave him a bath. John Pope, her grandson, had a few clothes there, and the little boys were about the same size, so she dressed him in clean clothes. Then she sat him down at the table where she served breakfast to the men and fixed him some coffee.

His coffee was warm milk, two spoons of honey, and two spoons of coffee. The coffee gave the drink just enough color to look like the real thing. While he was sipping on that, she scrambled an egg with two pieces of sausage. Next, she poked a hole in a big biscuit, poured syrup in that, and put it all before him. He ate every bite, eating slowly, sipping his coffee as he went. Miss Tilda was delighted. When he was through, she asked him did he need to go potty. She called to him in the bathroom, "Don't flush now, Aunt Tilda wants to see your stool." Satisfied that it was OK, she took him by the hand and walked him home. *Jack had to chuckle. That had made quite an impression on Willie!*

The next time it happened, Miss Tilda had had enough. After she got Willie cleaned up and fed, she walked him home, but this time, she went into the kitchen, fixed a pot of coffee, and sat at the kitchen table telling Willie little stories until Noreen woke up. When she walked into the kitchen and found Tilda sitting there, of course she had questions. Miss Tilda said to her, "You and I need to talk."

After a while, she and Jonathan gave up. Almost every morning, Willie showed up. They went through their routine, but finally Jonathan said, "No more. Let her come looking for him." He parked Willie on a box, gave him some nuts and bolts, pen, and paper, and told him to go to work. Every once in a while, Jonathan would stop and get him busy at something else. About nine o'clock, his mother showed up and in her sweet way, said, "Oh my, that child, what am I going to do with him." Then she went about that sweet scolding that made Miss Tilda want to spit tacks.

Miss Tilda said she could go on and on, but just one more little note. Her daughter was teaching in Hattiesburg and it was hard for her to get home except on holidays and during summer vacation. Well, one weekend, she surprised them and brought John Pope for a visit. Of course, she and Mr. Jackson were thrilled to have them there.

On Saturday morning, she let her daughter sleep late. She got John Pope all cleaned up and dressed, and who should show up but little Willie. Miss Tilda went about telling how she had introduced them and what name they should call each other. The first thing Willie said was, "You are in my place." The boys went through this "I ain't, you are, I ain't, you are" business before Miss Tilda broke in.

She laughed, "We were not off to a real good start." She then related the same tale Will had told Jack about the eenie, meenie, miney, moe game. With tears in her eyes, "They been the best of friends from that day to now. I am just so sorry that this race business can't be settled as easy!"

Jack asked about the time of the crash. He already knew from Will that soon after that, he had moved into the apartment with Jonathan and into the care of Jonathan and Aunt Tilda.

"Before we get to that," Miss Tilda said, "Jonathan, why don't you tell Jack about the Percival business. Keep in mind, now, this is before the crash. Willie was not in school yet. He spent more time at the shop than he did with his mama, and she did not seem to care. Most afternoons after lunch, I would clean him up some, then put him in my lap and read stories until he fell asleep. That is how I taught him to read too."

Jonathan proceeded to relate the incident.

The Lamar girls all lived on the same street, down from the post office. Jack knew this from Will, but he did not interrupt. The sisters did their best to help with Willie the many times that William, Jr. and Noreen were in Washington.

Most often, Willie would want to stay with Aunt Tilda and Jonathan, but often they insisted he stay at one or the other sister's houses. Usually it was his Aunt Jessie's, because he and his cousin Patricia were real close. Carole Anne spent more time in New Orleans with Beatrice, but this time she was in town for a few weeks. She preferred staying with Miss Annie.

The sisters all agreed that it would be nice if the two children would spend some time out in the country on a farm with their sister Nadine and her husband. The two of them had not been able to have children, and Nadine was just dying for the children to come there for a few days. On Sunday after church, Jessie and her husband packed a few things for each of the children and took them to spend a week. They both had been there several times and were familiar with the place. The promises of feeding chickens and riding a horse sounded OK.

On Thursday morning of that week, about six-thirty, Jonathan got a call from one of the men who worked at the sawmill; he just wanted to check. He thought he had seen Jonathan's boy walking alongside the road about four miles out in the country. By the time he could turn his car around and go back, the boy had darted into the bushes. Jonathan got the exact location from the millworker and hung up. That damn Percival had no phone.

Jonathan told Miss Tilda what was going on. He got in his old work truck and drove to the area where the millworker said he had seen the boy. The worker was still out in the same area, riding back and forth. Jonathan opened his truck door and drove very slowly, constantly calling for Willie. Then Jonathan spotted him. He was limping along, just barely in the road.

When Willie first saw the truck, he jumped off the road and into the ditch. Jonathan got even with the spot and started calling again. Out of the ditch came Willie, dirty, with tears and snot running down his face. He was hot. His face was as red as a beet, and he had fever. Jonathan picked him up and put him in the seat beside him. He looked at the boy's foot and thought it was muddy, then realized that that was blood caked with dust and dirt. Willie was whimpering; he was so tired he could not sit up. Jonathan laid him down on the seat beside him and put his head on his lap. Willie was asleep before they got to town.

It was too early for Dr. Rubin to be in his office, so Jonathan took Willie right to Miss Tilda. He carried the child in his arms, and when she saw him, she just cried.

Miss Tilda broke in. "Let me tell this, please," she said and completed the story.

He was filthy dirty, and she could tell he was feverish. They were both trying to get him to talk, but as soon as he had seen his Aunt Tilda, he started boohooing. At one time, he was crying so hard she had to pat him on his back to make him catch his breath.

She ran tepid water in the bathtub in order to soak him and lower the fever. As she took off his clothes, she saw what she thought were bad scratches on the backs of his legs. When she started to pull down his little underwear, there was blood on them. As she got them off, she saw that more of the stripes were there. She found the same welts were on his back and buttocks.

Jonathan was on the phone, talking to Dr. Rubin at home. The doctor would stop by on the way to the hospital. Miss Tilda called

Jonathan to look. She was trying to get Willie to tell her what had happened, but he was back to crying so hard that all they could get out of him was that he had gotten a switching and had to go to bed without supper. Miss Tilda wanted to know why he got a switching.

Jonathan broke in now and said, "I told her it did not make any difference what the cause, it would be the last time that son of a bitch whipped a kid." He got back in his truck and retraced his route. When he got to the road that turned to Percival's house, his anger had built into an unhealthy rage. He drove into the yard of the farmhouse, and out came Carole Anne, screaming that Willie was gone. Jonathan told her not to mind and that he was at home and for her to get her things and get in his truck.

Nadine came out, wringing her hands. Poor girl was upset, too. Jonathan asked where Percival was, and she said at the barn. Jonathan started there in a run. When he was halfway there, Percival came out and started walking toward Jonathan. Jonathan did not say a word. When he was in reach, he hit the man with his right fist, just below the jawline. Percival dropped like a rock. His poor wife was right behind. She told Jonathan she thought he had killed Percival. Jonathan told her he sure hoped so.

On the trip back in the truck, Carole Anne started crying. She had tried to comfort Willie. She had slipped into the kitchen and gotten a roll, but Percival had caught her and slapped the roll out of her hand. He ordered her back to bed with a threat of the same he had given to Willie. She held Willie close until he quit crying, and then they both fell asleep. When she awoke, Willie was gone. Nadine was upset, but Percival said the boy was probably hiding to scare them.

What happened to cause Willie to get such a lashing was asinine. Willie and Carole Anne were sitting on the steps to the back of the house. Chickens were running loose. While they were sitting on the steps, a rooster came right up to them. Willie was eating a piece of stale biscuit. When the rooster saw it, it pecked the biscuit out of Willie's hand, but pecked Willie's finger at the same time.

It hurt, and Willie lost his temper. He picked up a stick and chased the rooster all over the yard, swinging the stick every chance he got. The rooster ran through the henhouse and upset two old setting hens. Percival heard the entire racket and came to the back door.

When he saw the rooster with one wing down and broken, he lit into Willie with a heavy switch from a peach tree.

Back home, Dr. Rubin had come by and had managed to get two stitches to hold the toe together while Willie kicked and screamed like a banshee. He had calmed down when Jonathan and Carole Anne got back. Carole Anne went straight to him and hugged him close. He cuddled close to her.

"He was better already," chimed Miss Tilda. "He was on his third flapjack, and I was cooking him another one. Already he had eaten two pieces of bacon and sipped two cups of his coffee. He had his foot propped in the chair next to him, and Winston had cut a broom handle in half for a walking stick. He was going to be OK."

Jack asked about Percival and his condition. Jonathan replied, "Rubin called me mid-morning and told me he had just wired Percival's jaw together and pulled four teeth so he could suck food through a straw. Percival refused to pay. He told Rubin to send the bill to me. Rubin agreed, but at the same time told Percival that he would also like the sheriff to just go by and look at Willie. Percival agreed to pay the bill over time.

"Now to the crash," said Jonathan. "I think we all can add a little here, and I will start." Jonathan had had little to do with the political ambitions of either his brother or his father. He voted, and that was about it. His concern at the time had been the fact that Willie and Carole Anne seemed to be of little concern in the matter. What was going to happen to those two if they all moved to Washington? He said that he guessed he showed a lack of interest in the activity during those few days prior to the meeting and the subsequent air crash.

Winston, on the other hand, helped with getting guests back and forth from the hotel, greeting the airplane, making sure it was taken care of, things like that. He was on the scene at the airfield the evening the plane took off. As far as he was concerned, everything was OK. William, Jr., of course, was elated with the activities of the last two days. He in fact was going back to D.C. to become, in a matter of days, the US Senator from Mississippi. Noreen could not have been more thrilled.

The children were to stay with family. Willie was going to be staying with his Aunt Jessie, which meant he would still be coming to the shop every day. Jonathan and Miss Tilda could make sure he was alright. Carole Anne was already in New Orleans with Dr. Beatrice.

The plane was late getting in from the Gulf Coast. There was a lot of activity, many people, and some confusion at the airfield with everybody trying to get in the act of loading the baggage, and so forth. It was nearly dark when the plane lifted off. Only one person commented on the departure. William commented that the plane took too long to get off the runway. He felt it was overloaded but would probably be all right after they burned off some fuel.

At three the next morning, the terrible call came. Winston was the first alerted, and then Jonathan. They both gathered in the kitchen with Miss Tilda. Winston prayed, and Jonathan for the first time in a long, long while cried. All Miss Tilda could think of was her baby. What was to become of him?

After they had alerted Winston and Jonathan, William and Miss Annie went to Jessie's house to tell the Lamar family. They then came by the shop. William, Sr. wanted the family to assemble at the house as soon as possible. Dr. Beatrice was aware and was on her way. She would break the sad news to Carole Anne. They would leave at the break of day in Beatrice's airplane. They all discussed it and agreed not to talk to Willie until Carole Anne was present.

William was pulling out no stops. He started by calling the governor, to tell him of his need for assistance. He made phone calls to Washington to get an investigative team to the crash site as soon as possible. First reports were that the plane had hit a mountain west of Birmingham. William was arranging to go to the site of the crash. Before he could depart, a call from a CAA executive in Washington advised against his going. Officials who had found the wreckage had described the scene.

Miss Tilda could stand it no longer. She had to go to her baby. Miss Jessie would just have to put up with her. It was getting light, and people were already assembling at her house. Miss Tilda put on a better dress, combed out her hair, slipped on a new yellow apron, and headed out to Miss Jessie's.

Willie had been sleeping in the room with his cousin Patricia. Aunt Jessie awoke them earlier than usual. She told Willie that she wanted him to stay close to the house, and she also wanted him to put on nicer clothes. She had tears in her eyes and hugged him tighter than usual. Something was up. He was very confused by all the people, some of them crying softly. Once or twice, he caught people looking at him and shaking their heads. He ate a boiled egg and cereal and slipped out the back door.

The Lamar house stood on a lot that gently sloped to the back. The house was high enough off the ground to walk under, especially if you were a child. Willie crawled under the house and up to the area below the front room of the house. He could hear talking as plain as day. However, he could hear feet shifting around, so it was hard to hear everything said. The first thing that he clearly heard was a female voice, most likely that of his Aunt Violet. "It is so hard to believe they are not coming back. What about those poor children? What in the world will happen to them?" The next thing he heard was just barely discernible, but it was truly his Aunt Violet again. She had a screechy voice. "Oh, wouldn't it be good if they could go to Nadine and Percival; they can never have children of their own."

Willie did not stay to hear the rest. If he had, he would have heard His Aunt Jessie tell Aunt Violet that if she wanted to get her head bitten off, go mention that to any of the MacMorogh family. She told her further that she knew something that she had never told the rest of the family about Percival. She went no further.

Willie was halfway across the courthouse square on his way to the blacksmith shop when he met Aunt Tilda. She picked him up and he started to cry, then told her what he had heard. She was mortified and told Willie that he was never going to have to worry. She said that she would get right on a bus with him and they would go to Chicago and hide before Percival ever had a chance to see him at his house.

Willie then wanted to know if his parents were coming back. He had heard his Aunt Violet say they were never coming back. Aunt Tilda was about to cry herself. She held him close and told him she was not sure about anything he had heard. "Maybe we should wait and ask Uncle Jonathan." It was not her place to tell him, and she did not want to accept that responsibility.

Jonathan told about taking the children to New Orleans immediately after the crash. He and Beatrice knew there would probably be trouble with the Lamar girls over who would have guardianship. There was no need to have the children involved in that. He and Beatrice knew that they were the ones named. They had a lot to consider.

The first thought was to keep both in New Orleans with Beatrice. She had a wonderful housekeeper. Carole Anne, having spent so much time there, had friends. The school she would attend was near. Willie was the problem. Jonathan and Beatrice tried to keep a calm, pleasant atmosphere at all times. The children needed a feeling of security. Willie was shown the school where he might attend and was introduced to a few children in the neighborhood. He did not seem too impressed with either the school or the other kids.

Jonathan and Beatrice generally agreed on one thing. If possible, let the children decide where they wanted to live. Finally, as the school year approached and it was time to make a decision, Willie made his. He wanted to go to first grade with his friends. He would go back to New Cotswold to live with Jonathan. *Once again, Jack had heard this, but from a different perspective*

The MacMoroghs were always special guests on the trains, and for good reason. They traveled the route from New Cotswold to New Orleans so frequently that they knew almost all of the porters and conductors, and those workers knew them as well. It was well-known that the family owned a large amount of the railroad stock. Some of the older ones also knew there was a connection between the MacMoroghs and Mr. Jackson, who had schooled most of the porters and conductors in his role as chief conductor. Mr. Jackson had married Maudie Lee their first year at Tougaloo College, and it was Seamus MacMorogh who helped him get on with the railroad after college.

Jonathan and Willie took seats in a coach car and waited until the train crossed the lake near Slidell before going to the club car. There Jonathan ordered a drink, a Coca-Cola for Willie, and hamburgers with fries for both. Willie loved to ride back in the club car because of the windows that surrounded the car at the end of the train. It was possible to get better than a hundred and eighty degree view from the car. Willie liked it especially when the train was on long curves and he could see the engine puffing away.

After his supper, Willie snuggled up close under Jonathan's big arm. "We sure did have a good time at Aunt Bea's, didn't we?" Jonathan agreed, then said, "But I am kind of glad to be going home, aren't you?" Willie was asleep and did not answer. He did not have to.

Miss Tilda jumped in to tell the rest. The train pulled into the station at two o'clock in the morning, right on time. Jonathan had awakened Willie about twenty minutes earlier and had their bags together so they were ready to step off the train the minute it stopped. He picked Willie up to help him off, and the minute Aunt Tilda saw him, she let out a big "Whoop!" She and Winston had set the alarm and would not have missed this homecoming for the world. Aunt Tilda said she came into the apartment with Jonathan, helping to get the bags in. She got Willie ready for bed, and before she left the room, she kneeled down by his bed and held his hand while she helped him say his prayers.

It was raining the next morning, Saturday, and the crowds were in town despite the weather. The street and drive into the shop were wet, muddy, and splattered with manure from the animals standing in line waiting for shoeing. Jonathan had spent much of his time in New Orleans, working several hours each day at a drawing board he kept set up at Dr. Bea's house. He had almost completed a design he had been working on for several months. This Saturday, however, it was back to reality: pounding iron.

Since neither Willie nor John Pope was there, Letitia had not been coming on Saturday with Moon. After a bigger than usual breakfast, Aunt Tilda got Willie set up with a rocking chair next to hers. They shelled butter beans, shucked corn, and peeled peaches for the meal she would prepare for themselves and the prisoners in the jail.

Willie never shut up the whole time. He started with the first day he was in New Orleans and ended with the day they went shopping for school clothes. Aunt Tilda didn't care how much he talked. She was just glad to have her baby back home.

20

Jack could not recall having a more pleasant evening. They had laughed until they cried at some of Miss Tilda's stories and her antics. He had learned more today about the family than he could have ever hoped to gather in such a short time. Before they all wished each other well and said their good nights, Jack made tentative plans to visit New Cotswold again soon.

It was much too late to make his nightly call to Adrianna, but not too late for Jack to work an hour, getting his notes from the evening in order. It was almost one o'clock when the phone rang. He was just getting out of the shower and ready for bed.

It was Adrianna, and she was disturbed. She was not at the apartment and was afraid Jack had been trying to call her. She was at the hospital with Miss Penny. Penny had suffered a fall and was at Touro Infirmary. Miss Penny had requested that Adrianna be notified, and she had been there ever since. It was too late for a lot of discussion, but Jack did give Adrianna his plan for the next day. He would stop in Jackson to visit Mrs. Abernathy and then be on his way to New Orleans.

Jack left early the next morning after cleaning the bathroom and stripping the bed. On the way out of the lodge, he stood before the closed doors to the men's parlor. His curiosity was getting to him. He got a new tablet from his briefcase; this one he labeled "Mrs. Abernathy."

Jack called ahead: Mrs. Abernathy was expecting him at ten. Her attendant said she had been dressed for over an hour, primping and looking in her mirror every few minutes. Any fear that she might not be lucid went away the moment he stepped into her quarters. She greeted him politely, introduced him to her attendant, and then excused the woman. Before she asked Jack to sit, she informed him that she had been looking forward to his visit ever since her daughter-in-law called. She had even arranged for him to sit at her table for lunch. Though sitting at lunch with a group of old women was not a thrilling thought.

The two hours before lunch flew by. She inquired about her daughter-in-law and how well she might be doing at Mrs. Abernathy's old job. Then she started on an endless recounting of her life and times with Seamus and company. Jack asked if he might record their time together as well as take notes. There was no way he could have recounted his time utilizing notes only.

She admitted that early on in her job with Seamus, she'd had a relationship with him that she hoped and prayed would turn into something more than just a job. He confided in her more than he confided in anyone else. She signed his name more than he did. Being in the middle of things, she sometimes knew both sides of a situation when he only knew his own. She made some decisions for him that he would not have made on his own.

Yes, she knew Aunt Sophie, Maudie Lee's mother, and Maudie Lee as well. She also realized that when Mollie appeared on the scene, her own hopes of a future with Seamus were probably just that, hopes. Lunch with her and her friends was actually amusing. The small catfights between the old girls were funny. One thing Jack did notice was that Mrs. Abernathy was still using her executive skills. She was the boss at the table.

She hugged Jack tightly when he ushered her back to her quarters and then politely excused him. She knew he was probably more tired listening than she was talking. She extended an invitation for him to visit again. Maybe next time she would let him talk.

Jack could not wait to get into his car and take a long sigh that had been building for more than an hour. He said aloud to himself, "I'll be darned." He wondered why Maudie Lee had never mentioned Mrs. Abernathy. Now he knew. His suspicion, which had begun after meeting Winston and Miss Tilda, was confirmed.

Jack looked at his watch when he left the retirement home. He still had time to stop in for a few minutes to see his father. It had been several weeks. When he arrived, his father could not wait to hear how his project was going and started right off firing questions.

Jack asked his dad if he remembered anything about an air crash, around the year 1936, which had taken the lives of Senator Scoggins and some of his staff. His father put his hands behind his head and stared at the ceiling, trying to recall. Something was vaguely familiar. He had a thought; there was someone at the paper who might remember.

He called a fellow to his office; he appeared to be several years older than Jack's father was. He was a little man in a bow tie, wearing glasses with no rim and a white shirt with an ink stain in the pocket. He wrote the obits as a retirement job. Seeing him, Jack thought, "Mr. Milquetoast." That was until he opened his mouth.

Dolph White was his name. He had a smoker's voice and used the language of a sailor. "Hell. yes," he said. "Lots about that in political circles. Old man MacMorogh was a tough son of a bitch who went to any length to get his way. He was a political kingpin, had money running out his ass, and did not mind spending it. There was bullshit about the plane and whether there was foul play. Nothing ever came of it. But several people high up in political circles with grandiose ambitions went down the chute like a one egg puddin'."

Dolph thought a minute and then said more. "Take Hawkins, the lieutenant governor. He had his wife's family's money behind him and could have been the next governor. His old lady's family ended up on hard times, and Hawkins himself bit the dust. He still runs a white trash juke joint up near Inverness. Bastard must be nearing seventy. You ought to go see him sometime. You working on a story or something?"

Jack replied, "No, I just like studying political history." But he filed the comments.

He then used the phone in his father's office to call Adrianna again, to let her know he might be later than expected. It was OK; she had gotten an around-the-clock nurse for Miss Penny but was running late herself. Whichever one got home first—fix the martinis.

Jack's dad assured him that he would do more research on the plane crash. Jack was hesitant to tell him all he personally knew. Then on second thought, perhaps he should. He asked his dad to walk him to his car. His dad looked puzzled.

Outside the building, Jack said, "This is far enough. I did not want to mention anything else about the crash with other people in earshot. What I am going to tell you has to be confidential. It could jeopardize my position with the MacMorogh family."

"You know that I have a part-time assistant working with me. Her name is Jan Plow. She is an outstanding employee at the paper. In the very beginning, she started researching our archives for the name MacMorogh. Most of what she found was regarding Dr. Beatrice MacMorogh. She is Will's aunt and a prominent New Orleans pediatrician. There was a piece in our archives from 1936 about the fact that her brother, his wife, and Senator Scoggins died in an air crash near Birmingham. Without my asking, Jan called the paper in Birmingham, made friends over the phone with a young reporter there. She asked for his assistance in searching their archives for more information. Apparently, she made a good impression. The reporter called back the same day. What he found was that at one time, there had been suspicion of foul play. Later, the CAA said the crash was possibly due to an accidental explosion caused by a gas-fired heater on the aircraft. Nothing else was reported by the Birmingham paper at that time.."

"About a week later, the reporter calls again. This time, he tells her he has found something else interesting that took place a year after the crash. Two young rabbit hunters found the skeletal remains of a man. According to the County sheriff, the remains were less than a hundred feet from where the tail section of the airplane had fallen. There was not a positive ID. End of story. Next thing Jan knows, the young reporter calls again; he has more. According to a coroner's report, most of the bones in the skeleton were broken. The coroner concluded that the extent was such that it could not have occurred any other way than impact trauma of great force. The last time the reporter called, it was to report that after the required length of time, the remains were buried in a pauper's grave." Jack sighed.

His father mused, "And no one you've talked to so far seems to know anything about this? Are you thinking what I am, that this person might have been on the plane?"

"Correct. This could be an interesting story in itself. I would like to keep it quiet. However, there is one thing where I need your help. Will you see if possibly there might be a person that went missing at about that time from around the general vicinity? One never found."

His father grinned. "This may be the first evening I have not gotten home on time in several years. You have piqued my curiosity."

Outside Jackson, Jack called Will from a pay phone at a truck stop. He wanted to report on his days in New Cotswold and make his appointment to meet the following Monday. He would then be free to give Adrianna his full attention for the whole weekend. Will had talked to Jonathan earlier in the day and heard about the evening before. He was envious that he had not been part of it. After reviewing his notes, Jack asked Will to think back on a few things he had heard, just for accuracy's sake. Then they wished each other a great weekend and rang off. Jack could be home before Adrianna, if he stepped it up a bit. He would get flowers and stir up a pitcher of martinis before she arrived.

The weekend started with a bang. Adrianna did not beat him home. He took care of first things first, the martinis. Then he was showering, shampoo in his hair as well as his eyes. Suddenly, someone reached through the shower curtain and grabbed his penis. He let out a scream. Adrianna herself got into the shower, laughing but not turning him loose. They hardly dried off before they hit the bed. Finally, Adrianna was able to whisper, "I think that little fellow was glad to see me." All Jack could say was, "Very."

They sipped their drinks, both anxious to relate their tales of the past week. It was almost nine when they agreed that they were starving. It was not too late to go around the corner to Justin's for the Friday evening special, which would be Red Fish Courtbouillon.

Some of their regular Friday night gang was lingering, and they joined the booze-fueled party. It was in full swing. Justin the friendly fairy, as Jack called him, came over to the table with his string of insults for Jack. The house was full, and most of the people in the place were listening to the banter. Finally thinking he had gotten the last word in, Justin left the table to place their orders. He had made about three steps in his lighter than air slippers when Jack called to him, "Tinker Bell!"

When the other man looked around with his hands on his hips and a look of disgust, Jack said loudly enough for all to hear, "There is a fly drinking some of my drink." After which Justin turned and with a limp wrist replied, "Then make him spit it out, you selfish thing, you." The room clapped. Jack held his hands high in surrender. Another fun evening, and he could only think how great it was to be home. Even with as much fun as he had had in New Cotswold, he knew where his life was and with whom.

21

The Monday meeting with Will took a long time. They had catching up to do. Will had heard just enough from Jonathan to have many questions. In addition, he was amused at Jack's assessment of his grandmother. Jack wanted to hear Will's version of several points also. Had Will ever heard discussion of the air crash that had killed his parents? The only thing he'd heard was that of possible foul play. After all these years, there was never talk about it anymore.

Next, Will had a request. He would like to work on the project for the next two mornings. He was planning to be in London for a few days. This was great with Jack. He wanted to have time to visit more with Dr. Bea and Carole Anne. It was time to update Dr. Bea and get her response to the work done thus far. He still had not talked to Charles Chacherie. This would give him the opportunity. He did not tell Will about his other plans. He was going to revisit Maudie Lee Jackson in Mobile, then go on to Birmingham to see John Pope. Also, since none of the family seemed to know any more about the crash, he was going to call on the CAA office in Birmingham.

The information that Jan dug up was really eating at him. He was meeting with her after work that evening. She would be needling him about ignoring her discovery. In fact, he was afraid that if he did not pursue it, she would end up doing it herself.

The meeting with Will lasted almost to noon and allowed them to cover a lot of ground. Jack still would just shake his head at Will's ability to recall the many moments of his life. There was little pause. Occasionally, Jack would hold up his right index finger, signaling Will to slow down. Will would pause a moment, then move on. They finished their session early, and Will met with Mimi. Jack settled into his cubicle, well pleased with their progress.

He contacted Adrianna; she was due home on time. At seven, they met with Jan Plow at a small restaurant near her house. She was as excited as always to be a part of Jack's project. Adrianna could not be happier with the change that had come over her since she had started her after-hours work for Jack.

What she was finding in the document boxes was unbelievable. The restructuring of the giant conglomerate since the time of its inception was thrilling. The dry facts of the financial history were, to her, a wonderful story in themselves.

Jack expected Jan to ask, and she wasted no time. What he had done with the information she had given him? He pointed to the stack of pages he had handed her earlier. She understood that he had been busy. Then he told her of his plan to go to Birmingham, where he would interview the Rev. John Pope and follow up with the CAA.

On the next two mornings, Will and Jack worked steadily, with only short breaks. The time period covered was all the way through to Will's senior year in college. Talk about being blindsided. Jack wondered how much of *this* the rest of the family knew, and to what degree. Some of this must have been what Carole Anne was referring to as her concern. Jack was somewhat overwhelmed. He preferred to hear Will's version of the various periods in his life before hearing anyone else's version. He wondered if he should suggest that he keep copies of the manuscripts from the others until Will's return, when he'd have an opportunity to review them. Jack knew that he needed to keep Dr. Bea abreast, since she was in charge of approval and direction. But rather than ask, he made the decision that nothing else would go out until he'd spoken with her. Being so far ahead with

Will's story would have its advantages. He would have more pointed questions to ask as he continued his interviews.

On Thursday, Jack edited his notes and put things into correct chronological order. The following day, he made a call to Maudie Lee Jackson. She would be delighted to see him again on Tuesday of the following week, the same time in the afternoon. He was looking forward to his time with her and would probably see if Mr. Crow would like to come along. She said, "By all means."

He called next to speak with Winston Jackson regarding the visit with John Pope. Winston might give him a number where he could reach him. However, Winston had some concern. "You know that John is right in the middle of all of this mess in Birmingham. He is very close to the action; we pray for his safety every day. I do not know how advisable it is for you to visit at this time. Perhaps you should let us think about this a bit. Tell me when you will be in Birmingham, and I will call you back." They left it at that. Next, he called Jan Plow, got the name of the reporter she had talked with: Nelson Goodall. Then he called the CAA.

The weekend was a mess from the start. Adrianna had an appointment after work with Miss Penny's attorney, and then a downpour flooded the streets. She had to leave the car parked on high ground and walk home. She was exhausted; Jack, too. They did have a martini or two and relaxed a bit and caught up on all that was going on. They decided to forego their regular Friday night at Justin's.

They spent Saturday visiting retirement homes. Adrianna had had a long visit with Miss Penny's doctor, who'd been her physician and friend for years. He could be Miss Penny's doctor, but he could not care for her past that point. Someone had to take responsibility for her. There was no one else, so Adrianna had to do it, and she visited with her in the hospital. She ended up spending more time than she wished, but did not have the heart to leave her friend. Miss Penny was doing her best to communicate, but only a few words were discernible. It was an exhausting time.

On Sunday, they went to church again. Adrianna prayed for guidance in taking care of her old mentor. After church, they strolled home hand in hand. Adrianna asked Jack, "Do you love me?"

He immediately replied, "You know that I do. What brings that up?"

"You haven't told me in a long time. I do not want us to get so busy that we forget." She was silent for a long time. "I did not ask you if you loved me to see if you might do me a favor. But I do have one to ask."

"Shoot," he said.

"The next time we have a day or two we both can spare, will you go home with me to visit my parents? I think they wonder about us. You know that they do not approve of us living together. To them it is not socially acceptable. I want them to see you. I want them to see why I love you very much."

On Monday, they worked toward completing all their other tasks. That evening, the phone was ringing as he walked into the apartment. Fearing that it was Adrianna calling to tell him she was late, he grabbed it. Otherwise, he might have let it ring and go to his answering service.

The instant he answered, his dad came on the line. "You sitting down?"

"Yes sir, what's up?"

"Two nights before the MacMorogh plane crash, an inmate at Parchman, a Mr. Junius Abad, was given a thirty-six hour furlough. Know what for? Let me tell you. He got a furlough to go to a memorial for a one Henry Abad. You know who old Henry was, don't you?" Jack's dad was teasing him and stringing him along.

"No, tell me."

"He was a member of that Abad family that owned about half of the Delta." His dad paused. "Know what else? He had died three years prior." Then his dad started laughing. "That seem strange to you? A little late for a memorial service, right?"

"It does seem so; what else?" Jack was getting impatient.

His father kept the tease going. "Guess who he was released to? I'll tell you. Sergeant Bill Polk of the Mississippi Highway Patrol. And…"

Jack could tell his father was having a sip of his drink, probably Four Roses, and that he loved keeping Jack in suspense. "Did I mention that this Sergeant Polk had a specific job with the Mississippi Highway Patrol? I did not mention that, did I?"

Jack was getting more exasperated but knew it would make it worse if his dad could tell. The older man continued to drag it out. "Well, he was the driver and bodyguard for none other than Lieutenant Governor Hawkins. Now, isn't that something?"

Finally, Jack said, "So, what about it?"

"Oh now, Jack, don't get anxious. I'll tell you what about it. According to, and in the exact words of the person I spoke to at Parchman, Junius ain't come back yet!" and his dad roared.

It was Jack's turn. "So, it's only been twenty-four years. That's nothing to get anxious about."

Then they both got serious, Jack's dad first. "Do you think there is any possibility that he could have been the additional person on that plane? If so, what the heck was he doing?"

Jack asked quickly, "Any possibility you have a description of the guy, like height, weight, and so forth?"

"Just happen to have it," his dad replied. "Age thirty-six, height five ten, weight two sixty. He had four gold front teeth, a homemade tattoo of a naked woman on his right bicep. Probably none of that was obvious on the remains if there was nothing but bones.

"Listen to this," his father said. "Junius Abad had served two years of a thirty- year sentence for armed robbery of a small town bank near Jackson. The day he robbed the bank, he drove up in front of the bank in his mother's robin egg blue Pierce Arrow, wrapped a handkerchief around his face, and then boldly went inside the bank with a small twenty-two caliber pistol. He started shooting at the ceiling and hollering, 'Hold-up!'"

"He shot out two ceiling lights before hitting a ceiling fan. A blade on the fan fell and cut a customer. He stuck the gun in a teller's face, and she handed him a stack of ink blotters advertising the bank. On the way out, he turned to shoot at something again. In the confusion, he turned to run and ran through the glass door of the bank. The police had him before he ever got the car started."

Jack remarked, "Seems as though if his family was as influential as you say, he could have gotten out of that. Heck, any jury person would have to agree that he was insane."

His father said, "True enough, but that was not his first excursion into the world of crime. He had a record, including exposing himself to some school kids, peeping in the windows at the old folk's home, and another attempt at robbery. At any rate, the judge was tired of him."

Jack was silent for a minute or so, long enough for his dad to ask whether he was still there. He responded that he did not know for sure where to go from that point.

"Aren't you going to Birmingham this week to see the people at the CAA and the sheriff? How about the coroner, he still around? I think I would tell them what you know; see if any of them wants to pursue it," concluded his dad.

"Well, old boy," Jack said fondly, "you still got it in you! Thanks a million. I'll keep you posted."

Adrianna was flabbergasted when she heard. They discussed it at length, and Jack even dreamed about it. He had a new adventure waiting for him. He left early on Tuesday and made it to Mobile in time to have a quick lunch and to buy Miss Maudie Lee a quart of Old Crow. The visit with her this time was much more conversational than the last. Jack had many questions, now that he had met the other people. She recalled some things she had not before.

They talked at length about John Pope and his work at the church and with the Civil Rights movement. Maudie Lee had deep concerns. She also told Jack that she had talked to Winston. He wanted Jack to call him before he went to Birmingham. Meanwhile, Jack was apprehensive about mentioning Mrs. Abernathy. Maudie Lee had not said a word about her, but it was something he needed to know, so he came out with it.

"Miss Maudie Lee, I had a long visit with Mrs. Abernathy last week."

"So," Maudie Lee said. "You must have had fun talking to her. She has not had good sense for years. She is a lot older than I am. I will tell you for a fact, she does not have it," and Maudie Lee pointed at her head, "like I do!"

Jack replied with a smile, "Miss Maudie Lee, nobody has it," and he pointed at his own head, "like you do. But I will tell you she was pretty sharp the day I visited her."

Maudie Lee responded with a question, "Then I guess you came to some conclusions as a result?"

"I had come to a conclusion on my own, prior to my visit."

"And what is that conclusion?"

Jack looked her in the eye and said as sincerely as possible, "My conclusion will never leave my mouth or my pen without the approval of several people."

Maudie Lee looked at him, "Meaning the General?"

"No, Ma'am, meaning several other people."

Maudie Lee sat silent for a long while. "It has been another nice visit, Jack. It is probably time you go now. One last word, though. One day, the truth about a lot of things will come out. Whatever you decide about the value of true history and the need for your book, I for one approve. Nuf' said."

Jack stood and reached down to get her hand and help her stand. She wrapped her arm around him and gave him a hug. "You are a nice man, Jack."

Then all of a sudden, as Maudie Lee turned to go inside, she caught sight of a neighbor walking toward her house. The woman was several houses away, but coming at a good pace. "Oh my Lord," she said, pushing Jack out the door, "Run to your car. That old busybody asked me last time you were here who you were and what you wanted. I told her I decided to change my burial policy, and you would be the new debit collector. She wanted me to call her next time you came by. She wants to think about changing her policy too. You better git!" With that, Jack scooted to his car. As he drove away, he looked in the mirror. The neighbor was waving her arms for him to wait up.

He stopped at a service station to buy fuel and to call Winston. Winston inquired about his mother. Jack said, "No way can I keep up with her." They talked for several minutes about John Pope and Jack's plan to visit. "Don't go there right now, Jack. The next time you plan to be here in town, let me know in advance. John wants to talk to you, feels that it is important that he do so. However, not right now, not in Birmingham." Jack understood. But since he already had an appointment with Nelson Goodall, Jan's contact at the paper there, he would still continue on to Birmingham.

22

Early the next morning, after spending most of the evening talking to Adrianna and working on his notes, Jack was up ready to go. Nelson invited him to come by the paper first thing. They would plan their day from there.

The receptionist in the lobby was expecting him, and a visitor pass was ready. He was hooking it into a button on his shirt when Nelson came off the elevator and straight to him. He had a big smile, his hand out to greet him. He was a good-looking boy. Not that Jack liked pretty boys. However, Adrianna would definitely notice this young man.

After their brief greeting, Nelson led Jack up to a meeting room. He spoke to several people on the way and was quick to introduce Jack as a senior investigative reporter from the *SI*. Jack appreciated the fact that Nelson was proud to be in his company, humble as it was.

Nelson's battered briefcase and two large brown envelopes were stacked neatly on the meeting table. He invited Jack to sit. "I want you to know that I have in no way jeopardized your inquiry into this matter, but I have made some discreet inquiries on my own. I have these things for you to go over before you go visit any of these people." He took the first envelope and emptied the contents before carefully explaining each piece. "This is the report by the investigator who was first on the scene of the remains. You have here his full report, including interviews with the two rabbit hunters who made the discovery." He passed that along. Jack reviewed it as Nelson continued, "You will see there was no personal identification of any kind that the investigator could find. There was no wallet, no identifying marks on clothing, or anything else. You will see from these next photos that weather played a part. Also, animal scavengers had visited the body, if not human ones."

He then passed the photos to Jack. Jack gasped, and Nelson smiled," Pretty gruesome huh?"

Jack said, "Yeah, yeah, sure is." It was hard to keep his composure. There in the photos, obvious for anyone to see, were three gold front teeth stuck into what was left of the skull. There was a space where another might have been. Jack looked a long time without making eye contact with Nelson.

The next evidence was a stack of notes written by the investigator. He had made calls to the CAA, to the other law enforcement agencies in the area, and one to the people who owned the airplane.

The coroner's report was much the same, with more pictures. Close-up details showed the many fractures. Only pieces of clothing like the belt, the waist section of trousers, the collar section of the shirt, and one shoe remained. The coroner specifically stated that death was from trauma resulting from a severe fall or other massive force.

"Now, one other thing, here is the name, address, and phone of one of the original investigators from the CAA. He is retired and lives outside Destin, Florida. He has been out of town. Yesterday was my first opportunity to talk to him. He has some old files and will be glad to talk with you whenever you can make arrangements."

Jack mused a bit, "If he's available, I might just be able to make it there before the end of the day. I think I will try to do that."

After they reviewed everything, Nelson stood, "I am available to take you to visit each of these local individuals whenever you are ready."

Jack looked at him and said, "Why? You have done a far better job than I would have done. You obviously have the respect of these people. Otherwise you would not have this material." Jack patted the stack.

Nelson was pleased with the compliment. "Coming from you, sir, that is quite a nice thing to say."

Jack replied, "I am extremely proud of both you and Miss Plow. Jan started digging without my asking. You took the bull by the horns. My hat's off to you."

With that, Nelson said shyly, "About Jan, what is she like? She sounds awfully nice on the phone." He laughed, "We've become phone pals."

Jack grinned, "She is a pretty girl, a little quiet when she first came to work at the paper." Jack explained his own relationship with Adrianna, Jan's superior. Nelson said he knew all about that.

Jack went on, "Actually, we felt something was troubling Jan at first. She was very intense and did not smile or laugh much. Adrianna recognized, however, that she was the best worker and the least trouble of any of the others in the department. She started giving her special assignments. Her demeanor changed considerably for the better.

"Then we had a bomb scare, where she was about to open the door on the car where the bomb was. Thank God, we got the girls safely away from the car. Jan slid back into her morose state for several weeks. She has gotten engrossed in this extra work for me, and her real brilliance is becoming apparent. I may have to give her credit as co-author. "

Nelson responded," Oh, I heard all about the bomb scare. Wow! Tell you the truth, I have been thinking about going to New Orleans some weekend; maybe ask her out to dinner. But I haven't gotten to it yet." He paused for a moment. "I would like to have a picture too, but haven't gotten around to asking about that either."

Jack said enthusiastically, "I have an idea. Do you have a picture of yourself?" Nelson frowned in puzzlement. "I might just slip your picture in with some material I take her to type. Surely she will ask who it is. I believe that will get you a picture."

Nelson grabbed at his belt and the attached ID. "We just had these IDs made. Personnel may have a copy. Give me a minute." Off he dashed. In a few minutes, he returned, waving a color photo. "The photographer told me I was one of the few in the building who smiled."

Before leaving town, Jack rode through John Pope's neighborhood. It was definitely an all-black community. The church was large and well maintained. Jack would still like to talk to him, but would adhere to his wishes.

The drive around Birmingham got him off to a late start. He called Carlton Moore, the retired CAA accident investigator, to try to make an appointment for the next morning. The sound of dogs barking and someone trying to quiet them down welcomed him. The voice that came on was mellow and almost sounded like a radio voice.

"Carlton here, sorry about the animals. They always think the phone is for them. "

Jack introduced himself and reminded Carlton of his phone conversation with Nelson and the fact that Jack might be calling. Carlton had been expecting the call and was glad to hear from him. He understood that Jack had some new information. That crash had really gotten his goat. Never could figure it out.

Jack arranged to meet the next morning at Carlton's house. He checked in at the Frangista, a motel he had visited many times with his father when he was growing up. It sat on the beach side of the highway. Each unit had a bedroom, a small sitting room, and a kitchenette. His father had liked having a place to cook the fresh seafood they ordinarily caught themselves. He would load the car before going to work that last day before vacation. He packed their clothes, pots, pans, and condiments for cooking, and they would take off as soon as he was through work. There was always a quilt and a pillow for Jack to use on in the back seat while his dad drove straight through from wherever they lived. "No stopping at a motel on the way, costs too much money," his dad would say. Those were the days.

Carlton's house was inviting, for sure. It was Victorian, similar to many shotguns in New Orleans. The yard was large, mostly sand. Big oaks shaded the house. Two Irish setters met Jack at the car, Carlton calling after them. Carlton invited him around to the back of the house to sit on the porch; it looked out on Choctawhatchee Bay. From the porch, a pier fifty feet long went straight into the bay. At the end was a small, screened gazebo with benches on each side. An old shrimp boat, small enough for one person to handle, rocked lazily at the end of the pier.

A telescope stood on a tripod, and a marine radio crackled in the background. Carlton explained that the Intracoastal Waterway ran through the bay. He knew many of the boats by sight and often talked to the skippers when they went through. He had made friends with several of them. Often he got calls from downstream, asking if he would pick up a few supplies in town and deliver them out to the boats when they came along. He loved doing it. Sometimes he tied up alongside and shot the bull with the crew as they towed him along. Near the end of the bay, they would cut him loose. They paid him with fuel. Now, as he talked to Jack, there was more discussion about boats, fishing, storms, and the federal government before they got to the business at hand. Carlton did not get a lot of company.

He listened attentively at what Jack had to say about the possibly of a seventh person on the plane. That discovery had been made during the BCA days before the department had become the CAA. Carlton had already moved on to Memphis by then. Jack did not like the idea of telling Carlton about his dad's discovery until he could get Carlton's word that he would not reveal the information. A leak could jeopardize the whole project. Once he had this assurance, Jack showed Carlton everything Nelson had showed him. Then he told him about Junius Abad. Carlton was obviously surprised.

Carlton said, "Let me tell you what I know, but before that, I have to go get some old files I dug up last night. Can I bring you coffee on the way back?"

Jack agreed. "Black."

Carlton brought a can of tobacco, a crooked pipe with the stem chewed through, and a box of kitchen matches. The coffee was hot and strong.

"You know I talked to William MacMorogh after the crash. I am sure you know he was a veteran pilot. His first words to me after we began talking about the accident were that he had felt the plane had been overloaded when it took off. Maybe he thought there was too much fuel and baggage on board for the six people. Best we could tell, none of the passengers weighed over one hundred and eighty, and if that was true, the only other problem could have been baggage or other freight."

Then he gave Jack information that he had never heard. The airplane took off and was nearly to Meridian when the pilots contacted the tower there. They wanted to know the field conditions and which runway was active. The pilots said they were not declaring an emergency but that they were having trouble trimming the airplane.

Jack asked what that meant. Carlton explained. "Each airplane has a center of gravity, what they call 'CG.' In loading the plane, the pilot takes into consideration the weight of pilots, fuel, passengers, and baggage. You want to keep those things arranged so that the plane is not nose heavy or tail heavy. There are trim tabs controlled by trim wheels or levers on the aircraft that allow the pilots to make a fine adjustment to CG balance. The airplane then will fly straight with as little drag as possible." Carlton used his hand to demonstrate.

"Most of the fuel on that aircraft was in the wings. The pilots could not move their seats, so the only thing you could manage was placement of passengers and baggage in order to accomplish a balance for the CG."

Carlton then handed Jack a single sheet of paper bearing his own typewritten notes. "This is the report from that tower in Meridian. You will see that the pilots called again, once they were over Meridian. They reported that they were still having a problem but that they thought fuel burn off would help. Now, in my opinion, if the plane was tail heavy due to excess baggage or people, burning off fuel would likely make the situation worse.

"Somewhere between Meridian and Birmingham, the pilots were advised of turbulence en route. The pilots responded with the fact that they were having a persistent problem trimming the airplane and were planning an unscheduled landing in Birmingham. We know that the trim condition did not improve. Of course we know they never made it."

"What about your earlier thoughts about an explosion or foul play with the airplane?" Jack asked.

"There was some indication that some of the outside skin appeared to have bowed outward, indicating that a force from within could have caused the damage. However, none of the victims were burned." Carlton was staring off into space when he continued.

"The likelihood that the gas heater on the aircraft blew up was only a guess. First, it was not that cold, to have the heat on. We simply based that assumption on the fact it had happened on another airplane or two."

Carlton paused to reload the pipe. "You know, I am sitting here thinking about something. Evidence points to the fact that this person probably was on that airplane, regardless of MacMorogh's strong doubt. The remains were near the tail cone, right? As I recall, the tail cone was a good distance from the rest of the wreckage. Now, if there was severe turbulence and the aircraft was stressed because of the trim problem, it would be harder to control. Maybe they hit turbulence so rough that the plane broke apart. The tail cone and empennage could have easily drifted in different directions and therefore ended up some distance apart." Carlton clutched his pipe tightly in his fist as he made motions in the air, but still spilled hot ash on his pants leg. Jack looked closely at the pants. This was not the first time ash had fallen.

"My God," Carlton almost hollered. "What the hell have I been missing?"

Then he went on. "The other occupants in the airplane all were still belted in what was left of the seats. Your boy was not. That sucker was hiding in the baggage compartment! Sure as I am sitting here.

"Listen, but understand that I am just supposing. Suppose this man was on the plane, unbeknownst to the pilots. Somehow, he got on and hid in the baggage area, waiting for an opportunity to create a problem. For instance, the cables that run to the elevators that control the trim tab on the elevator run along and under the floor of airplanes of that model. Another thought, maybe he was planting a bomb. But why in the hell would he do that and not sneak off the airplane when he was done? Why go along to ride it down?"

Jack started laughing. "Kinda' like cutting off the limb you are sitting on. Carlton, you do not know about this guy. Let me tell you about him."

After he told about the bank robbery caper, Carlton bellowed, "Shoot, man, I think we might have discovered the problem."

Jack said, "I wish we had. I do not know where to go from here or whether I should."

"I tell you what I would do, and this is just another long shot. Find out if anyone still alive might have been around the plane when it was being loaded and serviced. Maybe you can place him at the scene prior to takeoff. Maybe the man did get on and was unable to get off without discovery. It might be possible that nothing more than his weight helped to bring the darn thing down."

Jack thanked Carlton for his time and invited him to lunch. The man declined, saying, "Thanks, I appreciate it, but there is a paddle wheeler working on the Intracoastal. It is due along here this morning. I want to see it. Good luck to you. I will keep thinking about this and call you if I come up with anything else."

Jack arrived back home after dark on Thursday night, tired but elated. This had been a very eventful and productive trip. He could not wait to tell Adrianna about everything.

She was having a tough time with work and trying to juggle Miss Penny's affairs. She needed to talk also. Jack saw the tension. After a light meal of sandwiches and beer, he asked her to tell him what the situation currently was and what had happened while he had been away.

She had taken off from work early on Tuesday to drive Miss Penny to one of the retirement homes that she and Jack had previously visited. Miss Penny loved it and was able to communicate the fact by clapping her hands together and smiling broadly. Her speech was still garbled, but she managed to get out the fact that she wanted to know, "How soon?"

Adrianna had gotten all of the information from the facility and then made a comparative analysis of all the ones they had visited. She took that to Miss Penny's attorney for his perusal. Mainly, Adrianna was concerned with affordability, not knowing Miss Penny's financial situation. She did know this much about it, however, and she passed that on to Jack. "Miss Penny has three more years lease on her fabulous apartment in the Pontchartrain Hotel. She paid the total amount of the lease in advance, right after husband died. By doing that, she got a small reduction in rate. Unfortunately, there is no refund."

23

On Monday of the following week, Jack arranged to meet on Wednesday with John Pope. Jack worked in his office until noon and then, after a quick lunch with Adrianna, departed for Jackson. He had promised his dad that he would be at his house by cocktail time; he was looking forward to his visit. They lingered at the table after dinner, enjoying their dessert while Jack brought his father up-to-date on the project.

Early the following morning, he slipped out of the house at sunrise and made his way to Inverness, a small town in the heart of the Delta country. He drove into town on State Highway 49 and cruised the short distance to the north edge of town before turning around. He drove back to a café with the muddiest trucks parked in front: the most likely place to have old timers eating breakfast.

Before he was even close to the front door, he smelled tobacco smoke. Inside, however, the smell of frying bacon drew him in. A cash register sat on a glass showcase to his right. The small sign on the counter read, "Welcome, seat yourself." There was not a vacant booth or table in sight.

Off to the left, Jack spotted a lunch counter with six stools; the end one was empty. A sturdy waitress waved a menu in the air as if she might be helping an eighteen-wheeler back into a tight spot. Jack headed her way. By the time he worked his way through the packed tables, Ilene, as her nametag announced, had placed tableware wrapped in a paper napkin, a tumbler of water, and a cup of coffee. A small jigger of cream tottered on the edge of the saucer.

"Special is four deuces," said Ilene. "Two eggs, two sausage, two bacon, and two flapjacks. I 'd get it if I wuz in a hurry. The cooks are behind. Special will come out quicker'n if you order off the menu."

"Bullshit, Ilene, ain't nothin' comin' out quick today. You got one cook with a hangover and the other'n workin' on one." That came from a voice at the end of the counter.

To Jack, Ilene said, "Don't pay no 'tention to the loudmouth. That's Charlie. The fellow next to you is Amos, next to him Ralph, then Junior, and next to Charlie on the end is Squirrel."

Charlie was at it again, "We been here since daybreak waitin' for the hens to lay and get a hog butchered." With that, Ilene poured more coffee and turned Jack's order in by yelling, "Nutha' Special, over easy, man's in a hurry!"

Amos turned to Jack and stuck out his hand; Jack shook it and introduced himself. Amos said, "You won't believe this, but we been sittin' at this same counter ever mornin' forty year or more and it's the same thang ever mornin'." Again Charlie, "Ain't the same neither, Ilene gets prettier by the day."

Ilene said, "Charlie, ain't you sweet."

"One thang ain't changed," said Junior. "Charlie's eyesight is getting' worse."

Ilene gave him the finger below the counter.

Jack said, "Forty years, huh? My dad had friends lived 'round here years ago. I told him I was driving up 49 to Memphis today. He said I should ask after those people."

Amos asked the name. Jack replied, "Abad, I believe was the name. Actually, a girl in the family. She ended up marrying a fellow who was some state official, lieutenant governor or something like that." Jack was playing it cleverly.

Amos was thinking, when Ralph joined in. "Abad, did you say?" Jack acknowledged. "That would've been Betty Lou Abad. Husband was lieutenant governor then. I think he got appointed to fill an unexpired term, then ran again and got beat."

Using the end of his spoon to make a point, Charlie interrupted, "Naw, Betty Sue was her name. Josh Abad's girl, big tits, blond, dumber'n a post."

It was Squirrel's turn, but he raised his hand politely to get his comment in. "Go ahead, Squirrel, you probably slept with her, right?" said Amos. To which Squirrel replied, "No, I knowed her, though. She's bad 'bout thowin' temper fits. Got her butt thowed outta' school for puttin' sugar in a teacher's gas tank. Evahbody was skeered uf uh. She's a mean un."

Then Ralph spoke, "Them Abads, they the same ones that spent all the money getting Betty Sue's husband elected lieutenant governor. Throwed a lot to the governor's race the same year too!"

Amos turned to speak to Jack. "If anybody would know them folks, Ralph here would. He's been a county supervisor since they first started building roads."

Ilene served breakfast to all but Charlie, and they started eating. Charlie continued grousing at her.

Ralph said no more while he poured syrup on his flapjacks and chewed a few bites. Then he took his empty fork, pointed it at nothing, and said, "Things are coming back to me now. Ol' Senator Scroggins got sick and was dying before his term ended. He decided to quit and let the governor use his power to appoint a successor. That would give the party a man in the office for a year before election time. Gave him the advantage of running as the incumbent." Ilene brought Jack and Charlie their orders. There was more silence as they all ate.

Jack had decided that Ralph was through talking, when he waived his fork again, dripping syrup across the counter. "Scroggins had his mind on a person he wanted the governor to appoint and thought he had worked it out with the governor. Now as I recall, these Abad people had another idea. They wanted Governor Ainsworth to appoint himself, leaving the job of governor to Lieutenant Governor Jenkins, Betty Sue's husband." Ilene poured more coffee all around; Ralph was silent again. Then he tapped his saltshaker on the counter to make a point. "Rumor was that money changed hands. Whether that's true or not, we don't know. But it did not matter no way, 'cause Scoggins got killed in a plane crash. So, the Governor did in fact appoint himself. Also he had a promise from the Abad family of a campaign chest strong enough to beat any opponent that ran against either him or Jenkins when they ran for re-election a year later." Ralph made no mention of the fact that Scoggins' choice might have been William MacMorogh, Jr., who had lost his life in the same plane crash. Jack kept quiet.

Another pause before Ralph continued, "Here's the kicker, times were tough. The economy hadn't recovered; cotton was not worth as much as it cost to raise it. Boll weevils, too much rain, not enough, same as today. The Abads seemed to have lot of money, but fact was, all they had was a good credit line at the bank. Well, wouldn't you know, the bank where they done business for years got took over by somebody else."

"These new people looked at their loans, and sure 'nough, called the note on the Abads. They had land and lotta' cotton, but no cash. They had their cotton stored with a broker outta' Memphis. That was no help, 'cause they couldn't sell the cotton for what money they had had in it. Nobody 'round here had money to hep 'em, and the family ended up losing evahthing. Short of this story is, neither Governor Ainsworth who was then Senator Ainsworth or Lieutenant Governor Jenkins who was then Governor Jenkins got re-elected. Another bunch with lots of money came in and elected the people they wanted."

Charlie was the first to ask, "What ever happened to Betty Sue and ol' Jenkins?"

Junior popped into the conversation, "That juke joint out near Swiftown called Floyd's Place is owned by a fellow they call Guv."

Charlie snapped his finger, "That's him, that's Jenkins. I think his wife left the area. If you drive by Floyd's and look out back near an old barn 'bout to fall in, you will see a red, white, and blue hearse. Sign on the side says, 'Elect Jenkins.' It still has some loud speakers on top if kudzu ain't covered it up."

Everyone was through eating. Amos turned to Jack and said, "Nice havin' you here today. Got us a real history lesson. If you have time, why don't you stop in out to Floyd's, ask Guv about Betty Sue. That is, if your father might be still interested." Jack laughed and said, "I think not." They all left the café together.

Ralph grabbed Jack's arm in the parking lot. "Now theys several more Abad families up and down 'long here in the Delta. Best I recall, one even got sent to the pen for something, don't remember much about that though."

Jack decided it might take Ralph too long to recollect, so he bid him farewell but not before Ralph had put a card in Jack's hand: "Re-elect Ralph Smith, County Supervisor, Beat Five, Big Levee County." Ralph walked to his muddy Cadillac and waved as he left.

Jack studied his map. Going by way of Swiftown was not too far out of his way. He would drive by Floyd's. When he did, he caught site of the hearse before he saw the juke joint. The hearse was as described; the joint was a surprise, however. It was barely ten in the morning, and the parking lot was full. The building might have been a house at one time. It was clapboard with a front porch. An old gas pump, no longer in use, lingered by the front steps, suggesting that the structure might have also been a country store.

Loud music came through open double doors. About four feet from the doors was an old attic fan, turned on its side, blowing air into the place. Jack had no intention of going inside. But he did pull his car under a shade tree on the back edge of the parking lot, to take a closer look.

He sat reviewing the landscape, mentally putting a little color into it, when he heard the sound of a rapidly approaching vehicle. The tires cried out, resisting the sudden braking and tight turn onto the gravel lot. Two men in a pickup drove up parallel to the front door. Both got out, leaving the vehicle idling. The driver was tall and skinny and had on jeans and a white dress shirt with the tail out. The other fellow was heavy, wore bib overalls, and mopped his face with a red bandana as they went up the steps.

Passing the fan, the big fellow took off sunglasses. The fan blew the tail on the skinny boy's shirt. They were inside no more than a minute when they came back out, supporting between them an older man obviously unable to motivate under his own steam. His head hung loosely. The front of his shirt looked like he had spilled beer, or puked, or both, down the front. They put him into the truck on the passenger side and closed the door. The heavy man went to the back of the truck, let the tailgate down, and sat on it before swinging his legs up into the bed of the truck. Jack did not blame him; he would have rather ridden in the back too. Skinny drove out of the lot. The older fellow was leaning out the window, a long lock of hair hanging across his face. The driver floored the accelerator; tires threw gravel until they contacted the pavement and screamed.

Jack sat a while longer and began thinking about what he might say if he went inside and did encounter the Guv.

He would walk in, stop near the door to let his eyes adjust to the darkness, then head to the bar. The Guv would be at the cash register counting change; he would see Jack in the mirror behind the bar, close the cash drawer, and then turn around. The Guv himself would walk up, wipe off the bar in front of Jack with a dirty wet towel, and say, "Hep' ye?" Jack would order a beer, chugalug it, and ask for another. By the third, he could act a little loose tongued.

He imagined his conversation. He would stick out his hand, say, "Name's Jack, sell notions out of Birmingham. You know calendars, pens, pencils, that sort of stuff. Do damn well at it too."

Guv would say, "I ain't interested." Jack would say, "Not a problem."

He then would say, "Funny thing. I drink a lot at this one little joint in Birmingham. I'm all time shootin' the shit with a funny ol' boy says he came from these parts. He told me the damnedest tale one time. Crazy son of a gun said he once was in the pen in Mississippi. One week, he got a two-day furlough to go to a funeral of a relative. He was under guard of a highway patrolman who escorted him to the funeral."

Jack imagined that the Guv would be looking at him suspiciously. He would go on with his tale. "Crazy guy says he went to the bathroom at the church where the service was held, climbed out a back window, and ain't been back to Mississippi since." Jack imagined the Guv staring hard at him.

Then Jack imagined he would slam him with the rest. "This guy says he borrowed a car and started driving. When he got over to some little town, New Cambridge, no, New Cotswold..." Then he would ask the Guv if that sounded like a town in Mississippi. Guv would answer, "New Cotswold," a cold stare now fixed on Jack.

"This is the craziest part," Jack would say. "This old boy said there was an airplane there at the airport, getting ready to load. He had his best suit of clothes on because of the funeral, so he just walks up sees the door open and gets on. He said there was only six seats plus the pilot's seats. Lots of folks were standing around outside, so he crawled through some curtains and into the area where they stored baggage. He covered up with suitcases, and soon everybody got on and the plane took off. He did not know where it was headed, nor did he care."

The Guv would be standing in the same spot, not saying a word, just staring. Jack would have him hooked.

Then he would finish his imaginary conversation. "This old boy says that after they got going, one of the pilots came back and discovered him. They landed in Birmingham to put him off. Before they landed, he heard one of the pilots talking to someone about having the police available when the plane landed. Then he said that as the plane got on the ground, it was going real slow toward the gates. He opened the door and jumped out with the plane still moving. He ran as fast as he could across the airfield, jumped a fence into a backyard, and hit a garbage can, knocking out a tooth. Gold one too! He hid out for several days and has been in Birmingham ever since. He said he later heard that an airplane crashed near Birmingham. He always wondered if that had been the one he was on." Jack would laugh to himself, That was the one he was on all right, but it had a real hard landing before it ever got to Birmingham.

Jack would be through with his third beer by now and would say, "Ever hear such a tale?" The Guv would say he had not. Jack would leave a small tip, say, "Nice talking to you," and walk out the door.

Jack sat there in the car a little longer and started laughing to himself. He imagined one other thing. As he came off the front porch, headed to his car, the Guv would come around the corner of the joint, a pistol with a long barrel pointed at him, and he would say, "Who the hell are you?"

He started his car, turned to leave the parking lot, and stomped on the accelerator, slinging gravel just like the pickup driver before. He was laughing aloud at himself, trying to get the heck out of the way of that imaginary pistol.

Further down the road, he stopped for gas, got a Coca-Cola and a package of Tom's Toasted Cheese Crackers with peanut butter for his lunch, and continued on his way to New Cotswold.

He had talked to June the day before, to arrange to stay at the hotel for at least one night. He thought he might try Will's little rehab cabin for a night or two also. Settled in his room and sipping on ice tea that June had sent up, he got busy making notes from the morning. In his mind, he rehashed the tale Ralph had told and went back over the hard times that the Abad family had encountered, the bank loan, the worthless cotton, and going broke. Then he wrote a note at the bottom of the page.

To Miss Annie and the General – I know something on you.

24

Jack telephoned Winston and then Miss Tilda, to let them know he was in town and to ask what time supper was. Both were happy to hear from him. John Pope was at their house, looking forward to meeting him. Winston had a meeting after work, but should be home by six or six-thirty. He said that Miss Tilda would tell him to come right on, but suggested that Jack give her a chance to brush and curry comb John Pope. Then Winston laughed, "You know what I mean," he said.

As Jack was walking through the small lobby, the desk clerk called, "Mr. Ward, you have a phone call. Just take it here if you like." It was Jonathan, welcoming him to town. He wanted to know about Jack's schedule for the next day. "What's the possibility of meeting me for breakfast," he asked, "then maybe spend the morning with me?"

They would meet at seven, and that pleased Jack. That would give him the afternoon to make an appointment with Miss Annie for Thursday. From there, he could play it by ear. He had several more things he wanted to do, including spending another night or two at the lodge or the little cabin.

Winston gave Jack the code to his gate and, as suggested, he did not go out to the house until about six. John Pope was a real surprise. He looked nothing like the only picture Jack had ever seen, John as a senior in high school. His head, except for a ring of hair above the ears, was bald. He had on comfortable jeans with a V-neck tee.

Smiling, he put a hard grip on Jack's hand; it was like the grip of a bear. Jack could not help but grasp John by the forearm and comment, "Those ten-pound hammers."

John laughed. "You heard about that exercise, huh?"

Miss Tilda whispered in Jack's ear, "We already had light toddy, you care for something?" Jack agreed, and they sat in the living room.

Miss Tilda, of course, did most of the talking, mainly about her two boys, Willie and John Pope.

Winston arrived soon enough to have a toddy before supper. They chatted all through supper about one thing or another. John had many questions about Jack and his career. He was sincere in his excitement about the project.

After dinner, Miss Tilda suggested that she and Winston turn in for the evening and let the boys visit. She said to Winston, "Come on old man, I will read you a story to help you go to sleep." Winston just smiled and shook his head as he caught John's eye.

John recommended, since it was still light, that they take a stroll down to the pond. On the way, he mentioned that his great grand-mother, Miss Maudie Lee, had spoken highly of Jack. He said that coming from her, that was a real compliment. She had told John that Jack never came alone, though; he always brought a Mr. Crow with him. Could be it was Mr. Crow that earned the compliments?

Jack explained his project, the facts, and the fiction. John said that he was pleased that his input was of importance. Because of Willie, he had always felt close to the family. They had drifted apart after they both started to school, but they managed to see each other some in the summer when he visited with his grandparents. He and Willie exchanged notes. "Mainly to prove to each other how many big words we knew," he said.

John's mother was a schoolteacher and then a principal. His father had left when John was about ten or eleven. His mother had moved several times in her jobs and then finally went back to school to get her masters. "Thank God, she was kind enough to drag me along. There were times I did not deserve it."

He remembered several bad incidents and even one where he called on Willie to come bail him out of jail. He could laugh about it now. It sure was not funny then. He got caught speeding in a small east Texas town, used the MF word, and had the crap beaten out of him. Then along comes this smart-mouth white boy to rescue him. He was driving a chartreuse Ford convertible and dressed like a bas-ket of pink and blue flowers. Will almost ended up in jail with him. "Willie and I share this special bond that few boys of different races have." Over the years, they often went months at a time without contact, but he managed to keep up with Willie. Will began to have troubles, but John never believed anything he heard and stuck by him. John Pope said, "I guess you know all of that story and his problems in the war and all."

Jack said, "No, we are not that far along."

John Pope responded by saying, "In time you will hear it from Will. Just let me say this, for the last several years, since the Korean War, I have been his spiritual conversant. Notice I did not say advisor or counselor. We just talk; I know that he loves me as much as I love him. Sometimes it takes someone to ask you for help before you really learn to love them."

Jack asked about Letitia and the tales that he heard. John started laughing. "Oh man, she is such a lovely lady. I still get embarrassed around her when I remember the first time I saw her. Here was this fat little girl, both elbows hanging across the windowsill on her daddy's big car. She was staring right down at Willie and me fighting over how to put pop bottles in a case. Willie looked up at her and told her she was "so purdy." I fell on the ground and rolled around laughing. She was far from being "purdy.""

Then John went on. "She turned into a lovely person inside and out. A lot of that is because she had wonderful parents. You do know that her father was a bootlegger?"

Jack replied that he did and that he knew that her father had caused Letitia some embarrassing times in school. He also knew that her father and Jonathan were best of friends.

John said, "Mr. Moon died when I was in college, and I drove a rat trap old car six hundred miles round trip to go to the funeral. I felt like we owed it to him to have a big turnout. There were as many colored at the funeral as there were whites. Many people probably thought that was because he was their favorite bootlegger. That was as far from the truth as you could get. Let me tell you the story about 'Piano Boy' Potter, or have you already heard it?" Jack had not.

The Potter family had come to the state along about the same time that Seamus brought the Dishmans to the area. The Potters, the Youngs, the Washingtons, all came at about the same time. Piano Boy was the grandson of one of the first families of Potters. The family members were light in color, but there was no doubt about their heritage.

"Piano Boy" was just a nickname. His real name was Paul, and from the time he was eight, he played piano by ear with never a lesson in his life. He was playing at church by the time he was eleven or twelve. By the time he got out of high school, he was playing in the "jukes." As soon as he could escape, he did. He went to Detroit, got a shift job in one of the plants, and played piano in the clubs there. The name "Piano Boy" stuck.

He easily passed for white, and he ended up marrying a white woman. They had a child; there was very little indication that she was of color. But unfortunately, Piano Boy forgot his roots and how awful things could be in the South for a colored person, especially one so brazen as to marry a white.

Forgetting those roots, he came home to visit, showing off his new Buick and his white wife and baby. All were having a good time. His family had a big get together one evening at their house in the Quarter. Piano Boy was hammering out tunes on the front porch, and people were dancing in the yard.

The news got out and just after dark, six or so men in white robes and on horseback, rode into the yard. They threw flares into the house and pulled Piano Boy off the porch. With their own fists, feet, and the hooves of their horses, they beat him to death.

At first sight of the Klan, the family called the marshal; right behind came the fire truck. Jonathan MacMorogh was driving. Moon Mullens, who happened to be making an in-town delivery, followed with others to help. It was too late; flames engulfed the house. Whoever might have been inside would have perished also. When they accounted for the family, two people were missing: the white woman and her child. The news spread through town like wildfire itself. Before long, it was all that the marshal and a few volunteers could do to keep a riot from breaking out. The situation got worse as each day went by. No one was ever charged; no one came forward even to accuse anybody. Hands off the Klan. Today, you could mention Piano Boy Potter and still feel the hate.

As the story went on, and some say it was just fable, there was no evidence that anyone had died in the fire. There were no remains of the white mother and child. Some say that someone saw a white man and a woman run across the highway just north of town near the Old Church. Their coat tails were smoking. Others say they saw a man running along the road near Naps Store with a child under his arm. His pants were smoking. Still another story goes that someone passed Nap's store after closing time. One man was putting gas in a big Lincoln car. Another was stuffing what looked to be groceries in the trunk.

Then there was the story that when the fire was out, the fire truck was sitting in the street, and Jonathan was nowhere in sight. People began looking for him. Tilda Jackson said he had come from the fire and gone to bed, dead tired. Several days later, he was at work. He was wearing a long sleeve shirt, even on one of the hottest days of the year. Another person saw Mrs. Mullens getting a prescription filled for a salve at Irby's drug store. The pharmacist explained to Mrs. Mullens that it was the best thing for burns.

Jack asked if that was the end of the story. John Pope responded, "No, but let Will tell you the rest; he was there for the end."

"Anything else you can tell me about the MacMorogh family that you think deserves saving for history's sake?" Jack asked.

"Nothing more than what I am sure you already know. Seamus established one thing. I do not believe the MacMoroghs have ever had a deep religious belief. That bothers me some. On the other hand, I have never known anyone who lived as believers more than they do. Their companies support this whole area. Even during times when they were unfairly treated by the townspeople, and there have been a few, they stood by the town. There were several times when they might have been better off to move elsewhere, but the town would have died."

Then Jack said, "Tell me about you."

"Not much to tell. Pore old preacher man just getting by," John grinned. "I guess you know that I have a law degree also?"

Jack looked surprised and said," No, I haven't heard that."

"Never passed the bar, never hung out a shingle. I had opportunities, but I was wrestling with other things. I couldn't decide if I wanted to represent the good guys or the bad guys. Just finally decided that I would represent them both and see how many I could put in heaven."

"So that is all you are going to tell me?' Jack asked.

"Maybe not. Let's see how your book comes out. You and I might co-author a book together. I am serious. Someday things will change. I want to tell about it."

They walked back to the house, John reaching out at lightning bugs and laughing about catching them as a kid. "We would put them in a jar and go out in the woods and all of a sudden someone would go 'Woo, WOOO,' and we would hightail it out of there." Back at the house, they half hugged each other and said good night.

It was not too late to call Adrianna when Jack got back to the hotel. She was still wrestling with getting Miss Penny settled and laughed that she also had a day job. Jack relayed part of the Piano Boy story. It had really gotten to him. He thought back on the statement that had come from Seamus' day, that locating the railroad where he did would have long-time effects. The Quarter and the Bottoms were not two compatible neighborhoods.

Jack met Jonathan for breakfast. June joined them for a few minutes, and they discussed the plan for the day. Jack would get another look at the big picture: MacMoCorp. At the plant, they again went to Jonathan's office. Jack remembered another door in the office, but did not know what was behind it. Today, it was open, and there was activity inside and he could hear voices. Shortly, an attractive young woman appeared at the door.

"We are ready, sir!" she said cheerfully, then turned back into the room.

The room was impressive. There was an elliptical desk cut out of solid wood. By Jack's count, it would seat fourteen. At the end was a podium where the young woman stood smiling. Behind her, the entire wall was a blown-up map of Mississippi, Louisiana, and East Texas. A pull-down screen hung from the ceiling. There was an overhead projector above their heads. Jack and Jonathan had pads, pencils, water, and lighted pointers before them.

Jonathan nodded; the young woman began a presentation. "Good morning. My name is Cathy Cannizaro, I am a second year co-op student from Mississippi State College for Women. This morning, I will present a brief overview of the MacMorogh Corporation."

"Behind me you will see…," and she began her presentation. In twenty minutes, she had presented in detail each of the MacMorogh companies, what they did, where they were located, and the number of employees in each. The map was magnetic, and different icons represented the various businesses. *Trees* indicated timber land, *Mills* represented sawmills, *blocks of ice* with frost represented ice plants, *dollar signs* were the banks, *gas pumps* indicated the fuel distribution business and gas stations, *factories* with smokestacks represented manufacturing, and finally, a *steam train* represented the railroad interests. But in her presentation, there was one row of red blocks that she didn't cover.

She closed, "That concludes my presentation, gentlemen. Are there questions?"

"Yes, what about the red blocks?" asked Jack.

Smiling, she said, "I think Mr. MacMorogh would prefer to answer that."

Jonathan clapped, and Jack joined in. Before she left, Jonathan had to tell a little more about her. She was fourth generation Lamar family. Her great grandfather, Tadlock Lamar, had been hired to come to town to build and operate the first sawmill that Seamus owned.

Her mother was "Tootie," sister to Will's mother, and therefore Will's first cousin. Jonathan explained that her relationship had nothing to do with their hiring her, however. They were pleased to have her, but the school had selected her for the co-op program because she was tops in the field that applied.

After she left the room, Jonathan said, "Somewhere in the history, I think it is important to reveal just how large this company is. We touch many people. It is not only our employees; there are products that we supply that enable someone else to profitably use them in business, and they too employ a lot of folks.

"One other thing, and this is not for publication. These are some rather impressive numbers." Then he showed Jack a financial analysis indicating the net worth of the company. It had increased every year for the past ten years. It was an astronomical number.

The presentation and the numbers were evidence enough that this small profile company was truly a large force throughout the region. These numbers, combined with some of the work that Jan had already done on the earliest days of the corporation, would be great for completing the financial history.

Next, Jonathan presented Jack with projections for the coming year, five years, and ten years. These included the growth of existing companies and expansion into other fields, including oil and gas. Manufactured housing was already underway on a small basis. What Will was bringing into the company with the aggregate business, cement, and dredging, was all new and had great potential.

Once again, Jack asked about the red blocks. He was curious because there were so many of them.

Jonathan said, "I would prefer that we discuss those at a later time. Chronologically, those indicate a more recent acquisition of a lot of property with a lot of potential. I have a very definite opinion that the events surrounding the acquisition could be among the most portentous of any in our family or company history. I think it would be best to first hear Will's version, and then it will be interesting to see how you interpret it."

Jack was content with what he had learned so far, but was still curious about the General. He expressed his apprehension about an interview with the man. One concern he had was what part the General played in the company. It seemed that Jonathan was in control. Was the General still the main decision maker?

"Yes, he is the final decision maker." Jonathan did not say this with any indication that there was dissatisfaction on his part. "He stayed in the army long enough to get another star before he retired, but he made good use of that time as far as the company is concerned. He made so many contacts in Washington that he keeps an office there," Jonathan said.

He went on, "The company has a lot of business that has been generated by him as a result of relationships formed over the years." Jonathan pointed out the first, the box factory. It had come about because of the war. It was the first government contract for which the General was responsible. They made boxes to carry huge cannon shells. Then there was business for the forge and the machine shop. Even though it was a small facility, they were competent and made small parts for tank armor.

Next, and as little as it now seemed, the surplus inventory auctions were a godsend at a time when the companies needed cash. Jack was not familiar with the auctions and had been unaware of them. Jonathan suggested that they walk across the lot to the fire department. He had not been over to inspect that day. Afterward he would tell Jack the story of the auctions.

There was a time immediately following World War II that the government wanted to dispose of all of its surplus equipment and facilities no longer necessary for the war effort. The War Assets Administration formed for that purpose, and many of the real assets were disposed of at public auction. The General was well aware of the auctions, prior to public knowledge of them. He knew where they would be located, what was going in the sale, and the intended method of operation. He alerted Jonathan, gave him as much information as he could, and suggested that he consider the opportunities. With the war over, Jonathan was anxious to get on with building his dream logging machine, but they did have a problem. Cash was short. If Jonathan was going to build anything other than a prototype, he needed more money. He contacted the General and expressed his interest in the auctions.

The first opportunity they had was almost in their backyard. It was at Camp Shelby, the same place Jonathan had reported for duty when he went into the army. The General got what was yet an unpublicized notice of the auction and the equipment in the sale.

The General heard of some shenanigans that had taken place at some of the earliest events. The government people responsible for the auctions were on a tight schedule and had limited time to get them all done. They preferred to sell in lots rather than one piece at a time. Most of the buyers were heavy hitters and capable of providing the cash to buy in lots. It would be a good idea to go well funded.

In addition, there were caveats. Unscrupulous individuals followed the auctions with every kind of rumor they could manufacture, to discourage people from attending the sales, therefore reducing competition. As it turned out, this was valuable information.

The rumormongers carried a variety of tales: tales like equipment having been in seawater or having been fueled with incorrect fuel, which would create a huge repair bill before the engines would run.

In addition, they spread the word that big players were in attendance who had conspired with government officials to award the entire inventory to the highest bidder. These tales did discourage a few. It would be good to beware.

Jonathan took a certified check for two hundred thousand dollars from the bank in New Cotswold, and from another, the same amount. Moon Mullens' name appeared on both. Moon and Jonathan would collaborate on what to buy, and Moon would do the bidding. The object—no revelation of the MacMorogh name or of the General's possible involvement.

Jonathan and Moon arrived a day early. It had been raining for two days, with no end in sight. The equipment sat on open fields scraped out of the red clay and sand, and mud was ankle deep. A preannounced, mandatory buyer registration took place at a hotel in Hattiesburg. One of the rumormongers was easy to spot. He was big and red-faced, and sweat poured off his bald head. He was loudly holding court. In his opinion, it was outrageous to hold the auction under such weather conditions. "This ain't my first rodeo," he kept saying. "If nobody shows up, the government boys will have to delay the auction, and by God, that is what I am going to do. I ain't going."

Jonathan and Moon made reservations at a cheap motel near the front gate of Camp Shelby. On the morning of the auction, they were among the first to arrive. "The Cowboy," as Moon dubbed him, was there, spouting off, "Ain't nobody coming."

He was not far from wrong. Very few showed up, but the government announced that the auction sale would go forth. Its representatives made their required announcements prior to the start. They covered check guarantees, lot sales, and mandatory removal of purchases from the premises within six days and then announced, "Let's have a sale!"

Moon and Jonathan had a plan. Moon threw up his hand to ask the auctioneer if it was possible to see if there were others besides him who might like to bid for the entire inventory. "The Cowboy" almost croaked. His rumor had come around to bite him on the ass.

The auctioneers stated that they appreciated the suggestion but felt it would be unfair to the other buyers, so they would prefer to sell in lots if possible. "The Cowboy" looked annoyed. The method of sale was simple. One item in a lot went on the block. The winner of that first item could have the entire lot or any portion for that same *per each* price. Moon always took the whole lot, according to his and Jonathan's plan. He bought all of the lots Jonathan signaled him to buy. Those consisted of the most desirable equipment, Jeeps, two and a half ton trucks, bulldozers, draglines, motor graders, and Plymouth four door sedans. The "Cowboy" had a bad day.

As soon as the auction was over, Moon made an announcement. He would be on hand for the next five days to sell all items he personally did not wish to keep. He promised he would sell on a one-to-one basis. The minimum amount would be ten percent over what he paid; other items could run higher. This was still a tremendous buy. Cash or check was fine, no certified checks required. Checks would have to clear, however, before the purchaser could take possession. A cheer went up from the crowd. It took a while for even the government men to catch on. Jonathan could wait until day six to pay for and remove his equipment, but he sold much of it prior to then. He paid the government without using much of his own money, and he made a nice profit.

For his effort, Jonathan gave Moon the ten Plymouths. Those Moon put in his taxicab fleet. They remained in natural, olive drab, military color. He painted an American flag on the door of each and renamed his cab company, "Veteran Cabs." Many other companies in other towns did the same, insinuating that veterans were involved. Moon boasted to all that the car itself was a veteran. Moon also said, "Only in America. I sell scrap iron for dollars, buy it back for pennies!"

Later the General advised Jonathan of an aircraft auction at Mineral Wells, TX. Jonathan reviewed the list. There was nothing of particular interest to him, but he did show the list to Dub Schooner. Dub was an air force veteran and knew the type of aircraft for sale in the auction. Dub needed something to add to his farm supply business and struck on the idea of a crop dusting operation. The aircraft for sale would be perfect. There were several lots of PT-13 and PT-17 bi-wing trainers.

Once again, Jonathan provided the certified checks. Off they went to Mineral Wells. More interested parties attended, and the competition was keener. Again, the planes sold in lots. Dub Schooner bought ten of the PT-13s and ten of the PT-17s. The only difference was that one had Jacob engines and the other Continentals. In addition, he bought spare engines; a few were 450 Pratt & Whitneys. There was a truckload of tires, wheels, props, wing ribs, and a few instruments.

Dub convinced Jonathan that these were not too many planes to be buying at one time. He would like five, and he had an idea of how to sell the rest. That depended on Jonathan. Dub knew the capability of the aircraft and knew they would make good crop dusters, especially if they converted some to the 450 Pratt and Whitney engines. He teased Jonathan, "You are the one with the aeronautical engineering degree. You can handle it." That was true. Jonathan and Winston went to work. Several months later, they certified the first prototype, and Dub started using it with terrific success. MacMoCorp, Aircraft Conversion Division, came out of that. Jonathan later sold that division for a large but undisclosed sum.

Jonathan laughed, "Out of those auctions, a cab company was formed as well as an aircraft crop dusting service and an aircraft conversion business. When Will opened his first sand pit several years later, he used an old dragline and a bulldozer purchased in the first auction."

"So the General is still very active," Jack commented. There was no question.

"He is," Jonathan replied. "Winston and I do have responsibility for day-to-day operations. Mother still goes into the bank a couple of days a week. We have a very capable young woman overseeing the banking operations. She too is out of the Lamar family and is a first cousin to Will. Her Name is Patricia Moore. Her husband is our county attorney as well as an attorney for the company."

Jack thought for a minute and said, "Would it be more convenient if I tried to make an appointment with the General in Washington?"

Jonathan told him that that would not be necessary; the General would get to him in time. "Believe me." That caused Jack more apprehension.

It was almost noon. Jonathan still had a question or two. The first was why there had not been any copies of the rough drafts lately. Jack explained that some of the material Will had given him on their last visit was rather personal. He wanted to double-check before he sent it out to everyone. That was fair enough for Jonathan.

Next, he wondered whether Jack was still investigating the crash. Jack explained that some interesting things had developed.

Jonathan said seriously, "Jack, you might want to leave that alone in discussions with the General. I know from my mother that the General is carefully reading all of your drafts. Over the years, I have gotten the impression that the crash was not a subject for family discussions."

Jack responded, "I think it is an important event that made a definite change in the history of the family and the company. I'd hate to leave it out. I would like for you and the rest of the family, including Dr. Bea, to discuss it. My plan is to talk to the General about it. I will not, only if instructed by Dr. Bea not to do so."

Jonathan looked at Jack and grinned," You have found out something, haven't you?"

Jack agreed, "Yes, and I am not sure the General is aware of some things we have discovered. I would like to at least let him know that."

Jonathan inquired about Jack's schedule for the rest of the week. When was he planning to talk to Jonathan's mother again? Was he planning to move out of the hotel? When was he leaving town? Had he talked to Nap at Nap's store?

Then Jonathan made an appointment with his mother for the next morning. He was pleased that Jack wanted to stay at Will's rehab center. He would find that interesting. "Be sure and drop in on Nap. You will be close by."

Then, "One other thing I almost forgot, and it is probably most important of all!" Jonathan said, slapping the top of his head. "You have to go talk to Maureen Mullens, Moon's widow, Tish's mother. Let's see if I can set that up right now; maybe you can go out there after lunch. She is here getting her house painted, and I do not know how long she plans to stay."

Jonathan called his secretary and told her to get Maureen Mullens on the line. Within minutes, they were talking. The first thing Jonathan said was in a low, serious voice, "Maureen, honey, I have just thought and thought and thought about it. Let's me and you run off and get married." He held the phone back from his ear, and Jack could hear her in a serious voice, low and sultry, panting on the phone, "Oh Jonathan, yes, yes, I thought you would never ask." Then, in a louder voice "Don't you know I am painting my house, and I do not have time for any of your bullshit?"

Then Jonathan told her what he really wanted, lined up a visit for Jack that afternoon, and told her he would give Jack directions. Before he hung up, he said, "Yeah, love you too. We'll see you for supper." They both laughed.

He was grinning. "About a year after Moon died, I gave a lot of thought to seeing if I might court Maureen. Then I thought more. Even with my best friend dead and gone, I could never think of her other than as his wife. I told her about it once, and she had actually had the same thought. So we just pretend. She and June are good friends. She and my mother are more than friends now, and in a different way altogether, she is part of the family."

25

Maureen Mullens

The directions to Maureen Mullens' house were easy enough to follow. Without them, however, Jack probably would have ended up lost in the deep woods. Simpson's Store was at the turnoff on County Road 12 E, eight miles from Nap's store. The terrain changed to rolling hills, cedar, and limestone outcroppings. Once Jack turned, he went two miles to a fork in the road. That section was asphalt, but not well maintained. At the fork, he saw a white arrow about two feet long with one word: "STABLE." He followed that arrow. The road was wide enough for one car, but two would have to slow to give each other room. The asphalt was new. Crepe myrtles were planted every hundred yards or so, and the grass was fresh cut.

He crossed the cattle guard two miles further and saw the white board fence on both sides of the road. A quarter mile on stood a white barn with a row of low stables. A small racetrack was next. A harness horse and driver were rounding a turn closest to the road. Light reflected off the chrome spokes of the sulky wheels. Jack slowed, and he could hear the horse's heavy breathing; the driver was calling to the horse, "Good gal, good gal."

Then Jack was in the deep shade of a heavy leaf canopy. He came to a tall brick fence painted white and within the wall, a closed, wrought iron gate. A bell box was at arm's length from the driver door, so he pressed the button and the gate slid open. He drove onto a brick lined drive that led to the house. It too was white, almost identical in outward appearance to Winston and Tilda's house. It had the same tin roof and wide screened porches all around, but closer inspection proved it to be made of brick.

The screen door in front was propped open, and two men in white painters' pants were in the yard, stirring paint, while another stood on a ladder painting the eaves of the house. A man called to Jack as he stepped out of his car, "She said come on in, she is out back. Just go through the house there and out the kitchen door."

Jack did as directed, and as he stepped out the back door, Maureen called from a beautiful garden, shaded all around with a variety of trees. She sat on an iron bench with deep cushions, next to a stream. A pitcher packed with ice cubes and some dark purple liquid sat on an iron table next to the bench. Maureen stood and stuck out her hand. "You must be Jack." She was tall, almost eye level to him. Her hair was blond with some gray mixed in. It was in a bun, with a blue ribbon wound tightly around it. No makeup, clear skin, with a few lines but not many for a woman he figured had to be over fifty. She had on jeans and a man's white shirt with numerous paint stains.

Jack could not help but admire his surroundings. The stream came from a small waterfall maybe fifty yards upstream and wound down through the rock-lined gardens. Several seating areas along the stream provided a view of the gardens from different angles.

A bridge crossed the stream, and Jack could see a short distance up a gravel path. More blooming bushes, more flowerbeds, bird feeders, bird baths. This was an absolute showplace. Maureen saw that Jack was taking it all in, and she let him admire everything before she spoke. "Something isn't it? It was my husband's great love, besides me and our daughter," and she laughed. "I think we were first, most of the time anyway."

Then she asked, "Jack, do you drink?" and then paused. "Alcohol, I mean."

Jack confirmed that yes, he did.

Maureen poured from the edge of the pitcher, filling two tumblers with the purple liquid, along with some ice cubes. "Shine does not get any better with age like bourbon or scotch, but this *is* very old. I call this plum punch. It is a mixture of a brandy made with locally grown plums and moonshine. If you are a lightweight drinker, just sip on this, otherwise I may have to put you up for the night."

Jack took a sip. He had never tasted anything like it. The temptation was to take a large swig, but he took Maureen's advice.

He began to explain to her what he was doing, the chronicle of the MacMorogh family, and how he was going about it. But Maureen was already aware; Miss Annie had discussed some of his manuscripts with her.

She liked what she had seen. She had tears in her eyes when she said, "If my husband had only lived for this day. He would have been the proudest person in this world to know how things have turned out: he and his best friend tied together in even a greater way.

"There are some things that I know, however, that I am not sure the MacMorogh family knows. I am talking about Jonathan, primarily. He has told me to be as candid as possible. He thinks I should not hold back anything. So, here goes."

Maureen met Charles Mullens at the University of Tennessee. She was a junior, and he was classified the same, but when she met him, he had just transferred from a small junior college in far east Tennessee.

It was Friday night, and she had a date. They were at one of the favorite college kid hangouts, a burger joint with a jukebox and a dance floor. No alcoholic beverages, but there were setups on the menu at fifteen cents. Everybody brought a bottle. Friday nights, there was a band; the cover charge was fifty cents.

She and her roommate were double-dating. It was a fun night, except that her boyfriend at the time did not dance well. They sat out many of the numbers, especially if they were fast.

"Not long after we arrived, up comes this boy, who leaned over and asked my date if he minded, then asked me to dance. Poor thing, this boy was so homely looking. I have to admit, I was a little embarrassed. He was not as tall as me; most boys weren't.

"It was warm weather. He had on brown wool slacks. The alteration was obvious. The cuffs were thick and not pressed. Then when he turned, the pants had been altered so much in the seat and waist that the back pockets were almost one."

"His shirt was clean and well pressed, but the collar was frayed. He had deep blue eyes, curly auburn hair, a big grin, and dimples in his cheeks. He could have been a handsome boy, except he had a mouthful of the most crooked teeth I had ever seen, and they protruded. They were awful. At first I thought they were some of those funny teeth that we could buy, the ones made of that awful sweet wax."

"He took my hand, introduced himself; he was Charles Mullens. I introduced myself. We got on the dance floor, and before I realized it almost everyone else had quit dancing. I began to look around and realized they were watching us. Then the beat turned faster, and everyone was clapping. Talk about dance, this boy could dance better than anyone than I had ever seen.

"He came back several times. We danced slow, fast, and one time he just held my hand while he did a down and dirty tap dance. Everybody in the place clapped and yelled, Go Charlie, Go!"

"Before the evening was over, Charles came over to our table, stuck out his hand to my date. As he shook it, he told him how much he appreciated him being kind enough to let him dance with me. I was impressed."

Maureen did not see Charles for several weeks, but once again ran into him at the same place they had been before. They danced several times, and then he excused himself for the evening. He had to go to work.

One of her classmates asked her the following week if she was dating Charles Mullens. She had seen them dancing together. Maureen explained that he was just a fellow who asked her to dance.

Her classmate told her that he was in several of her classes. By far the brightest person in the class, she said. In one Economics class, he solicited the poorer students for free tutoring. Besides that, he could be a riot. He was the funniest person she had ever encountered. Then she told Maureen that on top of all of the hours he was taking, he worked in the bookstore.

Maureen said she did not know what made her do it, but she walked to the bookstore that evening, about fifteen minutes before it closed. Charles was there. He smiled when he saw her and told her she was just in time. He was closing the store in fifteen minutes. He would like to buy her something to drink at the Student Union.

Of course, she went through the act that she was so surprised to see him there and she hadn't known that this was where he worked. He told her about himself. His family lived in a little community in east Tennessee. His father raised tobacco.

There were eleven kids in the family. Three were younger than he was. His older brother and sisters helped some, but he had to work or not go to school. He was studying business and hoped to go on to grad school to get an MBA.

Maureen told him she was getting a degree in elementary education. She planned to teach when she graduated, first grade if possible. Her parents both were teachers back home in Mississippi. She was at UT to get as far away from them as possible.

She ran into him off and on through the school year. He asked her out once; she told him she was going steady. Their only encounters were at the bookstore or out dancing. He was always his polite self. During her senior year, she hardly saw him at all. He was taking as many hours as he could manage. He had a better job writing ads for an advertising agency.

About a month before graduation, she ran into him at the Student Union. She had broken up with the boy she was dating. She told Charles and admitted it was for the best. She already had a teaching job for the next fall; they would have parted anyway. Charles too had applied for employment. He had given up on grad school for now. The three younger siblings at home were going to need financial help. Graduate school could wait.

That was the last she saw or heard of Charles for almost a year. She had taken a job as first grade teacher at a school in Memphis. One evening, she was looking for another teacher's phone number in the faculty handbook. As she was searching, she noticed something in the bio of one of the teachers, a Mrs. Anders. She was from the same town as Charles.

The next day, she approached Mrs. Anders. Did she happen to know of a Charles Mullens from Fox Hollow, Tennessee? The teacher was surprised. She said, "He is one of my younger brothers. How do you know him?" Maureen told her the story about their first meeting and their dancing and chatting from time to time. Mrs. Anders told her she had to get to class, but she wanted to meet Maureen for lunch. She had something to tell her.

After they took seats in the school cafeteria at lunch, Mrs. Anders began. "You are not going to believe this," she said. "I think you may be the girl Charles talked about at Christmas. We teased him about not having a girlfriend. He said he met a girl at UT that he thought could have been the one. He danced with her and wanted to ask her out, but she was going steady. She was the most beautiful girl he had ever known. He was too busy with school and work, and he let her get away."

Then Mrs. Anders said, "This may be hard to believe, but Charles is the most timid person you may ever meet. I think it is in part due to his teeth. My parents are not well-off and could not do anything about the teeth. However, Charles had a great attitude about his teeth. He said it was enough to be born into a big, loving family. If God wanted him to have prettier teeth, he would have given them to him.

"I think he covers his shyness with his talents. You know he can tap dance like crazy, and if he wanted, he could be a standup comedian. He can get before a crowd, take on that old east Tennessee twang, get to spitting and sputtering and acting like he is stuttering, and have a crowd in stitches."

The last thing Mrs. Anders asked Maureen was whether it would it be all right if she let Charles know about their meeting. Could she give him Maureen's phone number? Maureen agreed. Mrs. Anders wasted no time.

Mrs. Anders had become fond of Maureen as a teaching colleague and had even thought a time or two how nice it would be if she could meet Charles. When Mrs. Anders found out that Maureen knew him already, she could not wait to get in touch. She began trying that evening, but Charles was not easy to locate. He did not have a phone of his own. The only number she had was the rooming house where he had a room. Besides that, he was on the road with his job all week. He might not check in every night. She called the rooming house twice before she got an answer. The woman who answered said she would give Charles a message if he should check in with her. However, her tenants did not expect her to be an answering service.

Charles did check in and returned his sister's call immediately, fearing a family emergency. When he found out why she was really calling, he could not believe it. He was dialing Maureen's number before the receiver was on the cradle to end the call with his sister.

He and Maureen talked for half an hour, with Charles feeding coins into the pay phone all the while. He wanted to visit as soon as possible. He had a few small towns in Mississippi in his territory; one was not too far from Memphis. The next time he was close, he would try to end his week there. Perhaps he could spend a weekend.

Two weeks later, he made it work. He arrived at his sister's house about five-thirty, cleaned up, and was at Maureen's apartment by seven. He suggested that they have dinner that night, and the next night, maybe dinner and dancing. He was more than excited; he was ecstatic, and it showed. He brought a small bouquet, and Maureen was amused at his enthusiasm. She realized that she had missed him too.

They went to a restaurant overlooking the river, ate four courses slowly, and talked the whole time. Afterward they sat on a bench outside the restaurant with a beautiful night view of the river and the parade of boats passing. Charles talked about his job. He had gotten two promotions and two raises. That was rewarding; however, he did not know if the corporate life was for him. He hated the travel. Besides that, he did not think she would want to marry a fellow that was never home.

Maureen heard the last statement, but let it pass. She made no response. He had never even kissed her, for goodness sake. Back at her apartment, they spent more time sitting in his car chatting. She had three roommates, and had she asked him in, there would have been little privacy. When it was time to call it an evening, Charles walked her to the door, told her good night, and turned to walk away. Maureen took the lapels of his coat and pulled him closer. She put her hands on his cheeks and kissed him. She thought he was going to bolt. She then told him good night and quickly went inside.

Charles had not seen his sister in months and wanted to spend time with her family on Saturday. That evening, Maureen wore a new dress and low heel slippers that would be good for dancing, and also, she would not be more than a head taller than Charles.

Maureen had one of the best times she had ever had on a date. They dined in a restaurant on the roof of a new hotel. Several times during the evening, people stopped dancing to watch them cut a rug. They parked again in front of her apartment. This time he kissed her several times. He admitted that he was a little shy. She told him she thought they might have made one step toward getting him out of that.

Charles wanted to get an early start the next morning. He had to drive all the way across Alabama to be at his starting place for work on Monday. They made no definite plans for a future trip, only that he would make it as soon as possible.

Several weeks went by before he returned. Maureen felt they were both more excited to see each other than before. They had only talked on the phone once. Their weekend was a repeat of the first, but with a little more serious conversation. Charles was definitely looking at other job opportunities. He had her in mind.

A few more weeks went by. She had only one phone call from Charles. Then one morning, Mrs. Anders approached her with some news. Charles had quit his job. He was going into business with a man he had met in his travels. The job was going to be in New Cotswold, Mississippi. That was only a two or three hour drive away.

The job would be operating a distilling business. He would be full partner. Maureen laughed when she related her conversation with Mrs. Anders. She told her the only distilling business she knew about was whiskey. Mrs. Anders threw her hand to her mouth and said, "Not Charles!" Maureen had agreed, "No, not Charles."

He was busy settling into his new occupation, and it was almost three months before he made another trip to Memphis. He phoned two or three times, but said little about his work. Then he called to say he was coming to see her. Maureen found the change in him appealing. He was thinner and had a tan, and she was surprised at how rough his hands had gotten. He was actually somewhat handsome in a rugged way.

The weekend went too fast for both, and he rushed off Sunday morning. He explained little about his work other than the fact that he was doing it all. It was important in this start-up not to spend any more money than possible. Help in the form of additional labor would come later.

He told Mrs. Anders the same thing—not much. She was concerned he was working too hard. She did say, however, that it was not anything new to Charles. Tobacco farming was a hard life, and he was accustomed to it.

These quick visits went on for almost a year. Christmas came and went. He came for one night before Maureen left to go home to her parents for the holidays. He brought her a beautiful desk set with pen and pencil. In addition, there was a small box of stationery. Inside was his address. Charles Mullens, C/O Simpson's Store, Rt. 4, New Cotswold, Miss. She often wondered why she did not question that.

Spring break came around. He called and talked for a long time about how much he cared for her. He was quite happy in his new work. He knew she would be on spring break soon and wanted her to come to New Cotswold to visit. She had planned to go Vicksburg to be with her parents. Her mother was having a hard time with her father. She needed to spend time with her. She looked at a map: it was almost a straight shot from Memphis to Vicksburg. Going by New Cotswold would mean another hundred miles. Then she thought about it; she had a new Chevrolet coupe and was anxious to get it on the road, what the heck.

Charles made a reservation for her at the hotel in town. She thought that was sweet. He was not being presumptuous, even though they had reached that stage where she might have been tempted to stay with him had he asked. They arranged to meet at the hotel for dinner at seven. She wore a frilly new summer dress. He arrived in nice slacks, and a pretty sport coat. He looked nicer than she had ever seen him.

The hostess took them to their table in the hotel dining room. On the way, several people smiled and waved to Charles. She was impressed that he had made acquaintance with people in town. The two of them had been there for only a few minutes when Charles waved across the room.

A big, good-looking man came over to their table. He was casually dressed and had arms on him like hams. He had a crooked grin when Charles introduced him. This was Jonathan MacMorogh, his partner in business, though he made no mention of that fact. Charles asked him to join them. He declined, politely welcomed Maureen to town, said he had heard a lot about her, and left. Maureen liked his looks.

After dinner and a lot of catching up, Charles asked Maureen to come out to his place the next morning before she left for Vicksburg. She agreed. He gave directions; stay on the street the hotel was on until she came to Nap's store. From there it was eight more miles to Simpson's Store; he would meet her there at nine.

There was a late model Ford parked in front of the store. Charles was sitting in it with a big grin on his face. He got out, opened her car door, and told her to leave her car there. The road down to his place was rough and dusty; he did not want her to get the new car dirty. The car he was in was one of those business coupes like traveling salesmen drove. It appeared to have larger tires on the rear than the front, not an important thing for her to question.

The first two miles were not that bad; the road was gravel and not too rough. But at the crossroad, things changed. Maureen explained to Jack that they had paved the road since, but thirty years ago, it was almost impassable. The car was either in the old ruts or on the high ground alongside. They bounced, and dust settled all around them. She did not know how anyone could challenge the road when it was muddy.

They finally came to an area where the road was sandy and much smoother. Corn grew on both sides. She could see an old barn in the distance. Up ahead there was another group of trees making a canopy over the road. They passed under the canopy and arrived at a lot outlined with logs. Charles jumped out of the car, ran around, and opened the door for Maureen.

She said now, "You could see Charles beaming with pride at what he was getting ready to present. About twenty paces, he parted some shrubbery. This is what I saw." She waved her arm, taking in the garden where she and Jack now sat. "Not quite all there is now, but at least half as much. The most beautiful gardens I had ever seen. Charles planted most of these same flowering bushes, the same perennials. I was amazed. He guided me to this very settee, sat me down, and put his arm around me. He told me he had done all of this plus the vegetable garden. He pointed it out. There were butter beans, corn, carrots, turnip greens, cucumber, onions, you name it. We sat by the stream for a long while, saying nothing. It was idyllic. Then he told me to follow; he wanted me to see his house."

She took Jack by the hand and led him over the bridge and up the path. First he saw the tin roof, and then as the shrubs parted, there stood the cute house. The paint was a pale yellow with light blue shutters. French doors stood open. The glass in the doors as well as the windows sparkled. The windows were old sash windows with the bottom half raised. The lace curtains swayed gently with the breeze. As they got to the steps leading to the porch, Jack could see that the inside of the house was stark white.

Inside, it was a studio and gallery. There were Choctaw Indian artifacts displayed on shelves, some in glass cases. Many of the paintings, signed by Maureen, were quite good. Quilts lined several walls. There were clay pots on a shelf and a small placard indicated that Letitia Mullens had fired them. Some were dated. Maureen let Jack wander around the rooms.

"When Charles and I got to this point that day," she said, "this little house was the typical tenant house of the time. Board and batten exterior walls, tin roof, screened porches and windows. Inside was sparsely furnished but very clean, very comfortable. Everything including the tiny kitchen was spotless. It was spring, but there was wood in the fireplace, ready if the weather turned cool. Of course, there were vases of fresh cut flowers. Charles was beaming with pride. I was so excited, so pleased."

"Then we sat on the front porch and admired the view from this side of the stream. Charles showed me where he planned to build the big house. He showed me where he would put a dam and make a lake. Then he told me more. There were five hundred acres in this tract. It belonged to Jonathan MacMorogh, whom we had met the night before. Jonathan was his partner, but that was never to be public knowledge. Their venture together was outside the MacMorogh Companies. This was Jonathan's own money, with no ties to the corporation."

"Charles had put up no money. He had very little and certainly not enough for much of an investment. His equity was sweat equity; he did all the work. They split profits fifty-fifty. With Charles' portion, he could buy Jonathan out at some point. He would own it all."

It was then that Maureen asked Charles several questions, all at once. Where was the business, where did he work, how in the world did he navigate that road every day.

Charles turned to Maureen and took her hand before he dropped the bomb. He told her, "On this property are cool springs for water. I grow my own grain. I have four stills and five cool caves for storage. I make whiskey."

Maureen said that a big battering ram slammed into her breastbone when he answered. All the air rushed from her lungs. She could not get her breath and felt she was going to faint. She shook her head to try to clear it and not pass out. When she caught her breath, she could not speak.

"This man, this man who only moments before had successfully shown me enough to convince me he was the man that I would marry someday told me he was engaged in an illegal activity. He was a damn moonshiner!" Maureen was reliving the day, and tears welled in her eyes.

Then she began to laugh, wiping her eyes. "That fool, God I miss him." She continued, "I looked at him and asked him didn't he know that he was going to end up in jail. Did he not know that what he was doing was illegal? No wonder he lived at the end of the damn world! Those flowers would one day line his grave! That was what he was doing, making his own cemetery."

Jack was chuckling. "Maureen," he said, "it sounds like you were really mad."

She cackled, "You better believe it."

Jack asked her, "Then what happened?"

"I stormed out to that little Ford to get my purse. I was going to walk out of here. When I opened the door to get the purse, I saw that the keys were still in the car. Charles was a little dumbfounded by my fast exit. He was following along behind me, 'bout fifty yards, saying. 'Now Maureen, just wait.'"

She said to him, "No, you wait, mister!" She got the little Ford started, but killed the engine trying to turn around. He caught up with her before she could get the car started again. "He opened the door, politely pushed me across the seat, and then drove me back to my car.

"On the way, he talked. He said that it was evident by the amount of whiskey they were selling that there was a huge market for moonshine. They were selling in large amounts to others who actually distributed the liquor. They sold as far away as Memphis and New Orleans. If they were not doing this, someone else would be. He seemed to think that made it alright."

He told her that Jonathan had many connections. The sheriff might raid occasionally, but there was no problem; he looked the other way for a few bucks. Charles did not see any great risk in what he was doing. People in town did not seem to think badly of him, except maybe the Baptists. It was not just the money, he said. It was the work; he loved the hard labor. He was outside all the time and was healthier than he had ever been.

He felt challenged to make better and better product. He made some of the best scuppernong wine ever tasted, and his peach brandy was supreme. Maureen was ready to scream, and she did. "You are a damn fool!"

Even before the car stopped rolling, she had the door open. The minute it stopped, she jumped out to run to her car. Charles just sat there. She pulled her car around next to his. "Good-bye, Charles, take a good look now. You will never see this face again!" She went to Vicksburg.

Back at school, she did not have the heart to tell Mrs. Anders about her discovery. When asked about her trip, she said simply, "I do not think it is going to work out between Charles and me."

However, by the time she had gotten back, there was also a letter from Charles. She ignored it. The letter lay around on Maureen's bedside table for several days, maybe a week. It was long enough for her anger to subside enough to make a decision about whether to open it or not. She decided to rip it up. She placed the thumb and forefinger of both hands together across the envelope to rip it in half and then stopped. She took a nail file, used it as a letter opener. The short note dropped out.

Dear Maureen,

It was obvious from your anger and rapid departure this morning that you were not pleased with my occupation. Nor do I believe you heard anything else I had to say.

There is one thing that I must know and I ask you please to give me an answer. If, when I took your hand to tell you in all truthfulness about my whiskey making, I had instead asked you to marry me, what would you have said? I have been honest and forthright with you. Please do the same for me.

I will love you for as long as I may draw breath.

Sincerely,

Charles Mullens

It was Sunday morning. Maureen fully intended to go to church. Instead, she crawled back in bed and began to cry. One of her roommates tapped on her door and asked her if she was going to church; she muttered no. She stayed in bed all afternoon, alternately napping and then waking and crying more. Why had she fallen for Charles? God, what a mistake.

The more she thought about it, though, the more she decided she should at least respond to his note.

Dear Charles,

Yes.

Your friend,

Maureen

The ball was back in his court. Apparently, it was there to stay. He did not respond for several weeks.

Dear Maureen,

Thank-you. When I shake hands with somebody to seal a deal, it is a contract, a contract as tight as the promises made in wedding vows. I shook hands with Jonathan MacMorogh to seal the deal to be his partner. I cannot, nor will I, break it.

Your friend,
Charles

When the school session was over, she took a summer job with the Parks Department managing a swimming pool. It was simple; she oversaw the lifeguards, tested the chemical content of the water, and made sure the facility was clean. She had lots of time to think. She relived that day at Charles' beautiful little house: the stream, the gardens, and Charles.

He was as happy as lark doing what he was doing, carefree as a bird about the thought of going to jail. He had friends in town, and Jonathan seemed likable enough. How lonely could it possibly be out there all by himself? That was how Charles kept busy, the flowers, the cute house spic and span, his whiskey making. With that, she muttered to herself, "Damn fool."

Her mind often wandered back to Moon. One day, on the spur of the moment, she called information in New Cotswold for the office of the Superintendent of Schools. She asked the operator who answered for the number.

The operator replied. "No need to call there, ain't nobody home, honey. Herman and Lessie went to Mobile; Janelle had her baby, a girl, six pound five ounces, twenty inches long. They named her Sally. That Janelle was up walking around two hours later. If I was you, I would call back to the house late Saturday. You know Herman well as I do, he ain't going to miss Men's Bible Class Sunday morning, he ain't ever missed, and you know that."

No, Maureen did not know all of that, but she did not let on. She needed more information. She asked for and got the residence number of Herman Hewitt, Superintendent of Schools. Saturday afternoon, as suggested, she called.

He answered. "Grandpa Herman here, they are all fine, baby is prettiest I ever saw." The Hewitt family was still on cloud nine.

Maureen introduced herself and told Mr. Hewitt why she was calling. She would like to have an application for employment. Mr. Hewitt asked a few questions. She told him where she had gone to college. She had taught first grade for two years in Memphis. She wanted to move a little closer to her parents, who lived in Vicksburg. They were both teachers also. Then Mr. Hewitt asked if her parents were Kate and Hugh Wilson, and she responded that they were. He knew them both.

Mr. Hewitt sounded elated. He told her that rather than send an application, why not just come on down for an interview. He bet that they could work something out. He needed a second grade teacher for the fall.

The pool was closed on Mondays, so on the following Sunday, Maureen drove to New Cotswold. She had seen a boarding house across the street from the school when she had been there before. She was sure that that was where single teaches stayed during the school year.

Mrs. Farmer had a room for the night. Supper was at six. Within twenty minutes, Mrs. Farmer knew everything she could possibly need to know about Maureen. When she found out she was in town for an interview with Herman Hewitt, she rolled her eyes. She said, "Honey, you are now the new second grade teacher for next year. That Herman, he has a thing for pretty teachers, and you sure fit that bill. I feel so sure of it that I will give you the front room upstairs on the east corner. Good view of the street, you can see all the coming and going, and being on the east, it is cooler in the afternoon."

Mrs. Farmer was right. Herman Hewitt hired her on the spot. Teachers meetings would start the last week in August, right after the county fair. She took the room, paid a small deposit, and drove back to Memphis, composing a letter of resignation from the Memphis School as she drove. What would she tell Mrs. Anders; what would she tell her parents?

Maureen arrived at Mrs. Farmer's boarding house in the middle of August, one week prior to the beginning of teacher orientation meetings. Sure enough, the front east corner room was hers, as Mrs. Farmer promised. Three other teachers checked in early, including one male, Kim Lockwood. The boarding house was female. Two houses down from the main house was a duplex with six rooms for males only. All meals were served in the main house; the only rooms open to both male and female were the dining room and the parlor.

Kim seemed nice enough, actually too nice to suit Maureen. She would bet on him wearing lace underwear. It was Kim, however, who suggested that the three other girls along with he and Maureen take in an afternoon at the county fair. There would be harness racing. That appealed to Maureen. They all piled into her Chevrolet, Kim sitting in the back seat between two of the other girls. He seemed happy as a lark to be in their company.

They arrived at the fairgrounds half an hour before the races began, giving them time to stroll around and look at some of the exhibits prior to race time. In the agriculture barn were exhibits of every vegetable and fruit known to man. At the corn booth, Maureen laughingly asked the woman who was working the booth if they had any samples of corn whiskey. The woman pinched up her mouth as if she might have bitten into a green persimmon. She managed to squeeze out a "No" between her tight lips. Later, Maureen told the others that the woman's mouth looked like the thing under a cat's tail. Only Kim laughed. This would be the first of a number of times that she would shock the rest.

After they took seats for the races, a man and woman took seats several rows in front. The man was Jonathan MacMorogh. As he was working his way to his seat, he glanced back and for a moment made eye contact with Maureen. He did not seem to recognize her. However, several times during the races, he turned again to look back. He never nodded or smiled to acknowledge recognition. Perhaps he did not remember who she was.

Two weeks later, school started, and Maureen began teaching a full second grade with twenty-six kids. They had parent-teacher night and introduced the teachers to the parents attending. The following Thursday, the weekly newspaper had a brief article welcoming the new teachers to town. There was a picture along with a brief bio of each. Maureen decided that if Charles Mullens did in fact read the newspaper, he had no intention of making contact. Two weeks passed, and she had heard nothing from him.

A few weeks, and she settled into a weekly routine that did not include a lot of activity outside the schoolroom. She met several other men besides Kim who lived in the all-male boarding house, but she dated none. She even got so bored that she went to Vicksburg one weekend to visit her parents.

One of the other teachers, Carla, was a Methodist and insisted each Sunday that Maureen attend church with her. Maureen had grown up in the Methodist Church, but during college, had gotten out of the habit of attending regularly. There came a Sunday when it was pouring rain. Carla usually walked the three blocks to church, but that day it was not possible. Maureen agreed to attend services for no other reason than to give her a ride.

Seating was already close to full capacity when they arrived. The usher led them down the left aisle along the outside windows. Halfway down, he found a row of pews with vacant space. He extended the Sunday Bulletin to the women, and they slid into the row. Maureen sat on the aisle. Carla sat alongside, with room for another person or two in the center.

Maureen was busy reading the items in the bulletin when the usher again appeared at their row. He extended his hand in a motion to ask the two girls to slide inward on the pew to allow another worshipper to take a seat. Maureen took hold of her purse. Carla slid down, and so did she.

At about the same time, she glanced to her left to see who was moving into the seat she had occupied. There, with a big grin wrapped around those awful teeth, was Charles Mullens. He nodded to Maureen, then leaned forward to look past Maureen and greet the other girl. He leaned toward Maureen's ear and whispered, "Sorry I am late." Maureen was red as beet.

There was a clearing of a throat somewhere. Down about three rows in front, a head turned and looked back. Then that head leaned to the one next to it, and in a minute, that head stole a glance back also. Then across the aisle, the same thing happened. They were looking back at her, at Charles, or at both.

The organ played the opening for the first hymn. Then as the singing began, the most beautiful baritone voice she could ever remember came from her side. Not only could the man dance; he could sing.

Maureen could not relate one single word from the sermon. She was stunned. All she could think of was what she was going to say after church. She sure had not expected this to be the venue for meeting up with Charles. Time came for the collection plate to pass and the singing of the offertory hymn. As it began, the woman directly in front turned and smiled her approval at Charles. Maureen opened her purse and crumpled two one-dollar bills in her hand. When the plate passed, she laid them down alongside the brand new fifty-dollar bill that Charles contributed.

The final hymn, was completed, and the minister said the dismissal prayer. The woman in front of them immediately turned to Charles, stuck her finger toward him, and said. "We have to get you in our choir, young man." Her husband behind made eye contact with Charles; he knew him for more than his voice.

Charles stepped into the aisle, allowed the women to pass, and followed as they worked their way toward the vestibule of the church. The minister and his wife were shaking hands and wishing all well in the coming week.

Maureen heard her name, "Miss Maureen, Miss Maureen," and sure enough, hastily squeezing through behind her was one of her students. Past the child, Maureen saw her mother, president of the PTA. She was waving a hand and a hanky. Behind her stood the father, the local pharmacist and president of the Chamber of Commerce. He nodded and spoke, "Morning, Miss Wilson, howdy, Moon." What better two than these to spread the word all over town.

"Guess who we saw at church this morning. Why, it was Miss Maureen, and with the bootlegger. Now my husband is the one who says he is a bootlegger; that is why his nickname is Moon. How in the world would I know?"

Maureen put her arm around the shoulder of her student. They all worked their way out of the church, receiving their greeting from the preacher. The rain was still falling, and umbrellas unfolded. Maureen was speechless. She had to introduce Carla and actually stuttered as she did so. Charles bowed slightly and said, "My pleasure, Carla. Now, I would be pleased if you ladies joined me at the hotel for their famous Sunday buffet."

Immediately, Carla said, "Oh no, I already put my name on the list for dinner at Mrs. Farmer's. That would be a waste."

Charles turned to Maureen. "Then will you join me?" She accepted. She drove Carla back the three blocks to the boarding house before joining Charles. He waited under the cover of the hotel gallery. As she parked, he ran out to open her door and cover her with his umbrella. Inside, Charles spoke with the hostess and motioned toward a table in the far corner near the windows. The crowd was sparse today. Maureen at this point saw no one she knew. After they sat, she gained enough composure to ask, "How did you know I was in church today?"

"I didn't," Charles said. "I saw a white Chevrolet coupe outside and remembered it was like yours. Then I looked closer and saw the red 'T' from the University of Tennessee in the back window. That was a real coincidence. When I got inside, I would not let the usher seat me until I spotted you.

"Now my turn," Charles said. "What are you doing here?"

"I teach second grade in the grammar school."

"And how long have you been here?" he asked.

After they had gone through the buffet line, Maureen told him the whole story. How she thought about his letter, how she made the decision to leave Memphis. No, she did not tell his sister where she was going, nor why. She only said that she needed to be closer to her parents and was going to look for an opening in a school that would be closer to Vicksburg.

Then Charles said, "Then you have not totally written me off the books because of—"

Before he could finish, Maureen interrupted. She said, "No. Somebody's got to love you; it might as well be me." Charles caught on to what she said. He had told her somebody was going to make whiskey and it might as well be him. They both laughed, and he put his hand across hers.

That began the reconciliation. Maureen, with Charles' help, was very discreet about their romance. She never let him pick her up at the boarding house. Most often, she drove to Simpson's Store, and he met her there; the road was still a mess.

At Christmas time, Maureen asked Charles to go with her to Vicksburg to meet her parents. They drove over early on Christmas Day. Charles had a large basket of food items from Nap's store: smoked ham, sausages, fresh fruit preserves, and small homemade fruit pies.

During the day, they did not talk about Charles' occupation other than to say that he farmed. Before they left, Maureen's mother whispered to her that she approved. She also advised her that an expensive wedding was out of the question. Maureen told her not to worry.

After New Year's, when school was back in session, she received a note in her box to make an appointment with the principal as soon as possible. She went in that same day.

He assured her that it was not the place of the school principal to delve into the personal lives of the faculty. *Unless*, of course, there might be something that would affect the teacher's ability to effectively teach. That meant more than just classroom activity. It meant setting a good example.

There had been conversation from faculty as well as parents, suggesting that her relationship with a known bootlegger was not setting a good example. Children heard things at home, and what impression might they have if they heard disapproving remarks about their teacher? He reminded her of the meetings that would occur in February to discuss next year's contracts. Then he emphatically stated, "You must be more discreet; we would hate to lose you."

Under her breath, she muttered, "So much for the idea of stocking my desk with half pints to sell to second graders."

She and Charles continued to be discreet, so much so that no one knew when they were married. The week after the conversation with the principal, they drove to Biloxi, and a Justice of the Peace married them. She did not move out of the boarding house, mainly because of the bad road from their house to down. She spent weekends in that house and not in Vicksburg, as most believed. She got a new teaching contract for the following year.

During the summer, she helped harvest and grind corn, fire the stills, make home brew and corn whiskey, and ferment wine. She got better at the wine making than Charles was and experimented with various fruits and berries. Charles graded the road, spread gravel, and bought an old truck for her to use if the weather was bad and the road muddy. The following school year, she commuted. The principal again warned her early on in the school year that her contract was in jeopardy. She offered that it would be a shame to have to fight it in court. However, that would not be necessary. She was pregnant, and she would not seek a position the next year anyway.

The school administration thought they were through with her then, but just wait. Six years later, she would have a student in school herself. God help them.

26

Jack took a few notes and taped most of the visit. He was eager to hold the thoughts and to transfer Maureen's feeling to paper. It was a typical Wednesday, with everything in town closed for the afternoon. It was quiet, his room cool. It was almost seven by the time he quit working, and he was hungry. The Bus Station Café around the corner never closed. A hamburger and fries would suffice. Then maybe he would bring home a big container of ice and then imbibe a bit more of that wonderful concoction that Maureen sent with him. Better call Adrianna before doing that, however. He wanted to tell her about the wonderful life of Maureen and Moon.

Adrianna reported the latest on Miss Penny. She was fine, but the Bentley needed servicing. She felt that Jack would prefer to do that rather than have Adrianna do it.

With that, Jack exclaimed, "I might rather neither of us did that."

Adrianna answered back, "Come on, Jack, she has adopted us. There is no family other than the worthless niece. We are the only ones who seem to care for her." Then she had a question. "Are you returning to New Cotswold next week?"

"Yes, I have some legwork left to do. I still have people to talk with, and I need to check some courthouse records."

Adrianna then asked, "What is the possibility of me tagging along? I need a day or two away from here."

Jack was elated, "Oh, you sure may. That is terrific!"

"The way you describe Laura's Lodge, I thought maybe I could sit on the front porch and read, snooze, and explore while you work. Then maybe after you are done, we could go skinny-dipping in that cold creek you mention. Maybe come back to the house for some you know what."

"Why not some you know what in the creek?"

"If it is as cold as you say, your little pee pee might not be up to it," she teased.

"Right you are!" Jack replied. "Let's talk more when I get home."

He went around the corner to the bus station and got a hamburger and fries and the ice as planned. Back at the room, he raised the bottom half of one of the high windows to step onto the balcony with a view of the street below. This was a day of information overload. He would be glad for Will to be back and to finish the interviews. Each person he interviewed raised more questions in his mind as to what was ahead.

The following morning, he found June in her office and thanked her for the wonderful room and the service before heading for another visit with Miss Annie. He enjoyed the morning; Miss Annie was such a delight. He loved how she did not mince words. As promised during his first visit, she wanted to talk about her girls, the doctors, Beatrice and Carole Anne. Oh, she was so proud of both. The fact that neither was married did bother her. She related the story about Dr. Bea and her fellow, an RAF pilot who had died early on in the war. Miss Annie had met Beatrice's friend and companion, Dr. Bradshaw. It seemed to her that they had a good relationship.

Carole Anne was another story. She might never get married. In the opinion of Miss Annie, she was too self-centered. She was going to be high maintenance, and that would take some patience. Carole Anne had never had to worry about anything; whatever she needed or wanted at any time in her life, she got. Miss Annie was very emphatic. "She has her own money, and lots of it."

Carole Anne pleased her in another way, however. She had a wonderful diversion from medicine. She enjoyed studying the company and the many facets of the businesses. In telling this part, Miss Annie revealed how much she herself was involved.

It was interesting that when Carole Anne and Jonathan got together, they might talk for hours about business. Carole Anne was visionary, and Miss Annie said, "She continually looks into the future and what the company might be doing ten, twenty, fifty years down the road.

"For example," Miss Annie pointed out, "Look at Jonathan's idea for small drive-in grocery stores incorporated into some of our gas stations. Immediately Carole Anne wanted to call them convenience stores. Over a period of a month, studying as time allowed, she came up with not only an inventory for such a store but the placement of items in the store."

Jonathan wanted to consider a drive-in type store where clerks came out on roller skates, took orders, and filled them while the customer sat in the car smoking a cigarette. Very quickly, Carole Anne had said no. She had figured the cost of carhops; she'd talked to owners of drive-in hamburger joints. The conclusion was that the worst part of the business was carhops. There was tremendous turnover, injuries, and squabbling among themselves, with men hanging around.

Then Carole Anne showed Jonathan how she perceived placing inventory. She wanted impulse items along the way to the milk, or the bread, or the cigarettes. Those would be primary sellers. People would see gum, candy, and potato chips on the way to them. Jonathan was very impressed. The first model would open in the fall. Carole Anne planned to cut the ribbon.

When she and Jonathan discussed the cost of one of those stores, it was apparent that one company, even as large as theirs, could tie up a fortune rather quickly. Carole Anne had an answer: get three or four of their own operating successfully and then franchise them. The company attorneys were presently researching that plan. Miss Annie's conclusion: "If we were in need, Carole Anne could and would take over a leadership role in the companies."

The last thing Jack discussed with Miss Annie, or tried to, was the crash that killed Will's parents. Miss Annie diverted from that very quickly. "You need to discuss that with my husband."

To which Jack responded, "I get the feeling that may never happen."

"Oh shush," Miss Annie said. "He is reading the same manuscripts as the rest of us. He is impressed with how thorough you are. However, I will assure you of this: he will be the final interview. He will see to that." Will left Miss Annie after learning more about Dr. Bea and Carole Anne. He did feel better about the General after Miss Annie's comment.

Jack went to the cabin Will called his rehab center and found the key where Jonathan had told him to look. The place smelled musty. He opened windows, turned on ceiling fans, and started a window air-conditioner in the bedroom. He laughed at the cupboards in the kitchen—completely stocked with booze. Will had called it his security blanket. He could always escape if need be. Sounded like Maudie Lee and her cigarettes.

Jack puttered around the little house and then walked a ways down the path toward the back of the property. What a beautiful site. By the time he got back to the house, he was hungry and thinking about the great hamburger he and Will had enjoyed at the Toot. He closed the house and reminded himself how to get to the drive-in. He pulled headfirst into the parking spot and then flashed his lights. Through his rearview mirror, he could see that the girl Will had introduced as Holly Porterfield was not the one skating to him. The girl glided up, leaned on the window frame, and asked, "Can I hep' ya," a standard carhop sales approach.

Jack asked about Holly; she was on break. He asked if she might come to the car when she was through. He explained that Holly was an old friend, and he wanted to surprise her. The girl smiled and glided away.

Holly came moments later, looked inquisitively at Jack. "Since when're you my ol' friend? I don't believe I know you."

Jack explained that he had been there a week or so before, with Will MacMorogh. Then she remembered and wanted to know where Will was. Jack told her he was in Europe. She was amazed. Then she said, "How you comin' with your reportin'? Will told all yet?"

Jack said, "How well do you know him?"

She stuck her hand out flat and wobbled it a time or two, "So so. Why'd you ask?"

"Trying to get a little background from people he knew growing up. Have you always lived here? "Jack asked.

"All my life."

"Did you know Jack back during his school years?"

"I knew who he was, that's 'bout all. He was a football star, good lookin', rich, but I 'm younger. I was only in sixth grade when he was a senior," she said.

"When I was in here with him a while back, he seemed to know you pretty well."

"That come later." Then she said, "Look I gotta' get an order or get goin'."

Even though he was hungry, the thought of a greasy hamburger and fries no longer was appealing. Instead, he ordered a chocolate milk shake. Holly skated off. When she came back, she placed the tray on the windowsill and handed Jack the bill. He paid and then gave her a ten-dollar tip, "For your time." he said.

Before she left, she asked, "What all 's Will tellin' you? Lotta' people have heard about you writin' a book 'bout him. That scares the hell out of a few folks."

"What is there to be afraid of?" Jack asked.

"Oh, he knows stuff 'bout a few people that would be bad to get out, even now. Thanks, nice talkin' to you, gotta' go."

However, later, before she took the tray away, Jack said, "I would like to talk to you some more. Think that might be possible?"

"I git off work here at four, then go to my second job and don't git off 'til eight. Sometimes I go to the Six Mile Club after work. You know where that is?"

"Yes," Jack said, "I am staying at Will's cabin not far from there. Maybe I will see you at the Six Mile Club later."

"The rehab center?" she asked.

Jack replied, "Yes, you know it?"

She looked at him and winked, "Do I ever!" and skated off.

Jack drove out of the Toot, his appetite not satisfied. He realized that he probably should have gone ahead and eaten something. He would think of something more substantial for supper. There was a fifty-five gallon drum converted to a grill out back at the rehab center. He remembered seeing charcoal in the pantry with the booze.

Maybe later he would go by Nap's store, as Will had suggested, and get a steak and something to go with it. He would cook his own dinner and sip some more of Maureen's concoction.

Nap's store was a big white two-story building. Jack determined from the curtains in the upper windows that Nap might live on the premises. Inside, the store was unusually dark, but it was cool and looked well stocked. The meat counter was in the rear of the store. He could hear a meat saw running.

He made only a couple of steps inside when a booming voice startled him. Jack did not see the man behind the voice, but he kept walking toward it. He got closer to the cash register, and sitting on a stool behind it was one of the blackest men he had ever seen, whose head looked as though it could have been carved from obsidian. There was a small rim of white hair above the ears, and the man had chiseled frown lines in his forehead. He had a big grin, with gold teeth.

"Well, come on in, stop at that box and get you a cold Coca-Cola. No money, just mash down on that handle, one will tumble out." Jack did as instructed, and out tumbled a bottle. As he opened it, the drink immediately turned to slush, and before he could take a sip, it started running out over the top. Jack put his lips to the bottle and captured the wonderful iced drink.

"Just like I like them," Nap said. "Wish I could make 'em that way all time. They need to stay in the box about twenty-four hours. I told the Coca-Cola man he could make more money if they could figure out how to sell 'em frozen like that."

Nap went on, "Not two of ya'll, so you ain't from the Church of Latter Day Saints. Ain't three of ya'll, so you ain't trying to get me registered to vote. So I say one white boy by hisself must be lost." Then he chuckled. "So what can I do for you?"

Jack extended his had to shake. "I'm a friend of Will MacMorogh; he suggested I stop by if I ever wanted to buy good meat. Said you had the best in town. "

In order to shake Jack's hand, the man had to get off the stool to reach across the counter. He was taller than Jack had thought, with wide shoulders and narrow through the chest. Again, the booming voice, "Best you turn around and get right out the door. I know you lyin'. That Will ain't got friends in this part of the world." A big grin crossed his face before he stuck out his hand to take Jack's. "Nap Marrs," he said.

"You must be the famous journalist from New Orleeeans," he drug out the name. "I expected you might drop by. Let's go sit." Nap led Jack to two old cane bottom chairs propped against the wall. "My friend Winston says you are alright for a white boy from the big city. Miss Tilda says you are a dahlin'."

Jack told him that he had had more fun with them at supper one night than he had had in a long time. He cherished their friendship.

"So, tell me what I might do to help you?" asked Nap. "I do know that your objective is to chronicle the family history from as far back as you can to the present day. You are going to chronicle the business as well. That correct?"

Jack verified that it was. He could tell from the man's speech and the clarity of his voice that "Nap" was well educated. He just enjoyed falling into that "Po' ole darky" role on occasion.

"Beginning with Seamus, the family has had its share of financial success; it has also had its share of family tragedy. Now, you are not going to find any family connection to any other MacMoroghs before Seamus. I know, I have spent many hours researching. I have not been successful." Jack agreed with that statement, but still it puzzled him.

"The big question I have, and probably you also, is where did Seamus acquire all of the money he came here with? Some said whiskey making. Maybe that is true. My theory is based on something I read about England sending lots of money over at one time in history and the ships were lost. Some say that he might have gotten away with some of it."

Nap continued. "Fact is, though, wherever the money came from, Seamus laid the foundation for a great company and all the wealth. Course, he almost lost it, William came along and helped salvage it. He and Miss Annie, and give her lots of credit, made it stronger. Now, in my opinion, Jonathan and Winston Jackson are taking it to a much higher level.

"You may not know this. There was a time when Winston Jackson's money and that of his mother, Maudie Lee, was an important part of the survival of the companies. When Seamus died, he had many folks in his will. Darn near everybody that had been important in his life got something. Most all of them took their money and ran." Jack was well aware of that fact.

"The family was wealthy, but cash poor. Cash was important for the bank to survive, especially with the plan William had. Nobody trusted William. Winston kept his share of the inheritance in the bank. So did Maudie Lee."

Jack had wondered about Winston's involvement. It now was clear. He had not only been a great mentor to Jonathan as a boy. To a degree, he shared ownership.

He told Nap that he had shed a new light on things and that frankly, he had wondered about Winston's position. He knew Winston was a good businessman, a very good man all round.

Nap replied, "What you wondered was how a colored man could be sitting in such a responsible position in that company." Nap said emphatically, "Let me tell you one other thing, and I expect you already know about this. Miss Tilda had a very responsible and an important part also. She practically raised both those boys, Jonathan and Will."

They chatted longer about various things. Most of what Nap told Jack was repetitive. However, what he heard from Nap made it more credible, based on how Nap got his information, first hand.

It seemed that Miss Annie usually went to bed early. William had trouble sleeping, regardless of when he went to bed, especially after the crash that killed William, Jr. and his wife.

"William," Nap seemed to dislike calling him 'General,' "would walk the mile down here from the house and sit with me 'til I closed. Sometimes we talked. Others, we just sat and smoked our pipes. This was when my wife was still here, God rest her. She would call down and tell William to go home. It was time for me to be in bed."

"Was there ever much discussion about the crash?"

"Like what?" asked Nap.

"I have read old newspaper accounts from the Birmingham paper. At one point, there was suspicion of foul play," said Jack.

"Well, I will tell you what I do know. After the accident, the town was a mess. The tragedy hurt many people. The Lamar family that William, Jr.'s wife came from was large; they had close friends. Then there were all of the people working for the company. Talk was about nothing else for days. Every rumor you can imagine circulated about and added on to."

Nap went on to give Jack a long list of rumors. He did tell him something he had not heard. With all of the upheaval in town, nobody seemed to pay attention to the fact that a lone car still sat at the airport. It sat there for a week or so. Miss Annie's help mentioned it to Nap. He made a mental note, but did not think much about it. He had seen it there also, a big Chrysler. Then one day, two men drove up to the gas pumps in front of Nap's store. They were in the Chrysler. A Mississippi Highway Patrolman followed in his car. Nap went out to wait on the men in the Chrysler. They wanted the car filled with gas, the oil checked, and windshield cleaned. Nap went to work.

The Highway patrolman asked if Nap might have a big paper bag. Nap directed him inside to his wife. The patrolman returned with a bag and instructed the two men to collect everything in the car. Nap made note; there were candy wrappers, paper cups, a map, and things like that.

When it came time to pay, the patrolman paid from a fold of money bound with a rubber band, and then went to a pay phone inside the store, made a long distance call. His wife heard him say they had the car with no problem and it was on the way.

Jack surmised that Junius might have been the driver. He did not care to share that thought. He asked Nap if William knew about the car.

Nap responded that he had advised William, who made no comment whatsoever. William was bitter after the deaths and admitted that he and Miss Annie were having problems. She was blaming him. Nap said that many others beside her were doing the same, maybe with good cause. According to him, William had become very powerful because he had the money to do so. He spread his money around in political campaigns to get favoritism. He also made some enemies. That was for sure.

A month or so after the crash, William sat with Nap, drinking a little, but not drunk. He told Nap that Governor Jenkins' old lady was running her mouth. She had a penchant for the booze, and young highway patrolmen who were supposed to be her bodyguards. She had gone out to a club in Jackson…

Jack had heard this same story from Miss Annie, but out of courtesy to Nap, he let him reiterate it again. Jack made no comment. Nap's version added credibility. Then Nap talked about the airplane. William told Nap that he had felt something was wrong. Nap had never flown, was not going to, so what William told him about the airplane did not make a lot of sense, but he related it to Jack anyway.

Jack asked Nap, "Did William ever say anything about foul play after he heard the comment from Jenkins' wife?"

Nap replied, "All he ever said was, he who laughs last, laughs loudest." Then he changed the subject. "How do you feel Will 's getting along?"

Jack said, "I have only known Will for five or six weeks. I know enough to know life has not been kind to him at times. He seems to be doing well now."

Nap said, "Well, you have a lot in store; he has had a hard time. What I hear is good, and I pray that it is true. He has had enough tragedy in his life." Nap went on to say, "Come back sometime, after you and Will talk some more. I might be able to add a few things. Only for credibility, you understand."

When it was time to go, Jack said, "I really did come here to get a big steak."

Nap called back into the butcher shop and ordered up several T-bones for Jack to see. He selected one about two inches thick. Nap had the butcher wrap it, and then Jack went up front and got a couple of ears of fresh corn, a big red tomato, and a loaf of bread.

Nap said, "I would send along a little somethin' to sip on, but knowin' you are at the rehab center, you got all you need."

Jack tried to pay, and Nap refused. "I done got it on Will's charge account."

That evening, Jack prepared the steak, corn, tomatoes, and French bread all on the grill as Nap suggested. He sipped more of Maureen's concoction, straight over lots of ice. The steak was perfect, which was a surprise, since this was his first attempt on a barrel pit. He would have to treat Adrianna to a fine dinner, maybe on that same grill. Afterward he sat in a rocker on the screened porch, listening to cicadas and watching lightning bugs. He was at peace.

At a quarter to nine, beams from the headlights of a car washed across the front of the little cabin. The car, a late model Allstate from Sears and Roebuck, drove up the sandy driveway. Jack walked across the porch to unlatch the door, a New Orleans habit. Holly Porterfield trotted up the path to the front steps and stepped inside when Jack opened door. She stepped close and kissed him on the lips.

"Ummm, smells good, what're we drinking?" asked Holly.

"Plum punch," Jack replied and then showed her the half-gallon jug that Maureen had sent with him.

"It ain't near as pretty when it comes up," said Holly. "How 'bout I have a rum and Coca-Cola?" She went right to the cupboard, took down a half-full bottle of rum, then went to the refrigerator for a Coca-Cola and ice cubes. From another cupboard, she got a glass tumbler and bottle opener. She filled the tumbler with half rum, half Coca-Cola, and three ice cubes. She stirred it with her forefinger and took a sip. "Jus' right!" Next, she opened a drawer and got out two party napkins. She knew her way around.

Holly's hair was still wet, her cheeks shiny clean. Regardless of the obvious mileage, she was still quite pretty. What she had on, or more, what she did not have on, disturbed Jack a bit. He would welcome an informative visit, but nothing else. She looked like she might have other intentions. Her shorts might be paint, they were so tight. Her tube top covered very little.

They sat down in the front room, she in a big leather chair across from Jack. "So, what all do you do at night when you are in town?" she asked Jack.

"Catch up on my work and go to bed early," he said.

"I told you I go out to Six Mile club a lot. That's where I was going when I noticed your lights on. Lotta' dancin', lotta fellas lookin' for a good time. Most know me from the Toot. I 'm very popular out there."

Jack said he bet she was. He did not tell her why he thought so.

"You married?" Holly asked.

Jack held up his left hand to show there was no ring.

"Don't mean shit," Holly said. "Girlfriend?"

Jack said, "Yes."

"Steady?"

"Very!" Then Jack asked her, "You married?"

"You shittin' me? You'd seen my Momma and Daddy like I seen 'em, ain't no way. I seen that movie way too many times. Never git me into shit like that."

"Boyfriend?" Jack asked, duplicating her line of questioning.

"Lots," she replied. "Any time I need one."

Holly threw her right leg over the arm of the big wicker chair, exposing a thin line of red shorts bordered by a patch of white panty on each side. Jack glanced, and she grinned. Then she sat up, looked directly into Jack's eyes, and said, "What's Will told you about me?"

Jack said, "He only mentioned that you and several other girls had had a bad experience when you were growing up. I think it bothered him that life might not have been so easy on some of the girls as a result."

She took a strong swallow of the rum and Coca-Cola, leaned her head back in the chair, and closed her eyes. She said nothing. Jack thought she had dozed off; maybe too much booze.

"Who would've believed me anyway?" she said and then paused. "Me, the daughter of the town slut and her famous town drunk husband. Everybody in town knew that Momma would drop her panties for a quarter, and if you didn't have a quarter, she'd loan you one. I wasn't too squeaky clean either, had tits big as Momma when I was thirteen. I knew how to get whatever I wanted from boys. Besides that, it was always the warnin'. No one'll ever believe you. It was your fault to begin with. You should've been ashamed. Teasin' got you into this." She'd heard that over and over. "The others, same crap."

Holly said all the other girls felt the shame. Always it was their fault. Or the one that went, "We are not sinnin'. God has sent you to provide the love and affection that comes natural between two lovin' humans." Holly said that that was the common thread among all the stories.

Jack had to assume that she was referring to whomever or whatever it was that happened in the lives of all of them. He did not ask any more questions. Holly just started talking. Jack did ask if Holly knew how many more girls there were.

Five, that she knew of, maybe more. One would tell her closest friend, who had a close and dear friend that she would tell. The talk went on among them until most were aware of who the rest were.

"Oh, what the shit, I 've turned out better 'n the rest. I didn't have a lot goin' on for me, anyhow. What could you spect with my background?" Holly shrugged. "I ain't doing too bad, got two jobs, and git all my meals free where I work. I got a room that costs me eight dollars a week. I bought my car with money I saved from tips. Got it on time at Sears and Roebuck and did it without having to git anyone to kiss the note." Jack looked puzzled. "Cosigner, you know?" she said.

Jack asked about the others.

"Oh, some of them could still git hurt if the story got out. They always scared, still believe it was their fault. Who 'd believe them? One girl committed suicide when she was eighteen. I will always believe it was over that," she said. "Then another, she 's the worst off right now. She 's the daughter of a prominent family and engaged to a very religious young man, also from an equally prominent big man in town. There 's no doubt the boy thinks she is a virgin, wants to save her for the big night. She 's a nervous wreck. She 's talked to me and I am sure the others. Actually got down on her hands and knees in front of me and prayed to God that I would never forsake her. Sick, man, sick."

Jack then asked, "Why are you telling me all of this?"

" 'Cause Will knows 'bout it all. Everyone is afraid he 'll tell. You do know, regardless of the war hero and all that stuff, there are many people in this town think he 's no good. If you wanna' believe a lot you hear, he had a bad reputation with the ladies."

Holly stirred together another rum and Coca-Cola, mostly rum. She talked about what she might do someday. To leave New Cotswold was one of her greater ambitions. After a while she yawned, said she had to get home. She was too tired to go to Six Mile.   On leaving, she said, "It 's nice to be 'round a man who is not constantly tryin' to get in my pants. But lemme know if you 'd ever like to."

Jack tossed and tumbled through the night. He could not get over Holly and what she had to say. Jack was somewhat puzzled. Maybe Will would clear this up later.

27

As usual, Jack was up early, itching to get going. He wanted to catch Jonathan at breakfast at the hotel to discuss his plans to return the following week. Jonathan was at his usual table. Seated with him were two other people. He waved Jack over and introduced him to the two, but did not invite him to join them. He said they were having a quick meeting; Jonathan would join him in a few minutes. The other two people were Tom Moore, an attorney, and his wife Patricia. Jack made a note. He needed to interview her. She was Will's cousin on his mother's side.

When Jonathan did join Jack, he gave him good news and a message. Will was back and had been since Tuesday. He'd had problems to solve immediately upon his return, and the previous night was the first chance he'd had to call. He wanted Jack to call as soon as it was convenient.

Jack drove until after nine before stopping for gas at a service station with a row of phone booths. He got Will on the line, and the first thing Will asked was about his plans for the following week. He was anxious to get back to work on the project. Jack told him about his need to go back to New Cotswold for a few days and said that his plan was to do that the following week. Will changed that a bit, asking that they spend most of the day together Monday and Tuesday, working all day and having lunch together. Then maybe Jack could return to New Cotswold on Wednesday. That worked for Jack.

He got home in time to do what he had done several Fridays earlier. He showered, shaved, and dressed lightly, then mixed martinis. As soon as Adrianna arrived, they took care of the immediate and most pressing needs. Getting that out of the way took longer than expected. So long, in fact, that they decided to skip their Friday night social with friends. They grilled cheese sandwiches, lay on the couch in each other's arms, and talked until past midnight. Jack listened attentively to her week in review. Not much different at the paper; no new gossip.

Saturday was as usual. Jack caught up on some work. Adrianna made her weekly jaunt to Schwegmann's. In the afternoon, they visited Miss Penny. Jack committed to take the Bentley in for service as soon as possible. Yes, he would drive it himself. Yes, he would stay with the car until they completed the work. No, he would not put a scratch on it.

Sunday morning was tennis, then brunch at the Camellia grill. They spent the afternoon poring over all of their newspapers, editing some articles they read, and making notes of things to do the next week. Jack was back to his relaxed state. He loved his routine and could think of nothing better to be doing.

On Monday morning, Will was beaming when Jack got to the office. He had been in since seven, had had coffee made, and a couple of calls were out of the way. He was ready to hear about Jack's week in New Cotswold and then get their work underway.

Jack inquired if Will was up-to-date on reviewing his manuscripts. He was, and he liked what he had seen. He was anxious to move forward. Satisfied that he had read them all, Jack advised Will that he had not sent out the latest manuscripts to the others until he had verification, once again, that Will was willing to tell the world what they had last covered. Some of that material painted Will in a less than admirable light.

"It happened," was the only comment Will made.

They went to work where they had left off. There was no interruption until shortly before noon.

Mimi stuck her head in to ask if they were having lunch with Mr. Chacherie. Will had forgotten to mention it. They did have plans. They were meeting Chas and Sammie D'Antoni at the shop across from the French Market, the one owned by Sammie and his brothers.

Chas was in rare form. He told one tale after another in a Cajun accent that had them laughing until they cried. On a serious note, he touched on his plans to run for governor. During that discussion, he told Jack that he had a place for him on his campaign staff if in fact he did run. He wanted to discuss it later.

For the remainder of the two days, Will went from one year to the next and from one event to another, as if he was reading from a script. He was amazing. Once or twice, he turned silent and had to think a bit about what he was going to say next. A time or two, he almost lost his composure. He would sit still, look away, and wipe a tear from the corner of an eye. Then take deep a breath before plunging ahead. Jack could not believe that anyone other than a savant could have such memory.

However, in all they covered, there was never another word about Holly Porterfield. Twice Jack started to come right out and ask about her. But maybe this was something that had best be left alone for the time being.

After the two days, Will's contribution was drawing to a conclusion. Another morning or two together, and they would finish. Jack still had interviews and additional research of public records to do in New Cotswold. He might easily sum up his work in a week or two and then get busy putting his manuscripts together.

Tuesday evening when he got home, he found Adrianna with bags packed. She was humming and had her road map out. She was ready to get on the road. They left early Wednesday, stopping only long enough in Jackson to have lunch with Jack's father. They arrived in New Cotswold at mid-afternoon and went straight to the lodge. The fact that the house played such an important part in the history of the family was amazing. Adrianna had had a vision of the building based on Jack's description. Her vision was dead on. The mystery of the locked room intrigued her.

Jack prearranged dinner with Jonathan and June, who joined them in the hotel club at seven. June had a table set up in an alcove off the main room in the club. It was set for six. She explained that she knew Jack had not yet met Dr. Rubin. She had invited him to join them. Whether he showed up on time or at all, they would not know until he got there. In addition, she made sure there was room for an additional person, in case Dr. Rubin decided to bring a friend.

After they took seats, June summoned a waiter to order drinks. She sat so that she could see the bar and the door from her position. She was always working, always monitoring what was going on. No sooner did drinks arrive than she reached across and grasped Jonathan's forearm. "Don't turn around now, but you will never guess who Dr. Rubin has with him." She then said, "Here are our other guests." She stood, as did Jonathan and Jack.

Jonathan grinned broadly and said, "Imogene, what a pleasure to see you." He then acknowledged the doctor and made introductions. Jack smiled inwardly. He immediately knew who Imogene was. He also knew she was at least twenty years younger than the doctor. Jonathan sat there grinning. Dr. Rubin had been acting a little mysterious lately. Now he knew why.

Dinner was wonderful and the company outstanding. It was impressive to Jack that neither June nor Jonathan ever intentionally spoke of themselves or their own activities. They wanted to know more about their guests and talked about things that they thought would make them more comfortable with new friends. Before they departed for the evening, Jack arranged to meet with both Dr. Rubin and Imogene while he was in town.

After dinner and back at the lodge, Jack and Adrianna sat on the front porch, holding hands, watching the lightning bugs and listening to crickets and frogs. They talked a bit about Jack's manuscripts and how the history was going. They both began to yawn. It was time to turn in. They walked down the hall, passed the closed doors to the parlor, and were at the bottom of the stairs when Adrianna said, "Let's peek."

Jack said, "No. There might be a way that the General can tell. It could spook the whole project."

Adrianna playfully went back to the door. She looked closely at the handles and tried the handle that secured the huge pocket doors. The doors did not appear locked, but Jack urged her to leave them alone. She kept teasing. She turned the hall light off so they were in complete darkness.

Jack emphatically said, "No, Adrianna!"

He moved from the foot of the stairs back to the middle of the hall directly in her path. Her eyes had not adjusted to the dark. She felt her way along the wall to the doors. Slowly and quietly, she turned the handle. The doors were unlatched.

She put her fingers to her lips and whispered, "Here goes."

Jack said again, "No, damn it!"

The doors parted about six inches. Her timing could not have been worse. Fate was in charge. At that instant, the fire siren in town started wailing. Adrianna jumped back from the door. A single wail, then another, then another. Three wails. A fire in quadrant three of the town. Jack knew exactly what it was.

He said to Adrianna in a high-pitched, panicked voice, "Close the doors, close the doors!"

She slammed the doors shut and turned to Jack in the darkness. She had begun to cry. "Oh Jack, what will they say? Ohhhh, my Lord, I have screwed up! Jack, I am so sorry. Why didn't I listen?" And she moaned on. "Somebody will be here any minute. I will tell them I did not know anything about the room. I will tell them it is all my fault. I will tell them I will go back to New Orleans first thing in the morning and never come back. Can you ever forgive me?"

He wanted to string her along and chastise her severely for her poor judgment, but it was too funny. He could hold it no longer. He slid his hand along the wall and found the light switch. When the light came on, he was laughing. He held her in his arms and told her what had happened. Adrianna started laughing.

Jack whispered, "Shhh. Let's just slip into bed and be very quiet, act as if we have been asleep for hours. Just be calm."

In bed, Adrianna was still a little apprehensive. She whimpered, "I am so sorry." She was awake for a long time, but nothing happened. No one came to investigate.

The next morning, Jack made coffee and sat on the front porch, watching the sun come up. Adrianna heard cups as they rattled and came down and got a cup. Instead of joining him on the porch, though, she had another idea. The scare was over. What the heck.

Jack started for another cup of coffee and as he stepped back inside the hall, he realized that something was amiss. The doors to the parlor were open. Adrianna sat at the head of the horseshoe table, and surrounding her on all the walls, on the tables in front of her, and on easels placed around the room, there were "MacMorogh for Senator" placards and signs, everywhere.

She said, "This is unbelievable. It is true. The General sealed this for eternity. His hopes, his dreams, dashed. How sad."

Jack had a full agenda for the days they were in town, and as usual, he made sure Adrianna was well aware of his plan. As for her own plan: read, sleep, and be available when he had time to spare.

She was looking forward to exploring the area and perhaps meeting some of the other people about whom she had read. Before leaving, they arranged to meet back at the lodge at noon. Jack wanted to have lunch at the Toot.

He had no trouble finding the County Clerk's office. He introduced himself to a young woman who seemed to be in charge. After he told her what his mission was, she smiled and said, "You are planning to be here a day or two aren't you?" Many of the records were stored in the basement, some were in another building, and some might be water damaged if they went back a long way. She suggested that he give her a list of what he needed, and if she was not too busy, she would help. By noon, Jack had made little progress. He had been in the basement all morning in dust and cobwebs and had little to show for his effort. He informed the young woman that he was going to lunch and would return shortly after.

The Toot was a busy place; the day crowd was mostly workers, the vehicles mostly work trucks. Come night, though, the kids took over. Jack boasted to Adrianna that the Toot had the best hamburgers and fries in the state, but the real attraction was the girls, Holly and friends. Short shorts, tee tops, and roller skates on lithe young bodies beat hamburgers hands down.

They backed into the parking place so they could watch the action. Adrianna asked about a menu. Jack pointed to the big board painted on the little building in the center of the lot. It was compliments of RC Cola. She decided on the cheeseburger with onion rings. Jack took the same, with fries.

Luckily, Holly was the one who drifted up to Jack's window. "I thought I recognized this car. What canna' git ya'll?" Jack ordered, and she skated off.

"Jack, I think you may be spending too much time here," Adrianna said sternly. When Holly returned with their order, Jack introduced her to Adrianna. After Holly left, he told Adrianna about the young woman's relationship with Will. Adrianna had read enough of Jack's latest manuscript to know that Holly had also shared a bad experience in her life with several other girls in town. Jack did not discuss that part. After lunch, Adrianna dropped Jack in town and agreed to pick him up around four.

When he arrived at the courthouse door, Jack came face-to-face with Will's cousin Patricia. She wanted to chat a moment and guided him to a well-worn wooden bench. She was glad she'd had the opportunity to meet him, the week prior. Her question, "Are you planning to interview any of the Lamar family?" caught Jack by surprise.

"Absolutely," he responded. "I am glad I ran into you. I want to visit with you at length and with your mother. I have heard most about you two, but I might want to interview some of the other Lamar sisters also. I am sure you can steer me in the right direction as far as the others are concerned."

He explained that he was on a mission that day to search public records and had another interview or two on his schedule. He told her that he was planning to stay in town for several days. So when might be a convenient time to get together?

Patricia replied, "If you are churchgoers, why not join us at the Methodist Church on Sunday? If not, why not come to lunch at mother's house anyway? It is known as the Lamar Sunday Buffet."

"We would love to join you for church, but my girlfriend is with me, and she is Catholic. We will attend Mass at the Catholic Church first."

"Splendid," she said. "I'll tell Mother. She will be delighted; she thought she was going to get left out of this project." Patricia gave directions. "See you Sunday."

When Jack returned to the County Clerk's office, the young woman at the counter smiled and said, "Come back tomorrow, about this time. I will have everything you need."

Jack looked at her questioningly. "I can't ask you to do that."

"You have a friend in town," she smiled. "See you tomorrow."

With that, he had ample time for other things before meeting Adrianna. He strolled across the square and stopped off at Upton's barbershop. The first chair was empty, and in the second, the barber was busy cutting hair. He told Jack to have a seat and that he would be with him in just a few minutes.

After the barber was through and the customer gone, Jack introduced himself. He did not actually want to get a haircut; he wanted to meet Mr. Upton.

Mr. Upton tilted his head back to look at Jack through the bottoms of his bifocals. "And who did you say you were again?"

"Jack Ward. Will MacMorogh is a friend, and he brought you a tape of the most famous football game in the history of Leeville and New Cotswold. I announced that game."

Mr. Upton's mouth broke into a big smile. "Sit, sit, let's talk awhile. Matter of fact, I 'm goin' to put my sign out that says I'm on break. Let's go to the drug store for a hot cup of coffee."

Mr. Upton wanted to talk about Will and the times when all that bunch were kids. Then he wanted to know more about what Jack was doing. He had heard rumors. He was afraid Jack might be finding out some unpleasant things about the MacMorogh family. He wanted to help set some of that straight. It took over an hour.

Jack had not taped anything, nor had he made notes. When they were done, he had to get somewhere and write it down. Mr. Upton had been a pillar in the Baptist Church for many years, but came a time he had to resign. And he told Jack the reason.

This happenstance meeting was one of the most informative meetings of any. Jack walked back into the courthouse, found a bench, got out his note pad, and began to write. When he was through, he sat there musing. To himself, he said, "How could I have missed this?"

The courthouse clock chimed three times. Jack might still have time to go the Mercantile Store to meet with Imogene. A bell clinked when he stepped through the door. "Come in!" came a greeting from the middle of the store. A tall, older woman, maybe in her sixties, greeted him. "And how may I assist you, sir?" she said.

From another part of the store, he heard another voice "Well, hello there." Imogene approached and introduced Jack to her mother. She made no mention of Jack's occupation, only the fact that they had met the night before at dinner. Mrs. Swenson excused herself to go about her business.

After she was out of earshot, Imogene said, "I would like to visit with you, but now is not a good time. If you could come back tomorrow afternoon, my parents will not be here, and we can visit a bit. "Jack agreed and after shopping around, left the store. Adrianna picked him up as promised only minutes after four.

"Are you through for the day?" she asked. He responded that he was, but was behind on his agenda. He would have to take on more the next day. "Then let's go to the creek with a pitcher of martinis."

Jack remembered that there was a barrel grill at the lodge, similar to the one he had cooked on at the cabin. He drove to Nap's store. "Come in with me; we have to select our dinner."

Adrianna said, "Not in there?"

Just as it had been on his first trip, it was dark inside. "Come on in," Nap boomed. "Ya'll the second group of white folks come by to collect, though. I gave already."

Jack threw up his hand in a wave. Nap responded, "Get ya'll a Coca-Cola out of the machine there. Don't need money. Just push down on the handle." Jack already knew the drill. He warned Adrianna to be ready when the cap came off.

Jack introduced the two. Nap was very polite. "You have to take me with a grain of salt, young lady," he said. "I am just another smart-mouthed colored boy you folks always writin' 'bout. Come sit down and tell me 'bout yourself. This boy here tells me you the societeeey lady for the paper in New Orleeeeans. Believe that's the *States-Item*" he mused. "You come to interview me, find out we had any parties lately, here at the club?" Then he laughed and stretched out his hand to Adrianna, "Come on, sit."

They talked for almost an hour. Nap was interested in serious conversation about what was going on in cities like New Orleans with a large colored population. How were people reacting to the Civil Rights Movement? Was there trouble in the schools? He offered his own personal convictions. In addition, he offered up his prayer for peace in the world. It was something he was afraid he would not be around to see.

For their supper, Nap picked the same things as he did before for Jack, except he added some very ripe peaches. "Slice those in half, get the seed out, but leave the skins on. Put them face down on the grill until you get some grill marks, then top the halves with a scoop of this ice cream I am going to send with you."

He had the butcher wrap the steaks. Jack offered to pay, but as before, he could not. Nap said, "On Will's bill, remember?"

"We have one more stop to make," Jack said. "I left something at Will's rehab center." He stopped the car in front of the house. "Wait here; I will show you around later." He came back with the cold jug of Maureen's concoction, or what was left of it.

Back at the lodge, they decided to postpone the creek and get busy with their supper. Jack got a fire going in the pit while Adrianna sliced tomatoes, shucked back the corn, and buttered bread to toast on the grill. That done, Jack introduced Adrianna to the "Ain't that just like Maureen" concoction. He warned her, "Take only a sip."

She did just that, took one sip, puckered, licked her lips, and said, "My, that is so good." Jack explained what it was. She had read his account of the visit out to Moon's place and now understood what he meant about "Now, ain't that just like Maureen."

They sat on the back steps of the lodge, watching the smoke curl from the pit, the concoction beginning to take effect. The steaks were perfect, caramelized outside and red inside. The corn, buttered and sprinkled with a little cayenne, was juicy and seasoned just right. Per Nap's instructions, Adrianna put the sliced peaches on last and left them over the smoldering coals. After cleaning their plates, Adrianna retrieved the lightly charred peach halves, scooped ice cream onto each, and returned to the porch with the beautiful desserts.

"What a day," she said. "The meeting with Nap was fascinating. I really like the man. He seems very sincere in his beliefs."

Jack said, "Since we left Nap, I keep thinking how much I like it here. There is something I like about the peace and quiet that we do not feel in the city. Then I think about how much I miss that life, the city, the newspaper. Then I realize that regardless of where I am, if you are there also, my life seems to be at ease." Adrianna cuddled.

The next morning, Jack stayed busy in town until noon. He went to the small museum in the house that Will owned and studied maps, pictures, old letters, and a few rusty weapons. The woman who served as docent introduced herself as Mrs. Barker. She was half-Indian, the daughter of a Choctaw chief. She brought out more literature and pictures and regaled Jack with one story after another. Her information was a treasure trove to tie in with the Seamus years.

At noon, he stopped back at the courthouse. The young woman in the County Clerk's office had all his material stacked and ready to pack in boxes. Before she did so, she gave him a brief overview of the contents in each stack. Once again, he had hit pay dirt. He had verification that was necessary to add validity to the chronology he had established for the MacMorogh family as well as for the company.

He joined Adrianna for what he thought might be a quick lunch at Mrs. Farmer's boarding house. It was open to the public and considered the best family style lunch in town. Guests sat around a large lazy Susan and served themselves from multiple dishes. But instead, Adrianna had another invitation. Aunt Tilda Jackson, who did not miss much that went on in town, had heard they were at the lodge and had paid Adrianna a surprise visit. She wanted them to come for lunch at her house that day. She explained that the coming weekend was the start of the annual revival at her church. Because of her responsibilities with food preparation, she did not know if she would have time to meet with Jack and Adrianna otherwise. Nothing could have suited Jack more.

They arrived at the house just as Winston was arriving. Aunt Tilda met them at the door and made proper introductions. She hugged Jack as if he was one of her own and spoke immediately to him. "I had the pleasure of meeting Miss Adrianna earlier today, and I need a word with you in private before you leave today." She turned to Adrianna and winked. She led them on into the dining room where the table was already set. From the kitchen came a pretty voice, someone singing to herself. Jack had met the young pregnant girl on his first visit. She sounded happy.

After a wonderful meal and pleasant conversation peppered with Aunt Tilda's wit, it was time for Winston to return to work. Jack, realizing the work Aunt Tilda had going on for the weekend, insisted that they not tarry long. Tilda would have nothing of it. She was not through visiting.

She politely asked Adrianna if she might have a word with Jack in private. She invited her to sit in the parlor for a few minutes; it would not take long. Then Tilda sat next to Jack on the sofa, her hand to her chin in thought. She stated that she was sincerely concerned that Will might leave out some things about his life that she felt were important. She simply stated, "I know some things that Will may never tell you. As a result, there could be questions in your mind, or the minds of future generations, about his character. I cannot let that be. I am going to tell you something that nobody but Will, Winston, and I know. I beg that in some way it is included in your manuscript." Then she proceeded to tell him.

When she had concluded, she wiped tears from the corner of her eyes, smiled, and patted Jack on the hand. "I did not raise my babies to be mistreated. I have never in my lifetime felt that I could take another life. It was during that period of time I just told you about that I was really put to the test."

Then she stood, "Now on a lighter note, When you gonna' ask that sweet girl to marry you? You know she loves you to death."

Jack smiled, "The feeling is mutual; maybe soon."

It was past three o'clock when they left the Jackson home. Jack left Adrianna at the lodge and rushed to Swenson's Mercantile to talk to Imogene. Upon entering the store, a most attractive young woman greeted him: blond, with a big bosom, no doubt Imogene's sister Marlene. Imogene came rushing to where the two stood and introduced her. "Marlene and I are sharing management responsibility now. She is a buyer for our work clothes lines and takes care of outside sales. I handle inside sales and am buyer for hardware and building materials. We are not completely in charge, but we are getting there."

Marlene had to suppress a laugh. Then she said, "Nice meeting you. Ya'll excuse me."

Imogene directed Jack to a group of desks on a dais that enabled them to see all corners of the store. She sat behind one of the smaller desks; Jack sat across in a visitor's chair. "I have wondered ever since I heard about your PR project if I might have an opportunity to visit with you. I am pleased that you have included me."

Jack said, "I am interested primarily in the history of the company. How it has grown over the years and become one of the largest companies in the South while headquartered in this small, somewhat remote town. I know that the MacMorogh family holds your family in high regard. I was hoping maybe you could give me some insight."

Imogene answered, "First, let me say that we have a very strong business relationship with their companies. They make up a big percentage of our business. You might expect that all of my comments would be favorable, and they will be. The company has invested millions in this community. If you go back to the time of Seamus MacMorogh, as I am sure you have, you can see that if it were not for him and his vision, this town might not even exist. I would say that the one most important thing about the family is that they have continued with that vision, and they have shared it. In so doing, the vision is no longer just theirs; it belongs to the people who accepted the vision as their own. The town has become a partner with the company in many ways. The MacMoroghs are not the only wealthy people in the area, but they have kept a very low profile. Most of the others have followed suit."

She said, "One more thing: history will show this partnership has not gone without some hard love. Moving the new MacMoCorp facilities across the county line got the attention of some very complacent city fathers. They soon lost their position, and others took over. As a result, we formed an Economic Development Committee. I am chairwoman of that committee. We have attracted new businesses to the area that would not have relocated here had we not sought them out and made attractive offers. It probably has worked to our advantage that the MacMoroghs moved their facility and got our attention. One other thing: guess who has funded fifty percent of the costs of the economic development expense? The MacMoroghs."

Jack sat for a minute or two and scribbled notes. He was thinking about Seamus' discussion with William, Sr. when he was just a child. *"Surround yourself with people who can do the job better than you. Share your vision, it will become theirs and they will be you partner forever."* Jack said, "I think you have summed it up in a nutshell. I am pleased to hear those comments. It does go back to Seamus."

Imogene chuckled and said, "Now on some personal notes. I could see the surprise in Jonathan and June's faces when we came to dinner the other night. I have been dating Dr. Rubin for about four months. We have been very discreet about it. Did you hear any comments?"

"None," replied Jack. His thoughts were about Aunt Tilda's story that Jonathan bought June from Dr. Rubin for a case of moonshine.

Adrianna came for Jack at four. They were tired from the day and both had eaten too much at lunchtime, so they were satisfied to have a drink and munch on fruit, crackers, and cheese for their evening meal. On Sunday morning, they did attend mass at the Catholic Church. It was a small parish, with a small group of parishioners.

After mass, a good-looking young man with pretty wife and three kids made a beeline to them. "Hi," said the young man. "I'm Tommy Schooner. I'll bet you are Jack."

Jack acknowledged that he was and introduced Adrianna. Tommy introduced his wife and children, then said, "Patricia called me last night to tell me you might be at church this morning. Just wanted to say hello, and I hope you are enjoying your visit." He then turned to his wife and said, "Honey, Jack is the guy who announced our ball game our senior year when we beat Leeville. You and Will sure made old man Upton's day with that tape. He plays it often."

Tommy's wife said, "Nice to meet you; stop by if you have time. We are just two streets over from Patricia and Tom."

Patricia was at her mother's house, watching for their arrival; she ran out to greet Jack and Adrianna as they got out of the car. Three of the families of the Lamar girls were in the backyard under the screened tabernacle where they held their Lamar Sunday buffets. They met Patricia's mother, Jessie, Violet, who had gotten her face slapped by Miss Annie, and Tootie, the city councilwoman.

Jessie said, "I am the one the others call 'Sister' because I am the oldest. My husband will be here shortly."

"I 'm Thelma, but everyone calls me Tootie. I am the youngest. My husband will not be here shortly. He goes to fisherman's mass at seven a.m. and is...fishing." Then she smiled. "Did you get the things I had copied for you yesterday?"

Jack grinned, "So it was you? Yes, and thanks so much. It saved me a day or so. You do not know how important the facts are to our project."

Tootie replied," Anything else you need like that, let me know. I have a keen interest in some of the same things on your list. I may already have copies." Interesting, thought Jack.

After a grand lunch of too many different dishes, Jessie asked Adrianna and Jack to accompany her and Patricia on a little tour. Patricia drove. Jessie sat on the front seat with her body turned, so she could talk to them in the back seat. And talk she did.

She told them about her grandfather, Tadlock Lamar, one of the first people that Seamus brought to town. He brought the first saw-mill with him. Her grandmother had hated it here and had little use for Seamus. She was the bane of his existence.

The grandmother griped about anything and everything she could. However, her griping got her into trouble. Seamus found out that the best way to keep her off his back was to put her to work. He told her that if she wanted a school, get it built and he would pay for it. He told her that if she wanted a schoolteacher, go find one. He would pay for it. He said that if she wanted a church built, he would build it. One thing she could never get him to do. That was to go inside the church.

Jessie said that her grandfather became the first mayor, her father had been mayor at another time, and no doubt, Tootie would be mayor someday.

According to Jessie, the relationship between the MacMoroghs and Lamars had had its ups and downs. She asked if they knew that Jonathan had dated Noreen before William, Jr. had. That was news to Jack. She said that her father did not like Jonathan from the very start. When William brought the family back to New Cotswold to live, times were tough financially for everyone including the MacMorogh family. William put Jonathan to work at the blacksmith shop. He was a great big boy, and size was to his advantage when it came to black-smithing. He seemed to like it best when he was hot and sweaty with horse manure on his shoes. He was also mean as a snake. Because of his size and the fact that he liked likker, he took it upon himself to beat the heck out of anybody who wanted to take him on.

Mr. Lamar was not a drinking man, and fighting was not a respectable sport. He was a master craftsman and a model father and family man. When Jonathan came calling on Noreen, Lamar hit the ceiling. He threatened to send Noreen to a convent or a home for wayward girls if she dated Jonathan. Then along comes William, Jr. He was bright, good-looking, and studying to be a lawyer, and best of all, Mr. Lamar approved of him. Luckily for everyone concerned, Jonathan lost interest in Noreen. William, Jr. took over.

Jessie would pause in her talking to point out various structures built by the Lamar men. It was true; they had built most of the early homes and businesses. Then it was Patricia's turn.

According to her, the relationship with the MacMorogh family was much better these days. She and Tootie's daughter worked for the MacMorogh enterprises. Her husband Tom was the corporate attorney. Patricia told Jack that if he needed any information about Will, she knew a lot and would be happy to share it. "One thing you do need to know and perhaps are already aware of, Will got a bum rap from this town."

Jack and Adrianna left early Monday morning, stopped in Jackson for lunch again with Jack's dad, and were home in New Orleans by five. Adrianna slept most of the way. They had little conversation. After they gathered their mail and their papers and had fixed martinis and settled down in the apartment, Adrianna said, "Jack, I honestly think I could live in New Cotswold. What would you think about us buying the weekly newspaper and settling there?"

On Tuesday, she was back at work. She hit the ground running, and by Thursday, was knee deep in her job, a hundred things going at once. In addition, she had to worry about Miss Penny. One or two more days, and the thought of leaving New Orleans passed.

In the meantime, Jack spent two more days with Will and was through with his interviews for the present. Much of what Jack learned was about Will's life after the crash that killed his parents. That was the time of early school years and the friendships he developed along the way. He grew intellectually during his college years, not only from his studies but also from the time spent in the household of Dr. Bea. Under her guidance, he grew culturally and learned to take pride in his heritage. However, the summers that he spent back in New Cotswold were his most memorable. He felt a certain tie to his roots and was continually amazed at the dichotomy in life resulting from his exposure to two different worlds.

With the many notes and tapes Jack had from innumerable interviews, it was time to tie it all together. He found it hard to overlook some of the repetitive stories due to the different perspectives of the persons interviewed. He would have to work through it.

28

January, 1943

Willie adjusted well to life with Jonathan as his guardian. He loved school; learning was easy. He was growing socially due to exposure to more people. Before school, his friends had been Letitia Mullens, John Pope, and a few cousins. Now there was a whole school of people.

The war in Europe was raging, and then there was Pearl Harbor. War was the major subject of everyday conversation. The prevalent news in papers, on the radio, and on movie newsreels was the war. Schoolchildren learned through civics classes and constant drives for such things as scrap metal, blood, and war bonds. Willie heard talk about rationing and knew of the draft and the fact that local men died in the war. It had never concerned him that the war might affect his own life.

Then it occurred. His grandfather announced that he was going back into the military to help the war effort. Willie's grandmother would be taking over as president of the company. Shortly thereafter, Aunt Bea came to town for a weekend. She, his grandmother, and Jonathan spent hours talking privately. Jonathan and Will's Aunt Bea also spent endless hours alone talking. They had a great responsibility. Finally, the time came to make a decision; then came the dreadful announcement. Jonathan was going to enlist in the army also.

Willie was devastated. No reasoning could eradicate the hurt. His life was about to be turned upside down again. However, after a lot of conversation, he was convinced that he was growing up; after all, he was twelve years old. His grandmother was definitely going to need a man at her house. He needed to step up to that responsibility. That very evening, they loaded his clothes and his bicycle and moved him into the big house with her. Jonathan came along also and stayed there until time to leave for the army.

Five days later, Willie, his grandmother, Winston and Aunt Tilda, along with his grandmother's servants, Lillian and Baxter, took Jonathan to the bus depot. There he joined a whole group of men on their way to Camp Shelby for induction into the military.

Willie's routine did change a bit. It was too far to ride his bike to school. So every morning when his grandmother left for work at the bank, Willie rode along. Baxter dropped her at the bank and then Willie at school. After school, he went to the blacksmith shop. There was always a snack and a big hug from Aunt Tilda. That evening, when his grandmother left work to head home, she and Baxter came to fetch him.

Things began to fall into place, and Willie was comfortable. Then his aunt Violet opened her mouth again. Willie was at a birthday party for his cousin Patricia. Several other cousins were there along with their mothers, including Aunt Violet. They were playing games in the yard, when he overheard her say to another aunt, "Jonathan may not come back, and what if that happens?" Those words, "not come back" reminded him of his parents not coming back. He left the party. He was doing his best not to cry when he passed the drug store next to the bank. It was three in the afternoon, the exact time each day that his grandmother went down to the soda fountain at the drug store for an ice cream cone and a visit with the store owner, Mrs. Irby.

Grandmother just happened to look up and see Willie pass by. Realizing that he should be at the party, she ran to the door and called to him. She questioned him, asked why he was tearful, and he told her. She consoled him as best she could and invited him in for ice cream with her and Mrs. Irby. He calmed down and went on to the blacksmith shop. That evening, on the way home in the car, she said to Willie, "I do not think your Aunt Violet will be making any more such remarks to you, young man."

Then she asked, "What do you think, Baxter?"

He just shook his head and smiled, "No, Ma'am, I ain't believing she will either." *Jack had heard a little different twist to that story and liked the other version better.*

Then the next blow came. They were quietly having dinner one evening when someone drove under the portico of his grandmother's house. Baxter was the first to hear. He opened the front door with the first chime and greeted the guest. When his grandmother heard Dr. Rubin's name, she slid her chair from the table, to go to the foyer. At about the same time the phone rang, and Baxter took the call.

Willie heard Dr. Rubin tell his grandmother that Jonathan had been hurt. Willie's heart sank, and he dashed from the table and into the foyer. Dr. Rubin put his hand on Willie's shoulder as he and his grandmother talked. Jonathan had received a foot injury in a collision between two trucks. It was not life threatening, but it was serious.

At that moment, Baxter announced that Willie's Aunt Bea was holding on the phone. As soon as he was able to make a call, Jonathan had called Dr. Bea, who in turn had called Dr. Rubin. She was on her way to Camp Shelby. Dr. Rubin also planned to leave as soon as possible. He did not know if they would let him in the gate, but maybe he could join Dr. Bea in talking to the doctors. His suggestion was that Miss Annie contact the General. He needed to be involved.

His grandmother called Winston and gave him the assignment to contact the General. She would leave immediately. She then told Baxter to get clothes for himself; she packed her own bag with Lillian's help, and off they went.

Lillian stayed in the house with Willie that night, then drove him to school the next day. Willie was in a miserable state. He heard nothing else and was terrified that the news would not be good. Noon went by: he did not eat. School was due out at three thirty. At three o'clock, the principal came to the classroom. He knocked lightly; the teacher glanced toward the door and went to him.

The principal glanced around the room until he spotted Willie. As he was whispering something to the teacher, he signaled Willie to come forward. At the door, he wrapped his arm around him and told him he had a phone call; his Uncle Jonathan was calling. Willie ran to the principal's office, the principal himself in a trot.

When Willie picked up the phone and said, "Hello," Uncle Jonathan came on in his strong voice, "Hey Willie, did you hear I hurt my foot?" Then he went on to assure the boy that he was OK. He might be in the hospital a few days, but everything was fine. He was not to worry; his grandmother had been to see him, and she was on her way back home.

Willie walked back into the classroom and asked the teacher if he might be excused. She told him that it was OK, but first he should tell the class what had happened. He did, and then he ran as fast as he could to tell Winston and Aunt Tilda.

Jonathan was in the hospital a much longer time than anticipated. The army doctors were convinced that the crushed foot was beyond repair and wanted to amputate. Jonathan would have none of it. Several months later, the army discharged him and sent him to a veterans hospital in New Orleans for further treatment. Dr. Bea was close by for assistance and soon was instrumental in getting some of the most competent physicians in the area to examine the foot.

The private doctors agreed with the military group. The best thing would be to amputate. Again, Jonathan refused. The doctors had a challenge and began what would be a long series of surgeries. Dr. Rubin arranged to be present each time. By the time the doctors were through, Jonathan was walking, but with a noticeable limp and obvious discomfort. The foot would never be the same, but he still had it.

Jonathan did not sit still during the time he was recuperating. Dr. Bea set up a workable office in his bedroom at her house. When he finally did come home, he brought detailed drawings of the first of the logging machines that would change the lumber industry and the method of harvesting trees. That machine would go through one transformation after another, one improvement after another, one more patent after another. That was the beginning of MacMoCorp, Heavy Machinery Manufacturing Division. It was also the beginning of Jonathan's becoming a driving force in the company.

Though he preferred to move back into the house to be with his mother and Willie, it was not convenient. Miss Annie had the master bedroom downstairs; all others were upstairs. That presented a problem. So he moved instead into the small apartment attached to the main hangar at the airfield. It had once been quarters for an airport manager. There was a small kitchen and lunch counter in front of the apartment. It had served as a working café before the airfield closed due to the war. In addition, there was a meeting room, two bedrooms, and a bath. It was perfect for Jonathan. He was on the premises with his mother and Willie, but he had his privacy. Dr. Rubin and June were daily visitors to treat the injured foot with a series of remedies, including painful physical therapy.

He could not get comfortable in the apartment until he had work-space. He moved the few aircraft in the main hangar into another on the field. He then transformed the main hangar into a large shop where he could work without leaving the premises. Winston moved lathes, welders, and a small yard crane for heavy lifting. Soon, construction of the first logging machine was underway, but for now, it would be for the war effort only. The General probably could take credit.

Willie was delighted to have his uncle home. To show him just how happy, he was the man's constant shadow when not in school. He took over as chief "gofer." In order to get Willie out from under-foot, Jonathan gave him more responsibility. At the beginning of the war, they had turned the airfield over to the government for use as an auxiliary emergency field. There were certain requirements nec-essary to maintain it as such. The rotating beacon required frequent service and inspection. Fence posts at each end of the field had to be in red and white stripes that were always bright and clear. The wind-sock and wind tee had to be in good condition at all times.

The sod field had to be always mowed to a proper length and drainage ditches kept clean. Baxter had taken on much of the respon-sibility, but when Jonathan moved onto the field, he took charge. He assigned a lot of the work to Willie, including climbing the tower to service the rotating beacon. Baxter was happy to give that up.

Baxter moved the seat on the tractor as far forward as possible. With the help of a cushion, Willie could touch the clutch and brake pedal. He learned to drive in less than an hour; by the end of a day, he was mowing the field. He was so adept at driving the tractor that Baxter put him in the old truck and let him drive it on the airfield until he felt Willie could safely drive on the highway. He was thirteen.

Jonathan's foot stayed swollen and pained him most of the time. A normal shoe would not fit, even if he could have endured the pain. Dr. Rubin made plaster casts of both feet. When the casts hardened, he cut them off and then taped them back together to form a mold. Using a light cement, he made molds of each foot. The local cobbler used those to make a pair of soft high-top shoes. In time, Jonathan could wear both.

It was also bothering Dr. Rubin that Jonathan was standing for long periods. He was constantly on crutches. With Winston's help, Dr. Rubin designed and made a prosthesis of sorts. The result was a device that Jonathan could rest his knee on while belting the device with two belts to his thigh and a belt around his waist. He was actually kneeling with his left knee on a peg that was as long as the lower leg on his left side. He could completely take the weight off the bad foot. It was much more comfortable and gave him greater freedom with his hands. He could walk on it fairly well, and Willie was soon calling him "Peg." That was only in the presence of Dr. Rubin, however.

Jonathan went through periods of depression, complaining that he was not doing anything toward the war effort. In order to have some part, he volunteered for civil defense. He took responsibility for monitoring sections of town during air raid warnings. This required roaming a particular section to be sure all lights were off and that nothing was visible from the air. That required use of a vehicle. Because of the foot, he could not drive easily, so Willie took over. In addition, Jonathan sold war bonds and collected money for the Red Cross. The most important thing he did, according to Willie, was teaching people to identify enemy aircraft. Willie and Tish often climbed to the top of the rotating beacon to watch for enemy planes. They expected a Jap Zero or Nazi Messerschmitt to appear at any moment; they would be the ones to sound the air raid warning. Will and Tommy Schooner learned to send and receive Morse code and built their own telegraph keys.

Jonathan was always cognizant of Willie's need of a father and devoted a lot of his time to him. Many were the times that he and Dr. Rubin made plans to do something, only to have Jonathan cancel because Willie had something going on at school or needed his presence. Dr. Rubin realized that there were other boys and girls alike that had fathers serving in the military. They did not have a Jonathan, and they needed friendship and guidance as well. He wanted to help.

One Sunday afternoon, he drove by the school grounds on his way to the hospital. There were about a dozen boys playing touch football. Several other boys and girls were spectators. He stopped to watch for a while. The next Sunday, the same group was back, and it included Willie and Tommy Schooner. Dr. Rubin had played football in college and had even had a scholarship to Ole Miss. He loved the game. On that particular Sunday, there were more boys playing. Dr. Rubin walked right up into the midst of them, pulled out a whistle, and blew it and stopped play. Everyone knew him, but this was a surprise and even, to some, an annoyance.

He gruffly started pointing at one player after another, "You here, you there, you here, you there," until he had two teams that he considered an even match by age and size. Next, he assigned positions. "You are center, you are a tackle, you are the quarterback," and so on.

He walked over to the several girls who sat on the sidelines. He did the same with them, "You here, you there, you here, you there," he said, until he had them divided. To one group he said, "You are the cheerleaders for the Mad Dogs," and to the others he said, "You are the cheerleaders for the Wild Cats." He said to the rest of the group, "Unless you all have a bugle in your pocket and can be the band, then you are fans. No tickets required."

With that, he called loudly "Quarterbacks around me, *now!*" Just a few short years down the road, out of that same group of boys came a championship high school football team. The next Sunday, more players showed up. Letitia brought three friends to be cheerleaders. Tommy Schooner's mother brought a windup record player and some fight songs for a band.

Jonathan had played football in high school but was too intent on his studies to play in college. But he did know the game. He joined in to coach one of the teams. On the third Sunday, Letitia's dad, Moon the bootlegger, brought a whistle and flag and became the official referee.

Each Sunday after the games were over, Dr. Rubin and Jonathan would take the teams to the ice cream parlor. The winners got double cones; the losers got singles. The best reward for both Dr. Rubin and Jonathan was a letter that Tommy Schooner's father sent to the local weekly newspaper, praising the two for helping take care of his boy while he was away.

Driving required a license, but hardship situations took preference over age. Because of her father's occupation, Letitia lived a long way out in the country, and so far, the school bus did not go there. For all her early years, her mother drove her to school in the morning and came back in the afternoon. At fourteen, Letitia got a hardship license, and not only that, she got her own car, such as it was.

During the war, the whiskey business got better. As long as he could get black market ingredients, Moon was still making shine and money. He also knew how to get gasoline and recap tires for old cars. Moon bought the only taxi business in town. With it came four completely worn-out but still running 1939 Ford sedans. In addition, there were two others sitting on blocks due to lack of tires and parts. From these, Moon put together Letitia's first car.

Along with the old cars, Moon also got possession of a shack at the rail depot for use by the drivers waiting for fares. In town, there were three taxi-only designated parking spaces, one each at the hotel, hospital, and bus station. To Moon, these were additional spots at which to market his product. It was so easy. A drummer would get off the train, take a taxi to the hotel, and alight with a fresh jug of "shine" in his sample case. Little old ladies needing to go to the grocery store did the same. For many people, the taxi number was at the top of their phone list.

The first day Letitia came to school in her own car, she was the hit of the class. On the doors, using white adhesive tape, was printed the word "TAXI." Below, printed with the same tape, "ph. 41" (meaning "phone for one"). Moon had paid special to acquire that number—a whole gallon of moonshine.

Moon also felt the need to do more for the war effort. He owned an old flatbed truck. Jonathan installed a winch and an A-frame that gave Moon the ability to lift heavy pieces of scrap iron onto the truck without aid. Scrap iron was a necessity for the war effort. If one did not mind hard, dirty work, there was money in collecting and selling it. Moon traveled the back roads looking for old tractors or other rusty farm equipment. Soon he was operating a scrap iron yard near the railroad. It was also a good outlet for shine. He often traded white lightning for scrap metal.

Jonathan soon realized that his mother had her hands full, trying to run all of the companies, and was too proud to ask for help. One evening he ate supper with Winston and Miss Tilda. He discussed the situation at length and made a decision. He went straight to the house and found his mother in her robe sitting quietly listening to the radio, her knitting in her lap and Hardly the dog at her feet. He asked if she felt up to talking. This was something that rarely happened between the two.

Jonathan began with his sincere concern for her and the strain he felt she was in. She was touched. By the time he had become shoulder high to her, he had shunned away from motherly affection. Was it possible, he asked, that she would consider spreading some of the responsibility around? She took off her glasses. Jonathan was perched on a footstool, and she asked him to pull it closer and took his hand. She admitted that she was overloaded, but she felt everyone was.

She worried about the General; she worried about Jonathan, the girls, Willie. The war was exacting a lot from all of them. She could not place more burdens on any of them. Jonathan pointed out that not only was she heavily stressed with the MacMorogh Companies, but that she and her sister were managing their own cotton companies as well. It was just too much.

He told her he could no longer sit by and watch her destroy her health. She was too important to the family. She sighed deeply and said, "Jonathan, we have needed to have this discussion for a long time. Tell me what you have in mind." At her suggestion, they moved to the large dining room. They sat, and she took pen and pad. Jonathan began to spell it out. It took almost an hour for him to lay out the details of what he and Winston had discussed. She interrupted often, never with a negative but just for clarification. Jonathan was amazed at her knowledge of all of the different facets of the business. He finished with his thoughts, and she sat silently for a few minutes, her hands clasped in front of her mouth as if in prayer. Then she spoke, "Fix us a pot of coffee, and let's write this out." It was after one o'clock in the morning when Jonathan walked down to his apartment in the hangar, so proud of his mother; she was one brilliant woman.

The next morning, Miss Annie went to her office at the bank and got her day started. At promptly ten o'clock, she summoned both Jonathan and Winston. First, she presented the fact that there was a lot for which to be thankful. The MacMorogh Companies owned the banks, the lumber mills, the machine shop, Jonathan's fledgling machinery operation, the gasoline distributorships, ice plants in three towns, a box manufacturing plant with a government contract, and lots of land. There was no way one person could oversee all of the entities effectively. She had concluded that she had valuable talent within the organization, namely Jonathan and Winston. She needed them to come to the forefront and take more responsibility.

Then she presented the plan she and Jonathan had discussed the night before. That day, a new form of management went into place. She delegated responsibility. Not only would Winston be in charge of the machine shop, but he would look after the ice plants and the box factory. Jonathan would look after his machinery manufacturing, the mills, and the gasoline distributorship. Miss Annie would look after the banks and would confer with each of them daily. Each morning after the workday was under way, the three of them would meet to go over each segment of the business. Cash flow would be on the agenda each day.

Winston had reservations. How would the people in the businesses he was responsible for react to a colored man for a boss? Miss Annie looked directly into his eyes. "Do not tell them you are their boss; tell them you are now their leader. If they cannot follow the leader, perhaps another game would be more to their liking."

Within weeks, all of the operations were running more smoothly. Winston had no problems and lost no people. In time, he was their leader, and recognized in town as a leading citizen.

It made good sense to Jonathan to start slow with his machinery manufacturing operation. The machine would be in much greater need when the war was over. But the government contract was ideal for a beginning. He devoted much of his time to building better relations with all of their customers.

The first challenge was gasoline rationing. It was a hard task for anyone in the position Jonathan was, as a distributor. Jonathan could easily have pocketed a lot of money by selling on the black market. He contacted each of the small gas station owners, country storeowners, and two large stations in town who relied on him for gas. He discussed distribution with them individually and then as a group. He voluntarily opened the books of the distribution company to assure them that he was being as fair as possible. This seemed to pull the group together and resulted in more cooperation between them.

In one of their group meetings, one of the country storeowners suggested a way he was saving money. When his store converted over to electricity, only one switch controlled the lights for the store. They were either all on or all off. He installed four switches that each controlled the lights for quadrant of the store. Now, if no one was in the store, which was often the case in a small store like his, he only kept the lights on in one quadrant. If a customer came in, he would switch the lights on in other quadrants if necessary. He had cut his light bill in half. In time, they were all exchanging other ideas. What other services could they offer? Could they make better purchases by buying as a group? Out of the group, several mergers and partnerships took place. When the war ended, they were all stronger.

29

Fall 1946: The Class of '47

William III, since birth, had been Willie, thanks to Uncle Jonathan. By the time he was in high school, he had grown into a handsome young man and a better than average athlete. "My, my, have you seen that Will MacMorogh lately?" became a familiar comment from many a mother who wished her daughter might be the *one*. It probably did not hurt that his family owned the town also. So Willie now became Will.

Letitia, or Tish, was the most popular girl in the school annual, her senior year. But although she had a pretty face, with dimples in her cheeks, she was not on the most beautiful list. Like her father, she had horrible protruding teeth. She was also a bit chubby, and because she worked alongside her mother in her flower and vegetable gardens, she usually had a sunburned face with lots of freckles. However, her personality made up for it. That and the fact that she operated what she called "the fun taxi." There were usually at least eight or nine of her pals packed inside like sardines.

Tish grew even more in popularity due to knowing every popular dance step of the day. Between her and Kacky Kaplan's mother, they taught most of the kids how to dance. Willie was curious as to how Tish knew so many steps. She danced like a professional. It was easy; her parents danced a lot, and her dad danced with her too. Moon was quite a man, but no one knew just what a good man he really was.

Mrs. Kaplan was a strange one. Even in appearance, she looked to be as young as most of their classmates at school. She wore the same clothes styles and sizes. Not one single event took place at school that she did not participate in. She volunteered to chaperone, bake cakes, decorate the gym, drive her yellow Buick convertible in parades, raise money for any cause, and pay up if more became necessary. She could have been president of the PTA time and again, but some mothers, even though they appreciated her devotion to the kids, were jealous of her.

There was something else about Mrs. Kaplan and her relationship with Kacky's father. It was obvious that she was much younger. Will would find out about that in time.

School functions usually meant dates, but the senior class consisted of only twenty-one people. It really did not matter if you had a date or not. Most everything they did was as a group anyway. Matter of fact, often a boy went to a party with one girl and left with another. Will always made sure Tish had someone to escort her if the function did require pairing off in couples. Sometimes he would work all week, urging, sometimes coercing, some of the other boys to escort Tish so that she would not end up alone.

During eleventh grade, Kacky was Will's steady. All their friends were sure they would be the first in their group to get married someday. But it was not to happen. Will arrived at a point where he felt mother and daughter were trying to manipulate him. Kacky was planning to go to Stephens College, an all-girls school in Missouri. Her mother was already suggesting colleges nearby that might be good for Will.

But Will had his career planned. He was going to Tulane to take the Naval ROTC, and upon graduation, planned to go into the Navy Flight Program. Mrs. Kaplan did not think a naval career was fitting for a young man with his family business responsibility. Nor could she imagine her daughter traveling the world with a career soldier. Will should join the family business and build a large house near hers.

Will knew that his family was probably better off financially than most in town. Even so, he never considered the fact that he might not always need a job. He did not know a single person his age, girl or boy, who did not work at something. They had paper routes, cut grass, helped on the family farm, or in Tish's case, bottled moonshine. This work was a part of the times and an accepted way of life. If you wanted spending money, you earned it. For some of the poorer kids, it even meant that if you wanted to eat, you earned it.

As for college, he and Carole Anne knew that there was a fund provided by their deceased parents. Either of them could go anywhere they wished. Unbeknownst to Will at the time was just how many years he could go—maybe all his life, if he had wanted to.

Will brought the romance with Kacky to a halt. Within their small group of friends, however, Kacky did the dumping. Will did not care; he just needed breathing room. That was the summer before his senior year.

For Will and all his classmates, the beginning of their junior year marked a new era. By May 1945, the Germans had surrendered, and World War II was over on the European front. During the summer that followed, the Pacific war ended. It came to a conclusion in the aftermath of the Americans dropping the atom bombing on Hiroshima on August 6, 1945. Three days later, on August 9, 1945, another atom bomb fell on Nagasaki. And six days later, the Japanese surrendered.

That fall, at the beginning of their senior year, Will and Tish made a pact. Their goal was to be the top two students in their class by graduation, and they would flip a coin for valedictorian if they tied. It was destined to be a tie from the beginning. They studied together and prepared each other for tests and quizzes. Tish edited the school newspaper. They co-edited the yearbook. Tish played the bass drum in the band. Will was the quarterback on the football team, and made history by leading the football team to the first district championship in seven years. Four years earlier, the team had won only one game all season. Dr. Rubin deserved much of the credit for the championship.

Leeville was the neighboring town, twenty-two miles to the north, and they had forever been archrivals. For as long as anyone could remember, the game usually ended in one big fight. Will's senior year would be no different.

Jack enjoyed writing this part of the history because he was a part of it. At that time, Jack's father was a reporter for the Leeville newspaper, covering everything including sports. Jack tagged along to all games and loved being a part of the action. He had befriended the owner of the local radio station and watched him during his broadcasts of the games.

Jack began to mock him. He became good enough to earn the man's respect. The broadcaster was kind enough to give Jack the opportunity to do a small bit of announcing during the games. And on the eventful evening of the greatest game anyone could remember, the regular announcer had an emergency, and Jack took over. It was a battle from the start. Neither team had enough players to field both an offensive and a defensive team. Many of the players played offense and defense and played the entire game. The first half was tied 21 to 21. There was no score by either team in the third quarter. It was obvious that both teams were exhausted. If this had been a boxing match, the referee would have called it a tie and sent them to their corners.

Late in the fourth quarter, Leeville scored, to lead 28 to 21. Only minutes remained. It had to be the end. Fans on both sides started streaming out of their seats toward the parking lot. Drummers on both sides beat time as the band members headed for the school buses. History had taught the school officials to prepare for a fight. What few police there were in town were on hand to at least attempt to keep peace.

Then Leeville kicked off for what was surely the last time. Four minutes remained on the clock. "Little Joe" Graves, the team scatback for New Cotswold, received on his own twenty-two yard line. He was off and running like a deer. Adrenalin fueled him as he darted between tacklers until stepping out of bounds on the Leeville thirty-five yard line. The crowd went wild.

Breathlessly, Jack depicted the game in his coverage.

If you have left the stands and are in your car headed home, shame, shame shame! You are missing the most exciting two minutes of the game! Number twelve, "Little Joe" Graves receives the kickoff and carries until he is out of bounds on the Leeville thirty-five. The whistle blows, time out, New Cotswold. Fans, if I know Coach Wiggins like I think I do, he is going to fulfill the promise he makes to his senior players every year. Every one of them WILL get to play in the final game. This has to be a tough decision. It is a critical moment. This could mean losing the game...Will he do it this year? Hold on! I am right – there they are, four clean jerseys on the sideline, getting last minute instructions. Going into the game will be number 34, Billy Rogers, tackle number 46, Hodges Moore, tackle number 55, Moses Jones, guard, and Senior Bull Dozier number 48, guard.

New Cotswold fans stood and cheered the decision. Dozier was the biggest kid on the team at six feet, two hundred twenty pounds. Unfortunately, his IQ and jersey number were not far apart.

If you have followed this unbeaten New Cotswold team this year, you know that much of that success has been due to the dynamic duo of quarter-back Will MacMorogh and wide receiver Tommy Schooner. They have taken their air game to new heights. The whistle blows, both teams line up, the center snaps the ball. Oh my goodness! The New Cotswold line collapses, it is going to be another sack – but NO! MacMorogh gets off a wobbler, Schooner is in the clear, but the ball just will not go the distance.

Leeville Tiger number 44, Big Bill Horn jumps, intercepts! NO, NO, he could not hold on, he deflected the ball, it hits Dozier number 48, in the face. But Dozier HAS THE BALL! He has it tucked in tight, OH NO, he's turned the wrong way, NOW he is turned around, he's charging like a runa-way bulldozer. Three men can't pull the big man down, he is loose, and he is at the thirty, the twenty-five, and is finally out of bounds on the Leeville eighteen! There is not a single fanny in a seat in these stands!

New Cotswold lines up, the ball is snapped, once again Schooner out to receive, he is in the end zone, he is clear, the ball is in the air, TOUCHDOWN! My, oh my, oh my, this is going to tie it up! Coach Wiggins has kicker Pete Williams number 3, giving last minute instruc-tions. Quarterback MacMorogh is waving the coach off, Coach Wiggins is trying to shove Williams on the field. The whistle blows, they line up, the ball is snapped, Bull Dozier plows into the line leading the push, and MacMorogh is right on his back and he tumbles head over heels into the end zone! NEW COTTSWOLD MAKES THE CONVERSION AND WINS 29 to 28!

And, to all of you Friday Night Football fans who regularly tune in! Finley-Moore Funeral Home in Leeville and Bradley's Ice Cream Parlor in New Cotswold brought this game to you. This is Jack E. Ward signing off for Finley Moore Funeral Home and Bradley's Ice Cream!

The game was over, but the fight had just begun. Players and fans alike joined in the melee. It was in the process of turning into a full-scale riot when someone had the presence of mind to shut off the stadium lights. The field was in total darkness before the lights finally came back on. The goalposts were down and the field littered with trash, but the fight was all but over. Coaches had managed to get their players off the field into the locker room or onto the bus headed for home.

Bobby Lou Mills, the part-time school nurse, was at the game and had had the foresight to run to the school bus carrying the team. Coach Wiggins called ahead, alerting Dr. Rubin to be at the field house when the team arrived; they had injuries. Bobby Lou used a flashlight to examine the injured, and by the time the bus arrived home, she had determined which of the players needed immediate attention. Dr. Rubin sent most to the showers after a quick examination. Several did require more than minor patching. Bull Dozier had a severe cut on the arm by a knife or perhaps a broken bottle. Will had a badly bruised calf, a shoulder injury, and a deep cut over his left eye. Dr. Rubin put something on the cut to reduce the bleeding and sent him to the showers.

Will refused to have his injuries taken care of before Bull. He was the quarterback; he was still in control. So Dr. Rubin took care of Bull first before looking after Will. The cuts and bruises would heal. He shined a light in both of Will's eyes and felt the huge knot on the back of his head. That gave Dr. Rubin concern.

Tish stood outside the locker room the whole time. Dr. Rubin knew she was there and called her in. He explained that Will's Uncle Jonathan was out of town. He did not want Willie being alone when he went home. He was concerned that the young man might have a slight concussion. The doctor was not going to put him in the hospital, but instead was going to send him to stay in the apartments Dr. Rubin owned. Several nurses, including Bobby Lou, lived there. One of the spare rooms had a hospital bed where Will could spend the night. Bobby Lou could keep an eye on him.

Dr. Rubin understood that all of the team and most of the school would be at the Toot. He knew that telling Will or Tish not to go would be a waste of his breath.

"Go to the Toot, but no more than thirty minutes, and then deliver him to Bobby Lou. Understand? No more than thirty minutes, and no booze."

Tish was on the horn of the old taxi the second she turned into the Toot. There were so many kids that the carhops were having trouble working through the crowd. Everybody gathered around the fun taxi to cheer and talk to Will. His right arm was in a sling, and his left eye was swollen shut. Most of the other players were in similar shape. Tommy Schooner appeared with a big RC and handed it to Will. "Drink!"

Will took one big swallow and realized it was rum and RC. He did not need more of that; he was dizzy enough as it was.

Will asked about Bull; where was he? Someone answered that he had had to go by to tell his grandmother about the game. He was on his way. Shortly after that, an ancient Dodge Brothers truck turned into the parking lot. One headlight looked up, the other down. The muffler was a thing of the past. Bull's older brother, who had looked out for him for most of his life, was driving. Before he could get the truck stopped, Bull was out with both arms pumping in the air, still hollering. "We won, we won!"

Will, who had remained in the car until now, struggled to get out and stand alongside Bull. With his left hand cupped around his mouth, he began to yell, "Dozier, Dozier, MVP, Dozier, Dozier, MVP!" Soon the whole crowd had joined in. Tish was first to notice Bull's older brother. He was back in the old truck, his head down across his hands folded across the steering wheel, tears flowing. This might be the proudest moment in his life.

"Enough?" asked Tish. Willie agreed. She started the old taxicab. Slowly they worked their way through the crowd, kids slapping the car, others clapping for Will as they left.

Tish came around to the passenger door and held out her hand for Willie to pull on, so he could get out of the car at the apartments. He really hurt. Bobby Lou heard the car doors and was at her front door by the time they got up the walk. Her robe was tight around her, a towel wrapped around her head. She thanked Tish for bringing Will by. She would take over from there. She had liniment and some painkiller; he would feel much better by morning. Once inside, she led Willie to the room with a hospital bed. She threw him a towel and told him to strip. He was hesitant. She told him she could not rub the liniment on through his clothes.

"Just get your clothes off and lie flat on your stomach. Will, I am a nurse. I have helped deliver more than a hundred of you little boys. I have seen every kind of pecker you can imagine; I doubt yours is much different."

He did as instructed while she went into the kitchen. She came back with rubber gloves. "This ointment is going to sting a bit, but when it quits burning, you will feel it taking the pain way. By morning, you won't remember even hurting." First the shoulder. She was rubbing hard, the pain was intense, and he swore he was on fire. She told him to quit moaning or she would rub it on his balls. Then he would know how hot the stuff really was. He kept still. After she rubbed as much as she could into the shoulder, she started in on his calf. He moaned. She slipped one rubber glove off, slipped her hand up his thigh, and grabbed his scrotum. He screamed in anticipation of the fire that was going to burn his balls off. But nothing was on her hand, and she thought it was very funny.

She then told him to roll over on his back. "Move over a bit, please." Will moved over. She slid in beside.

Jack surmised, "No insurance claims were filed?"

Will laughed, "No claims were filed."

The next morning, Will woke to the smell of coffee. Bobby Lou brought it in and put it on the table next to the bed. She then took a small flashlight and peeked into each of his eyes. She held up two fingers. "How many?"

Will muttered, "Two."

She clucked her tongue, "Oh my, you are still not seeing well. I only had one finger up. You are going to need more care."

They drank coffee with her sitting on the side of the bed.

"Was that your first time?" Bobby Lou asked. He admitted that it was.

She said, "I thought so. If that was not the first time with a girl in this town, then that is the best kept secret since the atom bomb." She lifted the sheets and peeked underneath as she said it. He got dressed and felt amazingly good, with very little pain.

"Your taxi is here. And Will, hon, best there be no talk about your treatment."

"Not a word," he said. "Not a word."

Jonathan returned on Monday. Nothing else could happen until he could hear all about the game. Will relived it several times. All over town, it played over and over. Everybody in town had a point of view. Why didn't Bull play all year? Why did they wait so late in the game to use "Little Joe" Graves? I would have done this, or I would have done that. Jack knew; he had been one of the guilty participants.

30

End of May, 1947: Graduation

Graduation was as Will and Tish had planned. They tied for valedictorian, but there was no coin toss. The principal made the decision. He announced that they were co-valedictorians. Both would speak on graduation night. Before the big event, Kacky, who was not dating anyone special, begged Will to be her date for graduation. He felt that since he and Tish were co-valedictorians, it was only fitting that he escort Tish.

Kacky did not give up easily. Even her mother interceded. "Will, you and Letitia are co-valedictorians, but you and Kacky share something also. You were selected Most Handsome, and she is Most Beautiful. Isn't that important?" Will said he thought not.

The agenda for graduation night was a big one. First, the ceremony itself, then pictures with friends and family. Afterward, a dinner at the hotel with dancing until midnight with Spooky and the Alley Cats. Next, there was a hayride ending with a swimming party and breakfast at the Kaplan home.

Tish hated hay and sneezed at the word. She and Will took her taxi and snuck off to one of their favorite spots, the pond on the airfield. Oh, for those nights they had sat there watching for enemy airplanes. They had first tried smoking there: cigarettes rolled by hand in OCB papers with tobacco from a cloth sack with a drawstring. Later they had tried a cigar, a little too strong; Tish got sick. Then corncob pipes with Prince Albert out of a can; not too bad. The first taste of whiskey was "shine," pilfered from Moon's inventory. Later, wine; their favorite, "Thunderbird." They sang in unison,

Tish said, "Remember when I asked you to meet me here one Sunday night to help me plan how to burn down the Baptist Church ?"

Will started laughing. "I don't even remember what it was over. I did learn it would be a mistake for me to ever make you that mad."

"Lord, I wanted to burn the damn church down with that moron of a preacher in it." She went on to relate the story once more.

"I was invited to a slumber party at LuLu Osborne's house. It was a Saturday night. LuLu invited Candy Moak, Billy Sue Bridges, and me. We were to spend the night, play records, girl talk, all that stuff. Sunday we would go with LuLu and her mother to church. It happened to be time for the Sheriff to be running for re-election. A good time for him to go raid my daddy. It was nothing new to me; it was what it was. Ironically, the same paper had a notice of a raid on Kate's place where the prostitutes hung out. To top that off, the Catholics had advertised their bingo again."

"Gambling at its worst," Will said.

"Other than getting the jitters and needing to go to pee, the service went well. That is, until the final long-winded prayer. The preacher asked God to watch over the children of gamblers, whoremongers, and bootleggers, and give them peace. Let them not suffer for the sins of the fathers. I was furious. That preacher singled me out in church. There was no way to control my temper. As soon as the dismissal prayer was over and the congregation dismissed, I scrambled to go by the others on the pew to get out of there. However, there was no way out. Lulu's mother had her arms out trying to gather up all us girls at one time.

"'Now girls, not so fast,' she said. 'I want all of you to speak to Rev. Procter. I want him to see what a sweet bunch of Christian girls we have visiting our church today.'" Tish mocked her in a prissy, high-pitched voice. "I was building up saliva in my mouth so that I could spit in the preacher's face. Before we got to where he was standing, I had to swallow. It was a good thing."

"'Brother Procter,' Lulu's mother said, 'I want you to meet some of Lulu's friends that we brought with us to this lovely service this morning.'

"He began to speak to each of us and had that prissy little spiel. When he got to me, he said, 'I hope you will worship with us again and get to know us better.'

"So I said 'Oh, I know a great number of your congregation already. Most of them buy their whiskey from my daddy. You know, Moon.'

"He was stunned, so I repeated it. 'Sure, you know my daddy, Moon Mullens the infamous bootlegger.' I don't know whether Lulu's mother croaked or farted. I just know I heard all of the air go out of her."

By that evening, when she had met Willie at the pond to smoke, she had not cooled down. She had gas, rags, and some whiskey bottles. She was going to torch the damn church.

Back in the present, they went to the Kaplan house and had breakfast with everyone else. All said their "Good-byes" and "We will always stay in touch," but that was a promise seldom kept. Many never saw or heard from each other again.

For a graduation present, Tish's parents gave her a solid gold Lady Elgin watch with a diamond bezel. In addition, Moon presented her with a college fund. It would be all she would need to keep her in college for four years. His only requirement was that she continue to lead the class.

Will expected Jonathan at his graduation, but not so, Aunt Bea or his sister Carole Anne. He was accustomed to the medical profession. However, everybody in the class received some memento of this milestone. Watches, rings, and in Kacky Kaplan's case, a car. Will thought he might have at least received a card of congratulation.

He had another concern, however. Only half the class had college plans. Most had started sending out college applications during their junior year or no later than early in their senior year. Some like Tish had started visiting campuses in their junior year. During the last half of the senior year, his friends were coming to class with the exciting news, "I got accepted!"

Will heard nothing from Tulane. Being very confident, he had not applied anywhere else. The sour taste of arrogance was hard to swallow. His grades were tops, and he was above average in school activity participation. He had not asked for any financial assistance. It was hard to believe that they might turn him down. He even gave his address as being his Aunt Bea's house on Exposition Boulevard. It was right across the street from the school. How could they turn him down?

Will went from the graduation breakfast to work as if it was any another day. Jonathan tried to get him to go home and go to bed, but he hung in there and worked all day. He did crash that night. Early Sunday morning, he awoke to the sound of a big radial engine. He sat up, startled, and went to the window to look out on the airfield. He looked just in time to see his Aunt Bea's bright red Beechcraft no more than one hundred feet off the ground as it pulled up in a steep turn to come around to land.

He slipped on pants and shirt and bounded down the steps to find Jonathan in the kitchen, coffee and juice already set out for guests. "Surprise," he said. "Did you think we were going to forget your graduation?"

Aunt Bea was the first to hug and congratulate him, then Carole Anne. They also had presents. Carole Anne brought a gold pen and pencil set. Aunt Bea also said that she had ordered a few new things for the room he would be using over her garage, among them a different desk, some bookshelves, better lamps, and a telephone.

It was at this point that Will had to face up to fact. Tulane had not accepted him. The disappointment in his voice was real. He was about to admit that his arrogant attitude of thinking that he need not apply anywhere else had backfired on him. It was then that Carole Anne opened her purse and told him she had forgotten that he had mail. She handed him the letter from Tulane. His hand was shaking so badly that Jonathan took the envelope, sliced it open with his pocketknife, and handed it back. It was the acceptance letter. Will whooped like Aunt Tilda.

He had grown up with a good work ethic. He liked being busy as long as he was productive. Many days, he went to work not knowing what assignment Jonathan or Winston might give him for the day. Some days, he left home clean and energetic, only to return home at the end of the day, dog-tired and filthy dirty.

He had learned enough by the time he graduated from high school to make a good hand at many different things. He could drive large trucks and operate heavy equipment, bulldozers, and motor graders used for maintaining the airfield. Stocking and accounting small parts used in the machine shop had been his responsibility. Both Winston and Jonathan taught customer relations. Jonathan expressed the fact that the best asset he found in Will was that he would accept a job, follow directions, get it done, and never complain.

Summer of '47

The last summer before college, he did about the same work he had done in other summers, with one exception. He qualified in a new skill, piloting. He had flown numerous hours with Aunt Bea, Jonathan, and Carole Anne. He learned a lot under their watchful eyes. That summer, since Jonathan was neither an authorized instructor nor an examiner, he turned Will over to Tommy Schooner's father. Since returning from the service, Schooner had become a flight instructor and a designated flight examiner for the area.

Dub, along with Jonathan, had purchased a group of Stearman bi-wing training planes at a government surplus auction. Jonathan, having a second degree in aeronautical engineering, had converted most of them to aircraft used for crop dusting and spraying. The first dual instruction that Dub gave Will was in Jonathan's Piper. He soloed in that airplane and built hours in it while taking additional ground school instruction. After he acquired enough hours, he got his private pilot's license. Jonathan kept one of the Stearmans in its original military configuration as a trainer. As trainers, these planes were two-holers, meaning there was an open cockpit for the student and one for the instructor. Jonathan flew several hours with Will in the airplane, and Dub gave him a check ride and determined he was qualified to fly it safely. Later he would qualify in Aunt Bea's Beechcraft.

Tommy Schooner, Will's good friend and football teammate, had learned from his father and was well on his way to becoming a duster pilot. He and Will spent what time they could talking flying. However, Schooner was on a short leash. He was still dating his high school sweetheart. By summer's end, Will was best man at his wedding, two days after Tommy turned eighteen.

Fall, 1947: First Year at Tulane

Will reflected on his college years, admitting that he was amazed that he ever made it past the first month or two. In reality, the day school started, he was just an eighteen-year-old country boy from a small rural town in Mississippi. In that town, he knew everybody, and they knew him. Except for the time after he moved into the house with his grandmother, he had resided in the living quarters of the old livery and blacksmith shop, under the same roof with colored. Will was well aware that some might find that unusual. To others, it was downright objectionable.

He had a textbook example of a southern drawl. He sounded like a hick from the sticks; he even used colorful slang. He was nicknamed "Country" by his classmates. Some snickered behind his back. Worst of all, he was afraid some of his professors looked upon him in the same vein as many of his classmates. Many of those students who teased him were from the north or from large metropolitan areas. They had not yet experienced the large numbers of languages and dialects they would hear in New Orleans. But he did not let the nickname bother him. It was not long before most of his critics realized that their first impressions were far from correct.

One of the greatest advantages in overcoming the false impression was his past exposure to the city during the times he had spent with Aunt Bea and Carole Anne. Students new to the city found him to be the best source of information for directions. He knew the best restaurants, bookshops, and venues for cultural entertainment, and to many, he knew the French Quarter like a tour guide.

After the first semester, the professors knew: first impressions are often incorrect. Will established his goal with all who would listen; he would graduate in the top of his class. He would excel in Naval ROTC and then go right into the Navy flight program. His goal was set, and nothing would interfere.

Will had no desire to be a frat man, but by the end of the first semester, several fraternities were courting him. He expressed his appreciation but declined. He had too many activities as it was. This was not comprehensible to many of his friends, who had so much free time on their hands.

On Friday evenings, he usually joined a few other boys for a beer at a student hangout. During a conversation about dorm rooms, they asked about his. He explained that he lived in an apartment over a garage at a private home. That perked the ears of several. Was that terribly expensive? It was then that they learned where he lived and how he paid his rent.

Aunt Bea had had a long discussion with Will before the school year began. She had detailed his responsibilities. She moved Rose, her housekeeper, into quarters in her large home, enabling him to have the garage apartment.

It would be his to maintain, clean, and keep presentable at all times. He would also have other chores. One of his favorites was maintaining her automobiles. Besides the car she drove daily, there were twenty more collectible cars stored on a floor of a parking garage off Canal Street. He was to establish a schedule that would enable him to do a routine maintenance check and clean each car at least once a month.

Last, and far from least, he would serve as his aunt's escort when called upon. She attended numerous fundraisers, professional dinners, political meetings, and social events. Her usual escort, her friend and longtime companion, Dr. Benjamin Bradshaw, also had a large medical practice and was not always available. As long as it did not interfere with his class work, she would expect Will to be at her side.

It did not take long for Will to determine that his aunt had an ulterior motive. Accompanying her to her obligations, as she called them, exposed him to many of the most influential, well-educated people in the city. They attended cultural events that he would have not experienced otherwise. His social skills improved dramatically. He grew intellectually and socially to the point where it became apparent to Aunt Bea and Carole Anne that he was losing his drawl. There were times at dinner when he said things that made each of them smile when they made eye contact.

That first year ended with his mandatory summer cruise in Naval ROTC. His grades were such that he got the two weeks he requested, the two immediately following regular classes. He was off to Pensacola to get an introduction to the real navy: KP, swabbing decks, guard duty, marching, and the most strenuous calisthenics he could ever recall. Football in high school had nothing to compare.

That first successful year gave Will a sense of accomplishment he had not previously experienced. His self-esteem blossomed after those first few months at Tulane, at a time that it had been at its lowest. That year he also established the pattern for his college career. He followed through with the same determination each year.

31

Summer, 1948

There was never any question in his mind what he would do for the summer following his ROTC cruise. Jonathan had prepared him; he expected him to be vacation relief driver at the gasoline distributorship. What Will did not know was just how much fun it would be.

The manager of the fuel distribution yard was a woman rumored to be a tyrant to work for. The minute he stepped onto the property, she made sure he understood that it was not just a rumor.

"I do not give a damn if your name is MacMorogh. You are a truck driver working for me, not your uncle, not your grandmother, and not the General."

She explained her rules for maintaining the truck. "Check all fluid levels, tires, and safety equipment. For deliveries, double-check the load and make sure the proper bill of lading is in the truck. Do not dump fuel without cash up front. At the end of the day, wash the truck, refuel it, and be ready to take on a new load the next day."

One other thing she said. "No loitering around the yard before or after work. No, I am not married, and no, I do not like girls better than men. I dislike them both equally."

"You could have fooled me," muttered Will.

"Kiss my ass," she replied.

Will told Jonathan, and he laughed. "Good for her. You will learn to love her."

Each of the drivers gave him pointers about their routes before leaving on vacation. He learned the idiosyncrasies of the trucks and the best times of the day to leave, since there were days on which the first stop might be an hour away. Knowing a good place to stop for lunch and take a quick nap was important. He learned that to be good at what the drivers did, it was important to pay attention to all activity along his route. The second stop he made on his first day got his attention. "Had there been rain back at the previous stop the night before?"

On the next stop, "Had he noticed anybody out in the field at the Jensen place? Mr. Jensen sprained his back and was not able to work for a day or two."

Then the next, "Had he heard about the Harpers having a little spat in town? It was supposed to be a good one." Will learned to keep his eyes and ears open.

Another day, he arrived at a store out in Beat Four, a mostly colored area of the county. A white man owned the store, but most of his customers were colored. There was forewarning from the regular driver. A half dozen or so colored children, from toddlers to teenagers, always hung around and would surround the truck by the time it stopped. Will drove onto the dirt lot and got out to hook up his hoses. Kids were swarming like hornets, all wanting to help. They watched his every move with one question after another. Where was Mr. Tom? Was he dead? Was he coming back? According to them, Mr. Tom let them ride on the truck. Would Will do the same?

Tom had forewarned Will. "Be careful. They will try to get you to let them ride with you. The minute you start to drive away, they will jump on the running boards or the back of the truck, or run alongside, chasing after you like a bunch of young dogs. Be a shame to let one get under the wheels."

Will had an idea. He went into the store to look around and spotted a jar of candies, two for a penny, all wrapped in bright paper. Will spent a quarter. The kids knew when he was through and ready to leave; they took positions to jump on. Will pulled out his sack of candy and took a handful. He threw them as far down the road as he could in the direction opposite of the way he intended to leave. The kids were after the candy like hounds after a rabbit. He threw the second handful of candies even further, and the whole pack was gone. He jumped into his truck and fled. When he looked in his rearview mirror, they had caught on and reversed course. They were running after him, eating dust.

Remembering that he would be back there on Friday, he had another idea. When he got back to town, he went straight to the

Morgan-Lindsey Five and Dime to buy a dozen bright red rubber balls. Those kids would be too smart to fall for the candy again.

At the next to last stop, the storeowner asked if Will had room in the cab for four dozen eggs and thirty pounds of sugar. The man who owned the competitive store at his next stop had called. The Methodist Church was having an ice cream freeze, and he was running short on eggs and sugar. Will delivered them.

By the end of the week, he was thinking of what a dichotomy in cultures he was experiencing. A month prior, he had been to a garden party at the home of a millionaire attorney and his wife. It was at a mansion in the Garden District, where a string quartet played classical music. It was a black-tie event to raise money for something, he could not remember. He had rubbed shoulders with the city's finest. There was a catered dinner and three bars serving the very best in liquor and wine. But this Friday, he was in bib overalls and was dirty and smelled like gasoline. Lunch was a souse meat on a white bread sandwich with an RC Cola; dessert was a Moon pie. He thought about the people that he had been with all day. All poor, but they did not know it. Their interest in each other was genuine. This had been a far more enjoyable day for him than the garden party.

Toward the end of his work as a relief driver, he headed to a favorite shade tree to eat lunch and nap. A peddling truck that belonged to the Swenson store was already in the spot. Imogene Swenson, the daughter of the owner, was the driver. She was doing the same thing as Will, covering for the regular driver while she was on vacation. She shared the shade and a few homemade cookies.

Will had known Imogene for as long as he could remember. One of his favorite things about her was that she took interest in his pocketknife collection. In her father's store, she was responsible for the pocketknife display. If she was not busy when he was in the store, she would let him look at all the new inventory of knives. There was nothing like sliding open those little cardboard boxes with the metal corners. Taking a new knife wrapped in lubricated glassine paper and seeing the bright metal, the rich bone handles, and the smell of the oil was intoxicating. Seeing Imogene bend forward over the counter and looking down at the deep cleavage she exposed was not bad either.

Imogene was twenty-eight years old and not married. She and Kirk Massey, the son of a CPA in town, had been an item as long as anyone could remember. But they would never get married as long as Kirk's parents lived. His father had lost a leg as a boy and had a stump below the knee. He used crutches and let the limp, legless trouser leg flap in the breeze. His wife was a hypochondriac. Poor Kirk was obligated to see after them. Or that was his excuse.

Imogene inquired whether Will still had his old flatbed truck. He said he did, and asked if she needed to use it. She would really like to borrow him and the truck both. Her peach crop was about ready, and since half of it belonged to Will's grandfather, maybe he would help her get them to the farmer's market in Meridian. He assured her that he would.

After he completed the five weeks of relief driving, he had catching up to do on the airfield. Fence posts needed painting; he was behind on mowing. All the equipment needed servicing. That consumed his time until the day came when Imogene reminded him of her need to get her peaches to market.

Will met her on a Wednesday evening at her place, the property adjacent to Laura's Lodge. They loaded the peaches in order to get an early start the next morning. After the peaches were loaded, Imogene complained that the peach fuzz gave her a rash, so she invited Will in and told him to fix ice in glasses and get Coca-Colas out of the icebox while she showered. She returned to the kitchen with hair wrapped in a towel and went straight to the pantry. Out came a fruit jar of 'shine. She offered will a shot, and he did not decline. They made plans for the next day, decided on a time to leave, and after another drink, Will went home.

It was about ninety miles to Meridian. The old truck strained under the heavy load, and the trip took almost two hours. They unloaded most of the peaches into their booth and set about selling. Business was slow, and it looked as if they were going to be loading most of the peaches back on the truck. But as decision time neared, a buyer for a small group of grocery stores came up, looked over the peaches, and made a discounted offer if they would deliver the peaches to his warehouse. Imogene seized the opportunity, and as a result, it was late in the day when they headed for home. Imogene started scratching and complaining about the peach fuzz. Will was driving the old truck faster than he should, and under the strain, it overheated. Things were not looking up. They were approaching the river east of town, only twelve miles from home, when the radiator on the old truck started spewing steam. Will coasted to the side of the road and managed to get the truck down an incline and under the river bridge.

He took a bucket from the truck to draw water. Imogene bailed out of the truck on a mission. She beat him to the river and began peeling off her shirt. She told Will to get his water and go about his business. The truck was too hot to pour water into the radiator immediately. Will stood by, waiting for a clear signal from Imogene. When she told him he could turn around, her shirt was on, but she was still wringing water out of her bra.

She walked back to the truck and tied the wet bra to the truck mirror on the passenger side. Will explained that they would have to wait for the truck to cool, but they were in luck. He reached into his toolbox and came out with a pint of Four Roses.

Imogene smiled. "Four Roses with river water chasers. Life could not be better."

The old truck cooled enough for Will to refill the radiator. They got back underway, but not nearly as sober as when they had stopped. On the way into town, Imogene said she was starving. Why not stop at the Toot and get a hamburger? She would treat.

They pulled into the parking space front first. Will did not know if he could manipulate the truck into the space backward. He was a little woozy. They had been there only moments, when a car full of kids pulled through the lot. They honked and laughed. Then another did the same thing. The next car pulled in and stopped behind Will's truck, and one boy called out, "Way to go, Willie!" Imogene realized the reason for the attention and cried out, "Oh my God!" and then reached out and unwound the bra that had been blowing in the breeze. Will started laughing, and Imogene was in tears, laughing herself. "We will be the talk of the town," she exclaimed.

"No, we are already the talk of the town." Will nodded across the parking lot, where the kids in the car were pointing at Will's truck. It was only a week before Will would be leaving to go back to school. He had to figure out a way not to make any trips to Swenson's Mercantile and Hardware. He did not like the idea of facing up to old man Swenson.

Will's cousin Patricia was the first to get in touch following the bra incident at the Toot. "Willie," she said teasingly over the phone. She knew he preferred Will. "Just can't keep it in your pants, can you? First it was the school nurse and now a girl old enough to be your mommy." She squealed with laughter.

Then Will asked innocently "What are you talking about?"

Patricia said, "Don't play dumb with me; everybody in town is talking. By the way, Mr. Swenson caught up with you yet? You know he is looking for you, don't you?" Then she giggled again. Will said he had thoughts of getting his things together and heading on back to New Orleans.

32

Fall, 1948: Will's Sophomore year — Stephanie Morgan

Will told Jack that it might not be important historically, but it was important in his life. The young woman he would meet his sophomore year might have been the one, had circumstances been different. He thought it was interesting because of the way the MacMorogh family name had played an important role in his relationship with her.

That sophomore year was about like the first, the studies a little more intense. Will had developed good study habits the first year; he was well on his way to achieving his scholastic goals. Even though the studies were more intense, this was a more relaxed year, and he began to socialize more. He dated a few different girls he met through his Aunt Bea and her friends, but none seriously.

Then along came second year physics and Stephanie Morgan. The alphabet selected them to be lab partners. Miss Morgan told Will right away that she was in pre-med and needed to do well in all her classes. She preferred to have a female lab partner with her same ambitious goals.

Will told her he couldn't care less; find herself another partner. That was not as easy as she hoped. Then time came for their first lab experiment. Miss Morgan was less than efficient in putting equipment together. With Will, it was second nature. The first pop test also caught Miss Morgan by surprise. She missed three out of ten of the questions and made a "C." Will missed none and made an "A." Will left class as soon as it was over. It was raining, and he was anxious to dash home before it got too heavy. He was waiting to cross St. Charles Avenue when a yellow Chevrolet convertible rolled up. The driver reached across to roll down the window. It was Miss Morgan.

"Need a lift?" she called.

"No, I live just down the block here on Exposition."

Miss Morgan said, "Really, I live just around the corner from Exposition on Prytania. Get in; I will drive you."

In the car, Miss Morgan said, "Sorry about being a jerk and not wanting you for a lab partner. You are apparently a better physics student than I." Will accepted the apology. "Can we study together sometime?"

Will said, "You name the time." At his corner, he stepped out of the car and trotted down the block.

Their next class together was on a Friday. Miss Morgan, who Will now called Stephanie, asked what Will's plans were for the weekend. She said she usually went home to Baton Rouge but was staying in town for the coming one.

He explained about his usual Saturday trip to the parking garage to take care of his Aunt Bea's car collection. Stephanie said that she loved cars and asked if she might go along. He told her it was a work-day for him and not a social outing. She accepted that fact and still asked to go help.

After a few hours working together that Saturday morning, Will changed his mind about the girl. She might not be too handy with tools, but she sure knew how to clean and polish. At noontime, they walked across the street at to an oyster bar and ate foot-long po'boys with schooners of beer.

There was one problem with Stephanie. She wanted to tell Will all about her boyfriend at home. That seemed to be her main topic of conversation on several occasions. Matthew had been her steady since ninth grade. Their fathers were law partners; their mothers were college roommates. They did everything together on weekends. Their lives centered on the country club, golf, and Tiger Football.

She and Matthew were like another married couple. If she did not show up on weekends, it upset everybody. They expected her to participate whether she wanted to or not. Matthew seemed to love the togetherness; she preferred that they do things with other young people. She had put her foot down was refusing to go home every weekend. If she was not going to be in town, she did not mention it to Will. If she was, she started planning by mid-week. "Are we going to work on the cars Saturday?" she would say. Never was it, "If you do not have anyone else to help you, I would love to go with you to work on the cars Saturday." That bothered Will a bit.

On a chilly weekend in November, Stephanie did not go home and invited herself to help with the cars. They did their usual thing: work until noon and then go have a po'boy and a brew or two. Stephanie started in on her past weekend at home with Matthew. After lunch, they were working on the last car for the day, the Rolls Royce Silver Wraith. Both were sitting on the front seat. Will was cleaning windows while Stephanie was polishing rich burled walnut. Once again, she brought up Matthew. Will put down his cleaning material, reached across to her, took the wood polish rag out of her hand, and then kissed her long and hard. She pulled away, shock in her eyes.

"What, wh—" That was all she could say before Will exploded.

"Did it ever occur to you that I do not give one happy damn about Matthew, his parents, Tiger Football, or the damn country club?"

Tears welled into her eyes and she turned to Will, slid across the seat, and smothered him with another kiss, then another.

"Sorry," she said. "I did not know I was boring you." Then she kissed him again. That started a relationship that lasted well into their senior year. They were close during the school week, but she still went to Baton Rouge on many weekends. They studied together and before long began to rely on each other for help in other areas. Stephanie had concern for his comfort and well-being. She tried to please him and was very gracious for the things he did for her. She never mentioned Matthew, but Will knew he was still in the picture.

Then came a weekend of change. When Stephanie asked about cleaning the cars on Saturday, he told her that he had other plans. His aunt was planning a big party two weekends later at The Point. On Saturday, he was going to take a load of party supplies, silverware, dishes, crystal, and things like that. Then he would be supervising the people doing a major cleaning and grounds keeping. He planned to stay overnight.

"I thought you were going home this weekend," he said.

"I think I would rather go with you. That is, if you would like me to," she replied.

They drove up in his aunt's Packard Estate wagon. Will recalled fondly that it had real wood paneling. Stephanie was as excited as a kid looking for Santa Claus. She had often heard of The Point and knew some of the history. From Will's description, she had a visual image in mind and could not wait to see the place. She gasped when they drove through the black wrought iron gates. It was exactly like her vision. It looked like a paddle wheeler without the paddle wheel.

They unloaded the wagon and pitched in with the cleaning crew. By late afternoon, the place sparkled. A light going over the following weekend, and it would be perfect. Stephanie appreciated Will's desire for perfection, especially if it meant pleasing his aunt.

That evening, they cleaned up, dressed in fresh casual clothes, and had cocktails on the veranda. Afterward, they strolled down to Milton's Seafood restaurant on the river. Dinner was extraordinary; their spirits were high. Back at The Point, they watched from the veranda as a thunderstorm moved over the lake. After one more after dinner drink, Will announced that it was it was time to turn in. Stephanie excused herself and returned dressed in a short nighty. She took Will by the hand and pulled him along to the bedroom, where she went to work undressing him.

The next morning, lying with her head propped on her hand and elbow, she looked Will in the eye. "I care a lot for you. I would much rather spend my time with you," she said. "I do not know how long I can keep this charade going with my family. I have to tell them."

Will had begun to share the same feeling and told her so. However, he wanted her to know that any decisions she made about family had to be her own. He felt that theirs was a great relationship. Only time would tell where it might go. She would have to work it out. He would not pressure her. He left it at that. There was plenty of time to talk about the future.

Driving back to the city, she put her head on his shoulder. "I never expected this to happen," she said. "I am not prepared for it. Please be patient with me." Thanksgiving and Christmas came and went. During the spring semester, they grew much closer. Seldom was there any mention of her weekends at home. Stephanie gained the respect of Dr. Bea and Carole Anne and was frequently included when Dr. Bea called upon Will for escort service to one of her obligations. The school year ended; both had apprehensions about being apart for the summer. They agreed to correspond through the summer.

33

Summer, 1949: Mrs. Kaplan

Will once again got the earliest summer cruise dates for ROTC. He was looking forward to the summer responsibility. He would be taking care of the airfield so that Vivian and Baxter, his grandmother's servants, could take a month long vacation. His grandmother offered to let him stay in his old bedroom in the big house. He chose instead to stay in the little apartment alongside the big hangar, the one Jonathan had used after his foot was crushed.

The day his two week cruise ended, he would be leaving Pensacola by bus at five in the morning. The train from New Orleans to New Cotswold would depart at 6:00 p.m. Usually that would be a reasonable connection. However, dense fog slowed the bus, and it arrived at the Field House at Tulane at 5:00 p.m., two hours late. There was barely enough time to grab a cab to the station. He had planned to drop off his navy gear and change into civvies at his apartment, but time did not allow.

He boarded the train as it was pulling out of the station. The conductor, one of the old time fellows, recognized him and actually pulled him aboard. Will went back to the club car hoping to grab a drink and a seat. One seat was available. Once the train was underway and all the people in the club car seated, he ordered two beers and sat back down. The car cleared after each stop along the way and by the time it left McComb, Mississippi, one of the bench lounges was available. He could stretch out to sleep and did so, even through the routine one-hour stop in Jackson.

Will was conscious of the train slowing and looked at his watch. It was near time to be in New Cotswold. The conductor came back to inform passengers that the train had hit a cow and was stopping for a few minutes just down the line from New Cotswold. It would not look good pulling into the station with a dead cow across the front. Will gathered his gear, and with the help of the conductor, dragged it to the platform between the cars. A light mist was falling, but it seemed to be getting heavier as the train crept into the station. The mist was so thick that the lights on the station platform wore large haloes. The depot itself was scarcely visible.

Will jumped down from the train; the conductor dropped his duffle and two other satchels to him. He headed to the waiting room. The mist was heavier; he could see images of three people huddled under one umbrella, waiting to board. Suddenly, there was a squeal, and one of the persons darted from under the umbrella, calling his name. "Will, Will!" She got to him before he could drop his luggage, threw her arms around him, and kissed him. It was Kacky, his high school girlfriend.

"Mother, look, it's Will!" she squealed. "Oh my goodness, it is good to see you. This is my roommate, Joanne; we are on our way to St. Louis, can you believe it, do you need a ride, Mom, can you give Will a ride? We gotta' go, the train is boarding. I will see you later, love you, bye. Momma, give me a kiss, yes, we will be careful, bye now." All spoken in one breath.

The conductor was calling the last "All Aboard!" The train bucked and screeched. Will turned to Mrs. Kaplan. She pulled the scarf closely around her head. Under the open raincoat, she had on a cotton blouse with a solid row of buttons from neck to waist. Her skirt was a multi-colored, full-length wrap around.

She smiled, "Need a ride, sailor boy? I understand you are going to be my summer neighbor." Will confirmed that he was and that he looked forward to it. The Kaplan house sat on a hill a quarter mile from his grandparents' house. It looked out across the airfield from the east. The pasture of the Kaplan property adjoined the airfield.

Mrs. Kaplan said, "Please excuse me, I have to go to the ladies room before we leave. I will only be a moment."

Will needed to do the same and went into the men's room. He could hear the toilet flush in the next room and then water running. He went back into the waiting room and stood near the door. It took much more than a moment; it took a while to comb out her hair and apply fresh makeup.

He lifted his duffle, and Mrs. Kaplan insisted on taking the other two pieces. At the car, her usual yellow Buick convertible, she unlocked the trunk. Will shoved the duffle into the trunk. She heaved the two satchels in alongside, and as she did so, her breasts rubbed against his arm. Will opened her door for her, then went around to slide in on his side.

The heavy mist had turned to heavy rain, and visibility was poor, the windshield wipers struggling to keep the windshield clear. When Mrs. Kaplan braked, her long split skirt unfolded and revealed a lot of brown leg. She immediately pulled the skirt together, but each time she stepped on the brake, the same thing happened. She gave up.

When they arrived at his grandparents' place, Will instructed Mrs. Kaplan to drive to the apartment by the hangar. She was surprised that he was going to stay there. She thought he would want to stay in the house. He explained; too big, too much to clean.

It was pouring buckets. The outside light at the hangar apartment was on, courtesy of Baxter. Mrs. Kaplan said it was raining too hard to get out of the car and suggested that they wait until it slacked a bit. She turned in her seat and pulled her legs up beside her, then propped one arm across the steering wheel and the other on the back of the seat.

"Will," She said. "I have needed to tell you something for a long time. Seeing you and Kacky together tonight made me sad. I know that you probably still hate me for having a part in Kacky breaking up with you, and I need to explain."

Will wanted to say, "Whoa, lady, it was I who did the breaking up." However, he held his tongue.

Mrs. Kaplan continued. "I became a woman when I was twelve years old. By the time I was thirteen, I had a better figure than my mother, and more of it. We would walk down the street, and men would honk their horns or whistle. My mother knew they were whistling at me, not her.

"In those days, it was not unusual for department stores to lease out various departments to independent vendors. My mother owned the millinery department in the large Kaplan store in Jackson. It required long hours."

Lightning struck nearby, and thunder rattled the old tin hangars. Mrs. Kaplan paused until it was over. "My mother would come home from work and find me sitting on our front stoop, several older boys talking and gawking. She realized that this was going on from the time school was out until she got home. "

"She asked my grandmother to keep me after school. It was OK, but my grandmother had a weekend job, and I would be home alone. My mother's solution was to take me to the shop with her; I was big enough and old enough to help women try on hats. That was when I met Sturdivant Kaplan."

Mrs. Kaplan paused again. "What I am going to tell you has to be between us. Kacky worships her father. She should never have to hear this. Sturdivant worked at the department store with responsibility for advertising and promotion. He was also a buyer for ladies ready-to-wear."

She continued to explain in a matter-of-fact tone. On Saturday, he would bring in several models. They would parade throughout the store, modeling whatever he wanted to push for the week. It was easy work. The models dressed in rooms on the fourth floor and began their tour there, then went floor by floor to the ground floor. They then rode the elevator back up to the fourth, got a different outfit, and did it all over again. On a busy Saturday, two models failed to come in. Sturdivant asked Kathryn's mother if he might borrow her for the day. Her mother was delighted to have her busy. Kathryn had never worn heels except to play "ladies," like all little girls liked to do. She wore heels low enough to manage without looking too clumsy.

The part he played in getting the women dressed was a surprise. Ladies were running around in their bras and panties between changes, while he snipped here and tucked there, to make the fit just perfect. There was no time for modesty. The first time Sturdivant touched her was to get a better fit in the bosom of a dress: he stuck his fingers right down in her bra. She was shocked, but after several other times of his patting her butt or running his hand up her thigh to straighten a slip, she got accustomed to it. None of the other women even seemed to notice. They were busy combing their hair or putting on different makeup.

He told her she was a hit that Saturday. She was going to be a regular. Things progressed; she liked telling her friends she was a model. Many of them would show up on Saturday to see her.

Sturdivant boasted that she was good for business. As time went on, she became more comfortable with high heeled shoes. She watched the other women closely. Her posture and demeanor improved. Something else progressed also. Sturdivant took more liberty with his feels. In order to congratulate her, he often pecked her on the cheek. Sometimes the peck was on her mouth. She admitted she liked it. When he touched her, she gave an impish little grin.

In the fall, her mother and the other buyers made their buying jaunt trip to New York. Sturdivant suggested that her mother bring Kathryn along. He felt she had real talent, even enough to be a professional model. It would be good to expose her to the real world. In New York, her mother was paying her own expenses. They stayed in a less expensive hotel than the rest, but it was still convenient to the markets her mother visited.

The third day, he showed up at one of the rooms where her mother was picking goods. He told her mother he thought it would be good to take Kathryn to some of the other rooms for exposure. She agreed. They hit several before lunch, including a lingerie showing where the models exposed more than Kathryn had seen done before.

They left with a few packages. Sturdivant suggested that they drop them at his hotel and have lunch before continuing for the afternoon. After lunch, they went to his room, where he dropped the packages on the bed and told Kathryn they were for her. She was excited. There were sheer undies and a very revealing nightgown. Sturdivant urged her to model them. She did. She lost her virginity in New York City, just shy of her fourteenth birthday.

When they were back in Jackson, he arranged to take her places, job-related of course. He even picked her up at school a time or two. Then something went wrong with the magic. She was pregnant and only fourteen years old. She realized that she had a problem when she missed her period. When she began to puke her guts out in the morning, she told Sturdivant, and he told her not to worry. He would arrange to have it taken care of.

Before that happened, however, her mother became suspicious. Kathryn admitted the truth. When she told her mother that Sturdivant was going to take care of it, her mother not only threw a fit, but she threw a gun in her purse. The next morning, with loaded gun, she went in early, knowing she might find him alone in his office. She confronted him with the problem, and he also told her not to worry; he was going to take care of it. She pulled the gun from her purse and jammed it between his legs, telling him to put his arms in the air and turn around. When he did so, she shoved the gun in his back and told him to walk. She pushed him all the way to his father's office with the gun bumping his spine. The old man stood in alarm as they came into his office.

Kathryn said that her mother told her that that was when the negotiations began. She wanted Sturdivant to marry Kathryn. He would claim the baby as his daughter. He would put five million dollars in an account for Kathryn. The old man and Sturdivant both objected vehemently. Her mother told them she could see the headlines now. *Son of long time Department Store owner sentenced to life in prison for statutory rape of thirteen-year-old girl and violation of the Mann Act.* Then she reached for the phone on the old man's desk.

They negotiated the five million to two. In addition, they were planning to establish a small store in New Cotswold. They would divide the profits of the store between Kathryn and her baby. They would build a house to her specifications and buy her a new Buick of her choice each year. That was how she had ended up in New Cotswold.

"So Will, you might imagine what was going on in my mind when Kacky came from her dates with you. Her hair would be all mussed up, her lipstick smeared all over her face. My God, I just knew you two were being intimate. I could not stand the thought of her missing everything I missed. I never went on a date. I never went to school parties. I never learned to dance all the latest steps. I did not get to be a cheerleader or wear some boy's letter jacket. I learned to burp a baby and change dirty diapers."

Kathryn laughed. "I was so jealous of my daughter. I would think of her doing all of the things I missed. Then I thought, I will do it with her. That is the reason I volunteered for everything that went on at school. That is why I threw parties and chaperoned at everything that went on. I was living a life I never had experienced."

Will told her a funny story about what his friends used to say to him. "Mind if Mrs. Kaplan and I double-date with you and Kacky tonight?" She giggled at the thought.

The rain slacked. They got out of the car and waded through ankle deep water to the front door. Will opened the door, flipped on the light, and there on the counter was a big red cake box with a note resting on top. The note was from Vivian. It said, "Thanks so much for helping make our vacation possible. Enjoy your favorite cake. There is cold sweet milk in the icebox. Love Vivian and Baxter."

"Want some cake?" Will said.

Kathryn took the cover off the box. The center of the cake was rich white coconut, surrounded by a deep coating of chocolate icing. "How could I refuse?" Meanwhile, the storm got worse and the lights flickered several times, prompting Will to get out matches and candles.

"I do not like the thought of going into my house in this storm and having the lights go out," said Mrs. Kaplan. "Do you mind if I curl up on your couch?"

Will replied. "There is another bed. You are welcome to curl up in it instead."

Mrs. Kaplan insisted on the couch and urged Will to go on to bed. She realized he had been up for almost twenty-four hours. At seven fifteen the following morning, someone beat on the front door with such force that the glass in the door rattled. Mrs. Kaplan called out to Will. He got up and ran to the door in his shorts, wondering what was happening. He swung open the door. A Sheriff's Department cruiser with lights flashing sat behind Mrs. Kaplan's car; a deputy sheriff stood facing Will. The town marshal stood by his own car, hand on his gun belt.

"Is this Mrs. Kaplan's car?" asked the deputy. Will acknowledged that it was.

"Is she here?" asked the deputy.

"She is," Will replied. "She may still be asleep."

"I want to see her now; may I come in?" urged the deputy.

Will had no choice. He swung the door open, and there stood Mrs. Kaplan, wrapped in a sheet , her hair a mess, sleep lines on her cheek, her bare feet showing.

"You OK, Mrs. Kaplan?" the deputy inquired.

"Yes, I am fine, what is the problem?"

The deputy explained that Mrs. Kaplan's help had arrived for work and set off the alarm when she went in. The sheriff got the call and responded. The maid was flustered. She could not find Mrs. Kaplan and did not know how to disarm the alarm.

He had looked across at the airfield, spotted Mrs. Kaplan's car, and come to investigate. He asked again if Mrs. Kaplan was OK. She responded that she was. He insisted that he would rather she come with him. His excuse: they needed to disarm the alarm. The truth was that he still feared that she might not be there on her own accord.

Will was fully awake now. The situation began to sink in. He knew what he would be thinking if he were the deputy. There was hanky-panky going on between Mrs. Kaplan and Will MacMorogh. "Oh crap," he murmured to himself. What if these guys talked? It would be all over town before noon. He could just hear his cousin Patricia.

In about an hour, Mrs. Kaplan called. She had spent a lot of time with the deputy and the marshal. She had explained the situation and what she was doing at Will's apartment. She was unsure if they believed her. She agreed that if even they did, nobody else would. Hopefully, the two lawmen would keep their mouths shut.

34

Summer, 1949: Rev. Billy D. Simpkins and Christine

Patricia had been expecting Will in town and called in the afternoon. First, she wanted to invite him to go to church the next morning. Even though they were Methodists, they were visiting the Baptist Church. That church had a new choir director and a new music program.

Next, she gave him an invitation to the Lamar Family Sunday Buffet. He would be more welcome, however, if his Aunt Jessie saw him in church. Will was welcome, but he did not go to church. In his opinion, one choir sounded like the other.

Three of the Lamar girls, now all married, lived side by side on Lamar Street. Each Sunday during warm weather, they had their Sunday dinner buffet under the shade trees that cooled their backyards. Each family had a different church preference, Baptist, Methodist, and Presbyterian. Their ministers had open invitations to attend the Sunday soiree and often did.

Will was always nervous around the Lamar sisters. They were quick to notice anything he had ever done that was out of line. He knew that if the word were out about him and Mrs. Kaplan, he would not hear the end of it. But no one said anything; he was relieved.

The special guest that Sunday was the Reverend Billy Dee Simpkins, Minister of Music, First Baptist Church, and his wife. They asked him to say grace before serving lunch. The reverend and his Mrs. sat together at the table in Aunt Jessie's yard. Jessie was not Baptist, but her husband was. He usually dropped a twenty in the plate on Sunday. Even though she was Methodist, Aunt Jessie, along with Patricia, went to the Baptist Church a few times to hear the beautiful voice of Mrs. Simpkins. Christine was her name. She was beautiful, to say the least. Will might be attending church some himself, he thought.

On Monday, Will spent some time with Jonathan before he went to work on the airfield. Jonathan said nothing about Will's adventure. He was close to both the sheriff and the marshall, so if they were going to tell anyone, it would be him. Will felt a little better. The shit did not hit the fan until Wednesday. The General was spending more time in New Cotswold and had arrived from Washington the night before. He wanted to talk to Will.

Even though he was in town on other business, he indicated to Will that he had come to town specifically to talk to him. He was tired of his crap. The century old reputation of the MacMorogh family came from good behavior and service to mankind, not bad conduct. He was not going to let Will destroy even a little of that reputation. As far as the General was concerned, he would like him to spend his summers in New Orleans instead of coming to town to see how many women he could conquer. He did not mention the incident with Mrs. Kaplan, but surely he knew. Then there was one other thing.

The General wanted to make sure that Will understood that a young woman would be coming to town the next week. She would be spending time in their mills on an assignment with the Forestry Service. She was doing a paper on forestry products from planting, to harvesting, to utilization. Under no circumstance was Will to have any relationship with her whatsoever. She would be staying at Mrs. Farmer's boarding house. Will thought he was going to have to write a confirmation of understanding in his own blood. After his ass chewing, Will went back to work. Maybe it would be best if he stayed in New Orleans, especially if that old tyrant was going to be around all the time. He was depressed. He had a lot on his mind. Stephanie and he had agreed to write for the summer. He was going to miss her. Maybe he should go back. But things settled down after a few days. Winston sent him on an errand to Swenson's store. It was the first time he had darkened those doors since the peach trip with Imogene. He swore to himself that if old man Swenson even looked cross eyed at him, he would pack his bags and head back to the Crescent City. He already had incentive.

At the store, though, things were OK. Mrs. Swenson was the first to see him. She welcomed him with open arms and asked about school, his aunt, and his sister. She was genuinely glad he was home for the summer. Imogene came in from the warehouse, all smiles. She started laughing the minute she saw him. She had a big smile when she asked him if he was up for hauling peaches again this year.

Later, Jonathan took him out to look at a new hopper he had designed for installation on one of the Stearmans. He, Dub, and Tommy Schooner then went out to a new joint on the river, specializing in fried catfish. They laughed a lot, swapped flying stories, and caught up on each other's activities. Will felt better. Things were looking up.

Then a long letter arrived from Stephanie. She was worried about her relationship at home. *His* letter to her had prompted a confession to her mother. She played tennis with a friend one morning and then had lunch at the club before returning home. Her mother met her at the door with the first letter Will had sent. It was not open, of course, but the return address was enough to start an inquiry.

"Who is Will MacMorogh from Mississippi?" That was her mother's appalled greeting when she arrived home. Stephanie told her. Her mother put her limp hand to her forehead in tears. She was mortified to know that her daughter was seeing anyone other than Matthew. Her mother had all the questions. Stephanie reiterated them for Will.

Her mother asked if Matthew knew about this boy, Will. Then she had exclaimed, "What in the good Lord's name will Matthew's parents think? We do not deceive our friends. Matthews's mother and I are best of friends. We were Tri Delta together. Your father and Matthew's father are partners. What in the world has come over you?"

Stephanie told Will that she had simply shrugged her shoulders and told her it was another boy. Her mother went into seclusion for the rest of the afternoon. That evening at cocktail hour, her father was informed. He had summoned Stephanie from her room. He started in with his comments, which Stephanie included in her letter. Her father had told her that he had known better than to send her to Tulane. He had given in because she had insisted. He said he did not intend to send her back there if she could not get her head on straight. In addition, he told her that they had already bought season tickets for all of the Tiger games. Her mother had already bought her a new dress for the Harvest Moon Ball. Stephanie went on to write that by the time her father quit spitting and sputtering, he had demanded that she get Will out of her mind. She closed by saying she was in for a long summer.

Will set out to make the best of the situation with his grandfather. The man would be gone in a day or so. Maybe he could stay out of trouble for that long. But it was not to be.

He was mowing the airfield fence line that adjoined the Kaplan property when out of the corner of his eye, he saw Kathryn Kaplan's yellow Buick convertible easing across the pasture. He glanced in that direction. She was alone. All he could see was a big hat and sunglasses. He waved, and she waved back. She kept coming across the pasture until she was parallel to his tractor. She honked and he looked again; she was holding up two beers. Then she pointed downfield to the big oak in her pasture. She sped off in that direction. He followed on the tractor.

When he got down to the oak, he climbed through the barbwire fence and walked over to the car. She opened the passenger door, and he climbed in. Her brown shoulders were bare. She had on yellow terry cloth shorts and a white tank top; a six-pack of beer in a small cooler was on the seat beside her.

"You looked hot," she said. "Thought this might cool you off."

"Thanks, just what I needed."

Kathryn asked, "Have you heard any gossip?"

"Nope," Will said. "But I guess my grandfather has. He gave me a royal ass chewing. He told me it would be OK with him if I spent my summers in New Orleans."

"Did you explain?" she asked.

"No. What about you, heard anything?" Will asked.

She took a long pull on her beer before saying, "It's going around through the kitchen help. My girl, Prissy, said she had heard through her sister who works for your Aunt Tootie. I told Prissy the facts when I got to my house. I am sure she believed it."

"Well, if Tootie knows it, all the Lamar sisters know it. I am sure my cousin Patricia will be riding my ass about it anytime now. Look, my grandfather is leaving tomorrow. If he should come home now and see us down here, all hell will break loose again," Will said.

"Then you would like me to leave, I take it." She laughed. "Why don't you come up to the house for a swim after you are through?" Kathryn was serious.

"Not today, not today," he said. He went back through the fence and started back to mowing. At the end of the airfield, he turned the tractor and saw his grandfather standing at the back gate. He stood a long time staring in Will's direction. Then he turned and watched Mrs. Kaplan's yellow Buick as it drove through the open pasture to her house. But over the next several days, Will heard nothing more and was sure the little incident had blown over. Time would tell. Bad thing was, his grandfather was like an elephant. He forgot nothing.

A month went by, and Vivian and Baxter returned from vacation. Will went back to work at the machine shop. Late on a Friday afternoon, he received a phone call. It was his grandfather. His greeting was friendly enough, and his conversation to the point.

"Go to church at the Baptist Church this Sunday. I want a full report on what happens." Those were his instructions. Will tried to get some clarification. But his grandfather was short with him again and said, "Just do it."

Will went immediately to Jonathan to see if he could get clarification. He told him what his grandfather had instructed him to do. Jonathan responded by telling Will that he and his grandfather had discussed it. It would not be appropriate for Jonathan to go, but he did want someone he could trust to attend and report.

"He trusts you. Go."

On Sunday, Will put on nice trousers and a clean white shirt, no tie. He even polished his shoes. He made sure he was on time and paused in the narthex, looking to see if he saw his Aunt Jessie or Patricia. He spotted them on the middle aisle of the church. Patricia's dad was not with them. There was room on that row if everyone would slide down. He walked quietly down. Patricia sat on the end of the row, with her mother next to her. Will tapped Patricia on the shoulder; she turned to look up and seeing Will, bumped her mother's leg to move over. When his Aunt Jessie saw him, she faked a faint. The people in the row behind, knowing Will, started giggling.

He was at a loss as to why he was there. But whatever it was did not matter at that point. Christine Simpkins not only was a beautiful girl, but she had a tremendous voice. He really began to think his grandfather had decided that religion was going to be Will's salvation. Maybe going to church would keep him from ruining the years and years of wonderful MacMorogh reputation. He was a little miffed. The minister finished his sermon, and they sang the last song; it was time for dismissal. But before that, the minister had an announcement.

"Ladies and Gentlemen, it is my sad duty to inform you that today is the last day that we will have Ruby Holder with us. Ruby selected us for her temporary church home a month ago while she came here to work on a special project for the US Forestry Service. Since coming to us, she has been a strong voice in our choir and a wonderful contributor to our Sunday School Program. She asked that

I give her an opportunity to thank the congregation for making her stay such a grand experience.

"Ruby, come forward."

Ruby did come forward. In fact, she came around in front of the preacher and stood at the foot of the middle aisle.

"Thank-you, Reverend Procter. It is indeed an honor for me to have this opportunity. I cannot thank you enough for welcoming me into your church and into your hearts. I have been truly blessed."

She then looked around the room and appeared to make eye contact with someone in the back of the room. She paused a moment and smiled at the person before continuing. "I quite honestly did not expect to be treated so well, because on my last visit, I was not." She had not raised her voice any louder than what was necessary to hear her, and she paused again. There was a murmur or two. A woman in the front row looked at her questioningly.

"Some of you are too young to remember this, but the last time I was here, my grandparents threw a nice party for me, my mother, and my father. We were visiting a few days from our home in Detroit. My father was an accomplished pianist, so my grandfather moved the piano out on the front porch. Soon folks from the other houses in the Quarter gathered around to dance and sing."

When she said "Quarter," there was more stirring in the congregation. At that point, Will knew something was amiss. He had a pen; all he needed was paper. He opened a hymnal and started writing on the blank face page. Before it was over, he had written on four. He ripped all of them out of the books. Aunt Jessie was embarrassed. Frowning, she mouthed, "What are you doing?"

Ruby kept on talking. "Momma and my Grandma were in the kitchen, frying up chickens. I was trying to help, but like most four-year-olds, I was just in the way. All of a sudden, there was screaming and yelling in the front yard. Grandma ran to the front door and began to scream. My mother and I hid in the pantry. There was fire in the house, and smoke was coming in. I was terribly afraid.

"The commotion outside started when a group of men on horses, with white hoods and sheets around them, pulled my daddy off the front porch. With their fists and horse hooves, they murdered him."

With the last sentence, she raised her voice a bit, but was still in complete control.

The murmuring got louder. Some people stood. An usher came down the middle aisle. He drew his hand across his throat, trying to signal the preacher to stop Ruby. It was no use; she kept right on talking.

"The pantry door was jerked open. One of those hooded men pulled my mother out from under the table. Smoke was thick in the house. The man propped his gun in the corner. He slid everything on my grandmother's worktable onto the floor with a loud clatter. Flour, salt boxes, dishes went everywhere.

"Then he jerked the front of my mother's dress down. He pulled her skirt up and pushed her down on the table. He dropped his pants and crawled on top of her. She was screaming her lungs out, and no one came to help. There was a big frying pan full of chicken cooking on the stove. I was only four years old, and I could barely lift it, but I did."

In the back of the church a moan, "Oh no, oh no."

"I poured that hot grease and chicken down the man's back. He screamed as loud as he could and jumped off my mother. His big white hat came off." From the back of the church, there was a half cry, another loud moan, then sobbing from across the church. Several more people stood. Some people were trying to work their way out the back. Two burly men stood in the narthex. Two others stood by the side door. They would not let anybody leave.

Ruby kept on talking in her slow, controlled pace, no anger in her voice, no expression of anger in her countenance. "This man tried to get to his feet, but the floor was slick with grease, and he fell. Mother grabbed his gun. She had no idea how to shoot it, so she stabbed the barrel at his eye. All I remember is seeing a bright red circle form on his forehead and blood start to come out. I thought my mother had shot him in the head."

With that, a blood-curdling scream came from the same area as the moaning. A man tried to stand; a woman pulled him down. By now, the whole congregation was staring toward the area of the scream. Some stood to get a better look. Reverend Procter tried to get Ruby to stop. He held his hands high to the Lord and began to pray.

The organist started to play at full volume. Ruby had to talk louder. She was determined to finish.

"My mother grabbed me up and wrapped me in her arms. Her skirt was on fire, and I could feel hot grease on her clothes. Fire blocked the back door, so she gathered herself around me and ran through the flame and into the backyard. My mother started running, then two other men threw her to the ground. One started beating on her again. He rolled her over, and his shirt was on fire. Finally, one of the men grabbed me up, and the other, who was beating on my mother, lifted her up in his arms. We ran like the wind."

With that, Ruby nodded toward the back of the church and slowly walked down the aisle and out the church doors. Five dark blue Fords sat in the street. Ruby went to the first. Four men were with the car. A back door swung open, one man alighted, and Ruby climbed in. The man who held the door got in beside her. The car sped off.

Several men with badges held high came in the side door of the church. One came directly to the front and took the preacher's microphone. He calmed the congregation and told them to all sit. Two men went directly to the row where the moaning was. A man with a circular scar on his forehead sat motionless, staring straight ahead. The woman next to him had her head down almost to her knees, her hands covering her face. That row of people left the church. The other men with badges let the other members of the congregation leave, row by row. The agents pulled three other men from the congregation and held them for questioning. Later, they arrested all three.

Will, Patricia, and his aunt were in the middle group to leave. Aunt Jessie took each of them by the sleeve and said, "Just keep walking. We'll talk at home." Both Will and Aunt Jessie had parked near the church. There was far too much commotion. They left their cars behind and walked the four blocks to Aunt Jessie's house.

At home, the phone was ringing off the hook. As soon as Aunt Jessie had one inquiry answered, another call came. All of the Lamar sisters wanted to know what had happened. The regular Sunday buffet went on, but few could eat. There was rumor after rumor. No other talk was important.

At one point, someone called Will for a phone call. It was Jonathan calling to tell him to be at the curb in front of Aunt Jessie's. He was on his way. In the car, Jonathan's first words were, "You were there weren't you?"

"Yes, I was there. I do not know if I understand."

"We have to get to a secure phone for you to call the General. He is afraid the local operators might listen in to your conversation. We are going to take my plane to Meridian. We can call from there."

Jonathan knew the airport manager at Key Field. They used his office to make the call. Will related the entire story to his grandfather, reading notes from the confiscated pages he had torn from the hymnals. When he was through, his grandfather asked a number of questions. Had she mentioned anything past the point where the men beat out the flames on her mother's dress? Did she mention what happened after they started running again? Did she say she knew the men or had later learned the names of the two men? At any point, was the MacMorogh name mentioned? Was there any talk that the man arrested worked at our mill? The answer to those questions was, No.

Before Will hung up, his grandfather congratulated him and told him he appreciated what he had done. Then he told Will to give the phone back to Jonathan and to leave the room. Jonathan and his grandfather talked for a long time afterward. On the trip back to New Cotswold, Will flew the airplane while Jonathan snoozed. Will had many questions. But he knew that if there was more he needed to know, Jonathan would tell him in time.

The whole town was in an uproar. The mayor and the county sheriff made an appeal to the Highway Patrol to send additional troopers for a few days. They were sitting on a keg of dynamite. Several fires broke out in the Quarter for three or four nights after the incident. Crosses burned around the county.

The weekly newspaper came out on Thursday with a scathing editorial by the editor. Why did the Feds have to use the Baptist Church for their venue to make the arrests? There had been four more arrests, all done at private homes. A response from the FBI agent in charge said that Ruby did not inform them that she was going to make her pitch in front of the congregation. She had located and identified the man who had attempted to rape her mother almost immediately after her arrival. His name was Rupert Hackberry. She kept investigating and was confident that three other men who often visited with Hackberry were a part of the gang who had raided the house that night. She had snuck onto the Hackberry property late one evening and found five cases of dynamite. Furthermore, they all went to the same church. She was well aware that all four were brazen bullies. They carried guns and switchblade knives. It was her assessment that the best place to get all four at one time, without any danger, would be at the church.

The FBI agent had confirmed that Ruby was working on her own and had gotten the attention of the FBI when she gave them Hackberry's name. The agents were on hand that Sunday for the arrest of all four men. Ruby had surprised them all. It took several weeks for things to calm down even a little. But the incident did one thing for Will: the rumors about him and Kathryn Kaplan were no longer of interest.

Will finally asked Jonathan to explain the reason that his grandfather had selected him to go to church that Sunday. Why not Jonathan? He was around during the time it had happened. Jonathan told Will that he should ask his grandfather, knowing that that would never happen. By week's end, Will was so tired of having everybody he met up with tell them about the arrests that he strongly considered cutting the summer in New Cotswold short and returning to New Orleans. However, that idea quickly faded with a surprise phone call from Maureen Mullens, Tish's mother. Tish was coming in on Saturday night and would be around for almost two weeks before school began again.

35

Summer, 1949: Maureen Mullens and Tish

Will had not seen Mrs. Mullens or Moon since he had been back in town, but he had asked about them. Jonathan said that Moon had a new hobby. He was raising, training, and even driving harness horses. He was spending a lot of time that summer making county and state fairs. Mrs. Mullens was with him part of the time. Moon was still in the whiskey business; there was no doubt about that. However, he was branching out into businesses that were more legitimate, like his taxi business and the scrap iron business.

He now had two ice plants, one on a busy street in Jackson. Besides ice, he sold beer cheaper than any place in town, but by the case only. In a short time, he had become the biggest customer of the local beer distributor. Moon had a vision. He wanted to be a legitimate beer distributor.

On Sunday, Tish called to invite Will out to her house for supper. It was just she and her mother. They were thinking about grilling steaks, so Will insisted that he bring the meat. He would get it from Nap.

Will had not considered the fact that getting the steaks from Nap meant talking to Nap. He had not seen him since the past summer. That was going to take a while, so he went early. Sure enough, Nap was full of questions about the arrest. What was the reaction of those assholes? Folks had known for sure that those men were involved in killing "Piano Boy," but no one would do anything about it. It took that one little woman working alone to get it done.

Nap was mad by the time he got through talking, and he turned to Will, "It don't take long to figure that one out, Will. Now we got this whole mess out in the open again. I do not like to think about what may happen."

Will arrived at the Mullens farm about five. His heart thumped when he saw Tish. He had almost forgotten how much he cared for her and her friendship. Maureen had stirred up some of her "Ain't that just like Maureen" concoction. It was half shine and half wild plum wine. She kept it in the freezer compartment of the refrigerator and served it in frosted tumblers over ice. It was a superb drink. Moon had named the concoction. He said it was just like Maureen: one little kiss, and you were dizzy!

After a lot of catching up on each other and family, Maureen put the steaks on the grill along with potatoes wrapped in foil. Tish sliced beefsteak tomatoes, juicy yellow onions, and red radishes. Will monitored the steaks.

After the superb supper, Maureen poured a little more of the concoction. She had a surprise dessert for later. They sat comfortably by the creek, a nice fire going in the pit where the steaks had grilled. The subject of conversation got around to the latest news. Will, for what seemed like the hundredth time, related the events at the church. He shared with them the fact that he was mystified that his grandfather had demanded that he attend the service.

Tish laughed. "You certainly were not going as an undercover agent. You in church would stick out like a sore thumb."

He agreed. He had even seen some people snicker when his Aunt Jessie had faked a fainting spell when she saw him.

Then Tish asked him the same question that his grandfather had. Had Ruby said what had happened after they ran from the fire and the two men got them? Will said that that was as far as Ruby's story went. Tish looked at her mother questioningly. Maureen shrugged her shoulders slightly.

"Will, you really do not know what else happened that night?" Tish asked.

"No, I have never heard that."

Tish turned to her mother. "Will you tell the story?'

So Maureen began. "The night of the murder, Moon was in town. As he was getting in his car to head home, the fire siren sounded three blasts; the fire was in the Quarter. He was two blocks from the fire engine. He raced there in time to get on the truck with Jonathan. By the time they got to the house, fire had engulfed it. Somebody was screaming that people were in the house. Jonathan and Moon tried the back door, but flames were shooting out through the door. Suddenly, a woman carrying a child burst from the house and crashed into your father. Her dress was on fire, and he pulled her to the ground. The child tumbled from her arms, screaming. Jonathan lifted the child and beat out the flames of her dress with his bare hands. Moon rolled the woman in the dirt to smother the flames on her clothes.

"He lifted her, Jonathan had the child, and together they ran away from the scene. A huge culvert, almost large enough to stand in, went under School Street and came out alongside Mrs. Farmer's boarding house. They ran through and up the embankment on the other side. They ran to Moon's car, planning to flee the county. The car needed fuel, so they went to Nap's store. By then, their own clothes were smoldering, their skin beginning to blister. They knew Nap would help."

Maureen took a sip of her drink before continuing with the tale. "When Nap saw the situation, he wanted to call Dr. Rubin immediately. Jonathan thought better and told Nap that the telephone operators could not be trusted. He told Nap to go get Dr. Rubin in person and send him to our house. Nap snatched off his apron, ran to the door, turned the CLOSED sign around, and rushed to his car.

"It took me totally by surprise when Moon burst through out front door with a child in his arms. He smelled of smoke, there were blisters on his face, and his hair was singed. Some of his skin stayed on the child's dress when he put her down. Jonathan was right behind, with the woman in his arms. She was in shock. I got quilts to cover her and took the screaming child from her arms."

Maureen paused again and smiled, "Rubin's big feet sounded like thunder when they hit the front porch. I jerked the door open, and Jonathan began to explain the situation. Dr. Rubin gave the mother something for shock. I got scissors and assisted as Dr. Rubin cut her dress off. The woman had severe leg burns. They were greasy and bloody in places and smelled like burned flesh with a hint of chicken. Dr. Rubin treated the burns and gave her something for shock. The child was not bad, only a blister or two. Dr. Rubin gave her a sedative. I cleaned her up and put her to bed.

"Then Dr. Rubin went to work on the two men. Moon had the worst burns. Both his hands were raw, and in a place or two, it was third degree. Dr. Rubin treated the blisters on his face, treated them with salve, and gave him an antibiotic. He wanted to give him a shot for pain. Moon refused. Jonathan had less severe burns on both hands and arms, blistered mostly from contact with the woman's clothes. Dr. Rubin took care of those and offered both men a pain-killer. Dr. Rubin planned to stay the night, but at one in the morning, his answer service called, and he had to go back to town to deliver a baby. He was back before sunrise."

Tish sat on the bench by Will, holding his hand the whole time while Maureen told the story. He was mesmerized. When Maureen was through, Will said, "So it was Moon and Jonathan, and no one has ever known?"

Maureen said, "We never discussed it with other people. I called Winston Jackson after Jonathan and Moon got here, to let him know Jonathan was safe. A few people were suspicious. Jonathan had driven the fire truck, but was not there to drive it home. He went to work the next day, but with a long sleeve shirt to hide burns. I went to the drug store to buy salve. Dr. Irby said it sure was a lot of salve for one order. I told him it was for one of our horses. The woman and child stayed three more days. Moon slipped into town one night in one of his old 'shine hauling' cars. He put Mr. and Mrs. Potter in the back and brought them out to our place to talk to 'Piano Boy's' wife and to see the grandchild. It was a sad meeting. I cried at the sight and what was going on with the poor family." Maureen had tears in her eyes at the thought.

"Then what happened?" asked Will.

"When Dr. Rubin felt the woman was well enough to travel, Jonathan, Moon, and I drove her home to Detroit. That is the end of the story until now."

Will worked every day, but spent most of the evenings with Tish at her house. The Mullens family property was a showplace. Each member of the family had made his or her own contribution to its beauty. The creek now flowed into a lake that Moon had built using an army surplus bulldozer. The lake came within feet of the back of the house. He had built a pier and a gazebo over the lake. The gardens along the creek matched many big city arboretums. It was a lovely place to sit and relax.

While chatting one evening, Will commented on the fact that Tish sounded different. She explained that though she wanted to be a news journalist, she also was taking courses in broadcast journalism. She even went to a speech therapist and had a speech coach.

When he mentioned the fact that she sounded different, she came back with, "Me. I sound different? Will, with my eyes closed, I would swear, when you talk, you sound more and more like a white boy."

Tish asked Will if he thought he could ever live in New Cotswold again. "No," he replied, "not after what I have seen and heard these past few days. This town is full of hate on both sides of the fence."

She left for school two days before Will. He went with Mrs. Mullens to Jackson to put her on the plane. Will pecked Tish on the cheek, hugged her good-bye, and then went back into the terminal building when the plane arrived, so that Mrs. Mullens and Tish could say their own good-byes. Will and Mrs. Mullens were quiet for a while on the way home. Both were lost in their own thoughts. Mrs. Mullens did say she was very proud of both him and Tish. She felt they were growing into fine young people. She was so sorry that Tish could not be happy at home; she missed her terribly.

"And Will," she said. "I know that Jonathan misses you. I think maybe he does not show it, but he does. He talks about you a lot, your future and how he looks forward to the day you will come back to work with him. He needs you.

"While we are on the subject of Jonathan, he worries about your opinion of his relationship with June, since has he moved in with her at the hotel. I do not know how you feel about her, Will, but they are a good team."

36

Fall Semester, 1949: Will's Junior Year at Tulane

The junior year at Tulane was a repeat of the first two. It advanced progressively, and Will thrived on the challenge. As far as his relationship with Stephanie, that was another challenge all its own. They took up where they had left off. Same Saturday routine. Same studying together at night. Same act of ignoring or talking about Matthew. At Thanksgiving, Stephanie went home to Baton Rouge.

Will's grandparents, along with Jonathan and June, flew to New Orleans for Thanksgiving Day. Will drove Aunt Bea's big Packard Estate wagon to meet them at the airport. In the process of loading them and their baggage, he hugged June and said that he was especially glad that she had come along. Jonathan smiled.

They had a great day together. His grandfather was jovial and not too critical. His grandmother stayed out of the way and let the girls cook and serve dinner without interfering. Nobody drank too much. The mood was that of a close family enjoying a special holiday. The next morning when they were loading the car to go back to the airport, Will said to Jonathan, "There's something special about June. It makes me happy to see how much she seems to care for you. I am glad that you have moved into the hotel with her. You deserve someone like her."

Jonathan put his arm around Will and pulled him close. "You do not know how much it means to me. She is special." Will did not see them again until Christmas.

Stephanie came back to school with a request. Her parents wanted to meet Will. They would like to have dinner with the two of them the coming weekend. She felt it was necessary if she was going to resolve the Matthew issue.

Will asked about Matthew. No, she had not broken up with him, but that was her intention. If her parents could meet Will, they would understand.

Dinner plans were for Antoine's for Saturday night. The parents made a reservation for a suite at the Monteleone. There would be cocktails in the suite at 6:00; dinner reservations were at 7:15. Will wore his black cashmere jacket, grey wool slacks, and red, white, and black striped tie. He looked great on the arm of Stephanie in her simple little black dress.

They arrived only a few minutes late for cocktails. Stephanie's mother had a head start. She was smaller than Will might have guessed, but regal in her statue. She wore a camel colored pleated skirt, a white blouse, and a camel sweater over her shoulders. Reading glasses hung from her neck. Mr. Morgan was taller, with black hair with a touch of grey in the temples, parted in the middle. His dress was almost identical to that of his wife. His trousers were darker in color, and he wore tasseled brown loafers.

After introductions, there were drinks. Her father insisted that they try his Manhattans. As the couples seated themselves on twin sofas across from each other, the interrogation began. Name, place of birth, parents, guardians, grandparents, current course of study, career path, but never anything about the intentions with their daughter. That was a good thing in Will's mind. He had decided if that subject came up, he would just say he was going to ride that pony until it threw him. *Probably would have been a bad choice of words.*

The subject of his parents and their premature deaths brought the proper concern and consolation. That topic had started with his Mississippi home and whether his parents were close by. Will assumed that meant in distance, and his first thought was, yes, very close, only about four feet apart, and eight under. Again a bad choice of words, so he related their fate.

The way the questions were going and the expressions on Mrs. Morgan's face gave Will a strange feeling. They had been planning to ask enough questions that generated enough unacceptable answers for Will to see what a mistake this relationship with their daughter might be. But he fooled them.

He thought that what stumped them most was his desire to have a military career. "Very undesirable way of life for a young mother," stated Mrs. Morgan.

They asked what branch of service and how long his grandfather had served in the military. Will explained that his grandfather had refused to leave the service until he got his second star. He thought that maybe they gave it to him simply to make him go away. They all chuckled. Will was glad that they did not ask any more about his grandfather. He did not want to tell them that he and his grandfather were not on good terms because his grandfather thought he was screwing the mother of his first steady girlfriend.

The answer to the question about who had raised him after his parents died did not seem too appealing either. Will told them that his bachelor uncle Jonathan, his Aunt Bea, and Aunt Tilda had all shared the responsibility but that probably Aunt Tilda was the one that mothered him the most. He continued by saying that Aunt Tilda was colored, and that she and her husband lived in the same building that he and Uncle Jonathan lived in. Mrs. Morgan appeared to have heartburn.

At dinner, the maître d' showed the four of them to their table, placed napkins in the lap of each, and presented menus. As he was departing the table, he touched Will on the shoulder, "Nice to have you here again, sir. Say hello to Dr. MacMorogh for us, please."

Mrs. Morgan's left eyebrow went searching for her scalp. Will thought she would be a riot at a kid's birthday party. Ought to keep that in mind. After dinner, the parents suggested that it was rather late and perhaps they should say their "good nights" in the lobby of the hotel. That pleased Will to no end. Stephanie was quiet on the ride back to her apartment. They both agreed that it had been a full evening and that it was time to say good night. Before she kissed him, Stephanie said, "How do you think you did?"

Will could not resist. "You might prefer to ask how I think they did. I was not the one taking the test."

"Did they pass?" Stephanie grinned, knowing he would have to say, "Certainly."

"Time will tell," Will said. "Your father is still trying to figure out who my grandfather is. The whole landscape will change with that revelation."

"I do not get it," she said.

"Stay tuned."

Her parents were to have breakfast with Stephanie the next morning before heading home. He had not been invited. Not the night before, anyway. But things changed early on Sunday morning. Will answered the phone to Stephanie's sweetest voice. "Will, hon, Mother and Daddy want to know if you can join us for breakfast at the Camellia Grill. Nine would be great, if you could make it." Will reluctantly agreed to make it.

It was a long wait, as usual, since it was Sunday and the busiest time at the grill. That did not seem to bother Mr. Morgan. He never stopped whistling; Will thought it was the Tiger fight song. Will himself was constantly shaking hands or slapping backs. Mrs. Morgan was all smiles. Her most meaningful question so far was, "Will, darling, do you know everybody in New Orleans? I am pleased to be in the company of a celebrity."

After breakfast and when it was time for the Morgans to leave, they stood in a little circle with arms around each other's waists. Mr. Morgan offered the benediction. "Will, we are so pleased that we had the opportunity to spend time with you, and we sincerely hope the pleasure was yours as well. We look forward to seeing more of you." Mrs. Morgan smiled, "And soon now, you hear?"

They drove away. Stephanie was all smiles. "Well, I guess you passed," she said gleefully. Will mused to himself, "Perhaps my grandfather did."

Stephanie went home for Christmas vacation and, surprisingly, returned engaged. At least that was, as far as Matthew, Matthew's parents, and her parents were concerned. But the ring was still in the box it came in, in the top drawer of her dresser under her panties.

She called the minute she was back in town. Will went to her apartment; it took two hours to relate the entire episode. On Friday night there was a New Year's party at the club. The two families got together at Matthew's home before going. They sat in the den, drinks in hand; the beautiful Snow White Christmas tree glistened, the red lights aglow, the green balls sparkling. A fire crackled in the fireplace.

Mr. Morgan proposed a toast; Matthew sat next to Stephanie on the short love seat facing the two couches. During the toast, Matthew slipped Stephanie's left hand into his right and slowly slipped the ring onto her finger. She looked down, startled, and cried out, "Oh, my God!"

Stephanie said her mother looked stunned, Matthew's mother grabbed Stephanie's mother and they both started squealing, and then they went into some secret Tri-Delta signage or some other silliness. The fathers shook hands, pulled together, and slapped each other on the back. Stephanie just stood, staring down at the ring. Her mother could tell that something was amiss and should have known the reason. They had talked about it for hours the previous evening.

Matthew's mother would not shut up. She was breathless already with all that she and Stephanie's mother had to do before June. Stephanie was beginning to hyperventilate. No one had said one thing to her about when there might be a wedding.

Then Matthew's mother looked at her watch and screamed that they were already late for the club. She was anxious to get there to see how soon the word spread. They went over in one vehicle.

As soon as they were out of the car, Stephanie told her mother she needed to go to the bathroom. She left in a run, her mother at her heels. Stephanie was already throwing up when her mother got to her. Matthew's mother was right behind. Both mothers were trying to tend to her at the same time.

Her mother muttered that it was just all of the excitement, and Stephanie would be OK. Matthew's mother left. A shouting match ensued. Stephanie asked her mother whether she had had any idea that this was going to take place. Her mother replied truthfully; she had not. She looked her mother in the eye, and with clenched teeth said, "It is not going to happen."

Before her mother could speak, three girls burst through the door, squealing like banshees. Stephanie was in a panic. Her mother was aghast at what Stephanie had just said. More girls came in to join the banshee chorus.

It took a while for Stephanie to get back to the table. Matthew's mother looked at her so pitifully. "The excitement is just too much, isn't it?" she said. Stephanie told Will that she wanted to reply that the excitement had just begun. The evening was horrible. The news did spread like wildfire; boys were congratulating Matthew, and girls were gushing and squealing all over her. Their parents were getting attention. The evening drew on until the ball fell on Times Square. Then it was back to Matthew's family's house, where the party was supposed to go on all night. "After all," said Matthew's father. "This is one we will remember for a long time." Stephanie thought, "You just do not know how long."

When Stephanie and her parents got home, her father was the first to say something. He sensed that there was a problem and probably knew what it was. He said, "We are all a little tired, a little drunk, and I think we need to wait until morning to talk more about this." Her mother looked puzzled. She followed Stephanie to her room. "What did your father mean? He is acting strange. Is there something going on I do not know about?" Stephanie could not talk; she simply shook her head and bid her good night.

According to Stephanie, the next morning after breakfast, her father told her and her mother to bring coffee into the study. There he suggested they revisit the discussion the three of them had had the night before last. He said, "Was that discussion about the fact that your mother and I had a good feeling about Will? Did we not make it clear that we could understand that maybe you and Matthew might see less of each other for a while? Was that what we discussed? What I want to know is how did this progress from that point to being engaged to Matthew in less than twenty-four hours?"

Stephanie corrected her father. She said, holding up her naked ring finger. "No, how did I get a ring on my finger, not how did I get engaged, because I am not engaged." Then her mother started a low moaning.

The Tigers were not playing in a bowl, but there was going to be a big party at Matthews's house to watch the Sugar Bowl. Most of their friends would be there. Just before time to leave, Stephanie came down the stairs, not dressed, but back in pajamas. She announced that she was not going to the party. She said, "Tell Matthew that I am having my period. You may have to explain to him what that means." Her mother moaned, this time from deep in her chest.

She made it through Sunday. There was a brunch at their house with some of the same boring group of friends. She sat next to Matthew, wearing the ring. The excitement was still in the air for everyone but her. She was nice enough, however, not to let it show. The mothers were busy talking with others about weddings in their families. Matthew's mother was giddy.

On Sunday night, Matthew took her to a movie. On the way home, he told her how much he loved her. He then questioned if she thought there was any way they could pick a mutual school that offered both medical and law. He had been looking and had some suggestions. That was the last straw. She complained of cramps and kissed him good night. She stepped inside her front door, and the ring came off. Thank God she was leaving the next morning for school.

Will had just listened and made little comment. By Thursday, he was beginning to get worried. She was not studying; he knew she was not sleeping. If something did not happen soon, her grades would suffer. All she could talk about was, "What am I going to do? What do you think I ought to do? Tell me what to do."

After school that day, he met her at her car and said, "Let me drive." He walked her around to the passenger door and let her in. Then he drove through Audubon Park and down a road along the river to a point where they could drive onto the levee. He found a place to park, a place that he had come many times himself to think. He took her by the hand and led her down to the edge of the river. From that vantage point, the mighty Mississippi was awe-inspiring. It was much wider than it was in any view from a bridge. To Will, it was breathtaking.

He held her close and told her she had to get hold of herself. She had to make some kind of decision and then get on with her life. Once again, she said, "What should I do?" He shook his head.

Then she said, "What would you do?"

Will had been waiting for that. He said, "I have already done it."

"Done what?"

"Made a commitment," he said.

With that, Stephanie looked at him with a pained expression. "You have made a commitment to someone?"

Will turned her so that he was looking into her eyes. "Yes, I made a commitment to me. I promised myself I was going to Tulane to make the very best grades possible and then go into the Navy flight program upon graduation. Nothing can keep me from that."

Will continued, "Now, you tell me what, for you, the most important thing in the world is. Not who, but what?"

Tears began to flow. Will took her in his arms and held her for a moment, and then she pushed away. "There it has been all the time. I could not see the forest for the trees. I can't give up on my commitment to myself to be a doctor. I can't pretend I want to be a wife and maybe a mother. That has not been my goal. How could I ask someone to play second fiddle to *my* career? And that is exactly what it would be."

Back in the car, she looked at Will, a tear or two still hanging on her cheek. "You," she said, and just kept shaking her head. "Wonderful, smart Will."

As soon as classes were over on Friday, Stephanie headed to Baton Rouge. Her parents had a dinner engagement and asked her to go along. She declined and said that she had a few things to do. Her mother reminded her that Matthew's mother was having a tea the next afternoon for a few of their close girlfriends to start talking about priorities for the wedding. Of course, they expected her to be there. Nobody was listening to her at all.

Early the next morning, she went to the kitchen for coffee. Her father was already dressed in his golf attire. He had a nine o'clock tee time.

"You OK?" he asked as he put his arm around her shoulders. She sat at the bar in the kitchen.

She turned, brushed her hair back above her ear, and smiled. "Getting there."

Her mother came down for coffee and looked hungover. "You seem in better spirits. Did a week to think about it make it better?"

"Oh definitely, Mom, I am much better." Her mother said she was going back to bed awhile. Said she must have drunk too much the night before. Stephanie thought, not as much as you are probably going to drink tonight.

Promptly at nine o'clock, Stephanie got into her car and drove around the corner to Matthew's house. As usual, she parked in the compound behind the house and went in through the kitchen door.

The family housekeeper greeted her in the kitchen. She said, "Child, let me see the ring."

Stephanie held up a ringless finger. She whispered, "Oops, forgot it on the table by my bedside."

The housekeeper said, "Shame on you. Mrs. Blalock is in the den; don't fall down over all that mess in there." When Stephanie entered the room, she could see what the housekeeper meant. There were stacks of books on every horizontal surface. Travel magazines, party books, hotel and resort brochures, some of them lying open, others with markers stuck between pages.

Mrs. Blalock got up with her cigarette in her hand, half hugged Stephanie, and said, "Matthew is still getting dressed. Now don't you peep at any of this stuff. You might see where we are going to send you on your honeymoon!"

The phone rang, and Mrs. Blalock answered. From the conversation Stephanie could hear, she realized it was someone calling for information. The other woman said to the party on the other end, "I do not have that at hand. I will have to go into my husband's office and call you back." She excused herself. In a moment, Stephanie heard her back on the phone.

She glanced down on the coffee table, and her heart thudded and her head went light. There on the table, on the cover of a magazine called the *Dixie Business Gazette,* was a picture of a man in uniform, with two stars on the epaulets and with eyes like Will's. On his left breast, a long row of ribbons. On the right breast, a nametag, "MacMorogh." In large print under the picture, "Is This the Richest Man in the Deep South?"

Stephanie could hardly breathe. She started thumbing through the magazine. She did not have to thumb far to find a page turned. She scanned the article as quickly as possible. Some things were underlined in red: Headquartered in New Cotswold, Mississippi, timber, manufacturing , railroading, a multiple of businesses in a conglomerate headed by William MacMorogh, General, USAF retired.

In addition, in a sidebar, a quote from the General. It stated that the company was into its third generation of MacMoroghs at the helm. There were two in the fourth generation who might take the reins. They were Dr. Carole MacMorogh a New Orleans pediatrician, and William MacMorogh III, currently a student at Tulane.

She looked around again and dropped the magazine into her sack purse. Then Mrs. Blalock's voice from behind. "Sorry about that," she said. Stephanie froze. But if the woman had seen her take the magazine, she did not say anything. Stephanie had to get out of there, and fast. But in came Matthew, grinning, arms outstretched to take her in his arms. "How is my girl?" he said.

"Great, just great," she smiled.

"Had breakfast yet?" Matthew asked. "Want to go to the club for the Saturday Golfer's buffet?"

"Sure," she answered. "Meet you over there; I have to run by the house first." She had nothing to pick up, but she wanted to have her own means of transportation.

When she arrived, Matthew waited in the parking lot. She stepped from her car and walked up to him. From her purse, she took the ring in its box and pushed it toward him. His mouth dropped open, his brow furrowed.

She said. "Matthew, I have never loved you at all, and certainly not enough to marry you. I do respect you enough to tell you that I am honored that you want me to be your wife. Even if we were both in love, I would not subject you to the ten years of training it will take for me to get through medical school, internship, and residency. You would not be foremost in my mind. You deserve more." She took a deep breath and said, "Also, I would hate to marry someone who considered me to be a gold digging airhead who would marry someone for money. Will MacMorogh is, and always will be, one of my dearest and most respected friends." With that, she turned, got in her car, and went home.

Her mother was up, seated in the den, bleary-eyed, Bloody Mary in one hand and a cigarette in the other. Stephanie plopped down in a wingback chair, pulled the magazine from her purse, and pitched it on the coffee table. Her mother did not even look at it, but just inquired about the Golfer's Brunch at the club. Stephanie did not answer. She got up and told her mother she was going up to her room to lie down. Her mother called after her, "Don't forget the tea this afternoon." Her mother had not yet heard; the tea was not going to happen.

At noon, she went back downstairs when she heard her father's car in the drive. Her mother had made another pitcher of Bloody

Marys. Her father was all smiles: "Shot a sixty-nine." He too poured a Bloody Mary, then came back in from the kitchen and said, "You girls have a tea this afternoon, don't you?" Then sardonically added, "Whoopee, that should be fun."

He plopped down on the sofa and glanced over at the magazine Stephanie had dropped there earlier. He reached over, picked it up, and glanced at the address on the mail sticker. Then he blurted out, "This went to the office. I have searched high and low for it. I remember the cover. Where did it come from?'

By then her mother was interested. "What is it, darling?" she slurred. However, her father was too busy reading. Stephanie had gotten up. Her father stood also, looked at her, and kept scanning the article. "Tell me," he said. "Where did this come from?"

Stephanie looked at him. "You have read it before, haven't you?"

He answered, "I remembered the cover. That evening we had dinner with Will, he mentioned his grandfather. I put two and two together. I wanted to see what the article said. I couldn't find it at the office." Her mother picked the magazine up and started reading, and then once more came the moans.

Stephanie said, "I went over to Matthew's, and it was on the coffee table. Mrs. Blalock left the room; I read it. What I want to know is, how did they know about Will?"

Her mother whimpered, "I told Katie Nell that you were seeing him."

"Then that is why the sudden ring and wanting to get us married. They thought I might fall for the money, right?"

"Does Matthew know about this?" her father asked.

"Yes, sir," Stephanie said politely. "I told him very nicely." Then she told them what she had said. Everything, including the gold digging airhead bit. Her mother looked faint.

Her father took her in his arms. She explained what Will had told her about his own career. It had brought her to her own senses. The magazine article had sealed it.

Her father said, "Today you have made me prouder of you than anytime I can ever remember. Get in your car, go back to New Orleans, and have a nice dinner with Will, on me of course. Let this cool down. Your mother and I can get through it. You did the right thing."

Stephanie came back to school with an entirely different attitude. She was happy, with no worries about the outcome of her breakup with Matthew. Most importantly, she hit the books with a vengeance. The relationship between Will and Stephanie continued, but both had a better understanding about the future. Will did have a very strong feeling for her, more so than for any other he had dated. Maybe someday.

At the end of the school year, Stephanie enrolled in summer school and took a full load. She planned to be able to graduate at midterm the following year. Will went home for his summer job with the excitement of knowing that when this same time arrived the following year, he would be on his way to the Navy in Pensacola. That summer between his junior and senior year was, however, a pivotal year in his life.

37

Summer, 1950: The last contact with Tish

Jonathan discussed his plan for Will for the summer. He had built a water well drilling rig much like one he had purchased at a government auction. But this one was much bigger and would drill deeper. The most important improvement was that the rig was on a much larger truck. One or two men could haul the rig to a site, set the derrick in place, and operate it without a whole crew of men. This was not so with the surplus rig. The army had plenty of men, but a driller hoping to make a profit with a rig needed efficiency.

Not only did Jonathan plan to drill wells, but he expected to manufacture the units for sale. Winston had drilled two wells with the prototype; he would teach Will how to operate the rig with a hired hand. Meanwhile, improvements would continue on the prototype. By summer's end, Jonathan planned to market the machines.

Will arrived from his navy cruise eager to go to work. Little did he know that encounters with three different people during the summer would change his life forever. Of all of the summers he remembered, this one always stood out.

He worked with Winston for a week. The rig was in for some minor changes that took a few days. Meanwhile, Will pulled another assignment. The first Sunday in July was "Homecoming at Old Church." People who had moved away returned that weekend to visit relatives still in the area. A favorite of the event was church services on Sunday in the Old Church followed by dinner on the grounds. The highlight was strolling through the cemetery to visit the graves of departed relatives.

Each year on the Wednesday prior to "Homecoming," when all the stores closed for the afternoon, townspeople gathered at the cemetery for a thorough cleaning. They cut grass, trimmed bushes, and discarded leftover wilted flowers. It had been a custom for years that City Livery provided a supply of hoes, rakes, shears, and brooms for use if needed. In addition, they sent along a person with a pedal powered grindstone for sharpening tools. That person usually manned the burn area, making sure no fire got out of control.

The burn area was on the backside of the cemetery near the gazebo that sat at the edge of a bluff overlooking the valley below. Below the gazebo, in an area that locals described as under the hill, were two springs that fed the creek that flowed in front of Laura's Lodge.

Will arrived at the church thirty minutes before noon; women were spreading out dinner. He drove his old truck to the burn area where he would distribute the tools and keep an eye on the fire. The summer before, at one of the Lamar Sunday Buffets, Patricia had introduced Christine Simpkins, the attractive wife of the Minister of Music at the Baptist Church. Today she was dressed in her usual long sleeve, long skirt garb. She was busy pulling kudzu vines from the gazebo. He walked over and said hello. She said she planned to put a fresh coat of paint on the structure as her contribution to the forth-coming event. Will offered to help.

After lunch, Will made several trips from the burn area to the gazebo to gather vines to take to the fire. Each time, he chatted a moment or two with Christine. By four o'clock, most of the tools were turned in, and only a handful of people continued to work. Christine was not nearly finished with her painting. Will was putting the tools back on the truck when out of the corner of his eye, he spotted two women talking to her. One of the women tilted her head toward Will. Christine turned and glanced in his direction. The women departed. Christine began to gather up her paints.

Will went over to ask if she was calling it a day. She only looked at him, bewildered. "It has been suggested that I not stay here with you without many other *people* around. I am to understand you have a poor reputa-tion. There might be talk." Then she looked directly in his eye. "I hate this town!" *There was more to this story, and Jack would not hear until later.*

Will helped Winston drill two wells and then was on his own. He became very proficient at operating the rig, and even got to a point that after the rig was in place and the derrick up, he could manage most of a drilling operation without a helper. In addition, he began to make notes and advise Jonathan on improvements he felt might make the rig more efficient. By summer's end, Jonathan had rede-signed the prototype, and he gave Will credit for much of the change.

To top off his summer vacation, one more opportunity arose. Jonathan purchased three diesel engines in Kenosha, Wisconsin. He figured Will had enough time before heading back to school to take a truck to pick them up. Will looked at the map and figured the time on the road. He could do it with time to spare. He offered a deal. He would go if he could stay one night in Evanston, Illinois, to visit with Tish. Her summer school classes at Northwestern were over; she had a week before classes resumed.

It was a deal. He left early the next morning in a new Mack truck. The truck moved along very well without a load, and he made good time, but was too late to load the engines that same day. He was at the plant in Kenosha early the next morning and picked up his load and was back on the road by eleven. He had directions to Tish's apartment but was concerned about a place to park the big vehicle. A telephone call to her relieved that problem. She knew a safe lot near her house to park.

Will did not know who was the happiest to see each other again. From the time he walked into the door until well past midnight, there was constant chatter. Tish ordered Chinese, and they sat straddle leg-ged on the floor, eating off a coffee table, using chopsticks. At bed-time, Tish made up her sleeper sofa and got Will two pillows. They turned in for the night, he on the sofa and she in her bed. During the night, the sofa got more and more uncomfortable, and Will tossed and turned. Tish could not help but hear.

She got up and told him to get up; there was plenty of room for both in her bed. She felt he needed rest to drive the next day. She turned off the light, then turned to put her hand on Will's cheek. He rolled over and snuggled closer. She kissed him lightly, pulled closer, and asked him if he was more comfortable. Will kissed her on the mouth, and she responded with a little moan. For the first time ever, they made love.

When it was over, she laid on her side, her head against his chest. She began to cry. "Will, I always wanted you to be the first." She had lost her virginity. She could not be happier.

Will got up early the next morning, and they hugged for a long, long time before he left. She cried; she had hoped he would never leave. The big Mack truck was powerful, but there was no doubt that it had to work hard to do its duty. Each hill seemed harder to con-quer, the pace slow. Will had a lot to consider. He had never had any-thing come over him like the feeling he'd gotten in Tish's arms. There was no way he could explain it. He wished he could find the words to tell her. He spent the day mentally writing her a letter. He searched for just the right words to express what his heart felt.

After he got home, he composed the best letter he could, to express his feeling. He wanted them to see each other more often. All those years of being so close, he had not realized how much she meant to him.

Fall, 1950: Will's Senior Year at Tulane — The devastating rumor

Two days later, he was on the train, back to school. Stephanie was back, having completed a full load at summer school. She only lacked a few credits to have enough to graduate, and she would get those the first semester. She had her application in at Tulane Medical. She had also spent a lot of time visiting with Aunt Bea and Carole Anne. Both had written recommendations for her. She was confident she would hear soon.

Will and Aunt Bea talked in confidence. She had not told Carole Anne about their discussion. She confessed to Will that she feared what Jonathan might do if he knew. She had made a few contacts. She might have something positive working.

A week went by, with no return letter from Tish. He counted the days since he had mailed his letter. Then two weeks went by and nothing. Perhaps he was overanxious. Then the most distressing thing occurred. He came home from school in mid-afternoon. Aunt Bea was home early. She sat in the den and called to him as he came through the front door. He looked in; he could tell she had bad news.

His grandmother had called first, then Jonathan. The Rev. Billy Dee Simpkins had resigned his position as Minister of Music at the First Baptist Church in New Cotswold. His reason: his wife was having an affair with a college boy by the name of Will MacMorogh. He could no longer do the Lord's work under such stress. That was the story he had given to the church elders at four o'clock. By five, he was out of town.

Will sat stunned. He pleaded with his aunt to believe him. He had had nothing to do with Christine. Then word came the next day, this time from Jonathan to Will. Christine was gone. Her parents had arrived late the evening before. According to a next-door neighbor, within an hour after the parents had arrived, they had loaded Christine into the car and left. No one knew anything other than what the church elders reported. And, yes, the story was all over town. His grandfather was livid. Jonathan at that point was disappointed, but forgiving. He had not been beyond reproach all of his life either.

Will and his aunt ruminated over the situation. Finally, they concluded that at some point, the truth would prevail. Now, it might be best not to stir the pot. The truth might very well get someone killed.

Will was in the same position as Stephanie had been. If he could not get it together, his grades were going to suffer. Then more bad news and another blow. He received a letter from Tish stating that she also had felt as he did, but there was a lot to consider. He was nearing the time he would go into the navy. She was nearing the time she would go to graduate school. They both had made commitments to personal goals. They had to keep those commitments. Where had Will heard that before?

All attempts to call failed. Her phone was no longer in service, and repeated calls to her mother's house yielded no answer. He sent another note, and it came with a note scribbled on the envelope: "Moved — no forwarding address."

During finals at the end of the semester, Jonathan called to tell Will that Moon Mullens had died. Jonathan had served as pallbearer. Will was devastated that no one had informed him. Jonathan explained that Maureen and Moon had discussed it many times before. It had always been Moon's wish that they bury him immediately upon death; no embalming, no viewing, no church service, only a graveside prayer.

And Jonathan had more sad news. Tish was ill and bedridden and had not attended her father's funeral. Jonathan was unable to get more detail from Maureen other than that she was going back to take care of her.

Will had to ignore his shame and sorrow and go forth with his life. He graduated *magna cum laude.* Stephanie left school at midterm, having all the credits she needed to graduate. She would not begin medical school at Tulane until fall. Meanwhile, she was staying at home with her mother, who was fighting a bad case of depression. Will's aunt had invited Stephanie to stay at her house for three days during graduation. It gave Will and Stephanie some final time together. He told her about the dilemma he was in, but gave none of the prior details. Her father drove down the day of graduation for the ceremonies and left immediately thereafter. Things were not good at home.

38

Summer of 1951

Will got a July class assignment that gave him a short time to do nothing until he was to report for duty. He had not been to New Cotswold since leaving for his senior year. He stayed at the hotel as a guest of Jonathan and June. As he visited around town, he could feel the tension. He went to see Tommy Schooner and his wife and of course was welcome. There was no mention of the gossip, and for a short time he was at ease. But his grandfather made that quickly dissipate.

When he went to his grandparents to visit, he got a poor reception. Conversation quickly turned to the event, and his grandfather again expressed his disgust with Will. In a moment of anger, Will told him that he doubted he could ever live in this damn town again. His grandfather blasted him right back and said he saw no reason he would ever need to.

Will knew what to expect during primary flight school. He excelled. The fact that he was already a private pilot was not something he revealed. Instead, he approached his classes as if he had not flown before and knew that he benefited from it. He passed primary flight at the top of his class. He asked his aunt to come for graduation. He wanted her to be the one who pinned on his wings.

Will spent the next five months in advanced training, first in Beeville, Texas, and then on to a base in Louisiana. After advanced training, he joined the fleet and boarded an aircraft carrier on the way to Korea. Within days, he was flying combat missions.

The morning before they left on the fateful mission, Will had a premonition that he was not coming back. The mission was to destroy enemy infrastructure, railroads, highways, bridges, and power lines, anything that would make movement of enemy troops more difficult.

On their way to a target, the team leader spotted an enemy train; it was not one of their prime targets, but it was irresistible.

Will peeled off behind the team leader and followed him down. The team leader dropped almost to the deck and strafed the train from the caboose to the engines. Will followed, strafing from the opposite side. Then something the team leader hit on the train exploded, and suddenly, a shack as big as a truck loomed in Will's windscreen. He horsed back on the stick as he collided with the structure, but it was too late—the prop came apart, a terrible vibration set in, and the engine broke from its mounts. Will had to punch out.

Enemy soldiers were firing before his chute opened, and on ground contact, he failed to roll. Before he was out of his chute, soldiers were all over him and beat him unconscious. He woke after dark and found himself in a cage. He tried to sit up, but his shoulder pained so badly that he could not. Later, he tried to pull up using a bar on the cage and realized that he also had a fractured left leg. When he called out for water, soldiers came to beat him again. The next time he came to, he lay still. Finally someone came. He did know whether it was an enemy or another prisoner. His eyes were swollen shut, and he could barely hear. All he knew was that someone touched a cup of water to his lips.

The beating and torture kept on for days. Then other men came in, and his torture became less frequent. After the first of several forced marches, Will knew he could not survive another. The North Koreans had few, if any, permanent prisons, only shoddy, temporary stockades put together with anything they could use for material. Some were enclosed; others were in the open. When the battle line grew too close, they marched the troops to another location.

It was on these marches that the most men were lost. The guards lined up long columns to march and rode alongside in crude vehicles. Trucks followed at the end of the columns. If prisoners fell and could not get up, they were shot in the head. The truck picked them up. To stumble and fall was sure death.

The season changed, bringing rain and cold. Few men escaped pneumonia, including Will, his fever so high at times that he hallucinated. Death would be a welcome relief. His only regret would be not having one last visit with the people he so dearly loved. He started trying to remember each of them. It was this activity that Will had told Jack about during their first visit, after Jack asked if he had notes. Will had pointed to his head and said, "It is all right here." The following is the account that had convinced Jack.

Will told him how it started. He began trying to remember as far back in his life as he could. The first time he tried, the first thing that came to mind was that day in second grade when Tish Mullens got her feelings hurt so terribly. Mrs. Kaplan had invited everyone to her daughter's birthday party except Tish and Will, Tish because her dad was a bootlegger, and Will because he lived under the same roof as colored people.

Each time he started his memory exercise, that point was always where he began. First, he worked back from that point. Then he started working forward. He lived another day, so he repeated the exercise. In time, he was visiting the people in his daydreams. Soon he began talking to them, asking them how their day was and whether they were feeling well. Then one night, in the middle of the night, a voice came to him from the next cage. It said, "Shut the fuck up, you crazy son of a bitch."

His mind was always fuzzy, and much of the time, he was on the outside looking down on himself. Later in the night, the same person screamed out again. It was then that he realized he was visiting aloud. The next morning, he whispered an apology to the person in the other cage. He told him that this was the way he was holding on to life. Every day, he relived as much of his life as possible. And every day, he encountered some event or person he had not visited before. A few days later, the prisoner in the next cage, a colored boson's mate, stuck two fingers through the cage to Will. He wanted to shake hands with Will and tell him he was doing the same thing as he was, visiting everybody. The other prisoner told him that he had visited for a long time the previous night with his wife and an uncle he liked a lot.

Then he said to Will, "They just doing fine. My younger sister, she had her second baby last week, named her Kendra." The two of them visited each other through the cages. Soon they were relating news from home—all imaginary.

Time wore on; there were more beatings. Will was sure he had broken ribs. He could not open one eye, and he was pissing blood.

The stockade was crowded, and the North Koreans began packing more prisoners into each cage. They were practically sleeping on each other. Late one night, they threw another prisoner in on him. The man was near death. He could not talk. He was still in his blood soaked flight suit. There was stain from urine and feces. Will felt his head: he had a burning fever and desperately needed water. At first light, Will was able to read the nametag on the flight suit. Chacherie. Will did not think he would last through the day. He managed to catch rainwater in his hand and touch it to his fellow prisoner's lips.

The guards came through at dark. They poked sticks in to see if prisoners responded or were dead. Then a murmur went through the compound. Another march. It was raining and cold. He managed to get Chacherie to his feet, but the man was too weak to walk. Will had to drag him along. It got to a point where he could not manage him much longer. The road was slick with mud, visibility was poor, and every few feet, someone fell. Mass confusion was taking over. Even with the guards.

An hour or so into the march, two men broke from the column and slid down a ditch into the weeds. The guards did not see them. He shoved Chacherie down behind the men, and they hid out for three days. Finally, a company of American soldiers came down the road. Rescue at last.

Will had paused for a moment and then started to talk again, but Jack had held up his hand for Will to stop. He sat there staring intently at Will. After a few uncomfortable moments, Will asked, "Something wrong?"

Jack said, "You sure you are not leaving something out?"

Will shook his head, "No."

"I want you to hear another version of this, Will."

During an interview with Charles Chacherie, when Jack had begun hearing his account of this same march, he had made sure he recorded it. Jack had been taking notes, but as the account went on, Jack had become so drained by the tale that he had quit doing so. Later, he transcribed notes from the tape. He asked Will to listen as he read.

Chas said that he was unconscious from the pain of torture and from the fever from pneumonia. At times, he thought he was drawing his last breath. When he would be awake, he went from chills to burning up. He had never been so thirsty. After a while, he realized that he was in a crude cage and that another person was almost on top of him. At some point, the other person touched his lips with water. For a short time, he was lucid enough to know he was in prison.

Sometime after daylight, he came to, and the other man was in his face, trying to talk. The man said he was going to take care of him, but if he shook him awake, to try to stay awake. He told him that if they thought you were dead or near death, they would kill you. The other man managed to get water to him from time to time. Chas said that at some point, he came to again. It was dark, and the other prisoner shook him awake and asked if he could move. He said he tried but was hurting so bad that he did not see how he could get up and walk.

The other prisoner kept telling him that he was Will and that he was going to take care of him, but that Chas had to help. He said they were going to have to march. He said it would be great; they would be in the rain and could get water. Chas remembered little about getting to his feet and out of the cage other than that the pain was so severe that when Will moved him, he fainted. Then they were on a road. He could not remember getting there. It was muddy and slick. Every step or two, they would almost fall. He could not maneuver alone. Will had one of his arms around his neck and his other hand at the crotch of his flight suit, dragging him along.

He said that he begged Will to leave him, but Will refused. It was impossible to stay alert; he kept blanking out. Will kept begging him to help. At one point, Will told him he was nothing but lazy. He told him he ought to leave his lazy ass behind. He said that someday when he was out of there, he would find the guy's family and tell them the reason Chacherie never came home was because he was too lazy to walk a few miles. Chacherie said that those words made him fighting mad.

Chas said it made him so mad that he tried to take a swing at Will, but instead fell right on his ass. After he went down, something sharp caught his arm as he tossed around in the mud. His arm was cut and bleeding. Will dropped to the ground; it was raining harder, but he could see the blood on his companion's arm. Will felt around in the mud and cut his fingers on a long shard of glass. Other prisoners were stumbling over or around them. Will pulled the glass out of the mud and stuffed it up his sleeve.

They managed to get onto their feet again, but Will still had to drag him along. The next time they stumbled, Will himself fell face down in the mud next to Chas. A guard stumbled onto them himself and almost fell. He put his gun to Will's head. Will rolled his head at the same time that the guard pulled the trigger. He rolled over enough that the bullet grazed the side of his head, barely missing his ear. He swung his left arm out and pushed the guard off balance. The guard fell across Chas.

Will was on top of the guard in an instant, one hand on his mouth. The other he used to stab the shard of glass through the guard's eye and into his brain. Chas said the guard's feet and legs were kicking like those of a chicken with its head cut off. Other prisoners were trying to get out of the way before other guards got there. Will rolled Chacherie into the ditch at the side of the road and then pulled the guard in with them. He took the guard's weapon and a canteen of water.

They crossed into a field where the mud was so deep and sticky that Chacherie could not pull his feet out. Will laid him down on his back and used the collar of his flight suit as handle to keep dragging him along. The rain got heavier as they got further from the road. There was commotion at the point where they had left the road, and other guards were looking for them. With the rain, they were hard to spot.

When Will stopped to rest, they were still in an open field, with no cover in sight. Will told Chas that when it got light again, they would be easy to spot. He wanted to stop where they were and start digging. Chas was too weak to resist, but also too weak to help. So Will used his bare hands and a board he found to dig two trenches. He rolled Chas into one and then turned him on his back. He put Chacherie's arms alongside his body and buried all but his face. He smeared mud all over it. Will then lay down in the trench next to Chas and buried himself in the same manner. When light came, it was still raining lightly, but it had rained enough to cover their tracks.

They were a long way from the road. Enemy vehicles were still moving along the road, but at a more rapid pace. It did not seem that the enemy was attempting to look for them, but Will was still afraid to risk being in the open. They lay there in their muddy grave all day long. The rest restored Will's energy and determination, whereas Chas went in and out of consciousness.

At dark he remembered waking up, and Will was gone. He tried to rise up but could not. It seemed like hours, but Chas had no way of knowing. He was slipping in and out. His lungs were filling, and he was finding it very difficult to breathe. When he tried to cough up mucous, the pain was so severe that he fainted.

Sometime during the night, Will returned. He told Chas that he had found a hut but that Chacherie must help. He had to get up.

Will chided him along and told him that if he had gotten enough strength to take a poke at him, he had enough to try to walk. After what seemed like more hours, they came upon the shed that Will had found. Will got Chas in and leaned him against a wall. Then he got a piece of stale bread, dipped it in water, and stuffed it between Chas' lips. He put a canteen to his lips and wet them. He managed to get him to drink a little.

The shed was behind a tiny hut. It was obvious when Will found it that whoever lived there had left in a hurry. Will was afraid the owners might return, so they stayed in the shed the rest of the day. He could not sleep and was continually on guard. He slipped back into the house and found another small piece of bread and some kind of rotten smelling meat. They ate both.

At nightfall, Will heard noises, loud noises, powerful vehicles moving at a fast pace. He slipped out of the shed and lay on his stomach to try to see what was happening. In a moment, he crawled back into the shed. He got Chas' arm around him again, got him to his feet, and said, "Let's go home, lazy." The vehicles passing on the road were US.

Chas said it took a long time to get close enough to the road to wave a truck down. The US soldiers approached them with automatic weapons at the ready. Mud and blood caked their uniforms, and no one could tell what they were. Chas had said in finality, "Will MacMorogh saved my life."

While Jack read the manuscript, Will frowned a time or two and put both fists to his temples as if he was trying to stifle a headache. When Jack was through, there was a long period of silence.

Jack said nothing. After a while, Will said, "You know he is think-ing about running for governor. With the ability to tell whoppers like that, there is no telling what he will dream up to tell voters." Then he laughed and said, "Let's take a break!"

When their interview resumed, Jack asked Will if he felt like con-tinuing. He said he did, but he wanted to stop before noon. He had a lunch appointment; he would be gone the rest of the day.

Will continued. He said that he fell into a semiconscious state almost as soon as the US soldiers got to them. The troops got them to a MASH unit, and he knew from the sudden urgency of all of the medical staff that Chas was going fast. He knew enough to know that he himself was clean, his head wound was dressed, and he was feel-ing no pain. He drifted off.

When he came to, Chas was gone. Will lay there on a cot for a long time, with no energy to ask—afraid to ask. A nurse came to him and checked his pulse, his temperature, and his heart, and then she asked if he felt like traveling. They were going to try to transport him. He told them he was ready and asked about Chacherie. The nurse said he was critical but still alive. They had sent him ahead to a ship.

Will did not recall much more until he was on board a carrier and from there on a plane bound for a naval hospital in Hawaii. They checked him over and felt that the repairs he needed would require a long period of recuperation. He went by air again, this time to San Diego, where he would remain for seven months.

It was nearing noon; Will suggested that they touch base later in the week. He had a busy schedule and might have to skip their inter-views for a day or two. Then he left for his appointment.

As soon as he was out the door, Mimi approached Jack to see if he would be available after lunch. Dr. Bea was on the phone. She planned to be in the office in the afternoon and wanted to know if he would be available. He assured her that he would and that he looked forward to seeing her again.

39

Jack ordered in a sandwich and took the time to put the final changes on some of his notes. When Dr. Bea arrived, she admitted that she had some anxiety; she was concerned about Will. She knew about where they might be, chronologically, in the manuscript. Jack told her that they had quit that day with Will's arrival at the naval hospital in San Diego.

"Jack," she said, "I want to take it up from here. We will have to figure out a way to keep Will out of this until we are further along. I think you will see why as we go forward. We might need more than one session, so if it is all right with you, let's plan on another session or two. Perhaps we might meet an evening or two at my home." Jack agreed, and it did take three more sessions.

That day, she began. "Let me say that being a doctor, I have seen misery, lots of it. I have seen people in the most deplorable condition you can imagine. When I first saw Will, he was as bad as any I had seen in a long time. I wanted to cry! He was emaciated and probably did not weigh a hundred pounds. He had a bandage covering his head, cracked lips from the fever, eyes dancing and not focusing, and his skin had a yellow tone. Had I not known what to look for, I would not have been able to identify him. Those MacMorogh eyes were the only giveaway."

He was suffering physically and just as severely emotionally, if not more so. He was in a deep depression. He knew he was very sick. He was convinced he was going to be an invalid. The doctors immediately went to work on the physical, ignoring for the time the emotional. They felt that most of the emotional problem was the pain and sickness. They wanted to get the pneumonia and high fever under control before they started repairs on his shoulder. The leg was another problem. The fracture had not been treated and had mended on its own. The leg was crooked; he would have a limp.

Dr. Bea said, "I had been first to arrive in San Diego, then my father came, and Jonathan, and Carole Anne." Then she continued with the story.

Will began to recover. It took two months to clear up the pneumonia. The doctors were ready to start work on the shoulder. They warned Will that it would be immobile for several weeks after the surgery. They suggested nothing but rest. Eat well, get some weight back. They were observing him closely. Will was barely responsive. The doctors were now beginning to be more concerned about his mental and emotional state.

Dr. Bea flew back out, and after conferring with the doctors, she too was convinced that his mental state was poor. He had quit talking other than to answer questions, and then it was mostly just yes or no. He had nightmares and frequently said to someone that he was "so sorry, so sorry." Then, sometime when he was awake, he asked if anyone knew where Chacherie was. He was so sorry he did not get him to safety soon enough. He had to tell his wife how sorry he was. At other times, he would be wide awake and would scream for no apparent reason.

Once again, fate intervened. Dr. Bea set up a schedule to commute to San Diego every other weekend. Ordinarily, she left on Saturday morning and returned late Monday evening. She was in line to check in at the airline counter when in front of her, and already checking in, she saw a woman she knew she had seen before. Hers was not a face easily forgotten. She had to be one of the most attractive women Dr. Bea had ever seen. If only she could remember where.

The woman checked in and started across the terminal toward the concourse. Dr. Bea got to the counter, checked in, and tried to read the passenger list in front of the ticket agent, but she was unable to do so. She grabbed her bag and rushed ahead, hoping to catch the woman before she boarded an aircraft.

She spotted her and started walking faster, and then the woman turned her head in a certain direction, showing a different profile. Dr. Bea remembered. The woman had been boarding a cab at the hospital the day she'd left San Diego on her last visit. As she got closer, the woman turned into the same boarding area where Dr. Bea would be leaving.

Dr. Bea walked directly to the woman, introduced herself, and remarked that she thought she had encountered her at another time. Was she the same lady who had been boarding a cab at the naval hospital a couple of weeks back? With a radiant smile, she said she was, and then said she was familiar with Dr. MacMorogh. Dr. Bea had treated a friend's child.

"I am Adeline Chacherie, Addie for short."

Dr. Bea grabbed at her own heart and said, "Oh my, please tell me, is it your husband at the hospital?"

Addie replied, "Yes, he is there for quite a long time, I am afraid. And you, do you have someone there?"

"My nephew. His name is Will MacMorogh."

At that, Addie grabbed at her own throat, "Oh my God, Will, did you say?"

At that moment, the two women knew that they were kindred in a very special way. Dr. Bea was first to relay the situation with Will. She told Addie that he kept having nightmares and hallucinating, wanting to apologize because he had not gotten someone named Chacherie to help in time. By then, Addie was in tears.

"My Charles is wondering what happened to Will." The two women were overjoyed; both had tears streaming down their cheeks. They looked at their seat assignments: both were in first class, but not next to each other. On board, they got a man to switch with one of them. They talked nonstop all the way to San Diego. By the time they got there, Addie remarked, "We know far too much about each other now, don't we?"

Of course, their plan was to get the two men together as soon as possible. The minute they arrived at the hospital, they each made a beeline to the areas where they could find the main physician treating each of their men. Dr. Bea, familiar with hospital protocol, had some suggestions for Addie to use; she would approach their task the same way.

Dr. Bea went first to the nurses' station to inquire after Will's doctor. He showed her the utmost in professional courtesy, including asking if he might buy her dinner sometime. As they talked, Dr. Bea got a better insight into Will's condition. Yes, the doctor thought getting the two men together was a good idea. However, he needed to get with the physicians treating Chacherie to check on his condition.

He would get back to her. She asked if it might be OK to tell Will that Chacherie was there in the same hospital. The doctor discouraged that. He wanted to visit with the other physician first.

She went to Will. He acknowledged her and was glad she was there; hoped things were well with her. Past that, there was little conversation on his part. On each visit, she tried to be cheery, bringing pleasant news of all of the family, friends, dogs, cats, anything to try to make him smile. It was not easy.

Later in the day, Will's physician came by. He had something to consider. Chacherie might very well lose a leg. His team of doctors was evaluating that possibility at that very moment. If that were the case, would that be another reason for Will to go deeper into depression, knowing Chacherie might lose the leg? Would Will be blaming himself for that? Dr. Bea said she did not think he could go much deeper. She wanted to let Will know the man was alive. It was far better than thinking they might have buried him at sea, which was now the thing on Will's mind.

The doctor complied with her request. She asked for directions to where she might find Charles Chacherie, and then she went looking for Addie. Who better to tell Will than she? Dr. Bea also wanted to see what the doctor had told Addie about letting Charles know that Will was there also. She found the area, identified herself at the nurses' station, and asked if someone might go summon Addie.

Addie came from the room, a smile on her face. The doctor thought it would be splendid to let Charles know. She had been waiting to hear from Dr. Bea, and wanted her to tell him. Dr. Bea laughed; that was exactly what she wanted Addie to do for Will. They went into Charles' room, and Dr. Bea's heart sank again. The poor men, she thought, what they must have gone through. She thought, what a brave woman this beautiful one is. Charles Chacherie was a ghost. He was conscious and conversant, but barely able to speak above a whisper. A tube had been in his throat since he arrived, and even though it was now out, his throat hurt.

He looked up from his pillow when his wife introduced Dr. Bea. Charles whispered, "We haven't seen you here before."

Knowing his rank was Lieutenant Commander, she addressed him as such. "Commander Chacherie, I am not here as one of your attending physicians. I am here to give you news of my nephew, Lieutenant Will MacMorogh. Ever hear of him?"

A big smile crossed that terribly distorted countenance. "Will? Will, did you say? Is he safe?"

"He is," she said. She herself could not hold back the tears, as his began to flow. He just kept saying "Addie, my Addie, our prayers have been answered."

He regained composure, and in a strained voice he asked, "Where did they take him?"

Addie touched Dr. Bea's arm; she wanted to tell him. "He is here, darling. Right here in the same hospital." There was no way he could have gotten up. His worst leg hung high over the bed, but still he wriggled around and tried to rise up.

"I have to go see him," he strained.

Dr. Bea broke in, "In time, Commander, in time. Right now, you two have work to do. You have to get better." Then she explained Will's condition — not the emotional condition, just the surgeries scheduled.

Charles then tried to talk more, but could not. Addie knew what he was trying to ask, so she talked for him. "You want to know if he knows you are here. No, darling, we broke the news to you first. We want to go tell him now. Do you mind if I go with Dr. Bea to tell him?" He waved his arm in a feeble gesture. He wanted Addie to come closer. She did, and he painfully whispered, "Tell him I am not lazy."

When they got to Will's room, Dr. Bea asked that Addie wait in the hall a minute. She went in; Will was lying there staring at the ceiling.

"Will," she said, "I have someone to see you. She knows someone you know very well. May I bring her in?"

Will only grunted and made a motion with his hand.

Dr. Bea opened the door and asked Addie to come in. She walked to the bedside and leaned close to kiss him on the forehead. He looked surprised.

"My husband wants me to tell you that he is not lazy," she said, and tears welled into her eyes. "On behalf of three adorable children and me, we thank you for his life."

For the first time in a week, Will raised up. "Chacherie? You are not a dream?" And he was serious. He lay back against the pillow. Then he rocked his head from side to side. "I was worried," he said.

Dr. Bea and Addie talked to him more. They explained the physicians' prognosis for Chas and the fact that he was going to be a guest here for a long time, just like Will. They would have plenty of time to get together. By the time Dr. Bea said her "Good-bye" on Monday morning, she was sure he had a little color in his cheeks. He hugged her and kissed her hand. It was something he had not done in a long time.

Dr. Bea was not present when Will and Charles Chacherie got together, but she heard about it from Addie. Addie said it was one of the most joyous occasions in her life. Two grown men, in broken shells of bodies, holding on to each other as if they were the last two to survive the destruction of the earth. What she witnessed most was the immediate change that came over the countenance of both. She admitted that Chas had never seen Will smile. She said that after they had stayed in an embrace for a long time, clapping each other tenderly on the back, Charles looked at her and said in that croaked voice, "Sorry, honey, but it was love at first sight."

She said that Will then smiled and said, "Don't worry, it probably won't last. We have only known each other such a short time, two days and two nights at the most."

They were able to get together more each day. Their physical injuries began the long process of healing. Will, however, was having recurring fits of depression, still crying out in the night. Repeatedly, he kept saying he was "sorry, so sorry, so sorry."

In the office, Dr. Bea suggested a break. She and Jack got Coca-Colas and cookies, invited Mimi in, and chatted about irrelevant things, one of them being Jack and his girlfriend. Dr. Bea had run into her on several occasions and seemed to find her to be a real professional in her work. One thing she did say that amused Jack.

"Jack," she said, "You know that cute little girlfriend of yours has just the slightest Cajun accent. Child, you should hear Addie Chacherie." With that, Mimi chimed in, laughing, "She is pure bred, one hundred percent Cajun with papers to prove it." After the brief interlude, Dr. Bea told Jack that the hard part was coming up. It would be hard for her to relate, but it was important.

The prognosis for Will was good; he was improving physically. He was still wheelchair bound, and his shoulder was still in a cast, but all that would improve with time and rest. Now they had to deal with the other problem, his emotional state.

Charles Chacherie, on the other hand, had a long way to go with his physical problems. He had intestinal problems that he jokingly blamed on Will for feeding him rotten meat. His worst leg was past the stage of possible amputation; but several more surgeries would be necessary. The other was coming along well, and he was getting along with crutches.

His sprits stayed high because of Addie's alternate weeks of visitation. She had gotten an apartment near the hospital. When she was in town, she treated the hospital staff closest to Charles with Cajun dishes she prepared in the apartment. She arrived back in town for each visit with fresh seafood she brought from home, packed in dry ice.

There was one thing that the doctors had not counted on. Before Dr. Bea departed, Chacherie told her that Will was in his hands now. Will had saved his life; now it was time to reciprocate. With permission from the doctors, Chacherie would sit in the room with Will, sometimes two and three hours on end. He talked to him as if he was coherent and listening attentively to what he was saying. He chided him, he joked, he told foolish stories of accomplishment that only Cajuns might achieve. Will was seldom responsive.

The visits went on every day for almost three weeks. Chacherie was as patient as possible, but his attempts to bring Will around were to no avail. Then one morning he touched a button that made the lid blow off. He said to Will, "You know, you made me really mad when you accused me of being lazy. I wanted to knock you right on your ass. You had no idea how bad I hurt, and I could not walk. And now, here I am sitting here thinking what a coward you are, sitting there scared to death to face up to reality." Will made no sign of acknowledgement.

Then Chacherie said, "Oh, I thought you were really brave when you took that shard of glass and shoved it in that guard's brain. But, you know what, Will? The poor bastard was lying flat on his back.

All you had to do was fall down on top of him and shove that glass splinter in his eye."

Will was lying propped in his hospital bed, deep sunk eyes staring straight ahead. Then the bed actually shook. Will put his hands to his head and screamed, "I had to, I had to, I had to!" Then that wailing, "I am so sorry, so sorry, so sorry! I did not want to kill those men!" He was screaming at the top of his lungs and clawing at his own face with his fingernails. Orderlies rushed in and subdued him with a straitjacket. The nurses came, then one of his attending psychiatrists. His face was bloody; he was soaked in sweat, and tears were flowing. Charles Chacherie was sick that he had created such a problem.

Once Will was subdued and heavily sedated, the psychiatrists gathered around Chacherie. That was when what Will had said came out. The psychiatrist later repeated his words to Dr. Bea, and she too understood. Chacherie had hit the latchkey. Will had been repeatedly apologizing for his action. The doctors assured him that he had done nothing wrong. After several days, they reported that Will at last might be on the road to recovery. Chacherie was responsible for the fact that, at least then, Will was communicating. It was then that Chacherie told them about Will saying he had killed *those* men. Chacherie knew of only one. The head psychiatrist told him that what Will had said to his doctors was confidential, between patient and doctor. How Chacherie learned the rest was also confidential.

The evening Chas lay buried in the mud, Will left to look for safety. He came upon the shed where he eventually took Chacherie. He was cold, wet, and almost incoherent when he found the old hut and the shed. He observed the hut for a long time. He saw no activity — no smoke from a cook fire, no farm animals, nothing. He slipped into the shed first and was so exhausted that he slid down on the dry dirt floor with his back against the wall with the door. If someone came in on him, he would at least have an advantage.

Then it happened. Will awoke to the sound of footsteps in the mud outside. He stood erect, his back to the wall alongside the door. The door swung open, a soldier stepped in and swung his rifle from side to side, and as he did so, Will plunged a knife into the back of the man's neck. It went in just below the skull. The blade broke off;

the man dropped his weapon and tried to grab at the thing protruding from the back of his neck. Will clasped his hand over the man's mouth to stifle the scream, then with all the strength he could muster in his weakened condition, he wrestled the man off his feet. The man was unconscious when he hit the floor; Will pinched his nostrils together, and covered his mouth. The soldier smothered to death.

Will knew from the scream that someone else might be on the property. He took the man's gun, which was drier than the one he had in his possession. He crept to the hut. The crude door was ajar. Will peeped inside; a man was reclined on a mat, his eyes closed. He had his boots and socks off, his feet propped on a box. They were blistered and bloody, just as Will knew his own must be. The soldier had his hands clasped over his chest. Then Will accidentally bumped something with his foot, and the soldier became alert.

Will had not seen the gun in the man's lap. He raised it to fire, but Will shot him first. The man rolled off the mat. And that was when Will saw what the man had clasped in his hands. There were pictures of tiny children holding tightly to their mother.

The killing of the three men that took place during the escape, in addition to the constant fear that he had not gotten Chacherie to safety, had plunged Will into a depth of despair; his mind did not have the capacity. Charles Chacherie in his own way had accidentally made some compensation to Will for saving his life. The doctors allowed Chacherie to continue visiting Will, but for shorter lengths of time. They coached him on what might be best not to discuss.

The first time Chacherie went in to visit Will after what he called the "big boom," Will was again reclined on his bed. When Chacherie came in, Will looked at him and nodded. He sat silently for a while. Then he asked, "How are you?" Chacherie replied, "Better, You?" Will said, "The same." Day by day, Chacherie watched his friend slowly return to some form of being able to face the reality of what lay ahead.

Dr. Bea was ecstatic when she returned for her next visit. On recommendation from the psychiatrists, she had waited a whole month. The tremendous improvement showed. She sat with Will for an hour the first day. He was very lucid and even smiled some when she told him some silly things in which she and Carole Anne were involved.

She stayed five days. They did not talk much about anything serious, no discussion of the length of his treatment, nothing about any anxiety to go home. That last day, he asked her a question that gave rise to a belief that he was feeling well enough to be thinking ahead. He said, "I have not been behind the wheel of a car in almost four years. Have they changed much?"

Jack told Dr. Bea he could see why she wanted to cover this part of Will's history. He could not see what good it would be for Will to talk about it. It was important, and Jack was glad he had it, but at the same time, he felt a bit depressed.

In the final session with Dr. Bea, she related the story of the final days of Will's military service. The day that she left the hospital in San Diego, she went straight to a pay phone to talk to Jonathan. She was elated and wanted to share the good news. Poor Jonathan had gone into a mild funk himself, and she knew that it was due to his concern about Will.

Jonathan was anxiously awaiting news. Dr. Bea said, "I guess you need to be thinking about getting Will a car." With that, Jonathan let out one of Aunt Tilda's Whoops! She covered the basic facts about Will's improvement. Maybe they could begin thinking about his transition. He had not been free in a long time. There would be many things to get accustomed to again.

Six weeks later, he left the hospital in San Diego, and his records were sent to a veterans hospital nearest home. The navy showed that to be New Orleans. Shortly thereafter, he received a medical discharge.

40

1958: Jack and Adrianna

Jack did little other than his work on the documentary from the sessions with Dr. Bea. All he shared with Adrianna was that it was a sad story. One of the interesting things he discussed with her was Addie Chacherie, and the fact that she was also of Cajun descent. Then one evening, he finally told her most of the story. Now they understood the close bond between Will and Chacherie.

After hearing about Addie Chacherie, Adrianna spoke of her own heritage and her eagerness to visit her parents in White Castle. What about the coming weekend? They agreed: they would leave Saturday morning and return Sunday evening.

Adrianna was using Jack's car while he had the use of Will's company car. Since the White Castle trip was personal, Jack mentioned that he needed to get his personal car serviced for the trip. Adrianna replied that it was not necessary; they would be going in the Bentley. Miss Penny wanted Jack to drive the car so that when he took it in for the regular checkup, he could advise the technicians of anything that needed attention.

They were at the Villas, where Miss Penny was now saying she "was incarcerated," by 9:00 a.m. There was a long list of items to review before taking the Bentley. Promise to be careful, no speeding, and under no circumstance should they park where birds might roost on the car.

Jack did not say much about the forthcoming visit other than to say he was apprehensive. He felt ill at ease about being in the company of Adrianna's four brothers, her father, her mother, and eleven nieces and nephews. She assured him that he would be fine.

Her family was expecting them by mid-afternoon. The agenda was for a cookout in the backyard at her parents' home, a wild game extravaganza, according to Adrianna. Will knew that her father was a game warden and that the brothers hunted and fished. They were all contributing to the pot, and there was no telling what to expect. Adrianna drove the last half of the way and had to park the Bentley in the midst of half a dozen other vehicles, one car and five pickups. The gang was all there. Smokers were going, tables were set up, and a keg of beer floated in a washtub full of ice. A horseshoe game was underway. One of the nieces was the first to spot them and called out, "They are here! They are here!" Then the mob came to gather around.

First, there were introductions to father and brothers, all trying to shake hands with Jack at the same time. Then her mother in a bright apron came to hug him. All the nieces and nephews gathered around their Aunt Adrianna. Jack met the sisters-in-law one at a time and could sense them sizing him up.

After the meet and greet session, everyone got back to what they were doing. One brother and the father were tending the smokers; the girls went back to setting the tables and preparing food. They invited Jack to get into the horseshoe tournament. That was a good thing. He was very good at horseshoes. Soon he was one of the team.

Jack knew that his name was very familiar in the city but he did not gloat over the fact. He did not consider his profession to be different from any other. He soon found out that Adrianna's family held him in a lot higher regard than he would have expected. They lived closer to Baton Rouge. The Baton Rouge paper was their daily. However, because of Adrianna, they also got the *SI*. They knew a lot about Jack over and above the fact that he was living in sin with the only daughter in the family.

The horseshoe game ended, and the men all took chairs as they gathered around the big pit where the Breaux boys and father were cooking. No one specifically asked Jack questions about his job or anything pertaining to him and Adrianna. It was a surprise when one of the brothers had a request.

He asked Jack to elaborate, if he would, on one of the columns he had recently written. When Adrianna had made them aware of the column, they took it to be a sports column and probably just another opinion about baseball, football, or basketball. But even though it was supposed to be a sports column, Jack had taken a lot of leeway and was writing about some sports that were not those most in the forefront. He had recently written about the unlikely and illegal sport of cock fighting. In the column, he expressed his own disgust at the sport and at those involved in it. Adrianna's brothers and father wholeheartedly agreed.

From there, it went to the column on harness racing. Through Maureen Mullens, Jack had learned a lot about the sport and the training, not only of horse and rider but of handlers as well. It was very informative. Before long, Jack was one of the boys.

The evening meal was a feast to behold: rabbit, squirrel, alligator, doves, and venison, each prepared by a different household. There were also dessert contributions from each kitchen, made with nothing but wild fruits — plums, blackberries, persimmons — and even an after dinner dessert wine made with scuppernongs.

Adrianna's father blessed the dinner, and a period of silence fell on the table as everyone ate. With stomachs satisfied, the table began to fill with talk of the exciting things going on in each family, accomplishments of nieces and nephews, and a few tales of growing up, including tales of Adrianna and her life with five brothers. However, there was no gossip; Mother Breaux forbade that. No one felt in a hurry to leave the table; a little chitchat kept going on, another nibble of this, a little more wine, and finally it got quiet. They made plans as to which mass to attend the next day and who all was going to stay for the potluck lunch in honor of Father Boudreaux's birthday.

Then the highlight of the evening, if not the entire trip, took place. Chesney, the six-year-old niece of Adrianna and the daughter of her youngest brother, came around to the side of the table where Adrianna sat next to Jack. She wiggled in between them, and Adrianna lifted her onto her lap. She sat there a few minutes, staring all the while at Jack. After a few moments, she asked Jack, "Do you think I am pretty?"

To which Jack answered, "I sure do; you are gorgeous!"

She then replied, "Good. You know that I am going to be the flower girl when you and aunt Adrianna get married."

Chesney's mother screamed, "Chesney!"

Chesney answered back, "Well, it 's true, I am."

Adrianna glanced at Jack, and he was bright red. She bowed her head and put a limp wrist to her forehead. Dinner was over.

On Sunday morning, Adrianna and Jack attended mass with the family and joined in for the potluck at the parish hall. Several friends of Adrianna whom she had grown up with came up to greet her. One whispered in her ear, "I heard that last night, Chesney announced your forthcoming wedding."

On the way home, they were both quiet until Jack spoke up. "You know there were just my dad and I, one aunt and uncle, and no cousins when I was growing up. That was the first time I have ever been to a big, happy family gathering like that. I enjoyed it enough that I would like to be a part of a family like that." Then he said, "I guess you might be my ticket."

After a moment, Adrianna said, "Jack, is that a proposal?"

He replied with a grin, "Yeah, I guess it was."

"Well, I guess I will have to think about it."

There was a long period with nothing but the sound the Bentley's tires on the asphalt.

After a while, Adrianna said, "I've thought about it. Yes!"

She then leaned across and kissed his cheek. "My family loved you. They all have known for quite some time that as far as I was concerned, this had to happen." Adrianna said one other thing, "But we cannot get married until you're through with the book and have nothing else on your mind."

41

When Jack got together again with Will, he discussed the sessions with Dr. Bea and the fact that they had covered his hospital stay in San Diego. He asked if Will would review his manuscripts of those sessions with him. Will sat contemplating for a moment or two, then said, "Maybe I trust you to do what is best." He said nothing else. Then in a low tone, "I appreciate Aunt Bea wanting to protect me, and perhaps for the record, her recollection is far better than mine." Then, as he off his thoughts, he said enthusiastically, "Well, let's begin with my return."

He arrived in New Orleans with his ill-fitting dress whites and a small duffel with the total of his belongings. Jonathan knew of his impending arrival and was there with Dr. Bea and Carole Anne, all grinning just as he was when he stepped from the plane.

Plenty of rest was still the primary consideration; his old apartment at Dr. Bea's was the perfect spot. He dug through a trunk and found old bank records, his Social Security card, and some old letters. Some were from Stephanie, and one from Letitia. He read each of the letters, one at time. He wondered where they might be now.

The sessions at the VA hospital were not what Will expected. He was disappointed; all the young psychiatrist who'd been assigned to him wanted to do was go back through his file and read it to him, page by page. At the end of each session, the doctor would ask if he still had plenty of meds, and did he remember not to drink alcohol with the meds. The last time the young doctor told him that, Will asked whether that meant he could drink alcohol before or after the pills. The young doctor did not think it was funny.

Carole Anne aided immensely in his readjustment. She took him for walks in the park and trips to the zoo, things they had done when he visited as a child. She took him to nice restaurants, to movies, and on streetcar rides. He was coming along fine. As the last favor, she took him out on a country road alongside the river levee and let him begin driving again. Then she went with him to get a new driver's license. Soon he could leave the nest.

There had been much discussion about Will returning to New Cotswold. He was not ready to go to work, so what would he do? Jonathan was not too sure how welcome he might be either. There were still townspeople who would probably never forget the incident with Christine Simpkins.

Will was not going to have any concern about what townspeople thought. By damn, he had paid a dear price for his freedom. He would live wherever he pleased. Jonathan agreed. He found a piece of property outside of town on one hundred acres, where there was a barn and a house. He thought Will might like to have that piece, take his time remodeling the house, get some animals, rest, read, work when he wanted, and reunite with old friends. To Will, it was appealing, and he bought the property sight unseen, based on Jonathan's opinion. When he asked Jonathan if he would draft on his account for the money, Jonathan laughed. Will was quite wealthy.

He bought a new Ford pickup truck in New Orleans, bright red, with every possible option including a Mark IV aftermarket air-conditioner. His first excursion after purchasing the truck was to his appointment at the VA hospital. He sat patiently through the pointless session and listened to his medical history again and then minor points discussed. At the end of the session, the same young doctor as before handed him a new dose of pills and reminded him— no alcohol as long as this medication was in his system.

Will went to his apartment, got all of his meager belongings, and headed for New Cotswold. Near Slidell, he stopped at a bridge over a bayou, got out, and poured the pills into the bayou. In Slidell, he found a liquor store and shopped the bourbons. A clerk asked if he needed help, and he responded that he was shopping for a new doctor. The clerk frowned. Will selected Dr. Jim Beam and Dr. Jack Daniels. It was always best to have a second opinion. The clerk packed three cases of whiskey and put them in the truck cab for him. For the remainder of the trip, he briefed the doctor on his medical history.

He arrived in town late and went straight to the hotel. Jonathan invited him to stay there until he could get his house ready for occupancy. June was expecting him but was not expecting what she saw. He was hardly recognizable from the young man they had sent to war. It was hard for June to conceal her shock and her sorrow.

Jonathan raced from the office as soon as he knew Will was at the hotel. He went straight to his room and welcomed him with a big hug. June, Jonathan, and Will met later in their suite ; they had cocktails, but Will declined. After a brief catching up on family news, they adjourned to the dining room. Several people in the room waved as they came in. No one seemed to recognize the man with them, with his gray hair, pale complexion, and ill-fitting clothes. Will saw people at another table lean across to talk in whispers. One of the women turned to look.

Will was up at his usual 5:30 the next morning, as was hospital custom. They liked to wake patients up early to shove overcooked oatmeal and undercooked toast at you. Then it was time to give you pills to get you back to sleep. He was downstairs and waiting when the dining room opened. Jonathan arrived moments later. Other than "Good Morning," neither had much to say until they were through with their first cup of coffee.

Jonathan looked across at Will in his long sleeve shirt. It swallowed him. Jonathan asked about a jacket, but Will had not brought one along. He had forgotten how chilly it could get here in winter. It was February and still enough time for a freeze. He would find a jacket that day, maybe a work jacket from Swenson's Mercantile. He needed to say hello to the Swensons anyway.

The plan was for Jonathan to lead him out to his new property, show him around, and then get on to the office. Will was glad Jonathan was in his own vehicle; he was not ready to introduce his new team of doctors, who were resting peacefully in the cab of the truck.

He was familiar with the property location; after all, these were his old stomping grounds. He was not sure he had ever been on the property, but he had flown over it. Jonathan told him it was on School Road, the same road that passed in front of his grandparents' home and Nap's store. In addition, it was four miles west from Nap's, meaning it was only two miles further west to the Six Mile Club. He knew Nap's place well, but Six Mile Club had not appealed to him in

his youth. The clientele was mostly the older, rednecked, pool shooting crowd. Honky Tonk music was their forte. Will preferred music
that was like a seven course meal that got better and better, right up
to dessert. Honky Tonk music had a place, but to him it was more like
a condiment, similar to hot pepper sauce on collard greens. However,
his opinion of Six Mile Club would change.

Jonathan turned onto Will's new property, and he recognized the
site immediately. He had even been on it from another road. This
piece went all the way back to a spur that ran off Old Church Road.
On the rear of the property was a great little pond for bream. Only
a few knew about it. Aunt Tilda had introduced it to Will and John
Pope.

Will liked that there were no houses near enough to see, except
the one directly across the road. The house on his property sat at least
a hundred yards back from the road, making it very private. Jonathan
had not overstated the problems with the house when he'd given his
description of it as a run-down old tenant house of board, batten, and
shingle roof. The tilting roof needed repair. They mounted the board
steps onto a porch that slanted the wrong way. It was a dogtrot house
with a wide, open center section, not screened.

To either side of the open dogtrot were two rooms. Will followed
Jonathan closely as he showed him the rooms on the left: a big front
room that could serve as parlor or bedroom, and a kitchen large
enough for cooking, with room for a small dining table. The only
thing in the kitchen was the old wood stove, probably original to the
house. A rusty sink with only one faucet was set in an old wooden
work table.

Across the dogtrot hall were two more large rooms. Each had
muslin or newsprint stuck to the walls, indicating that that was the
only covering there had ever been. The interior walls were of wood
plank, what looked like oak. The ceilings in all the rooms were of
weather stained corrugated cardboard from old boxes, and they
sagged. But the floors were a surprise. They were thick, of something
more like two by twelves rather than ordinary flooring.

There was electricity, but poor wiring ran on the surface of the
walls through glass and ceramic insulators. The water supply was
from an inoperable windmill with missing blades. The toilet was

outside, about thirty feet from the house. From the back porch, they looked across at a decrepit barn, leaning to the east. Neither of the men said much until Will laughingly said, "This is a designer's dream."

Jonathan started to defend against that statement by telling Will he thought he had been very candid when he had described the house to him in the beginning. Will cut in before he could finish.

"First, level it, gut all the old ceiling out, maybe leave the wood stove, get new glass for the windows, rebuild the porch, put on a new tin roof, windmill blades, new wiring, new plumbing. There is enough room on the back porch to enclose an area for a bathroom. Just perfect," Will said with true enthusiasm.

Jonathan said, "You sure?"

"It is perfect for me. I need something to occupy my mind, something to afford exercise, and most of all, a place for peace of mind for a while." Jonathan was pleased as well as relieved. He then told Will to get in his truck, because there was more to see. The driveway from the road to the house was no more than a two rut trail. Will was not surprised that it continued along his fence line all the way to the back of the property, where it joined up with the spur off Old Church road. They passed another old home site. Now only a chimney stood there, and nearby was the roof of a well. They passed the pond that Will remembered. Three little colored boys left their fishing poles and scattered into the woods nearby when they heard Jonathan's truck.

Jonathan assured Will again, "You can stay at the hotel as long you need, until the house is livable."

Will remarked, "As I came into town yesterday, I spotted a travel trailer on a lot near Tony Cannizaro's store. It has a "FOR SALE" sign. I think I will look at it. If it is what I think, it would be perfect for the time being." Jonathan agreed.

Before they parted company, Will went over his plan for the day. He needed to call his grandmother and then Aunt Tilda. He was sorry his grandfather was out of town. He would catch up with him another day. Jonathan laughed, "Don't plan on seeing anybody else; that is going to take the rest of your day."

Jonathan left, and Will took his team of doctors into the barn. A tack room inside would do for safekeeping, and it would be cool and comfortable for the gentlemen. His first stop was to see his grandmother. She had been forewarned and did not show alarm at his appearance. His grandmother's maid, Vivian, came into the parlor; she had not been forewarned. To her he looked pitiful. She came to him, held out her arms to hug him, and said, "Oh Mr. Will, I am so sorry. You going to be OK?" Will was going to have to get used to this for a while and not let it bother him.

Jonathan was correct. His visit with his grandmother lasted until near noon. Even then, he had to beg her to let him leave. That day, she told him something that she would repeat many times over the next several months. She held his hands in hers and looked directly into his eyes. "Will, you have so much to live for that you know nothing about. Work as hard as you can to get strong again. We will help all we can."

Even though it was lunchtime, Will drove to Winston and Tilda's house. They had bought Mr. Swenson's property after he had decided not to build there. According to Jonathan, the property was a showplace. He also told him that the day's date was the security code at their gate. Will drove up the road alongside Nap's store, turned to cross a new bridge, and came face-to-face with the beautiful wrought iron gate. A post near the gate did indeed have a keypad. Will put in the date and drove along the winding pea gravel drive to the front of the house. He was puzzled; why did they need a security gate?

Hearing a car on the gravel, Aunt Tilda got up from the kitchen table where she and Winston were already having their noon meal. She was standing at the front screen door, peering out at the red truck approaching. They were not expecting company. Will's appearance when he stepped from his truck was a shock. At first, she did not recognize him. Then she bounded down the steps, running toward him with her apron in her hands, tears in her eyes, and called for Winston to come see. "My baby is home!"

Inside the kitchen, both Winston and Tilda were stumbling over each other, rushing to set a place for him. Not having enough food was certainly not a problem. Tilda had cooked for the jail for years before they built their home in the country. She was still accustomed to cooking more than they could eat at even two meals. She had smothered pork chops, fried okra, butter beans, stewed tomatoes, and refrigerator rolls. The corn bread was from breakfast; the iced tea was in quart fruit jars.

Will had not eaten so well in a long time, or as much. Aunt Tilda winked at Winston when she saw how much he was eating. "I'll put meat on your bones before you know it!" she said.

Winston could hardly make it through the banana pudding without nodding. Soon as he took the last bite, he excused himself to go to take a nap before returning to work. Aunt Tilda ushered Will to the sunroom and told him to stretch out on the sofa and take a little snooze. She sat in an easy chair and took up her crocheting. Soon both were asleep.

Will woke up when he heard the back door close as Winston was off to work. He sat up, and Aunt Tilda began to talk. "Hon, I am worried about you. You are so thin. You sure you OK, taking your medicines, getting rest, everything the doctors told you to do? What about your chest, any sign of congestion, any fever?"

Will looked at her with a grin. "What about tomorrow morning I bring you a sample of my stool?"

With that, Aunt Tilda rose up from her chair and slapped at his arm. "You and that John Pope, I never knew what you two would say. Remember when you called into the bathroom to that cute little Letitia, told her not to flush, Aunt Tilda wants to see your stool! You embarrassed her and me both."

Will looked far off into the distance, then back at Aunt Tilda. "I completely lost track of her. You ever hear anything about her or her mother?"

"Last I heard, her mother had moved to Kentucky to be near a sister. Someone said the girl moved to Europe. You do know they still own that beautiful place in the country. Miss Maureen has it leased to a man and wife who train harness horses."

Even though he had taken a nap, Will was surprised how tired he was. It was going to take time. He went back to the hotel, cleaned up for supper, and met Jonathan and June in the dining room. He had supper with them and they talked little, but June could tell that Will was tired. "Will, hon, you have had a full day; why don't you turn in early? He agreed, excused himself, and went to his room.

At breakfast the next morning Jonathan took a typewritten list from his shirt pocket and handed it across to Will. He explained: one of the men at the plant had made a list of tools he thought Will might need for work on the house. The entire list had a check by each item, indicating that those tools were available in the tool crib at the plant. If Will would like, Jonathan offered to have them sent out to his house. Jonathan suggested that he should pick up clasps and locks to put on all the doors for security until he finished the doors.

"Next," Jonathan said, "I called REA to get a power pole put up with six outlets for you to use until the house is rewired. You need to go by their office across from the high school to sign up and give them a deposit. Phones take a few days, so I requested one even though the house may not be ready."

Will leaned across to Jonathan and said, "Lord, I have missed you."

June was busy running here and there, getting the hotel up and running for the day. She did stop by the table to tell Will not to leave before she talked to him. When she returned, she had a big ring of keys and a list. She sat across from him for just a moment to tell him that she had something of interest. When they had remodeled the second floor of the hotel, they replaced all the furniture with new. She led him to the storage in the basement. There were beds, mattresses, end tables, coffee tables, armoires, even some linens and curtains.

June then pointed to one other closet. She opened it. Only one garment hung there: it was a jacket, red with white sleeves. It had the number "6" embroidered on the sleeve. It was Will's old letter jacket from high school. June said Jonathan had spent half the night going through old trunks stored in the livery building. Will was thrilled, even if it did fit loosely.

His first stop that morning was to check on the trailer. He liked it and called the number on the sign. Will told the person answering the phone that he was interested in the trailer and would like to see inside. The owner said he was minutes away and would be right there. The owner was Tony Cannizzaro, who was married to Will's mother's youngest sister, Tootie. At first, Tony did not recognize Will, and he introduced himself. When Will spoke his name, Tony put his arms around him. He was sorry; it had been a long time. Tony was asking four thousand dollars for the trailer, but he confided that he had taken the trailer in lieu of a two thousand dollar gambling debt. Will could buy it for that. He took it.

Next stop: Swenson's Hardware and Mercantile for a one and five eighths hitch ball for his new trailer and a few loose hand tools, clasps, and padlocks. The Swensons had been forewarned. The minute the little bell jingled on the front door, he heard a squeal, and Imogene came running. Mr. Swenson sat at his raised desk on a dais. He came down the steps at the same time, calling for Mrs. Swenson.

Imogene hugged him tightly, then Mrs. Swenson, then Mr. Swenson. He had to go sit around Mr. Swenson's desk with the three of them. He was welcomed home. God love him for his sacrifice. Then all the questions, was he going to move back here, what was he going to do, where would he live if he moved back? Will answered all in time.

When he mentioned the old house and the remodeling, Imogene's ears perked. She loved refurbishing houses and helping with it. When he needed materials, he was to come see her. Mr. Swenson urged him to do so. In his own opinion, she was an expert when it came to estimating materials and costs. She would save him money. Will left the store with the promise that she could stop by the old house anytime to start working up an order.

He took care of the things he needed to do at the power company and the telephone company, and he even got a Post Office Rural Route number. By noon, he was exhausted. He went back to the hotel, skipped lunch, and napped until supper time. Will and June were out with friends, so he ate alone and was back in his room and in bed by eight o'clock.

The next several days were busier. He got his trailer moved and connected his electric lines. Next, he rigged a drain for the trailer holding tank to the outdoor toilet, and he filled the propane bottles. All he needed now was water. That required windmill repairs. Meantime, he could fetch water from Nap's store. He was keeping track: five days without meds.

He ate supper again with Jonathan and June. Jonathan said that his Aunt Jessie was anxious to see him. Will was reluctant. She had never taken his word about Christine Simpkins. Will told Jonathan that he would see her in time, but that today, Schooner's was on his list of places to go.

The Schooners had gotten the word: "Will MacMorogh is back in town. You will not recognize him," followed by a brief description. Mrs. Schooner saw him come in first and greeted him warmly, with a big hug and a kiss on his cheek. She admired his jacket and laughed. Tommy would be thrilled to see it. They were working on a plane.

She directed him to the hangar and then called on the intercom to alert the men. After two hours of talk, while the men continued to work, Will did get his order in for windmill repairs. The Schooners would take care of it; Tommy himself would oversee it. They broke for lunch, and Tommy, who usually went home for lunch, offered to buy lunch for Will. His wife excused him if he would bring Will by to see the babies, now two of them.

"Let's go to the Toot and get a double burger with fries and a chocolate milk shake, see if they have any new sexy carhops!" When Tommy said this, which had been something oft repeated during high school days, they both laughed.

"Good to have you home, Will," Tommy said. Then he too wanted to know what Will would be doing. Since he was getting windmill repairs out at the property he bought, was he going to live there, what he would be doing, all of the same questions others had asked. Then he told Will that he had never believed any of the rumors after Christine had left town. He felt that it was all a bad memory and had about gone away. He went on to say, "This civil rights thing will keep most of these fools occupied."

That night was the last night Will spent at the hotel. The next day, he took up residency in his trailer. All he had to do was haul water from Nap's store. Probably one trip a day would do it until he got his windmill and water well operating. The next day, he had to go see Nap. That was another visit long overdue.

Will used blocks cut from old railroad crossties to use as footings for house jacks. He first leveled the front porch, then one rear corner of the house. It changed the appearance of the structure dramatically. It was also the first hard labor that he had done. The job took three days, and by the end of the third, he was sore all over and at the point of exhaustion. However, he ate like a horse and slept like a log. No meds, no ill effects.

Will had asked the pharmacist at the VA hospital why the warning about alcohol and the meds. She told him that he did not want to find out. Among the problems, severe gastrointestinal pain, vomiting, and splitting headaches. If someone was not present to keep the patient hydrated, he might well die. When asked how long the meds stayed in your system, she had told him twenty-one days, in an average metabolism.

Once the house was level, Will was ready to move to the next step. He wanted to get the roof on before spring rains set in. He stopped by the store to ask Imogene for her help in estimating the materials. She promised to come out that afternoon.

She showed up in tight overall pants, work shoes, and a MSCW sweatshirt that might belong to someone less gifted. She used Will's long ladder to climb to the roof for measurements; Will held the ladder. As she came down, and at the point when her butt was almost in his face, a car pulled up.

"Oh no!" said Will. It was his Aunt Jessie. He should have gone to see her first. Aunt Jessie had chastised Will severely about several incidents involving women. Imogene's bra incident at the Toot was one of them. His Aunt Jessie had told him back then that his inability to keep his penis in his pants was surely going to get him in trouble. The scandal about him and Christine had convinced her she was right.

Seeing the making of a bad scene, Aunt Jessie handed Will a sack from her garden containing fresh tomatoes and another of fresh corn. She invited him to visit her when he had time and bid him and Imogene farewell. They laughed it off but, it was the kind of thing that started rumors. Will did not need more of that.

Imogene was a tremendous help. Once her measurements were complete, she told Will how many sheets of the roofing tin were needed, what gauge she recommended, how many nails it would take, and how much time it would require. She had a piece of advice. Hire someone else to do the job. Will objected, but she continued with her reasoning. Old wood shingles would be difficult to remove. There would be some baseboards to replace. The worst job would be pulling the roofing sheets up on the roof and securing them before a gust of wind got under them. She told him he was not strong enough to do it.

He was not yet convinced she was right, but he would take it under advisement. It was getting late, and he would like to offer Imogene a drink. She would accept only if he was having one. He declined, giving the meds as an excuse. They both drank Coca-Colas instead. With bottles in hand, they walked through the old structure. Imogene would stop and look and then say, "Uh huh," or "Good," or "Wouldn't work," more to herself than to Will. After a while, she said that she had a great idea, asked Will if he was interested. Of course he was.

The basis of her idea was to raise the ceiling in all the rooms, and she explained how simple it would be to do. Will said it sounded easy enough, but what was the purpose? According to Imogene, there were two reasons. Most important, he would have enough height to install ceiling fans. That would help tremendously with cooling. Next, it would give the feeling of larger rooms that she felt the little house needed. She kept looking and decided she would like to come back again at another time with a sketchpad. It was dark when she left. No meds, no problems; he was closing in on twenty-one days.

The next day started a new regimen. He heard that the Six Mile Club now offered breakfast and lunch. He needed to build his strength. He would walk there, have breakfast, and then walk back home. By the time he got home, however, he realized that he would have to build more strength. He rested much of the day. That got him to thinking more about what Imogene had suggested, hiring the roofing to be done.

The next morning, he drove his truck halfway to the Six Mile Club, pulled it to the side of the road and left it. After breakfast, he walked back to the truck. Two miles were more like it for starters. When he got back home, he had enough energy to put the ladder up and see how hard the old roofing shingles would be to remove.

On the way down, he missed the last rung on the ladder and fell backward, pulling the ladder with him. He did not fall far, but the position he was in with the ladder when he fell was what did the damage. The pain was intense. He hurt the shoulder that had required so many repairs. Along with that pain, his hand was numb, and his collarbone hurt like hell. Not being able to use his left side made it difficult to get up. He managed to crawl to the side of the barn and use his right arm to push up. Once he was on his feet, he made it into the house, got his truck keys, and drove himself to the hospital.

There were three new doctors in town. Will asked for Dr. Rubin. Dr. Bea had sent all of Will's records from the VA to him, just in case there were emergencies. He knew all of Will's problems, medical and psychological, along with what meds he was supposed to be taking. Will was X-rayed from head to toe, and all the other vital signs were checked. He had not damaged any of the previous shoulder repairs. However, he had pulled a ligament, broken a collarbone, and had two cracked ribs. He would be tightly bound, with his arm and shoulder in a sling for a month. Someone else would have to do the roof.

To relieve pain, Dr. Rubin prescribed a painkiller. Will adamantly opposed any pills. Dr. Rubin assured him that the meds he wanted him to take would not interfere with his current regimen of medicine. That was when Will let him know he had quit all medications. Will stressed that he was tired of the out-of-body feel that the pills gave him. He was tired of the mental and physical slowdown.

Dr. Rubin tried to explain that the pills slowed him physically because his body needed rest and repair. The same thing applied to his brain. It needed rest and repair. He told Will he could not feel that his brain hurt, but in fact it did. He strongly advised Will to go back to the VA, check in, and get back on track. Will told him he would go home and take two aspirins.

He left the hospital under his own power, drove home, and did just as he had promised. He took two aspirins. The afternoon wore on. Dr. Rubin had called Jonathan, and he drove out to check on him. Will was still in severe pain. Jonathan left him with the promise that he would check back the next day. In the meantime, he should call if he needed anything. Will went to the cupboard as soon as Jonathan left. He asked Dr. Beam for advice. He put one finger in the glass and poured to the first knuckle.

He lay on his sofa and turned on the TV, but the antenna had blown in the wind, and he got nothing but snow. He got up, went to the front porch, lit up a pipe, and sat. After a few minutes, the pain subsided a bit. In another hour, he was asleep, sitting in the chair. Next morning, he drove to the Six Mile Club, drank three strong cups of coffee, had breakfast, and felt good. He went home and called Imogene with his latest problem. He thought he should take her advice. Could she arrange for the roofing repair people? That was the start of Imogene's project.

She came out again that very afternoon, sketchpad in hand, and went to work. She had many ideas that she thought were good. Will listened and agreed. The project got underway in earnest the next day.

She suggested that it might be more comfortable for Will to stay in the trailer during the house repair. He moved the doctors into a permanent place in the kitchen cabinets. The pain in his shoulder got worse as the day wore on, so after Imogene left, again he consulted Dr. Beam. His advice: another dose, but this time, one finger, second knuckle.

Two weeks went by; the repairs were finished, Will was able to move into the house. He went to the hotel and got June's help to select the furniture he would need. Jonathan got men from the plant to move the items.

42

The house was probably the cutest tenant house in the state of Mississippi as well as one of the most expensive. Imogene made other changes, with Will's permission. Two air-condition units came along with the ceiling fans. All windows and doors were new. The kitchen had a top line stove, ovens, and dishwasher. Instead of closing in a part of the back porch, she suggested making the back room of the two on the east side into a bathroom and large closet. Then they enclosed the front and back porches with screen, leaving the porches and dogtrot open and insect free. It was a great area for summer entertaining.

What came with the completion of the little house, however, was boredom. Will needed something else to do. He would get to work on completing the barn project until he recovered from his injuries. There was a problem, though. The healing process was going slowly. Dr. Rubin said it took time, and he urged Will to try some pain medication. But he refused. He could manage with his current medicine; it was just taking more of it to get the job done.

Summer was upon them. Because of the arm in a sling, driving was not comfortable or safe. Will found comfort sitting around the house watching TV or listening to the radio. Music was different now; some he enjoyed, and some he disliked. When he had lived in New Orleans during college, Dr. Bea had had music playing all of the time. It had been low, pleasant to the ear. She loved classical music, string quartets, classical guitar, piano, and some opera. Now all Will got on the radio was popular music, much of it loud screaming. By the time three in the afternoon arrived, Will was not only bored, but the pain was returning. He sought medical advice. The recommended dosage now was one finger, four knuckles. Sometimes he took two doses.

Slowly he began to heal, but by then the fact that he was drinking heavily was obvious. Concern for him turned to disgust or pure sorrow. Jonathan was disappointed, but kept his faith in him. He never chastised or criticized. He simply stated on more than one occasion that he knew Will was in pain physically and perhaps emotionally. Jonathan said, "I will never let you down; don't you let me down."

Aunt Tilda was hearing rumors she could not believe, so she came to see for herself. She was distraught. She prayed about it. When she returned the second time, she treated Will with a dose of hard love. The words she used and her tone did not completely sink in at the time, but as days went by, Will recalled what she had said, over and over.

His grandmother was the pitiful one. She kept telling Will there was something he had to live for, but until he straightened up, it was not going to happen. She literally begged him.

The healing progressed, and he got to a point where he was working most of the day. Though he was in pain, he was determined to do the work on the barn regardless of the fact that Imogene said he could not. First, he managed to get the barn standing so that it did not resemble the leaning tower. He stripped the old shingles off, one by one, and replaced the baseboards and then the metal roof. Last, he poured a concrete floor. This took weeks, and his daily routine continued. Three o'clock, medicine time. Between then and passing out time, he often drank much of a fifth.

One of the people he occasionally shared his booze with, he met by accident. He had begun having his evening meal, usually the same thing, rare steak, baked potato, salad, and plenty of booze, and always taken at the Six Mile Club. The person he met was a young woman by the name of Holly Porterfield. Holly had a poor reputation in town and earned it quite easily. She was second generation. Her mother was the town slut, her dad a drunk of the first degree. No one expected much of her, so she did not disappoint them.

She had one thing in common with five other girls in town, however. They were not all from poor white trash families. Matter of fact, she fared better than a couple of them had. One committed suicide; the other shot her brother in the face with a twenty-two pistol loaded with rat shot. It did not kill him, but he had a hard time getting dates afterward.

There were many nights Will stayed at the Six Mile Club so long and got so drunk that he could not walk. The owner of the club, Roscoe Durden, usually put him in his office to sleep it off. One night, Holly offered to drive him home if someone else would follow in her car so she could then drive herself home. She got him out of the truck with the help of another girl and the boy who followed in her car. She dismissed the others, then stripped his clothes off, all of them. She got a cold cloth, put it across his eyes, stripped off herself, and climbed into bed with him.

Will awoke the next morning, turned over and his arm fell over a sleeping Holly. She woke and explained how she had gotten there.

Will made the mistake of asking her how much money he owed her. She blew up. What she told him was not what he had expected to hear. She had brought him home for two reasons, she said. One, he could not get home by himself because he had passed out. Two, he started talking when he was drunk. She was afraid he was going to tell what he knew about her and the other girls. That confused Will.

She then told him that there were five girls in town, including her, who knew that he was aware of what had taken place. She told him there had been six, but one killed herself after several years of shame and fear that someone would find out. Holly said that she was at a point in her life where she did not give a shit anymore. But the others lived in constant fear. Now that he was back in town, was he was going to tell?

Then Will looked at her. "You were involved in that also?" he asked. Then he went on to tell her that he did not intend to say anything. He felt heartsick that one had died; who was she? She told him, and he moaned. He knew her family well. Holly told him that the family moved away in shame.

Then it was her turn again. "You mean that you have had your name and the name of your family drug through the mud and you are going to say nothing?"

Will shook his head back and forth. "No, I would never do anything that would hurt the girls. Too much water has passed under the bridge." Holly became his guardian. If he got too drunk, which was often, she got him home.

One other thing happened while he was in his drunken stage. It occurred only a few weeks before Thanksgiving, and somehow, the story got out. Will was sitting on his front porch one night when he was too tired and already too drunk to go to the Six Mile Club. He had Doctor Beam sitting on the floor next to him, with a bucket of ice cubes and his favorite snack, rat cheese and crackers. His glass made that delightful sound it made when he whirled the ice cubes and booze. He took a long sip, smacked his lips, and for a moment, closed his eyes.

The sound that caused him to open his eyes was a car slowing in the highway, then tuning into his drive. The car crept up the drive, near enough to the house to stop. The driver door opened, the interior light came on, and two men talked for a minute before getting out. They came up the walk muttering something, unaware that Will was sitting there in the dark. Will saw that both men had books in their hands, Bible sized books.

The light was on in his parlor, but the drape was drawn; little light escaped to the porch. The men stepped up to the screen door, and Will said in a loud voice, "Hallelujah, praise Jesus, someone has come to save my sorry ass." The men jumped back for an instant, then the one in front pulled the screen open and the other man followed. The first one said, "Shall we pray," and bowed his head. Will recognized him. He was the ruling elder at the Baptist Church when they had evicted Christine.

"Kiss my ass, Banks, what do you want?" Will said.

"Now, now, Will." he pleaded. "We want to overlook old transgressions and offer to you the same love that our God offers us. We want to pray with you."

Will swished his glass around, heard the beautiful music of the ice cubes, and then said in a strong, firm voice. "Transgressions, you say, you sorry son of a bitch. You are here because you are scared shitless that I am going to tell the world that you aided and abetted a crime, then lied to cover it up. Get your ass off my front porch and take your fucking dummy with you." The other man said nothing; nor did he have the opportunity.

The two men turned, and Banks ducked his head. They went toward the car, but before they got to the car, the dummy stopped, handed his Bible to Banks, and came back to the door, opened it, and stepped up on the porch.

"You do not know me.," he said. "I am Dr. Cash Whitman, newly appointed assistant pastor at the church. In three weeks, I will take over as senior pastor when Reverend Procter retires. I am coming to see you again, by myself, and if you treat me like you have tonight, I will kick your drunken ass all over this porch. And by the way, I am no dummy." With that, he turned, looked back at Will, pointed his finger as if it was a gun, and pretended to pull the trigger. "See ya." Will sat there a little stunned. The man had said enough that Will remembered it the next morning. He liked the man.

The first week in November, the weather changed, cooler, nicer to work in. Will was working in the barn, pouring concrete, needed more water, went to the faucet, and opened it. Nothing. He checked his windmill first, then the electric pump in his reservoir. Nothing was wrong. He called Tommy Schooner. Tommy arrived later in the day, double-checked everything again, and then gave Will the bad news. The well was dry.

The well on the property was a shallow, hand dug well that had gotten water from the groundwater that years before had run close to the surface. It was depleted from years of usage, and maybe even had caved in. The short of it was that Will needed to drill a new one.

Will went to Jonathan and told him his problem. Jonathan reminded him that he knew how to drill a well. He would loan him a rig and a man, but he needed to do the rest himself. He also reminded Will that rigs could kill a sober man, much less a drunk one. Drilling started on a Wednesday. Will recalled wells he had drilled with Winston. Surely, he would bring the well in at about one hundred and fifty feet depth. That was easy to do in a couple of days. But on Friday at noon, he was close to two hundred feet, and nothing. He called Winston for help. On the phone, Winston told him he was in a part of the county where the aquifer he wanted to hit was deeper. Keep drilling.

At three o'clock, a car drove into the yard across the road. The young girl, who Will had seen there, usually on weekends, got out and ran toward the house. She waved; he waved back. He had met the old man who lived there, but not the girl. In a short while, she came out in jeans and a purple and white Millsaps sweatshirt, her hair in a ponytail. She crossed the road to Will's mailbox, took out a stack of mail, and walked swiftly up his drive toward the house. She dropped the mail inside the front door and continued down the road to where Will and his helper were drilling. He had selected the spot, about two hundred yards from his existing house, thinking it might someday be a better home site for a larger house. Piping water from that point to the existing house would be easy. When the young girl got close enough, Will walked away from the rig and toward her. He took off his hard hat. She stuck out her hand and introduced herself. "Susie Scott."

Will reciprocated, "Will MacMorogh; my pleasure. I have met your dad."

She asked about the well, how it was coming, how deep was he, and when he expected to hit water. Will answered all but the last: he did not know when he might hit water. He told her he had drilled many wells, and they had all come in in less than two hundred feet. He was currently at two hundred ninety-five.

She smiled and said, "You'll come in at three and a quarter to three fifty,"

"And how can you be so certain about that?" Will asked.

She explained that she was a business major at Millsaps College, graduating the next May. She had taken geology classes and owned several books on Mississippi geology. She added that her professor was at one time the state geologist and passed on a lot of firsthand information. Will smiled and told her he would keep drilling.

At nine that night, the well came in. Will had let his helper go home at dark and was working alone. He was not paying close attention to the water coming up from the hole. He was using water from a tank on the truck to cool the drill bit and wash up cuttings. That water came out of the hole and ran off as thick muddy water. All of a sudden, he realized that the water coming up was beginning to clear, and soon there was a steady flow. He stopped drilling, pulled the drill stem up a few feet, and let the drill bit circulate.

Susie Scott heard the sound of the diesel engine running the drill when it went to idle. Will saw her porch light come on. She stepped out onto the porch, pulling her coat on, and came trotting up the road with a flashlight. Will greeted her with thumbs up. She looked at the drill stem and asked what the last section was that he had put on since she had left earlier. He told her that there had been one more plus that one. She backed off, looked at how far down the stem was in the drill table, then said, "Three hundred and sixty, approximately."

Will led her over to the control panel. Three forty-eight was what his gauge showed. She said to him, "Good job!" She then asked where his helper was. He told her that he was gone for the day. Then she wanted to know if he was just going to circulate the bit until morning and wait for his helper to pull the pipe. "If you want to pull the pipe now, I will help."

Will just shook his head. "You have done enough for today."

Susie kept a close eye on the drilling operation and came over the next morning to watch. After the rig was down and the men were taking a break, she added a little more information. It was her opinion that this property would make a great sand and gravel pit. She started talking about the yards of sand it might hold, how much gravel was also there, and how little overburden he would have to move in order to get to the sand. Will listened attentively. After the helper left, he asked her how she knew there was a lot of gravel there. She told him they should take a ride in his truck.

Will drove, and she directed. They got to a place where she said to stop. They got out and walked down a steep incline and through some kudzu. There was a stream bed and gravel everywhere. She then led him up another draw and through more brush to another outcropping, with even a better show. Will complimented her on her knowledge. He thought she had a great idea. He might think about it.

Back at the house, he thanked her and asked her how long she would be in town. She told Will that she came home every weekend to clean house and cook meals for her dad for the following week. Will had seen her father outside a time or two in a wheel chair and he walked poorly, with two canes. He had only spoken briefly to introduce himself.

Susie looked at Will and said, "My dad drank a lot too. He got hold of some bad whiskey called Jamaican Gin. Distillation took place through a car radiator with lots of lead solder. He got lead poisoning. We were lucky that it only crippled him. A lot went blind from it."

Will asked about her mother. She had died four years earlier. They got a small check each month; she was on a scholarship. She did not know what she would do when she graduated. She guessed she might have to find work near home so she could take care of the old man. She asked one other thing of Will. She had seen a book of coupons in the mail she'd left on his front porch the day before. If he were not going to use them, she would like to have them. Every little bit helped.

Will thought about Susie again about three that afternoon when he poured his first drink: one finger, four knuckles. "My dad drank a lot too," she had said. He sat on the porch drinking; too late to go to Six Mile, he thought. However, he did think of one other thing before he went to bed. He took an envelope, stuck a one hundred dollar bill in it, and put it by the coffee pot. The next morning he would write a note, "Consulting fee, Susie Scott, $100.00," and then put it in an envelope and stick it in her mailbox.

The next day he continued his daily routine: work hard until three. Go see Dr. Beam and spend the rest of his day drinking. He was doing that very thing on Thanksgiving Eve. He had not even considered that the next day was Thanksgiving, much less where he was going to spend it. His routine was his focus.

Dusk set in, and he saw activity across the road at his neighbor's house. Someone waved; he waved back. Then he closed his hand tightly around his drink, took another slug, and closed his eyes. At the sound of a car door slamming loudly, he raised his head to look. Baxter, his grandmother's chauffeur, stood beside the car, and his grandmother was walking toward the house, bent as if she was facing into a strong wind. She jerked the screen door open and stepped onto the porch. He tried to get up, needed help to do so, and fell back in his chair.

His grandmother drew herself up to her six feet, regal as she stood. "Will, I have told you over and over again that there might be something great waiting for you if you would get your life together." Then she began to tear up, something he could never remember having seen her do. "Now it is too late. It is over. You had your opportunity, it came, it went. I am beyond being sad or disappointed. To me, it is like death has struck our family again." She began to weep into her gloved hands, turned and stepped off the porch and on toward the car door that Baxter opened.

She crawled into the car; the last Will saw before Baxter closed the door was her, lying across the back seat. Baxter got in; the interior light was on, and he was talking to her in the back seat. In a moment, he got out and came back to the house. He opened the door, saying, "Mr. Will, I am not going to tell you what she told me to tell you. Maybe she will get over this. I hope so. I will tell you this. I have been her servant for almost forty years, and I have never seen her cry, not even when your mother and daddy died. So," and then he paused, "I am as hurt as I ever have been in forty years. Good evening, sir."

Will managed to get up without falling, got another drink, sat down on the porch again, and drank himself into oblivion. Somehow, during the night, he got off the porch and into bed. For the first time in months, he had that horrible nightmare. He shot the soldier directly, and the man rolled over, and the pictures of his children fell on the mat. Will's own screams woke him. He got up at mid-morning with a bad hangover, the dream fresh in his mind and taunting him. He sat at his kitchen table, wondering about his grandmother's comment. He spent the rest of the day alone. No one came; he went nowhere.

43

That night, he went to bed without a drink. He slept fitfully and was tempted several times to get up, but he did not. The following morning, he fixed a huge pot of coffee, shaved, showered, put on clean work clothes, and headed for a place he had not been, the new plant and headquarter offices of the MacMorogh Companies. For some reason, when he returned, he had not wanted to go there and pretend he was a part of it. He was not and probably would never be. At the gate, he told the guard he wanted to go in to see Jonathan MacMorogh. The guard asked his name. No, Will thought, I probably never will be a regular here.

The guard, hearing his name, looked at the other guard in the gatehouse. That one looked over his glasses at Will, and it was then that he recognized him. The other man said, "The score was twenty-eight to twenty-one; it was the last two minutes of the game." He came outside and leaned in the truck window to shake Will's hand. To the other guard, he said, "This is him, Jake, this the one they always telling about, him and Tommy Schooner." Will felt a little better.

Jonathan met him in the reception area and led him back to his office and offered him coffee. After they sat down, Jonathan said, "Missed you yesterday."

Will shook his head back and forth. "Sorry."

Jonathan asked the purpose of his visit. Will told him about his plan for a sand and gravel pit. He went over the sand pit and projections and what he anticipated he could pull out of the property and not totally destroy it. He was thinking of maybe landscaping the remaining property. Maybe establish building lots for homes.

What he needed was to see if Jonathan would sell him one of the old bulldozers he had purchased at a military surplus auction. Along with that, could he also buy the old dragline? Jonathan said he would think it over and let him know. He did not sound very enthusiastic. Then he told Will to follow him. He led him into the adjoining meeting room. He began to explain what they used it for, all about the audiovisual equipment they had. Then Will spotted the reason Jonathan brought him in the room: to see the portrait on the wall. It was of Will in full flight suit alongside his F8F Bearcat.

Back in Jonathan's office, he said, "Tell you what, I will send those pieces of equipment out to you today. They both need work. You can probably do it yourself. You are sober now; if you are still sober by Christmas day, I will give the machines to you. I know how badly you must need the money." He laughed.

Will left elated. He stopped by Swenson's to ask Imogene for a return visit. He had a new project and wanted her input. He had to get to work and fast, if he wanted to open the pit the first of the following year. It was only five weeks.

The next day, Saturday, Susie Scott walked across the road. He had not seen her since he had brought in the water well. "We went to my aunt's house for Thanksgiving; I haven't seen you outside since I got home." She handed the envelope across to Will. "I can't take this."

Will said, "But you can. If you had not come over that night when I was drilling, I was going to shut down and move the rig somewhere else."

"No, I can't take it. I do know a little geology, but the reason I knew how deep your well would be was because we drilled one behind our house a year ago."

Will started laughing; so did she. "Keep it for being honest, then." Then he told her about his plan, again based on her suggestion. She was excited and offered her help. She said she would not deceive him anymore, and help she did! The next weekend, she arrived back home with a dozen questions. Have you got your books set up? Do you have a tax number? Have you registered as a proprietorship or as a corporation? Have you gotten a bank account set up for payroll? What about phones and a mailbox? Do you have an insurance carrier?

Finally, Will held up his hand. "Whoa!" he said. "I am confused already."

Susie said, "I could do all of that for you. I could even do it from school. I could work here on weekends too."

Will saw that she desperately wanted him to say, "yes". "Figure out how much you want per hour, and let me know when you want to start," he said.

She suggested starting at minimum wage. When he saw what she could do, he could set her salary. She did not think it would be proper for her to do that. As for start time, it had begun. Things started humming.

Imogene came out the next day. She was so good at houses, Will wanted her ideas on landscaping. What he had in mind was to pull as much sand and gravel out as possible without destroying the property. Then he wanted to landscape the remaining area, let the pit fill to be a beautiful lake. Perhaps he could then subdivide the place for homes. Imogene loved the plan, and could not wait to start working on ideas.

The next weekend, Susie Scott came with stacks of things for opening an office. Her question: where is the office going to be? While Will pondered, she suggested the trailer, since he was no longer using it for living quarters. It was perfect. Before the weekend was over, she mentally removed all the furniture from the trailer. The living room would be the front office, the bedroom, Will's office. Will approved the plan and promised to store the furniture in the barn before the next weekend. That was easy enough, so she asked if he would get her a desk. "Not war surplus please!" she said.

Will commented on how well things were going together and how pleased he was with her help. Susie's comment was, "Feel good to be sober?" He smiled.

The old machines proved to be more of a challenge than anticipated, but he was determined to use them. If things went well, he
would buy better equipment later. The bulldozer was the first
machine to get operational. It arrived on a lowboy trailer, and even
though it was running, it had hydraulic problems. Will discovered
that the problems on the old dozer proved to be a training ground
for what he would find on the dragline. He had shortcomings as a
mechanic, but his skill grew.

Once he had the bulldozer operating, he put it to work removing
the overburden. Imogene suggested that the pit be as far back on the
property as possible. The pit itself would not be visible from the front
or rear entrance. Susie looked at the soil in the overburden; it was
sandy loam. It would be good fill for future lawns. Will piled it in
mounds to sell separately from the sand and gravel.

He had a few other concerns about operating a pit and drove to
a pit in another county to observe. That company used large hop-
pers to load dump trucks. In addition, there were gravel separators,
heavy-duty truck scales, and an escalator loader—all things he had
not considered. Seeing the need for those, he headed to Memphis
and to a dealer handling used dirt moving equipment. He made the
necessary purchases. Susie would be pleased; the equipment did not
look like military surplus.

Time was slipping away if he was going to get started by the New
Year. He had to scrape a better road from the highway back to the
pit, and he decided to use the Old Church road entry as the main
entry. That was another Susie suggestion. It would keep both his little house and hers out of the commercial truck traffic.

She came home on weekends and got the office operable, all
licenses obtained and permits granted. She was a whiz; Will did not
believe his good fortune. The last weekend before Christmas vacation was to start, Susie asked Will what he had done about a sign.
Nothing. She gave him instructions on size and color and then on
where to get it painted. He might consider business cards, also, and
letterhead. She had a few example designs. The next week, he ordered
them all.

The old dragline was the last major problem. Between scrap-
ing dirt all day and taking care of other chores, it was the last to get

attention. The ornery machine was frustrating; if anything, it made him want a drink at the end of the day. But he managed to abstain. Three trips to Memphis to buy cable, drum brakes for the main drum, and hydraulic hoses took more toll on his time. On the Thursday prior to Christmas week, Susie arrived home for the holiday.

She spent the day Friday and Saturday working at little tasks here and there. Her multiple questions seemed to annoy Will, and it showed. She was concerned and almost sure that he was drinking again. It was all she could do to keep her mouth shut. On Sunday, she did not see him; she was convinced he was off drunk. His truck was gone, and there was no activity at his house.

During the night on Sunday night, she saw lights. He was home. She was tempted to go see about him, but decided against the urge. On Monday, Christmas Eve, she got up early, took care of her dad's needs, and was at the trailer by eight o'clock. No Will. Thirty minutes later, he showed up, red-eyed and tired. She drew in her breath and was ready to give the same lecture she had heard her mother give innumerable times. Drinking was going to be his downfall. But she lost her courage.

She said, however, in a cheerful voice, "Missed seeing you yesterday."

"Should have been with me," he said gruffly. He drew a cup of coffee, pushed away a pile of office materials she had stacked neatly on her desk, and put his cup down before speaking again. His hand shook, and he spilled coffee on her desk. That annoyed her; she was close to exploding.

Then Will started talking as if he was sitting around the café talking to a bunch of men. "Saturday night, I worked on that damn dragline until eight o'clock, and then realized my problem was a broken part to make the brake shoes apply full pressure to the cable drum.

"I knew with Christmas coming, I probably would not be able to get that part until next week. I recalled a used part hotline from an equipment magazine and called the number. They had the part; problem was, they are in St. Louis. The place stays open twenty-four hours a day, but the fellow I talked to said it would be impossible to ship the part until after Christmas. I was still in trouble. So rather than go to Six Mile and have a drink, which I desperately wanted to do, I got in my truck and hauled off to St. Louis. The part is out there in the truck. All I have to do now is put it on." Susie sat in her chair, slumped back, and sighed. Will read her; she had been worried.

It was below freezing outside, with the threat of rain or sleet, much too cold to be on frozen ground under a dirty, greasy, and worn out dragline. But Will chiseled away at grease and dirt to get to the bolts he needed to remove. His wrench slipped, knocking the bark off two knuckles. He was having no success. He crawled from under the machine and went into the office to warm. Inside the trailer, he wiped blood and grease on the counter top and cursed. Susie could feel the frustration building in him. Going out the door, she was sure she heard him say he needed a drink.

Near noon, Will, still under the machine, heard a noisy vehicle with a diesel engine in a low gear coming up his road. It stopped, went to idle, and a door slammed. In moments, he heard Susie telling someone that Mr. MacMorogh was under the machine. He heard footsteps on the frozen ground, which was now collecting a light coating of sleet.

"Hey there, Mr. Mac, you under there?" a voice called out.

Thankfully, Will had managed to get the old part off and the new one on, busting only three more knuckles. His hands were filthy with black grease and blood. He began squirming his back and his side to a point where he could roll from under the dragline. The first thing he saw were brown and white wing tip shoes and red trousers.

When he was out far enough to sit up, the man standing at his feet reached down and extended his hand to pull him up. The rest of the man's outfit was comical. He had on a green coat, blue shirt, and a dirty brown fedora. The turned up hat brim had mistletoe attached with a rusty safety pin. Curly red hair hung out from under the hat. Had the man not been smiling from ear to ear, Will would probably have had some concern. Still, the man had a deep worry furrow in the center of his forehead. A scar, white from the cold, ran from the left side of his forehead diagonally across the nose and down to the jawline. He had a bag of roasted peanuts in his left hand and a few peanut crumbs on his crooked teeth. Will glanced toward the tandem axle dump truck idling nearby. It had seen better days.

"Nate Ludlow, Mr. Mac. Saw your sand and gravel sign a day or so back. Thought I might step in and say hello." Will made no offer to ask him inside. "How many trucks you got for delivering sand?"

Will said, "None. I figure whoever wants sand and gravel will come pick it up."

Nate said, "Oh, the bigger contractors will do that, but half your business is probably going to be old boys pouring a little slab at the house for a patio or sidewalk. They are going to want to call and get sand delivered." Like many other things, that had not occurred to Will.

"I have ten trucks, eleven including that one." Ludlow pointed to the Dodge. "I am taking that one up to my ex-brother-in-law for him to try to sell it for me. Going to my sister's house anyway for Christmas, thought I'd bring it on today."

Will said, "You are probably right about me needing a truck. How much do you want for that one?"

Nate smiled. "I'd like to be your friend; better not sell you that wore out thing. Tell you what I'd like to do. I would like to send you a truck and a driver. You keep the truck here and let me do your hauling. You can bill the customer for the sand, ask my driver how much the delivery will be, and then collect my money and yours at the same time."

It was agreeable to Will. Nate asked if he could use a phone to call his sister's house in Leeville, see if somebody would come pick him up. If so, he would leave the truck to use just in case. That sounded good, and Will insisted on driving him the twenty miles to Leeville.

Will poured gas from a can onto an old rag to clean his hands. He did not want to go back into the office and irritate Susie again. At the trailer door, he called out, "I am going down the road a piece with this old boy. Don't run off before I get back."

On the way to Leeville, Nate told Will a bit about himself. As a kid, he had loved trucks, and at fourteen, he had gone to work hauling pulpwood with his own truck. He had volunteered for the navy when he graduated high school, and after he got out, went to college on the GI Bill. After graduation, he went right back to his trucks. Besides the dump trucks, he had two big rigs with lowboy trailers to do heavy hauling. He felt like he was doing OK.

After this brief bio, he reached into his coat pocket and pulled out what was left of a pint of Four Roses. "You look like you could manage a drink, Will. Let's finish this off. You are a drinking man, aren't you?"

Will answered, "Only on special occasions."

Nate said, "What special occasions?"

Will said, "Three."

Nate asked again, "What three?'

Will grinned, "Three o'clock."

Nate caught on and laughed. "It is not quite three, but it is Christmas Eve. You can start a little early today, can't you?"

Will shook his head. "No. Especially not today."

Meanwhile, "Up the road," to Susie meant one thing. He was on his way to Six Mile Club. After an hour, he was not back. Two hours, and she went across the road to her house. She sat on her bed, with wrapping paper, scissors and ribbon scattered about. She and her father were going to her aunt's for Christmas; she had a few things left to wrap. All the time, she sat looking out the window toward the trailer.

A car came, turned, and went up the driveway to the house. The lone occupant got out, went to the door, went in, and then came right back out. The man got in his car and drove on to the trailer. Susie grabbed her coat and got back into her car; it was too cold to walk back to the trailer. At the trailer, she opened the door, and there stood the man, Mr. Jonathan MacMorogh, Will's uncle.

He asked if she knew where Will was. She was already clenching her teeth and tightening her lips around them. She was going to cry. She told Jonathan about the scary man, the long conversation outside, and Will taking off with the man in his own truck to go up the road.

Jonathan uttered one word. "Drinking."

Poor Susie leaned across her desk and said, "I have done everything I can to make this easy for him. The more I do, the more he gets frustrated. It is those old machines; they have about killed him trying to get them operating."

Jonathan felt sorry for her. He said, "You have done a great job. Look at it this way. This is Will. He has plenty of money, he could have bought the biggest and very best new equipment to dig whatever hole he wants to. Instead, he tries to get by as cheap as possible. And it is that one thing that may mean he is not off drinking."

The words had scarcely passed his lips when they heard a truck door slam. Susie went to the little round window in the trailer door to peep out. Will was trotting to the door. She stepped back as he burst in. He stuck out his dirty hand to Jonathan and turned to Susie. "Sorry, I got hung up longer than I thought. I am glad you are still here."

Jonathan said, "Will, your grandparents drove to New Orleans last Saturday. June and I are going to fly down early in the morning for dinner, then fly back tomorrow night. We would like you to go along. If you want to stay a day or two, you can do that and then drive back with Grandma."

Will said thanks and that he would come back with him and June. Jonathan departed, instructing Will to be at the airfield at seven a.m. After Jonathan left, Will went straight into his office and pulled an envelope and a tiny package from his desk drawer. Returning to the office, he handed Susie the package first. Susie figured jewelry, and opened it. Instead, it was a small box of business cards. An example was stuck to the front of the box: "Susie Scott, Office manager/Staff Geologist." She laughed and hugged him.

Then he handed her the envelope. She took it and thanked him. He had to tell her to open it. She took a letter opener from her desk and slit the envelope, and five one hundred bills fell out. Her hand went to her mouth. "Oh my," she said.

She stood there a minute, got her breath, and said, "I can't take this."

"Sure you can," Will said with certainty.

Then she caught Will by surprise. "I think my daddy already believes there might be something going on between us."

"Nonsense. Maybe he will feel better when he sees what I bought him. Go on home; I will be over in a minute."

Will drove down to the barn, went in, and came back with his present for Susie's father. It had a big red bow. He drove across the road and into Susie's yard. At the door, he knocked, Susie came, and he pushed a brand new wheelchair in through the door and into the front room of the little house. Susie shrilled in delight; her father came from the kitchen, walking poorly with the aid of his two canes.

"The chair is portable; it can be folded and put in the car," Will said "Besides that, it is a new design, and it goes between standard room doors, not like your antique."

The old man shook his head back and forth. Susie had tears. Will grinned.

Will said to himself, "*And I got a dragline and a bulldozer free.*"

He felt great. What he had done for Susie and her dad put him in the Christmas spirit. The family had long ago quit exchanging gifts other than a small token of some sort. Instead, they picked a favorite charity or other recipient, then did what they thought would make a difference. Sometimes it was cash, sometimes a home, a year of school tuition, medical payments, that sort of thing. Besides the gift for Susie, he had anonymously paid off the car loan on Holly Porterfield's car.

The next morning, he was at the airfield on time. Jonathan was preflighting the airplane. June was already on board and in the right seat. He would be riding in back, though he would have preferred being up front with Jonathan. But after takeoff, he realized the reason for the seating arrangements. When they reached cruising altitude, Jonathan handed off the controls to June; she was learning to fly.

Christmas dinner with Aunt Bea and Carole Anne was wonderful. They had both invited their gentleman friends. No one seemed to regard this as a Christmas different from any other, though they all knew that it was. This had been a tough year on all of them, tougher on his family than on Will himself.

44

The name of the business was simple: "SAND AND GRAVEL CO."
The sign on Old Church Road had an arrow pointing down to the
sand pit property. Will ran an ad in the weekly newspaper and ran
a few spots on the local radio station as well as one in the Leeville
weekly. Opening day was less than exciting. The day after New
Year's Day was hardly a day to expect people rushing in to buy sand.
The temperature was scarcely above freezing, and for sure, no fool
was going to be outside spreading sand or mixing concrete. Over the
next week or so, a few customers called, but there was not enough
business to keep one truck working full-time.

However, Will put the idle time to good use and started knocking on doors. He called on contractors, landscapers, and on county,
city, and state offices. The contact at the Mississippi State Highway
Department (MSHD) was the winner. Three weeks after Will's initial
call, he got a huge order, one large enough to keep three trucks working for several weeks.

The MSHD people, pleased with the quality of the sand, passed
the information on to a road builder. It was the one with the contract
to finish sections of the Interstate Highway System. The builder's
order was so large that it was more than Will had planned to take
out of the pit. He refused to leave a gaping hole in the landscape. The
only solution—look for additional land.

Using the geology textbook from Susie, he studied the areas he
thought had the best possibilities. She came home from school for the
weekend and reviewed what he had found. She agreed, but had the
best idea: she would pass their findings by her professor.

Will was collecting money and putting appropriate invoices in a
cigar box and keeping it in Susie's desk for her to post and file. For
the first month or so, she was discouraged at how little money came
in. Now the outlook was improving.

The professor Susie relied on at school informed her that Will was scouting in the right area. Will bought several small pieces that would get them off the hook for a few months, but he had to keep looking. Nate and Will had bonded, and Will respected his opinion. Together, they walked over a large tract south of Jackson. Will, accompanied by Nate, called on the listing agent. The terms were satisfactory; Will bought the ground.

Nate wondered where the money was coming from. Will found no reason to hesitate when he saw something he wanted to buy. Little by little, Will dropped enough information about himself for Nate to know that, one, Will had plenty of money. Two, it was his own. Three, he was not a part of the large MacMorogh group.

That day, leaving the realtor, they spoke to another man waiting for his own appointment. After they departed, the man asked the realtor if he was right, that he had heard the name, "MacMorogh." The realtor confirmed that he had, and as matter of fact, that he had the person's card. The man copied the phone number.

Will and Nate had gone to a café down the street for lunch. A few minutes after they sat, the man they had spoken to in the real estate office arrived. He glanced around, looking for seating, and spotted Will and Nate. He walked straight to their table, stuck out his hand, and introduced himself.

He was Whit Mason, an attorney and real estate broker from Memphis. He accepted an invitation to join them and wasted no time getting to business. Speaking to Will, he said, "I have been meaning to get in touch with you fellows for several days now. I have something you folks might want to take a look at." He said that he had all of his maps out at the hotel, and he invited them to come out and look. Will agreed, still not knowing what it might be about. Nate made note: Will was suspicious that the man probably thought he was talking to someone from the big MacMorogh group.

At the hotel, the man rolled the maps out one at a time. There were eight, each as big as his bed. According to this Whit Mason, they were the absolute final plans for the routing of the Interstate Highway from Memphis to New Orleans. They showed the exact locations of every on and off ramp along the as yet incomplete system. The shaded plats were pieces that Mason had options to purchase. There were ten, ranging in size from twenty to one hundred and six acres. When the highway was complete, these pieces could easily double in value. They were for sale, one or all.

Will had many questions. What were the terms of the options, the execution dates, and the price if he exercised the options? How much money was involved? Whit Mason said that if he were a serious player, he would list each piece individually, with necessary information about each. The listing could be ready the next day.

Will told him he was a serious player and asked where they could meet the next day. Whit Mason suggested Will's office. Will said he would rather meet right back where they were. Nate became more suspicious. Will drove Nate back to where he had parked his truck. Will said he would like to meet Mason the next day and then meet Nate in his little town of Moss Back, where he had his truck terminal.

Will used his home phone to call Chas Chacherie. He and Chas talked often. Chas was practicing law in New Orleans, with his office in the same place as the offices of The Chacherie Companies, a conglomerate owned by his father. The last time they had talked was when Chas called to tell him that they had named their latest newborn after him. Her name was Willa May.

Now, he was delighted to hear from Will and was eager to get together. Will suggested the next day, but Chas said it would have to be the day after that, Thursday, but even then, he had a lot going on. He established a specific time: nine a.m. That was agreeable. On the way to New Orleans, Will would see why he was so busy.

The next day, he met with Whit Mason. After breakfast at the motel, they went to Mason's room to look at the documents. Mason had done a superior job of assembling the materials: maps, plats with legal descriptions, aerial photos, taxes, zoning if any, the option for each piece, and the price. Some of the options were good for six months, some for a year. Will was well pleased. He asked how much time he had to make a decision; he needed to review the material with their attorneys. Whit Mason gave him a week.

Will mentally calculated the amount of money necessary. The man had sure gone to a lot of work putting the pieces together; the task had probably taken a year to complete. He was looking at several million if he bought the whole package. With as much as a year to go on some of the pieces, he might easily sell off a piece or two. Either way, he could afford to buy the options.

He was jubilant about the potential that lay ahead, and he was anxious to tell Nate, the only person he confided in these days. That was another thing that gave him a good feeling. The real man hiding behind that awful suit he had worn on Christmas Eve was no dummy. The most important thing Will had learned about him was that he was as honest as Abe himself. Nate worked off the premise that his word was his bond. His handshake sealed it. In addition, he was as smart as a whip in business. Will was interested in his ideas about the use of the property.

He had never been to Nate's house or place of business. The directions were easy: when he got to Moss Back, turn left at the Pure Oil station. Go past the post office, past the jail, then one and two-tenths miles from the jail. He would see the sign, "LUDLOW TRUCKING COMPANY." In smaller letters underneath, it read, "Dirt movers, heavy hauling."

The little square block building with "OFFICE" printed over the door was white with red lettering. Off to the rear of that building was another large metal building with overhead doors tall enough to accommodate big trucks. Part of the lot was asphalt and the rest slag. The trucks on the lot were in a neat row, all sparkling clean, and all had neat red decals showing the name of the company business.

Nate was in the office alone. He had on his usual clean and starched khaki uniform with "Nate" embroidered in large red letters over his heart. He was talking on two phones at once. He signaled Will to sit and said to him across the two phones, "My office lady will be back here in a few minutes," and he then got back into his telephone conversations.

The office lady, as he called her, did arrive minutes later, laden with a large basket of mail. She was tall and thin as a rail, gray hair pulled tight into a bun on back of her head. Will's first thought was that if Mr. Webster wanted a picture of an old maid schoolteacher for his dictionary, here she was. Nate was still on the phone. Will introduced himself, and she tilted her head back to look through the bottom lenses of her bifocals and said, "We aren't hiring, if that is what you are here for."

Will said, "No, Ma'am, I am a friend of Nate, just came by to visit."

"Well, as you can see, he is busy. Take a seat; he should be through in a moment. I am Mrs. Murrah. We are glad to have you visit, but do not take too long." With that, she went into her office and closed the door.

Ludlow took Will outside to show him around. He had overheard what Mrs. Murrah had said and apologized for her abruptness. "Would you believe she taught me in fifth grade, and I was her pet? Right after she retired from the school system, her husband took sick and died. I heard she was having a hard time making ends meet, so one morning I ran by her house, and she was sitting on her front porch. I walked up and asked her if she had time to take a little run out in the country with me. I put her in my truck and drove straight here. My office was a mess, and I asked her if she could help me out a little and get some of the mess organized. She has been here ever since that morning. Problem is, she decided she was still the teacher and me a pupil. She thinks she is boss."

They sat down in another office behind the repair shop where Nate said he often came to hide from the phones and Mrs. Murrah. Will described the documents he'd gotten from Mason, explaining what they meant, option times, etc. He then asked Nate for his opinion of the pieces.

Nate came right back. "I see three that I think would be good locations for truck stops. One south of Memphis but inside the Mississippi line, one south of Jackson, and one north of Hammond, Louisiana." Will raised an eyebrow. All he'd thought of was motels, restaurants, and gas stations for auto traffic. It took a trucker to think otherwise.

Then Nate said that he had some good news and some bad news himself. The good news was that he had remembered the name of the construction company on one of the maps that Whit Mason had. It was in St. Louis. He had called their office and finally got someone who would answer his questions. He told them he owned a dirt moving and heavy hauling company. He hoped he might find out when the construction company was going to start on its Interstate projects. He was soliciting work.

Without Nate asking any more questions, the man with whom he spoke said that the first project was the southernmost section near Hammond, Louisiana. He also told Nate that he was going to need to move twenty Euclid dirt movers from the St. Louis branch to Hammond. If Nate were interested, he would send him the information for bidding. The company had dump trucks of their own, but they always needed more. That was the good news.

The bad news was that the project would start in six weeks. That meant that Will needed some pits closer to Hammond if he was going to bid on the fill dirt, sand, and gravel. Nate said that there was something else; he would need a terminal in the area. Nate knew of a place north of the Lake Pontchartrain Causeway, but it was probably out of Will's price range. Since Will was on his way to being a real estate mogul, maybe he would like to partner up on a piece of ground. Will told him to find out who owned the property and to see if he could set up an appointment to walk over it. He told Nate that he had a meeting in New Orleans the next day and would check back with him before he left the city.

Within a mile of crossing the Mississippi line into Louisiana, Will saw what was keeping Chas so busy. The billboard read, "Vote Chas Chacherie, Candidate for States Attorney General." In New Orleans, he found the building he was looking for on Carondelet Street. The entire ninth floor housed the Chacherie Companies office. On a small sign outside the main entrance was a sign that read, "Office of Chas Chacherie, Candidate for States Attorney General."

There was a joyous reunion between the two who owed each other so much. There was a bond between them that would live as long as they did. Chas introduced Will to the people in his office and to his father. The older man hugged Will tightly and said over and over, "Thank-you, thank-you."

Chas gave Will a quick synopsis of his campaign, why he was running, and how it was going. Then a quicker review of Addie and the kids before they got on to business at hand. Will asked Chas to review the options he had in his possession. The short of it was that Chas thought the package looked great. He would have written some of the agreements a little tighter, but overall, he said he liked what he saw. That firmed it for Will. He was going to buy the options. He wanted Chas to act as his attorney.

He called back to Nate as promised. Nate had talked to a realtor about the property; they could meet her at the property the next morning. Will got directions and then drove across the lake and spent the night at The Point.

Early the next morning, the two met René Stedman-Bates. She arrived in a Jeep with four-wheel drive. She had on jeans, short, lace up boots, long sleeve work shirt, and a sun hat. She was blonde, tall, and curvaceous, with beautiful teeth and a dark tan. Will was smitten. What he had not noticed was that she also had a rock on her left ring finger as big as the bulb out of a headlight. Her company owned the property. Her dad had purchased it before he died. It was a perfect piece for Nate's needs.

Will and Nate conferred for a few minutes before deciding to make an offer. Nate did not know if he could come up with half without borrowing against property he already owned. That might take a week or so to arrange. Will offered René ten thousand dollars for a one-month option. She agreed, but she would not come down one penny on the price. He went to his truck and wrote a check for the option. Nate, seeing how smitten Will was, suggested that they have lunch at his favorite place, Milton's Seafood. Surprisingly, René agreed.

Over lunch, René revealed her intent to start a one hundred and ten house subdivision just across the river from where they were seated. However, she was having problems putting a project that big together. The Pontchartrain Causeway had created a new living opportunity for people in the city. The bridge was still a toll and was still only two lanes, but the second bridge was in planning. She felt that upon its completion, the commute would not be as bad. Her problems were mainly with labor and materials suppliers. What she needed now was curbs, gutters, and streets. There was not a ready mixed concrete supplier close enough to supply concrete at a livable cost. Will's ears perked. They finished lunch, bid farewell, and left.

Nate had not been alone with Will until this moment. He asked the question that was disturbing him. "What if I can't come up with my half of the money in two weeks? What then?"

Will replied, "Then I put it all up by myself until you have enough. In the meantime, I have to figure out how to lease enough trucks to get into the concrete business."

With that, Nate threw up his hands. "Look, I 'm getting scared here. The last two days, you 've obligated yourself for millions of dollars for property from here to Memphis. You have things to do with that property working in your mind. Now you 've started on another project. What about the sand and gravel business? I 'm a part of that, and I gotta' lot riding on it." Will told him not to worry; he would work it out.

He spent the night at The Point. There, alone, he sat on the top floor, smoking his pipe and enjoying the brisk breeze that blew in from the lake. Nate was right, he thought; I have bitten off more than I can chew. He spent most of the rest of the night figuring out what to do. By morning, he had his priorities in a row. First stop; René's office.

Stedman-Bates Realty was located in an old French style home with two levels. René's offices occupied the entire bottom floor. Will wondered if she and her husband might live on the second level. René was not expecting him. Was something wrong? Had he gotten buyer's remorse? Will had his checkbook with him and told her he wanted to go ahead and exercise the option on the property. She was stunned, and it showed.

He handed over the check and explained the reason for the urgency. He wanted to go ahead and complete the transaction so that Nate could get on with his plans. Next, he wanted her to find him a spot where he could put a concrete plant. If she could do that, he would go to work on getting it into operation as soon as possible so that she could go about her plans for the subdivision. One requirement was that she had to commit to use him for concrete and Nate for site preparation and dirt work. She readily agreed. She confessed to Will that she had other problems: cash. The sale of the property he was purchasing, which she herself owned outright, would take care of that. She could go forward. She had only one place to suggest for the concrete plant; she would start looking for others.

In the meantime, she wanted to show him the one piece that was available. When he saw where it was, Will knew that it could very well be the ideal place. It was far enough from other businesses and homes that it would be no problem. Best of all, it was a large plot adjacent to the local airport. The small airfield was one long grass strip, with perhaps a dozen T-hangars and a larger hangar that was home to a local aviation mechanic, and there was fuel available. They negotiated a price; Will signed a letter of intent to purchase.

He spent the rest of the day driving around the area. He could see potential everywhere. The next span of that causeway would cinch it. Now was the time to get in on the ground floor. That night, he slept better than he had slept in years.

Next on his agenda was to talk to Nate regarding the plan for the sand pits. He formulated one, late the night before they met. Imogene popped into his mind while he was wrestling for a solution. He thought of her and her peaches. She picked her own peach crop and his grandfather's; she picked his on halves.

He arrived back at Moss Back before noon. Mrs. Murrah said that Nate was in town at the bank and should be back shortly. Nate was grinning from ear to ear when he returned. He got Will by the arm and suggested lunch. He conveyed his good news as they drove back into town. The bank had verbally approved his loan. He did not have to give up any of his other property for collateral.

Will told Nate that that made him feel better. Now Nate could write him a check. He had paid for the property earlier in the day. He told Nate that he had given a lot of thought to what he had said the day before, and yes, he had bitten off a lot. He needed help, and he presented his plan. He asked Nate to take over the sand and gravel operation. Will would furnish the land for the pits; Nate would operate the business on halves. That would leave Will free to concentrate on his other projects. It was a win for both.

Nate was more than agreeable. All it took was a handshake. He told Will to go about his other projects. They had the highway order for about eight months of work. They could actually close the New Cotswold pit to nothing but their highway department order. Nate said he would continue searching for more land closer to the Hammond area.

In the meantime, Will planned to move his office to North Shore and planned to live at The Point. He would be close to the site where he wanted to build the concrete plant. In addition, he could help Nate if need be on his project to relocate his terminal. Things were coming together quite well for both of them.

When the two left the café where they had lunch, Nate took a different route to return to his shop. They drove on into town, past the post office and past the jail. At the Methodist Church, Nate turned one block north, then one block to the west, and then stopped.

"This is where I live and where I grew up," Nate said. "I 'd invite you in, but that old Chevrolet in the driveway belongs to my housekeeper. She comes once a week and cleans everything, including waxing the floors. If we go in there now, she 's liable to quit." They continued to sit in silence for a few moments before Nate spoke again.

"I was born on January 3, 1929, at Charity Hospital in New Orleans, to an unwed mother. Three days later, on January 6, she checked out of the hospital, and no one has ever heard of her again. As for me, at 4:30 in the morning on January 7, 1929, two minutes before the milkman came, somebody deposited me on the front porch here. I was in a bassinette that had been placed inside of a shipping box."

Will said, "Surely you are joshing."

"Nope," said Nate. "I 've plenty of proof. Whoever brought me opened the front screen door, laid the box right in front of the door into the living room, and left. They let the screen door slam, and it made a noise loud enough to wake Elbert Permenter. Elbert thought it was the milkman and called him a name. Only two minutes later, the milkman did come to make his delivery. Elbert heard the glass milk bottles tinkle and was about to give the milkman more abuse. Before he could do so, the milkman himself called out for Ruth and Elbert to come to the door. There I lay. So then, of course, all heck broke loose. Before you know it, half the town was out in the front yard: the city police, the county sheriff, the newspaper, they were all there."

Nate pointed across the street at the large home behind a brick wall. "Over there is Judge Lee's house. His housekeeper, Mrs. Morris, a colored woman, was in the kitchen when she heard all of the commotion. She got her husband up, and they both came over. Ruth Permenter was thirty-six years old, had never had kids, and never handled any babies. She had my bassinette out on the kitchen table, and I was squalling. Mrs. Morris walked in and they say that when she picked me up, I immediately quit."

"She sent Mr. Morris over to get their daughter who had a two-month-old of her own, and I got my first good meal. She wet-nursed me until I was big enough to be bottle fed."

Will said, "So I assume that the Permenters adopted you."

Nate acknowledged that they did. They named him Hubert Permenter. Nate said that he did not like the name, but that did not matter. No one would ever call him that anyway. He said the top board on each side of the shipping crate was missing. It looked more like a bed or cradle than a box. The second board on one side of the crate had "N.A.T.E." stenciled on the side. And "C/O Trailways bus depot, Ludlow, Mississippi was on the board below.

The local newspaper took pictures and printed them on the front page, hoping that someone could identify the box. The picture went out across the South. Apparently, that box had gone to somebody in the rural community of Ludlow, Mississippi. No one ever came forward. From that day on, he was Nate Ludlow. Before he went into the navy, he had had his name legally changed to reflect that.

That evening, Will drove back to New Cotswold and arrived too late to call Jonathan. He set the alarm and was at the hotel in time to catch him still at breakfast. After they finished eating, Will began his account. For some reason, he decided to leave off the major project, the options with Whit Mason. That could wait a day or two.

He did tell him about the concrete plant in North Shore and his plans to live at The Point for the time being. He would leave on Monday. Will spent the remainder of the day packing. It was a strange feeling to have so little connection with the place or people that he could so easily walk away.

45

Susie arrived from school for the weekend, ready to get to work. Will was not looking forward to telling her about committing all of the sand in the New Cotswold pit to one customer. There was not much work left for her. He felt like she depended on the money she was getting for her part-time work; that could be a financial blow. Then he reconsidered; there might be plenty of things to do for him.

After a light breakfast, Will went immediately to the trailer office. Susie sat at her desk, a frozen look on her face. The cigar box was open; there was nothing, no invoices, no money. She looked at Will. "Have we had a robbery? What is going on?"

Will held his hand up to calm her. Then he told her what he had done the past week and where he was headed. There was no doubt that she was upset. She had questions, but before she could get answers, he had questions for her. What was she going to do when school was out? Where was she going to seek permanent employment? What about her dad? Was she going to have to look for a job locally?

Her reply surprised and pleased him. She and her dad had talked about that at length. She was already sending applications to national chains such as Sears and Roebuck, J.C. Penney, Morgan and Lindsey, and others that might have a training program. She hoped somebody out there wanted to hire a girl with a business degree. She knew that if such a company hired her, she could not stay in New Cotswold. Her father could manage by himself; he had a small pension. He could hire a person for a day or two a week to come in and do what Susie did on weekends. She could help financially. She felt that she might have to supplement his needs, especially for repairs on the old house. The house would soon need a roof and a new septic tank. She would probably be in a position later to handle those kinds of expenses. She had only one concern. She needed some income until school was out. She asked Will if he might help her get part-time work at the bank.

Will presented her with another idea. When he had started the sand pit, she had taken care of innumerable things that he had had no idea he would need, and now he enumerated them. He was going to need far more help with the concrete plant. He felt that a lot could be handled long distance, like phone calls for permits and licenses, things she had taken care of before.

Susie's eyes lit up like stars. Then she started to squeal. "A business plan, oh my gosh, a business plan!" Will sat in the visitor's chair across from her desk. She stood and did a little dance.

"For my last semester, I have to do a business plan for a start-up business. May I use the concrete plant? I will learn a lot and maybe even be some help. I know that I can take care of other things in the process. As a matter of fact, that will be a plus." Then she added one more thing excitedly, "Oh, if we could only get the plant open before the end of the semester!"

Will looked at her and said, "Then I guess you have some income until the end of the school year."

Before he left for the day, she made a long list of addresses she would need. If he could get those for her, she would do the rest. She also wanted to know if she could go to North Shore between semesters to visit people like the members of the Chamber of Commerce, get a feel for the area, and visualize the plant. Both felt good about the idea. And down deep, Will knew something; probably she did too. She would be the business manager at the concrete plant.

Monday night, and Will was back at The Point. He unloaded his meager belongings and set up an office of sorts in the living room area. He called his Aunt Bea and Carole Anne and arranged to eat lunch with them the next day. He had not told anyone other than Nate about his large option purchase. He wanted to share it with someone. Aunt Bea and Carole Anne would be discreet.

They all gathered in the den at Aunt Bea's house. Will laid out the maps, one by one, pointing out the properties. His aunt and sister listened attentively. Aunt Bea still had concern about Will's psychological stability. She knew he had quit drinking or at least had slowed down considerably. However, he still seemed to have a great deal of anxiety.

She had seen it before. Someone comes out of a deep depression, rises to the top, and suddenly plummets. She asked him what in the world had he gotten himself into. She did not see how he possibly could handle a project of that magnitude alone. Carole Anne concurred and asked if she could help. She thought that the project was as exciting as anything she could imagine.

Dr. Bea raised an eyebrow and gave that some consideration. Carole Anne was a big factor now in her life; the younger woman was her medical partner and a grand one. She did not voice her concern at that point, but rather listened to this brother-sister banter. They went back and forth about usage. Will was thinking motels, gas stations. Will's friend Nate was thinking truck stops. Carole Anne threw in her idea.

Ever since she had heard of the small, self-contained ice plants that Jonathan had built, she had been thinking of a compact supermarket incorporated with gas stations and mini ice plants. Her vision was one with many of the same items carried in a full-sized store, but with far less inventory. She wanted to call these supermarkets convenience stores. What better location than on an interstate highway, using gasoline as the draw?

Will asked the question that was going around in Dr. Bea's mind. Where would Carole Anne find time? Her response was that she had already completed design of a store layout and the calculation of the inventory requirements. She had done that with the help of Tony Cannizaro, Aunt Tootie's husband. He was from a very successful supermarket family and was a good merchant himself. She had used her spare time on days off.

At first, Dr. Bea scoffed at the idea that Carole Anne would have time. She had to retract when Carole Anne pointed out that Aunt Bea had more irons in the fire than anyone she knew. She was an avid collector of classic automobiles, and she had logged a hundred hours of flying time the year before, a lot for a nonprofessional pilot.

Will's spirit rose with the enthusiasm shown by Carole Anne. He knew he could handle this project, but there were priorities. His first stop the next morning was at Stedman-Bates Realty. He got an update on the property he had contracted to purchase. Surveying was underway. Information about zoning was on the police jury docket. The title company had most of what they needed to begin work.

René still anticipated two weeks to closing. Before he left her office, he had to meet her husband, Baker Bates. That name rang a bell, and then he remembered: "Gator" Bates, LSU football star who later played on some pro team. He had gotten the nickname "Gator" due to a birthmark, a chocolate brown figure at his left jawline. Using imagination, one could visualize a long, thin alligator with its mouth open. Bates owned an insurance company with his father and brother; he had insisted on an appointment with Will.

Will spent the rest of the day chasing down the long list of items given to him by Susie. Then he began researching the equipment needed for a concrete plant. It was not a matter of mixing sand, gravel, and mortar mix. It was far more complicated than that as well as labor intensive. Here again, he would need his own water wells.

On Wednesday, he was deeply entrenched in the project, and nothing more seemed to enter his mind. He stopped by The Point at mid-afternoon to make some phone calls. While there, he received a call himself. It was not friendly. Jonathan was calling with instructions from the General to have Will in the office in New Cotswold the next day. No excuses. Be there. His grandfather was spitting nails.

It was a long drive. Will left at four the next morning, in order to arrive at the MacMorogh offices by nine. He first met with Jonathan. Will had a good idea why he was there, and Jonathan confirmed it — the options. He told Will that under no circumstance should he lose his temper. "Do not kill the rooster!"

He referred to something that had occurred early in Will's life. As a very small boy, Will had killed a rooster belonging to his uncle by marriage. The rooster had pecked at Will's finger, and it bled. So Will got even. Since that event, they used the remark, "Do not kill the rooster," to suggest not losing one's temper. It usually got a laugh and eased the tension. Will had to remember that several times during the following thirty minutes.

The General began by telling Will that he had received an interesting phone call. It was from a Mr. Mason, alerting him that there was another piece of property that they could option along with the other pieces. That was, if they were interested. The General had had no idea what Mr. Mason was referring to and had told him so.

Mr. Mason, realizing he was not talking to the same William MacMorogh he had dealt with previously, explained to the General that he had called the number on the card Will had given him. A person at that number referred him to the MacMorogh Companies number. He asked for William MacMorogh, and the switchboard had connected him with the only William MacMorogh present. The General then asked Mason what it was in regard to. Mr. Mason had given him an accounting.

That was when the General spit his nails at Will. "You used the name of this company to do business and probably win business that should belong to this company. You are not a part of this organization; you never will be a part of this organization. Now get your smart ass back to wherever you came from, and do not ever set foot on this property again." Will just sat there. He did not kill the rooster. He got up, saluted his grandfather sharply, did a crisp military about face, and departed.

Jonathan had not been in the room, but he could hear what was going on from inside his own office. What his father had said to Will hurt him terribly. Will was like a son to him. He was proud of him. What Will had done was deceptive; however, what his father had said was not necessary. What he had done was drive Will not only from the company but from the family as well. Jonathan sat for a long time, telling *himself* not to kill the rooster.

The General walked by his office, his face red as a beet. He stuck his head in and said, "That damn kid reminds me so much of Seamus." He stormed on down the hall. Jonathan smiled to himself; things were not that bad, after all. His father had had a love-hate relationship with his own father, but Jonathan knew one thing, The General had secretly worshipped the ground Seamus walked on.

Moments later, Jonathan had a call from Will. He was at the hotel and wanted to talk. Jonathan was at the hotel in fifteen minutes. The staff closed the dining room for the afternoon, and it was dark, cool, and private. Will apologized; he should have told Jonathan about the options when he'd told him about the concrete business. He related his story about Wilt Mason approaching him about the options. Yes, he probably should have made it clear that he was not part of the MacMorogh group.

Then he went on to tell Jonathan in detail what all was involved, the amount of the options, the lengths, the purchase money needed if he exercised the options. Then he told him about his plans for developing the property. In closing, he also told Jonathan he was going to need a lot of his money. At that, Jonathan whistled. Will and the General were both in for a little surprise. He would have to work it out. He asked Will if he minded if he told the General about the deals Will had made. Will said there was no problem. Jonathan stood, walked over, and put his arm on Will's shoulder. "I love you. Drive safely." Will drove slowly back to North Shore; his head was spinning.

Jonathan wanted to wait until the next morning to approach the General. He wanted the man calm and cool before he spilled the rest of the story. He walked across the street and found Winston in the shop, tinkering. He said, "Time to call it a day. We need to talk. How about we go out to your house and have a toddy?" Winston took off his lab coat and followed.

Aunt Tilda had her church group out in her garden when they arrived, so they went out to the cookhouse, where Winston pulled out a bottle, two glasses, and some ice. They went to two nice wicker chairs, turned on the ceiling fan, and got a cool breeze going.

Winston said, "What's up?" Jonathan told him all of it from the beginning to end, including Will's options and the General exploding. When he was finished, Winston groaned. Then he spoke. "Let's not tell Miss Tilda about this, just yet."

Jonathan laughed. "No, let's wait until the crap really hits the fan." Winston laughed. He knew what was coming up. The next morning, Jonathan went into his father's office. He told him he had caught up with Will and he now knew the details. The General put his hands behind his head and said, "Tell me." So Jonathan did.

The General said that he understood how Will might have the money to afford to buy the options. But where was he going to get the money to exercise them? He asked Jonathan, "How much money does Will have?"

It was then that the surprise came. Jonathan told him, "A lot." When asked how much was "a lot," Jonathan said, "In the area of ten million."

The General said, "That's a bunch of horseshit he is feeding you. How could he have that much money?"

Jonathan explained. Part was Will's trust; also, part was navy back pay." Then he dropped the next surprise on his father. "I have been managing his money since he became my ward. I have done rather well with it." He did not share with his father that he even at one time had had a lot invested in moonshine. Then Jonathan told him the rest. "Beatrice and I have teamed up on this with Carole Anne as well. She is not as well-off, but she has nearly eight million."

Then the General asked, "Where is all of that money? Is it in our banks?"

Jonathan grinned when he dropped the last shoe. "Part is in our banks; the bulk we have borrowed from Will."

The General sputtered. "He is a creditor of ours?' We owe him money? How in the hell did that happen?"

"When we made all of the capital expenditures in new plants, all of this property, you agreed that we should not use any operating capital. You said to borrow at the best rates possible. We did; we used Will's money. He has the mortgage on this plant."

"God damn it, Jonathan, I wish I could fire the whole bunch of you and start over!" The General stormed out of the office. He did not return for the rest of the day. He and Miss Annie left the next morning for their once a month weekend to attend services at the Episcopal Church in Jackson. The General had not spoken to anyone at the office since he had stormed out.

Something bore heavily on his mind. Miss Annie, as usual, did not press him. Eventually he would talk about what was bothering him. He always had.

When he finally did talk, what he said threw Miss Annie into a tizzy. She knew something that only she and three other people knew. Her husband and Will still had the surprise of their life in the making. She had to help resolve the problem, and quickly.

They arrived back in New Cotswold, but she would not let her husband stop at the house. She wanted to go to the cemetery and to the graves of Will and Carole Anne's parents. She led her husband to the graveside. Then she talked. "Tell them what you have done. Tell them that you have cast their son out of this family. Tell you are sorry. Ask them to forgive you. Then it will be easier for you to go to Will and do the same thing." She turned, walked back to the car, and drove away. He was standing at the graveside, his head down. Miss Annie left him to walk home.

She stood at her kitchen window, with a drink in her hand, gazing toward the far end of the airfield, watching. An hour had passed, and dusk was settling in. Then she saw him walking slowly across Old Church Road and onto the airfield property, his head still down. Instead of heading straight for the house, he turned at the little path that led to the small pond on the property; she knew where he was going. She poured a heavy bourbon over ice in a small fruit jar, capped it, then drove slowly down the airfield. At the path to the pond, she got out of the car, drinks in hand, and walked to where he stood on the small pier. She walked up alongside and handed him the drink.

"The day I threw him in here, he learned to swim. He was so damn mad at me, though, he did not even think about the fact that he had swum back to the pier. All he had on his mind was fighting me. I knew then he had spunk." That was all he said. Miss Annie took his hand; they drove back to the house.

The next morning, the General had his regular Monday morning meeting with Winston and Jonathan. He said that he was sure Winston had heard about his action, and he wanted to apologize to Will. They needed to discuss some things before he went to North Shore to talk to his grandson. What he proposed was an offer to buy the options from Will, even give him a profit if he insisted. Then he would like the company to exercise the options as they came due. Next, take Will into the company and let him head up the project. In his mind, Will's money was safer in the mortgage on the facilities. Furthermore, if the options did not have the same execution dates, they could do it with operating income. He asked Jonathan and Winston to put some numbers together and see what they thought about the idea.

What the General did not know was that that was not exactly what Jonathan and Winston had spent most of the previous evening preparing. Their version had been a plan to buy the General out of the business. The numbers they had put together were accurate; they had a very good idea of the viability of the General's plan. They could revamp the figures easily. By the end of the day, they gave him an answer; they liked his idea. They shook hands, and all three heaved a sigh.

Following the agreement, there was more discussion. Where would Will have an office? What kind of staff would he need? How much support would the three of them need to give him? Whether Will could live in New Cotswold was the main issue. Jonathan thought not. He did not think Will would want to; nor did he think the town had gotten over the rumors about him and the preacher's wife.

The General came up with a valid proposal that would include Beatrice and Carole Anne; both had responsibilities with the company also. From time to time, they needed secretarial support as well as office space. Why not open an office in New Orleans? He suggested that they could have conference calls regularly, to stay in touch. The General was looking out the window when Jonathan winked at Winston.

The General insisted that they had to meet with Miss Annie, Beatrice, and Carole Anne before they could go forward. Jonathan suggested that they set up a lunch meeting in New Orleans with the girls. They could meet, and if all concurred, they could then meet with Will.

As usual, once the General had his mind made up, it was time to get on with it. He was impatient. Later in the morning, he called the girls. It was possible to meet with them the coming Thursday, but for only two hours, from noon until two p.m. With that established, the General had Jonathan set up a meeting for Friday with Will.

Jonathan contacted Will and told him nothing more than that he felt that his grandfather wanted to apologize. Will said first to tell his grandfather to kiss his ass. Jonathan again urged him not to kill the rooster. Will agreed to be civil, but nothing more. The meeting with the women went smoothly, and they all agreed, with one exception. Neither Dr. Bea and nor Carole Anne wanted to miss the meeting with Will. Instead of meeting with him the next day, Jonathan called and asked him to come into the city that evening. Make it six o'clock at Dr. Bea's house. They adopted the plan—no roosters killed.

Over the weekend, Will sat with Dr. Bea and his sister. He had accepted the recommendations made, with one exception of his own. He wanted to be sure that Carole Anne participated in the real estate project in the same capacity that he did. Dr. Bea expressed her content that another generation was moving into positions of leadership.

Once over the hurdle with his grandfather, reconciliation would continue. Dr. Bea began to refer to herself, Will, and Carole Anne as "MacMorogh South." Will and Carole Anne quickly relinquished the reins to her, since she was senior; she gladly took them. Job One now: find an office, staff it, furnish it, decorate it, and move into it.

Will preferred to skimp and save. One room with a couple of desks, a couple of phones, and an answering service should be more than adequate. He suggested the Touro Infirmary area close to the doctors' offices. Dr. Bea disagreed. An office in the area of Canal St. and St. Charles, or Baronne, or Carondelet, any of those streets was important. They should be near the major hotels for the convenience of visiting clients. They had an image to keep.

As for staffing, she already had someone in mind: Mimi Ducharme. She was a dear friend and widow whose husband had left her quite well-off. She was bored. She was not happy just serving as a social secretary for Dr. Bea. She was bursting at the seams to have more to do. She knew everybody in town worth knowing. What an asset!

Décor and furnishing was next. Dr. Bea turned over that responsibility to Carole Anne, specifying that she search for military surplus office furniture for Will. Perhaps for decoration, he would appreciate a large black velvet piece with lots of Day-Glo paint, perhaps a caricature of a clown. They both laughed.

Will's responsibility, now that he knew the area desired, was to find the space. At least three offices, preferably four, with a conference room, reception area, male and female restrooms, and a small kitchenette. Parking in the building was a must. The next morning, he stopped by the Chacherie offices to seek out recommendations. He found at least a dozen people in Chas' office, all trying to talk at the same time. He thought, "Politics," and shuddered.

He turned to leave and ran head-on into Chas' father. The man stopped Will and asked him to visit a minute. Will told him why he had come by. The old man gleamed. "I am the person you talk to about that, not the New State Attorney General." He took Will by the arm, and instructed him to follow him out the door and down the hall: Suite 901 and vacant.

"We have this entire floor leased," said Mr. Chacherie. "We had these offices subleased to a foreign government for trade offices. They got into an internal pissing contest, and the fellows that we leased to ended up in smaller quarters, eight feet under. See how this would work. If this is not adequate, tell me what you want, and I'll see to it you get it."

Will wanted to jump for joy. Four offices, reception, large kitchenette, powder room for both sexes, and a mahogany paneled conference room. Great address, Carondelet, one-half block off Canal. He left a message at Dr. Bea's office. Let her make the decision and negotiate the rent. The old man was not going to be easy.

The next day, he crossed the lake and went right to work on things he needed for the concrete plant. A few days, and he began to think more about flying again. Lord, he missed it. He was soon to be regularly covering four hundred miles of real estate between Hammond, Louisiana, and Memphis. Time was of the essence, and driving would not work. He did what was necessary, took the physical exam, spent some dual time to get back into the groove, did a flight check ride with an examiner, and he finally had a new commercial license. The first plane he bought was used, a Cessna 180 with floatplane capability.

As months passed, Susie Scott became more competent and took on more responsibility. They did not get the concrete business up and running before she graduated, but it was far enough along that she won honors with her business plan. She came to work the day after she graduated. René Stedman found her a condominium; she moved in and took over the concrete operation as business manager.

Reconciliation moved further along. The General threw Will a bone. The Port of Gulfport was going to be dredging for the port; there was another project. This would involve dredging sand from offshore and pumping it to the beach. The State of Mississippi wanted the entire beach along the Gulf to be one large expanse of white sand. All Will needed was a dredge boat. The General thought he might be able to get the bid. It took almost six weeks and a couple of trips to South America, but Will found the dredge.

Next, the General called to tell Will that he had enjoyed meeting his friend Nate the last time he and Will were together. He had some inside information for Nate. Something was going on in the Pearl River area of the coast. It possibly was a large government project. But one thing he did know. There was going to be a lot of heavy equipment brought in, some by barge, some by truck. Maybe Nate should check into it. He gave Will a contact name and number, but he could not mention the General's name. He also told Will to tell Nate that he would need a security clearance.

That morning, after Will and Jack had finished the session and were caught up to that point in his life, Jack made a comment, "I do not see how life could get much better for you."

"You will be surprised," Will laughed. They made an appointment to get together two days later, on Wednesday of that week. They discussed the fact that the project was ending. Everyone seemed happy to this point. Jack said, "Everyone except the General. When am I going to get to visit with him?"

"He will let you know; this is the way he operates."

Later the same day, Jack received a phone call. Will had talked to the General.

"He wants to meet with you the same time you and I have scheduled for Wednesday. Let him have the time. He will be at my aunt's house. Please be there by nine a.m." Will said one other thing. "Jack, I told him we were through, with the exception of his review. See if you can get the manuscript completed and have a copy to him by tomorrow. Do not tell him we are not finished. I would like my last segment to be a surprise."

46

Jack parked in the alley behind the house and walked to the corner, then to the sidewalk that ran in front of the houses. As he neared the house, he heard laughter. Rose, Dr. Bea's live-in housekeeper, or home manager as she now preferred, was cackling aloud. Maybe the General was in a good mood.

Jack stepped up to the doorbell and heard the soft chimes deep within the house. The footsteps were brisk, heavier than Jack remembered Rose's to be. The General appeared through the distortion of the crystal glass in the door. Then the door swung open. "Come on in," the man spoke in a raised tone. "You must be Jack the Fibber." Jack relaxed. He was in a good mood.

What was a surprise was his height. He was about five ten, slighter than Jack would have expected, but ramrod straight, which he did expect based on the man's military career. He had a few lines in his face, especially at the corner of his eyes. Those eyes bore that strong family trait, deep-set, with the left eyelid slightly drooped. The General asked Jack if he minded sitting out back in the gardens. Jack had been there. He remembered it as green and lush, the gurgling fountain peaceful, almost as idyllic as Moon Mullens' stream. Rose had juices, coffee, pastries.

Leaning next to the base of the General's chair was a weathered leather briefcase. The ragged zipper was not performing its duty; instead, a small leather strap held the briefcase together. The General took the case, placed it in his lap, slowly unbuckled the strap, and took out the manuscript.

"Some piece of work here, young fellow. I have researched your background. Went to Mizzou, did you?" He began to search for what turned out to be one of many folded corners. This was going to be a long day.

"I want to tell you that I am well pleased with what you and the others have assembled here. For the most part, it is accurate and to the point. It is, by far, more than I thought it would be. There are a few points I want to clarify, just for accuracy's sake. Then, I understand from Jonathan that you may have a comment or two that you have not wished to express to anyone else."

It took until noon to get through the pages. Some points that the General wanted to make were as simple as spelling errors, or so the General thought. He would research several other points. The military career came out in the man: no stone unturned, attention to detail. Finally, the tedium was over, the General obviously well pleased by his own contribution.

Lunch was a chicken salad served in a French roll, with a lemon parfait for dessert. The General insisted that Rose join them for lunch. Then after lunch, he suggested a short stroll in the park to ward off what he called the drowses. It was interesting to see this old soldier, a man Jack had feared talking to, to be so relaxed, so at ease. He seemed very comfortable in his skin.

They had walked along in silence, stopping once to look at an odd bird making a nest in the low limbs of a tree. "Too close to the ground to be safe," said the warrior. Then they walked on, again in silence. Jack started to prompt, but then remembered a comment from Miss Annie: "He will eventually tell you what is on his mind." And so he waited.

"I read through your work and wonder what goes on in the mind of someone who is not a part of this family. What do you think of us? Then I wonder, what do we really think of each other? Then I think to myself, it doesn't matter. What is most important is what we think about ourselves, and is God going to approve?"

They walked a little further, and the General's comments turned to Seamus. He felt Seamus had done great things with the ability he had. He had vision and was steadfast in the pursuit of his dreams. He laid a great foundation for what was to come. He set fine examples of sharing the wealth. He saw each individual for his or her merit, not for color, not religion, and not politics.

The General felt that in his own life, he had realized early on that what you took out of the earth, you had to give back. Later, he applied that same thought to the economy of the family, the company. If he cut down a tree, he insisted on replanting. This was not a practice of the early settlers, including Seamus. In those days, people could only see an abundance of resources. All they needed was the taking.

He later proved that his theory worked not only with the timber. He applied it to money. If you harvested it, you had to put some of it back. He was proud that he had done so, proud that the next generation, Jonathan and Beatrice, had done the same. His belief of late was that the generation now coming into leadership, Will and Carole Anne, had accepted the idea.

He pointed out Jonathan's successes and those of Beatrice. Then he spent a long time on what he dreamed that his own son, William Jr., might have done. He could tell from early on in his life that the man was a true humanitarian. There was no doubt in the General's mind that he would one day have been president.

Then, as they strolled along, the General boasted a bit about his role in the company. He and his mother, Mollie, had saved the company when it was bound for ruin. Seamus was old and cranky and could not think well enough ahead to know that the terrible depression could not last. He had almost abandoned hope himself when Seamus had died and willed most all of the cash to everyone who had ever touched his life in a positive way. At this point, he gave a lot of credit to Winston and his mother, Maudie Lee. Had they not left the money they had received in the bank, it was destined for failure.

There was also self-assessment that showed the General's real side. He wanted nothing more in life than to be a soldier. At a time when it was not necessary, he had walked away from the company to go back to war. He had left the company in the hands and on the shoulders of Miss Annie, Jonathan, and Winston Jackson. Then he admitted that when he could have gotten out, he stayed. He literally had had stars in his eyes, four of them. He would always regret only getting two. He said he was able to wipe away some of the guilt for that by the fact that his Washington years had had their advantages. The company prospered from his contacts, things he arranged, people he knew. Jack did not disagree.

They turned around at the lagoon, where the Swan Boat took passengers, mostly kids, on short cruises. It was then that the General switched subjects. Was Jack ready to broach the subject that he had thus far not talked to the others about? He was.

Jack told him that it had to do with the crash that had killed William, Jr. and his wife. He had reason to believe that the General knew much more than he had let on about the crash and what had caused it, and that he had in turn taken retribution. Jack had lit the fuse. If the old man was going to blow, here it might come.

The General calmly stated, "You have it in your manuscripts that the cause was never clearly determined. I had to take the word of all of the investigators. I doubted their word at times. I have many hours flying all kinds of aircraft, have test flown aircraft. I can hear an aircraft fly over and tell you if the engines are running properly. I knew something was wrong with the plane; it might have been nothing more than pilot error. It took too long to get off the ground at our airfield. Believe you me, I can still hear those engines straining, throttles to the wall.

"As for retribution, I want to hear why you think that." Still the general was calm, his voice at conversation volume.

Will told him about conversations with his own father and the fact that his dad was city editor of the Jackson newspaper. His father did not remember anything himself about the time, but he'd had a staff person who did. The staff person had grown up in the Delta and was an avid follower of politics in the area and the state. From him, Jack had heard a tale about the Abad family. Here he paused.

He got some clue that he had hit a nerve with the name Abad. The left eyelid, the one that drooped naturally, almost closed. He then described his trip through the Delta to see if he might uncover anything. It was truly a shot in the dark. As fate would have it, he had gotten into a conversation with some old-timers over breakfast. Jack told the General how he had gone about getting in the conversation. He had never divulged to his breakfast partners his true reason for his inquiry.

Jack's accounting continued. "Several of the breakfast partners were longtime residents of the area. A couple of them knew the Abad families. One remembered a time when they were quite active in politics. As he recalled, they first spent a sizable amount of money backing their son-in-law in a campaign for Lieutenant Governor. He was Floyd Jenkins and was married to an Abad daughter. They then spent another sizable amount trying to sway a decision made by the governor at that time, Mark Ainsworth.

James Morrow Walton

"Governor Ainsworth knew that the incumbent senator was terminally ill and was planning to step down before his term ended. Ainsworth was thinking of appointing himself to fill his seat. If he did that, the Abad son-in-law would be governor. That would give him the advantage of being the incumbent at the next election."

The General listened attentively. Jack expected him to interrupt at any moment and say, "I know all about that; get on with it." He did not.

"There was another group, however, that convinced Governor Ainsworth to do otherwise. He decided to appoint another fellow instead of himself. Before the appointment took place, an airplane crash killed the other fellow as well as the ill senator. Scoggins was the senator; no one at the breakfast could remember the name of the other fellow. So in the end, Governor Ainsworth did appoint himself, and Lieutenant Governor Jenkins became the governor. "

Here Jack made a point. "Now it gets interesting." The General was attentive, poker faced. Jack said, "Jenkins, who was then governor, had the advantage of being the incumbent, but he still had to face a forthcoming election. They needed a lot of money. But it seems that the bank the Abads were deeply indebted to changed hands. Moreover, it happened about the time the campaign funds became necessary. The new bank, reviewed all its loans and called in the notes owed by the Abad family. On top of that, the cotton brokers in Memphis who held their cotton could not sell it for what the Abads had in it. The Abads went broke."

Speaking in the sort of tone he'd have used if he was lecturing a history class, the General said, "The Jenkins woman was a loose cannon, uncontrollable, vicious. When she was drinking, she was dangerous. She went to a nightclub in Jackson under the care of two plainclothes Mississippi State Highway patrolmen. That night, Mrs. Jenkins got knee crawling drunk. During the course of a friendly argument that turned unfriendly, she lost her temper and flew into a rage. What it was over did not matter. She threatened the person and said that the Abads did not get mad, God damn it, they got even. Then she went on to say that if the person did not believe it, he ought to talk to me."

Then the General took on a bit of a harsh look. "She was talking to the wrong person. She was talking to a young fellow who was an attorney in the offices of our company attorney at the time. I knew about the conversation fifteen minutes after the words passed her lips." They walked along another step or two and stopped.

Then the General said, "This was not the first time I had heard of threats by the Abad family. They controlled a lot of land, many people, and many votes. They did not always feel that playing by the rules was the best way to go. Turned out, neither did I." That was all that he said. Jack had to assume that retribution had taken place as he had heard.

Jack then asked, "So you based a lot on nothing more than what came out of her mouth? Did you have any other clues?" Jack knew he was skating out on even thinner ice.

Surprisingly, the General stayed calm. "I did not; none."

Jack went further. "General, do you remember that a car stayed at your airfield for over a week after the crash? No one knew to whom it belonged."

Then the General got a little impatient. "Seems I do, but I don't think anything came of that. Two highway patrolmen came and picked it up; a stolen vehicle was the assumption. You have something you want to say about all of this, I think."

"One more question, sir. Did you know of a Junius Abad?"

"Never heard of him. Was he a relation to Jenkins' wife?"

Jack began the tale of an intrepid reporter who had read about a body found by rabbit hunters in a field near Birmingham. He began to dig around and found one aviation investigator who put two and two together. The body was in close proximity to where the tail section of the senator's plane fell. The investigator felt that the person could have been a passenger on that plane.

Here the General broke in. "Impossible. I was on the airplane myself before it took off. Got on to shake hands, hug my son before they left. There were no other persons on that airplane other than the ones who were supposed to be."

Jack then revealed to the General his own concerns after talking to the federal investigators. "They had looked at the assumption that there was someone else on the plane. It could answer several questions, even your own about the plane having a hard time getting off the ground." Jack paused. "So they considered this. The plane ran into heavy turbulence. The flight controllers reported that fact. They were already having trouble controlling the airplane. That fact in combination with the turbulence might have overstressed the airplane, causing it to break apart."

The General said, "Go on."

Jack said, "I do believe there was someone else on the airplane."

Again the General said, "And what are you basing that on?"

"I began to consider all possibilities. If someone else was on the plane, why hadn't there been some inquiry or reports of a missing person?" Jack said. "And then I thought, maybe there had?"

Jack told him how he had once again enlisted his father's help. If there was a person on the plane, who was it? Why had no one ever come forward? Why had there been no report of a person missing? His father went through the tedious process of checking newspapers all across the state for information at that time about any missing person. There was nothing.

He had about given up when he stumbled upon a clue. About the same time as the crash, a short article in a Greenville, Mississippi, daily paper reported the fact that a prisoner from the State Prison in Parchman was missing. The prisoner was on furlough to go to a family memorial service, but authorities did not give out the name of the prisoner, believing he might be trying to hide out with relatives. According to the news articles, he had been under the guard of two Mississippi Highway Patrol officers. They had lost him at the church where the service was, when he had jumped out a bathroom window and disappeared. Jack's father had followed up by calling the penitentiary. Luckily, he got an assistant warden who had been at the prison a long time. His father asked him about the prisoner referred to in the article back then. His name was Junius Abad. The assistant told his father the truth. "He ain't back yet!"

The General had to laugh. "He ain't back yet," he said.

Jack related the rest of the tale. Junius Abad weighed two hundred eighty pounds. His only distinguishing marks were four gold teeth, upper fronts. His hair color was brown, his eye color, blue. Knowing about the last two was of no value; they were gone. Also missing was any identification: no billfold, no belt, no shoes. But the skull did have three gold teeth, plus a space where another could have been.

Interesting thing was, the two boys who found the remains were from a poor family, not likely able to afford a new Scott-Atwater outboard motor. But at the time, they had recently acquired one, plus two new twenty-gauge shotguns. They denied finding any more than what the authorities found when they arrived to pick up the remains.

The General questioned what had happened to the remains. Jack told him that after a specified length of time, they declared the remains to be those of an unknown pauper. The county had buried the remains in a gravesite in Birmingham. Jack and the General both agreed; there was not much way of knowing if the Abads ever knew of this.

"What good would it do now to open that can of worms?' said the General, who then said, "Excuse the pun." They both had to laugh.

They had used up most of the day. The General again expressed his gratitude for a job well done. Jack gathered his things, went to the back door, and called out to Rose to express his appreciation for the nice hospitality. He went out the back gate and to his car. He closed the driver door and started the engine, but then heard the squeak of the back gate. He looked in his rearview mirror; the General was walking toward him at a quick pace, and he called for Jack to wait. When he got to the car, he opened the passenger door and slid in.

"Listen to me a minute. I have another thought. What do you know about bombs?"

Jack laughed and said, "They go boom."

The General gave him a description of several types. The main difference was the way in which to trigger them. He explained one that could be set off in midair. An altimeter operated by barometric pressure triggered it. He gave an example. "The bomb likely would have an on/off switch for safety in transporting. To set it up to explode, someone would select an altitude, say, three thousand feet. The way the bomb would then work would be that as the airplane went through three thousand feet climbing out to altitude, a wire attached to the altimeter needle would arm the bomb. As the airplane descended back toward earth and went through three thousand feet again, the bomb would be triggered and would blow."

Then the General said, "Recall that in the very beginning, a so-called witness reported that he saw a flash, heard a boom, and saw fire falling to the ground. Let's take this one step further. Suppose your boy Junius was in the baggage area, let's assume with the bomb. The plane actually broke apart in turbulence. The bomb fell free just as Junius did, and exploded at some preset altitude. Was it supposed to go off with Junius aboard? Had he been duped?" Then he opened the car door, and said to Jack, "Interesting theory, huh?"

47

Will arrived at his office at his usual time of eight o'clock and plugged in the coffee maker. With that underway and the pot perking, he went across the hall to say hello in the Chas Chacherie offices. After catching up on the weekend and what was going on with Charles and family, he returned to his own office. His week varied, but it always included a Thursday trip to the MacMoCorp headquarters in New Cotswold, Mississippi.

Mimi greeted him with a hug and a smile. Today, however, she was a bit puzzled. Within the last ten minutes, she had received the second call from a woman with a slight British accent; she wanted to speak to Will. Mimi had told the caller that he would be in within the hour. The woman had been very polite, but still did not care to leave a message. And the persistent caller was back on the line within minutes.

"This is Will MacMorogh, how may I help you?"

"Hi Willie, Tish here." He too caught the slight British accent.

Will was startled and hesitant in his response.

The caller said, "Are you still there?"

"Tish, Letitia Mullens?" he questioned with excitement in his voice.

"Yes."

"My God in heaven, where are you?" His excited voice startled Mimi. She came to the door and peeped in. Will waved her off; everything was OK.

"If I am reading this map correctly, I may be just around the corner. Is your building close to the Roosevelt Hotel?" Tish asked.

"I can see it from my office window. How soon can we get together?" Will was practically shouting.

"We can get together later today if you are available. At the moment, I am on my way to do some work. I should be back here in my suite no later than two. How convenient would that be for you?" she asked. He could make that work. They agreed to meet at that time. She would already have had lunch with colleagues.

Will called for Mimi, and she rushed in. "My goodness, you are excited. Who in the world was that?" smiled Mimi. He told her about his lifelong friendship with Letitia Mullens, better known as Tish. They had lost track several years ago, and he had not heard from her since. He asked Mimi to send a bouquet and a bottle of good champagne to her suite. As far as work, he would take care of as much as he could on the day's agenda. If he did not complete it, he would ask her to reschedule any other appointments.

He was in the lobby at two and called the Mullens suite from a house phone. She was in; the door would be unlocked. Ever since she had called that morning, Will had wondered how she might be, how she looked. Was she still the wonderfully adorable chubby little girl with the dimples? He tapped lightly on the door, turned the handle, and stepped in. Tish stood several paces back, her arms at her sides. He almost excused himself for being in the wrong suite. She smiled; she did still have the cute dimples in her cheeks. Otherwise, he would not have recognized her. She was stunning; gone was that chubby little girl.

What Will had not considered was her reaction to him. Her right arm flew to her heart as if it had a mind of its own. She came to him and put her arms around his neck. All she could get out was, "Will," before she began to cry. She leaned her head onto his chest, and the tears flowed. She could not stop. She only sobbed, and again, "Will, Will."

Finally she pulled away, rubbed under her nose with the back of her hand. "Please forgive me." She pointed to the sofa. "Sit, please," she said, and then turned to the bathroom. In a moment, she returned with a box of tissues, her face wiped dry and her eyes still teary.

She sat on the cushion next to Will and turned to face him, but could not speak without her mouth trembling. She took her hand and softly touched the deep scar on his upper lip, the lump where his nose had been broken, and then the shoulder. Through the thin white hair over his ear, she could see the pink scar running from his forehead and back. She touched it ever so lightly.

Once she regained her composure, she spoke almost in a whisper. "There were many nights that I prayed for your survival before crying myself to sleep. Then I would pray that God would help us survive also. Now, here you are, that same fellow, just a little older, with a scar or two. Handsome as always, perhaps a little roguish." She managed a smile.

"And you, you are absolutely gorgeous! When did all of this happen?"

"What do you mean, when did this happen!" she scoffed. "As I remember, all my life, you have been telling me I was *sooo purdy*."

"That I have," he laughed. "Sometime I will tell you how often I have thought about that. But tell me, what are you doing here in New Orleans? How long will you be here? How much time will we be able to spend together?"

Tish replied, "I am a broadcast journalist with the BBC in London. We are here for several things, mainly some political issues we want to explore. In addition, we have a meeting with the British Consulate here. I have to fly to D.C. on Wednesday morning, then be back here on Thursday. Beginning Friday, I plan to take some holiday. Then," she paused, out of breath, "I will be taking over for one of our Washington bureau correspondents in D.C. for two weeks. After that, back to London."

She caught her breath and went on, "My schedule here is probably odd for you. We are broadcasting live for our morning and evening news in a cooperative agreement with a local TV station. Since the time difference is six hours, we finish our evening news at noon here. I then go back to the studio later in the evening to prepare for a one a.m. broadcast, which will be our seven a.m. morning news in London. In between, I try to catch some sleep. That leaves me free for about five or six hours each afternoon before my early bedtime."

Will replied, "I can make my schedule fit any free time you have. We have a lot of catching up to do. What are you planning for your week of holiday?"

"I have to play that by ear. My mother will be coming over from London on Saturday. We want to do some things together, maybe even go to New Cotswold. You know she still has the house and farm there."

"How is your mother? I was so sorry to hear about Moon and more sorry that I heard about it too late to attend the funeral."

Tish then told him about her mother, how important she had been to her in the past several years. Her mother was seriously thinking of returning to the States to live, but probably not to Mississippi. One of the reasons for returning to visit New Cotswold was to see if she had it in her to give up the last of Moon. Then Will asked, "How long have you been in London? Is that now home?"

Tish was silent for a few moments before she replied. "I have been in England since I graduated from Northwestern. I did two years graduate study at Cambridge. During that time, I did freelance for several news groups. By accident, I was asked to interview for a job at the BBC. Long story; I was hired. I was in London until two years ago, and then the company sent me to Russia to work out of our embassy there. I returned to London four months ago."

She paused again, as if choosing her words "I do not know about it being home. There are times when I think I need to come back here. I love my work, and I am very good at it, but several things are going on in my life that may make the decision to return not one of my own."

"Is there someone in your life?" Will asked. "You are still using the name Mullens. I have to assume you have not been married, or if so, that you kept your name."

"That too is another issue," she replied. "There has been someone in my life for quite a while that I must think of. In addition, I have had an on again, off again, relationship with a colleague at work. I guess right now it may be off, perhaps due to circumstances."

She looked at her watch and said, "What about opening the champagne, and then we can order a light meal here in the room. I will need to get some rest before I go back to the studio. Perhaps we can get back together tomorrow."

"Great idea," Will laughed. "I was so surprised , I forgot the champagne. It will be nice to order here. You may run me off when you wish. I will reluctantly obey." Again, he chuckled.

Tish excused herself again; he could hear her talking in the other room. When she came out, she said, "Dinner will be served at five." Then, "Tell me about you, where you live, what is now going on in your life?" Tish asked. To Will, it seemed she might want to change the subject.

"My aunt and my sister and I use an office here for convenience sake. Our headquarters are still in New Cotswold. I have another office over on the North Shore where I operate our construction aggregates business and do property development. Also, I have a dredge boat working on the Gulf Coast near Gulfport.

"As for residence, I still have the apartment over my aunt's carriage house. When I am in the city, which may be two or three nights of the week, I stay there. Weekends I spend in a little settlement across the lake. When my aunt was in pre-med at Tulane, my grandfather bought an old resort hotel with twenty rooms. It was at the point of collapse, but it is ideally situated. It has beachfront on Lake Pontchartrain. The Tchefuncte River is the west border. Grandfather spent a fortune remodeling it, then, a couple of years ago, he gave it to my aunt. She has spent another fortune refurbishing and making a showplace out of it. It is large enough to have more than one group of guests without one interfering with the other. It is quite comfortable; I cannot wait to show it to you."

Their dinner arrived. The waiter uncovered the table to reveal half dozen oysters for each, a small filet of redfish, green salad, rolls, and key lime pie. There was a chilled bottle of chardonnay and two glasses ready for pouring. Will was astonished at the amount of food for a light meal.

"Keep in mind that I will be working until past midnight." Tish said.

Over dinner, they chatted on about Will's grandparents, his aunt, his sister Carole and Uncle Jonathan, all the people she remembered. Then they talked about Moon.

"It was a sad time indeed. I was ill and could not attend the funeral. It was one of the worst times in my mother's life, and I was not there to support her."

She continued, . "People did not know my father at all: the county bootlegger, pudgy, red-faced, spitting, sputtering through those God-awful teeth, and slinging his arms when he talked. However, he and my mother had a relationship most people never acquire. He was kind and considerate and worshipped the ground she and I walked on. Bless his heart; he was generous to a fault."

"He graduated magna *cum laude* with a degree in business from the University of Tennessee. He worked for several years for P&G, but the corporate life was not his cup of tea. How he got into the whiskey business, I never knew. He converted whiskey money, and lots of it, into stocks, bonds, land, and an education savings program for me. He had a million dollar insurance policy when he died. Mother has done very well with it."

Tish looked at her watch and smiled. "We have covered a lot of ground. Suppose we call it an evening, and let me get a nap?" Will agreed reluctantly. At the door, he held her tightly; they kissed for the first time. They held tighter. Tish did not want to let go, and neither did he.

Looking into her eyes, he said, "Good night, but I do not know if can sleep a wink."

That night and through the next morning, Will thought of nothing else. The afternoon before was a pleasant surprise. He hoped that their parting kiss had left her feeling the way he did.

They met again at the same appointed time as the day before; she had gotten out of her work clothes and into slacks and a light blouse. Will commented on how chic she looked.

She responded that she had had a lot of help and a real incentive, especially since her illness. It had started at the beginning of her second semester in her senior year and soon after his visit to

Northwestern. It was the recurrence of a kidney problem, one that had plagued her since childhood. She had actually been bedridden for a spell. Once she was better, she had cause for a more active lifestyle.

Will took her hands in his. "I do not know where to start. I completely lost track of you after that weekend. I knew you were planning to move to another apartment. You said you would send the new address. I hate to bring that up, but when I tried to get in touch with you, I could not. From that point, I lost track. Then things began to happen in my life. I cannot tell you how sorry I am that you were only a memory, a very fond one."

"That night we were together meant more to me than you may ever know. All I could think about on my slow trip home was that the love of my life had been right in front of me for all those years and I had not realized it. I had never felt the love that came over me that night. I wanted you to be mine forever. All the way home, I composed and recomposed the letter that I sent to you."

Tears began to well into Tish's eyes. "Let me help you along a bit," she said. "Yes, I received that wonderful letter. I still have it; I slept with it under my pillow for a long time. I thought about what you had said, and I felt the same way. I was moving and trying to get a new semester started. I wrote several responses, trying to say just the right thing, but with the moving, I hesitated too long in sending it."

She took a deep breath before going further. "Before I got my response in the mail to tell you I shared the same feeling, I got the worst phone call of my life. My mother wanted to know if I had heard that the wonderful young minister of music at the Baptist Church had suddenly resigned. And you know his reason."

She began to shake her head from side to side. "He did not feel he could continue to do the Lord's work with what was happening in his life. His wife was having an affair. It was you. You broke up their marriage." She was speaking defiantly. Will hurt.

Then the tears began to flow, and she sobbed uncontrollably. "How could you have done that to me? I hated you for that." Will pulled her to him. She tried to pull away, but he held her close until the sobbing stopped. After a while, he let her pull back, and she sat on the edge of the sofa, facing him.

"Over the years, I have managed to let that pass. I have managed to keep up with you in various ways. I doubt that you have known that. With all the pain and suffering you have gone through, I finally found forgiveness. The worst thought that I had in my mind after all of our years together was that I could not trust you." The words stung. It was hard for Will to keep his composure. Tish spoke again, this time not so tensely.

"So, instead of a heartfelt note expressing my love, I wrote a letter stating that perhaps we should just continue to be friends. We had been focusing on exciting careers for a long time. Maybe it would be best to continue in pursuit of those careers and see what happened. You were going into the navy to fly as soon as the next school year was over. I was already applying for graduate school."

Will paused before responding. "What I have to tell you, I have never told to anyone other than my Aunt Bea. I hope you will try to understand before you pass final judgment on trusting me. Promise to let me finish. It was the last summer I was home, the same summer I came to visit you. Uncle Jonathan and Winston had constructed the first of their water well drilling rigs. They used it to drill three wells with great success. They were anxious to teach me to operate the rig over the summer."

"They scheduled the drilling of a well for Mr. Swenson. You remember the girls, Imogene and Marlene, very attractive women and quite buxom. Imogene was twenty-seven. Marlene was fourteen, and maturing rapidly. She was definitely going to be able to wear Imogene's hand-me-down bras.

"I went by Swenson's Mercantile to pick up keys to the well site, a hundred acres out past my grandfather's house. There was a small lake, many trees, and some open fields. In the midst of one copse of trees was a beautiful building site. That was where the well was to be. There were two ways to access the property. One was from the main road, and the other from Nap Road. The entry from Nap would have been easiest, but there was an old wooden bridge. It was a weak structure. Winston feared it would collapse under the weight of the drilling rig."

"We arrived at the site early in the afternoon. I was driving my truck with supplies. Winston was driving the drilling rig. Mr. Swenson's key would not open the lock on the chain that secured the gate. We decided that I should go back into town to see if I could get another key or get permission to cut the chain. Then Winston saw a reflection in that copse of trees. It was off a windshield. We thought Mr. Swenson had decided to meet us there and had entered through the other gate."

"I climbed over the fence. Red, Winston's dog, crawled under and went bounding off toward the trees, running back and forth, chasing rabbits. When I got to the trees, I spotted the back end of a car. It was Imogene's little red Chevrolet coupe. Three more steps, and another car came into view about a car length in front of Imogene's car. I stopped in my tracks."

"All four doors were open. A petticoat hung over one door, and at another, a man's coat. I dropped to the ground and then onto my belly. Red was sniffing and thinking I wanted to play. It was all I could do to keep him muzzled. All I wanted was to sneak out of there. After seeing the clothes, I realized that two people were on the back seat. I could see a long arm stretched high and two sets of feet, one toes up, the other toes down. Then suddenly, a man slid out of the car with nothing on but a pair of shoes and socks."

At this point, Tish said, "Imogene? Oh my God, who was the man?"

Will shook his head. "I slithered backward before getting to my feet to run. When I got to Winston's truck, he told me I looked like I had seen a ghost. I shook my head and told him it was nothing I could talk about, ever. I suggested that I go back into town for the correct key. I hoped that the people I saw would be gone by the time I returned. Winston said he would walk to Nap's store for a soda water while he waited."

"I took my time, driving back into town. I parked the truck in the back lot near the freight dock, the one the family used to park their vehicles. I opened the door, and the little bell over the door jingled, and there stood Imogene. She saw my astonished look; I told her that I thought I had just seen her out on the highway. She put her index finger to her lips, signaling me to hush. She stepped closer and told me it was Marlene driving her car. She said she would be fifteen the following week and would be eligible to take her driving test. Mr. Swenson did not approve. Imogene, being the sweet big sister, had let her use her car to practice."

Tish spoke, in barely a whisper, "Marlene, fourteen years old? Who was the man, Will?"

"I went back to the drill site where Winston was waiting. He told me that if the two cars he'd seen leaving the property belonged to who he thought they did, we had best leave it alone. We did not finish the well until late the next day, but the encounter would not leave my mind."

"On Sunday, I did not go to the pot luck dinner at the Lamar family gathering as usual. I could not; instead, I grabbed a sandwich, then went to go fly Jonathan's Piper Cub. I followed the railroad as far north as Leeville and made a few turns around the lake, wagging my wings at people. I turned back toward home, and a few miles out of town, I spotted the sand pit where you and I went one night to smoke cigars and drink cheap wine."

Tish chimed in, "And on the way home, I puked my guts up."

"As I flew over the sand pit, I saw a car pulled into the trees. Parked out in the open was a green and white Model 'A' Ford pickup, clearly marked with a dinosaur on the door. You remember the old truck T.G. Holt used to advertise his Sinclair service station. Clara, his youngest, was driving it. I made a slow circle around, flew back north a distance before turning back south. I throttled back to an idle to begin a slow, almost silent glide that brought me to an altitude of about one hundred feet when I crossed back over the pit. The same man I had seen with Marlene was naked as a jaybird, and so was Clara on the quilt beside him."

"Who was the man, Will?"

It took Will a moment or two to respond. He looked her in the eyes and quietly said, "The Reverend Billy D. Simpkins."

Tish could only mutter. Tears flowed once more. "No, no, no!" She covered her face with both hands and leaned her head back on the sofa. "And you knew about this when you came to visit me?"

Will nodded, "Yes."

"What did you do?"

"What could I do? Whom could I tell and not run the risk of getting someone killed? If the word got out, Mr. Swenson would have probably killed him. You know that T.G. Holt had a reputation of being one of the meanest hotheads in the county. He would have killed Billy D. with his bare hands. What would have happened to the church or to the town, for that matter? Half the town was and still is Baptist.

"I could not sleep. All I could do was worry about what I had seen. Someone needed to know. I had three young cousins, all enrolled in the junior choir at the Baptist Church. I had no earthly idea how to handle the situation. I called the only person I knew who could help sort it out, Aunt Bea. She mulled the situation over before contacting a person she knew at a Baptist College. She made an appointment and told the person about the incident. She alerted me; it was not necessary to tell me to keep quiet."

"The week after I visited you, I was back in New Orleans at Aunt Bea's house to begin my senior year. I had not yet heard back from you. I tried to call. Your telephone was no longer in service. I called your mother; no answer. You had moved.

"Within the same week, Reverend Billy D. was called to New Orleans for an interview. The staff there informed him that an investigation by persons from the church, including two child psychologists, had found proof of his conduct. He could go back to New Cotswold, get his business in order, and immediately resign, never again to step into a church in the capacity of a minister. He could handle it quietly and go his way."

"Instead, he went back, called his parents and Christine's parents, and gave them the bad news. Christine was having an affair. He was leaving his job. He could not continue to do God's work in his state of mind. He left the moment he turned in his resignation. He did not tell Christine what he had told the church deacons. They were the ones who told her. They did what they called *the Christian thing to do*. She could stay on in the parsonage for another week."

"Her parents were appalled. They drove immediately to New Cotswold, only to find Christine at the point of a nervous breakdown. The unfortunate thing was, neither set of parents believed her side of the story. It was all her fault. Billy D. had been telling his parents for months that she was unhappy. He feared that something was going on."

Tish listened attentively without interruption, but at this point, she placed her hands over her face, leaned her head against the back of the sofa, and moaned. When she rose, she was trembling and could hardly speak. Her lips trembled; she was about to cry. "I do not know where this is going, I am afraid I do not want to know. Maybe it was a mistake for me to want to know the truth. Maybe it was a mistake to come here." She said, "Just tell me, were you having an affair with Christine when this happened? How could you have possibly sent me such a wonderful letter?"

Will said, "Let me finish."

So he continued. "My aunt was the first to hear the news, and yes, she questioned me also. She was disturbed that not only was my name involved, but that this thing involved our whole family. Grandfather was furious. Grandma was beside herself.

"I did not have an affair with Christine. All I can tell you is what I told my family," Will pleaded.

"Why would Billy D. say what he said? Why would people immediately believe him?"

Will responded quickly, "Don't you think that went through my mind hundreds of times? The worst part was that I could not find Christine. I wondered if she could have said something to imply she was having an affair. Did I do something to tip off Billy D.? Did he know I was the one responsible for him getting caught?"

"How could he have known, Will?"

"It could have been all my own doing. I was still at Mr. Swenson's when Marlene returned. I was walking to my truck when she drove up. Long strands of grass hung to the underside of the car. I pointed them out to Marlene and told her she might want to get those out before anyone saw them and knew she had been off the road and in tall grass. Then I said something I should not have. I told her she might want to tell her friend about that also. I often wondered if she told Billy D. that I had seen them."

"The other thing was the day I flew the Cub so close. Most anybody in New Cotswold knew who owned that Cub. Billy D. might have figured it out for himself."

Then Tish asked, "Had you ever had any contact with Christine that could have caused you to be suspect?"

"Let me tell you all that I know. All of the contact I had with Christine or with Billy D., for that matter."

48

It was the summer between his sophomore and junior years. Every Sunday, he went to the regular Lamar Sunday Buffet at his Aunt Jessie's house. The Lamar sisters did not all attend the same church, and their ministers had standing invitations for the Lamar buffet. Occasionally some were there. The Sunday he first met Christine, he was at a picnic table with his cousin Patricia; she motioned toward the couple walking into the yard. It was Rev. Billy D. Simpkins and his wife Christine. They almost looked like twins.

Both were platinum blond. His hair was long and swept back, hers was down to her waist. He had on a snow-white suit; she was dressed in a full white, no waist dress over several petticoats. The hem was to her ankles. Will's comment was that she looked frumpy. Despite her attire, she was quite attractive. Rev. Billy D. was too prissy.

After they arrived, the reverend said grace, and then they sat at a picnic table several over from where Will and Patricia sat. After he finished eating, Rev. Billy D. excused himself to go take care of the Lord's work. According to him, it never ended; he had to visit the homebound, sick, and needy that needed God's blessing. After her husband left, Christine came to sit by Patricia. Patricia usually was the ringleader in getting the smaller kids all involved in games, so Christine joined in. Will said his good-byes and left.

This became a Sunday ritual, and it was Will's only contact with Christine or her husband. Patricia later told him that the marriage between Christine and the reverend had been an arrangement. Both fathers were on staff at a Bible college in Texas, and Christine was a student there. Billy D. was in another school, working toward a Masters in Music. The two met, the parents promoted their relationship, and they were married after Christine's sophomore year. Billy D. had not received a call to a church. One of the promises he made was that he would not accept a call unless it was in a town with a college so that Christine could continue her education. That did not work out; the closest school to New Cotswold was the junior college fifty miles away.

To make things worse, the church did not offer Christine a warm welcome. She had a beautiful voice, and Billy D. showcased her on many Sundays, much to the annoyance of some of the other choir members. In addition, Christine was shy. Some of the younger congregation misconstrued that as being aloof. Christine was at home alone each day without transportation. She bought a used bicycle, painted it blue, and rode it all over town. Many of the older people did not find that to be lady like; they whispered behind her back.

The following summer, another episode might have been suspicious. It was on cleanup day for "Homecoming at Old Church." Tish was well aware of the event and knew of the responsibility Will had for sharpening tools and tending the burn area. He had been doing it since he was old enough to drive. Will continued covering what transpired that summer.

Christine had taken it upon herself to clean up the gazebo and give it a fresh coat of paint. Will went several times to the gazebo to gather up the grass and leaves that Christine had cleared and to take it to burn. He was standing at the area when two women walked up to Christine, the Shelton sisters. They began to talk, and Will saw one of the women nod toward him. Christine turned to look at the same time. The next time he went over to collect her cuttings, she told him it might be best if he not help her. The Shelton sisters said he had a bad reputation around town. People seeing her with him might talk. Christine was furious. She stated clearly that she hated the town.

When Will was ready to leave for the day, only a few people remained, including Christine. He needed water to douse out the remaining ashes at the burn area. With a five-gallon bucket in hand, he took the trail that led to the spring that flowed under the hill. It had been a long time; tree limbs spanned the area, and kudzu enveloped them. The vine provided a canopy for a small room.

The area around the spring was clean. Bright green moss carpeted the ground on both sides of the stream created by the spring. Vases with dead flowers, apparently left over from past funerals, decorated the area. A pie pan was half-full of peanuts and birdseed, and a metal chair leaned against a tree. Someone spent a lot of time there.

Will continued to look around, then went back up the trail. When he reached the top, there stood Christine, wringing her hands. Tears ran down her cheeks. She muttered that it had been her secret getaway. It was her place to hide. Will assured her that it could still be her secret, that he would tell no one. In fact, he asked her if she had ever followed the creek around the bend.

She had not because there was a POSTED sign on the property. Will told her that if she followed the creek, she would come to a covered bridge. The trail across the bridge led up to a lodge that belonged to his family. Just before the bridge, there was a dam on the creek; it made a large swimming hole. Will invited her to go to the lodge at any time. She would find a big porch with rocking chairs, and she could see for miles. It was very peaceful there.

She thanked him, but declined the offer, saying it was probably not proper for her to do that. It was not long after that when Will caught Billy D. the first time. His next encounter, and the last before Christine and Billy D. both disappeared, was hard for Will to talk about, but he wanted everything out and on the table.

He had taken complete charge of the drilling rig and had hired a part-time helper. They worked all one Tuesday until dark. Will was having trouble with the drill and did not want to quit working. He let the hired hand go home, and he stayed with the rig, working all night and until noon the following day. Winston came out to the site and helped him and the hired hand finish up. By two o'clock, Will was through for the day.

That summer, he was staying in the small apartment alongside one of the hangars at the airport. He went there and put six bottles of home brew in a pail and along with them, a half-pint jar of moonshine. He cut a big hunk of cheese, loaded that and a box of crackers into a sack with Lava soap, towels, and clean clothes. Then went to the lodge. He had planned to sit on the front porch drinking beer and eating cheese and crackers until he felt like jumping in the creek to take a bath.

He popped a beer, took a big slug of 'shine, and then put the rest in the refrigerator. He took the cheese, crackers, and beer to the porch, slumped down in a rocker, and began to relax. The 'shine had put a numbness on his lips and cheeks. He was feeling no pain. He dozed off, and at first, he thought he was dreaming. He heard someone whistle. In a moment, he heard it again. The sound was coming from the woods near the creek. Then, all of a sudden, out of the bushes stepped Christine. Had it not been for the hair, he might not have recognized her. She had on tight black pedal pushers with a red sleeveless shirt. He had never seen her in anything other than the frumpy full dresses. He would never have guessed what was under all those petticoats.

He stood, welcomed her to the lodge, and asked if she would like something to drink. He offered Coca-Cola or water. She declined and said she would like a beer like the one he was drinking. He was surprised and suggested that Rev. Billy D. might not like her coming home with beer on her breath. She told him her husband was in Jackson at a revival. He had taken the girls' choir on invitation from the church there.

Will went to the kitchen to get her a beer, and she followed. He was still filthy dirty, with grease and grime to his elbows. When he handed her the unopened beer, she grabbed his arm and pushed it up. He had a long scratch from his elbow to his wrist; there was dried blood. He did not remember when he had done that. She asked about a first aid kit. He got it out of the cabinet, and she went to work cleaning the arm and smearing iodine on it. That was the first time he had ever touched her, or her him.

After cleaning the wound, they moved back to the front porch. He explained to her that he had come over to soak in the creek and then take a nap. Off to the west, they saw a streak of lightning and then heard thunder. It was a long way off, but the wind picked up, and then there was more thunder and lightning again.

Christine said that if he was going to bathe in the creek, he had better get to it before it started to rain. She stood, thanked him for the beer, and then started back the way she had come. Will gathered up his soap, clean clothes, and towels, and went to the creek. He jumped in at the deep end by the bridge.

He got his hair lathered and was soaking off more dirt and grease when a stick splashed into the creek. Then he heard Christine. She told him to turn his head and not look. He followed her instructions, and she waded in at the shallow end. When she said she was decent, Will turned to see her standing twenty feet away with only her head visible. She complained; the water was too cold, and her lips were blue. She kept her distance. Will had thought to himself, "What would the old ladies at the church think."

Out of the corner of his eye, Will spotted a ripple in the water. On closer look, he realized that it was a small water snake swimming at the edge of the creek; it was eating insects. He told Christine to stand still because a small snake was coming toward her. She turned her head and, seeing the snake, took three long strokes and grabbed him around his neck. Will reached behind him to get a small stick. When the snake was close, Will slid the stick under its midsection, lifted it up, and flung it into the bushes.

Christine pressed tightly against him. He could feel her firm breasts against him. He was getting an erection. She felt him against her and pulled his lips to hers, and they kissed. Will pushed her away. He told her they could not do that, or there could be no stopping. Slapping would not have gotten a worse response. She turned, made about four strokes to shallow water, and then stood and dashed into the bushes to retrieve her clothes. He could hear her sobbing bitterly. He needed to go to her. He got out of the water and slipped on his pants to go to her, but she broke into a run. All he could hear was her sobbing as she ran back toward the Old Church.

Will then said to Tish, "That was the last time I saw her."

Tish said, "You did not try to contact her?"

"Yes, I did. I called her parents' house. When her father found out who was calling, he told me I had my nerve. He did not know where she was and did not care. He said I would be in hell before he would tell me, even if he knew."

Tish was pale. She excused herself to go to the bathroom. When she came out, she had the tips of her fingers against her temples. "I feel compelled to say something, but I can't get my thoughts together. My head is pounding. It seems like a hundred things are all running through my head at the same time." Instead of sitting next to him on the sofa, she sat on the settee across from Will. "There are so many 'ifs,'" and she paused for a moment. "If I had done this, or if you had done that…"

Will interrupted, "Excuse me, but we cannot go back and hash through all of those 'ifs.' I do not think it would hurt from time to time if we reflect back, but we cannot bury ourselves in the past if we expect to go forward."

Tish said, "You have been candid with me, and I believe what you have said. We are not through, however. Remember, I came here because I have needed to include you in my life for a long, long time. We have gone through a lot since the last time we saw each other. You have suffered tremendously. What you do not know is that I suffered with you. More than you can imagine. We have a lot more to talk about, but not tonight. I need to get some rest before our broadcast tonight. As you know, I have a six a.m. flight to DC tomorrow. The meeting there is important to me. I have to be at my best."

Will smiled, "You are saying that it is time for me to leave."

"Yes," she said.

Before they hugged and Will departed, they arranged to meet again when he got back on Thursday. Will reminded her that he would be back by five. She said that she had arranged for someone else to sit in for her on Thursday night's broadcast. When she returned, she would actually be beginning her leave time.

With that in mind, Will asked if she would consider a change of scenery. He would like to take her across the lake to spend the evening at The Point. She agreed that it would be fun. All she had to do was gather her things and be ready to leave when he arrived. The hotel suite was on permanent lease; she could come and go as she pleased.

On Wednesday evening, Will had turned in but was not sleeping when the phone rang. It was Tish. She just wanted to say good night. Her meeting had been a real success. As for now, she still had a job.

On Thursday morning, Will, Aunt Bea, and Carole Anne flew to New Cotswold in Aunt Bea's airplane. Will flew the airplane up; either Aunt Bea or Carole Anne would fly it back. A headwind slowed them a bit, but they were still on time for a nine o'clock meeting at the office. Will taxied the airplane as close to the back gate of his grandmother's house as possible. She heard them land and stood waiting.

Of course, she wanted to chat, but they reminded her that they needed to get on to the office. The General would have a fit if they walked in late. She conceded; she would see them at lunchtime. The meeting was tense as usual; the General made it so.

At lunch, his grandmother announced that by the time they met again, she would have an important announcement. "Stay tuned," she said. Before leaving, she pulled Will aside to whisper in his ear, "I do not care what kind of rush those girls will be in to leave this afternoon. I must talk to you before you leave. Do you hear me, Will? All that business about those girls making rounds at the hospital, it is just to get away from me. They can wait for me to talk to you a few minutes. I mean it, now."

The afternoon meeting went without any problems. The General was considerate of the girls' schedule and dismissed them on time. His grandmother was watching from the gate. By the time Will was out of the car, she was calling to him.

Aunt Bea would fly the leg home. She told Will to go talk to his grandmother and be nice about it. She would preflight the airplane. Carole Anne went into the house with him. The moment they stepped through the back door, his grandmother told Carole Anne that she needed a few moments with Will in private. Carole Anne used the bathroom, came out, said, "Bye, Grandma," and was out the door.

"Now, Will, what is this I hear about the Mullens girl being in New Orleans? The best I recall, you two were best of friends growing up. Is she still that chubby little redhead with the awful teeth? My, my, I cannot believe that her parents did not get braces on that child. But she was such a sweet girl," said his grandmother.

She hardly took a breath and was at it again. "What I wanted to talk to you about is that you are not getting any younger. You have been through a lot, and you deserve a family. Now, the Mullens girl may not be up to your usual standard, tall, thin, blonde, and big breasts, but think about what is important. She is not a stranger."

Will got in a word when she took a breath. "Grandma, first of all, she is absolutely breathtaking now. And by the way, I did date some tall, skinny brunettes too, with big tits, of course."

"Will, do not make fun of me," she scolded. "You and that girl are the same age, I think. You have time to have children. You do not know how happy your grandfather and I would be to know there could still be a chance of another MacMorogh to carry on the name. Poor Jonathan, he will probably never marry. Your grandfather hounded him so much about an heir that I was afraid that he would go out and marry some old brood mare just to make your grandfather happy."

About that time, they could hear the shrill sound of the starter motor turning over the big radial engine in the airplane. The engine caught, belched a time or two, and went into idle. "I have to go, Grandma, they are getting anxious."

"Go then," she said. "Why don't you see if you can't have some kind of relationship with that girl? How long is she going to be in New Orleans, anyway?"

He assured her that he would try and kissed her good-bye.

49

Will called Tish's room. She was in, packed and ready; he could pick her up at the St. Charles entrance. When he pulled to the curb, the doorman opened her door and placed her bags in the car. Will reached across her to hand the bellman a tip and got a kiss on the cheek.

"I am so excited; this will be so nice, getting out of a hotel for a change. I cannot wait to see The Point." She seemed much more relaxed than she'd been when he last saw her. He was glad she was in good spirits and was eager to hear about her trip.

They were crossing the bridge across Lake Pontchartrain at the worst hour of the day. Traffic was slow, at times just a crawl. Will asked how things had gone; she had said last night that she still had a job.

She answered, "I was not in D.C. to talk about my employment. I was at the British Embassy. While I was there, I received a phone call from our London office. I will have a published reprimand to appease the Russians. It might be embarrassing."

"Appease the Russians?" Will questioned.

"How much longer will we be in the car?" she asked. Will told her probably another forty-five minutes. She began her tale about Russia.

She had not wanted to take the assignment, but it had come with the promise that she could pick her next posting if she would go for a year. It was a tremendous hardship and put undue responsibility on her mother. Tish would only be able to come back to London every other weekend. She was a fool for doing it, because as it turned out, the assignment stretched for over a year. It would have gone longer, had her problem not occurred.

According to her, all Russians, especially males, were only one generation past the time the species had started walking upright. She had had warning about the many occasions she would work outside the embassy headquarters. Other media people before had run into incidents. She should be doubly careful for several reasons. One, invitations to state functions were issued so the Russians could get worldwide coverage of their propaganda; reporting was tedious. The other problem: the vodka-soaked men could be abusive.

One evening, only two months earlier, she had been at such a function. She and the other Brits sat in the same area but at two different tables. An obnoxious diplomat, whom she had encountered before, passed by their table. He leaned over, breathed on the back of her neck, and uttered something she did not understand. Later he passed by from the opposite direction; that time he rubbed her shoulders, grinning like a damn baboon.

About halfway through the dinner, she excused herself to go to the loo. She had been told to never go alone, but two other women from her table had just left, so she did not consider herself alone. She started down a long hall, and the baboon came out of a door directly in front of her. She started to turn away, but he grabbed her arm and pulled her into a maid's closet. Immediately he put his hand over her breast. She wanted to scream, but he covered her mouth with his other hand. Then he took his hand from her breast, pulled her skirt up, and put his hand between her legs. Again she tried to scream, and he pushed his hand harder against her mouth, so hard in fact that his little finger went into her mouth. She bit down as hard as she possibly could.

He took his hand from her crotch and slapped her; but not before she had bitten hard enough to taste blood and to feel the crunch of bone in her teeth. He hit at her again. Then it was him doing the screaming. He flung his injured hand down as if he could throw away the pain. Spots of blood went across Tish's dress, across the floor, and up the wall on the other side of the closet. She was free and dashed as fast as she could to the lobby. There she ran down the stairs to the staff car. Their driver, who always stayed with the car, saw her running to the vehicle and opened a door. She jumped into the car, and lay on the back floor. She told the driver to go to her table, retrieve her bits and pieces, tell the others she was ill, and then hurry back to the car. She had to get to the embassy as soon as possible.

When he arrived back at the car, two others from her staff were with him. Once at the embassy, she called the chief of staff. She relayed the story; he called London. Within three hours, she was on an embassy aircraft and out of the country. The next day, things turned bad. One of the reasons she had come to the States was to get out of the country. The Russians demanded that she be sent back to face charges. The bastards would not let up. They barred the BBC from any further news gathering in the country. She had refused to offer up an apology, even if it meant dismissal. Management was in a quandary. What she had heard the day before in Washington was that the British Embassy was offering a formal apology.

The apology would state that the offending reporter had been relieved of her duties. What that meant was her duties in Russia, but not total dismissal. When she was through, Will started laughing, and Tish knew why. "You are thinking he is lucky it was just his pinky stuck in my mouth, right?" Will kept on laughing. They got off the causeway and then turned left on Highway 12, headed toward the Tchefuncte River bridge.

"How about we stash our things at the house, then have dinner? I will show you around the place later."

Tish agreed. "Yes, I am starving."

At the drawbridge, Will turned left into a small road paved with clam and oyster shell. To the right, after they turned, was a large parking lot full of cars. In large letters across the roof of the building was an ancient but well lit sign, reading, "MILTON's." Smaller letters underneath read, "Since 1916." Will explained that there was a restaurant there now. Before pollution had gotten so bad in the lake, there had been an abundance of fish, oysters, crabs, shrimp, and clams. Milton Adair had had a seafood processing plant at the dock. He'd sold fuel and supplies to fishing boats as well as purchasing their catch. Now the boats had to go out to Lake Borgne or down to Chandeleur to fish; the place was now only a restaurant, but it was a great one. They would eat there later.

They continued down the road past a dozen boat stalls with small apartments over each. These were weekend places for people with yachts and cruisers. The names on the docks were the same as the names of the boats in the stalls. "*Judge Not*" belonged to a retired judge. "*Fresh Meat*" belonged to a meat packer in the city. "*Cabooze*" belonged to a liquor dealer who had his stores in retired cabooses.

Another hundred yards and a white wall came into view; bougainvillea grew up much of it. They passed a point with a sensor, and spotlights came on over beautiful wrought iron gates. "Welcome to The Point" was formed in wrought iron above the gates. Will pulled to a box on the driver's side of the car and inserted a key into a slot, and the gates slid open. At the same time, all of the porch lights on both floors came on. The building looked more like a beached steamboat than a house.

The entire structure stood on ten-foot-high pillars. The ground floor was concrete; an enclosed area about ten twenty feet square stood in the center. This housed an elevator that Will said was his Aunt Bea's gift to Grandma. Inside the house, Will explained that what once had been a guest hotel now consisted of five individual apartments. Each had three bedrooms, two baths, a kitchen, and a small living room. Most of the living here was on the outside. Will put Tish's luggage in the hallway to the bedrooms, showed her around a bit, then suggested they get on to dinner. At the restaurant, they walked into a packed reception area.

Strawberry, the hostess, spotted Will as they came in and called out to him, "Mr. MacMorogh, I was about to give your reservation away. You are just in time. Follow me, please." After they took seats, Tish said she did not know he had made reservations. He had not; it was not necessary. The MacMorogh family had eaten there so much that over the years, they were like family. Suddenly a big man charged from the kitchen, red-faced, with a white rag on his head. He spoke to people along the way before getting to their table.

"Evening, Ma'am," he nodded to Tish, introducing himself, "Little Milton."

Will introduced her.

Then Milton then turned back to Tish. "Hungry tonight?" he asked.

"Famished," she said and meant it. She had not eaten much or well on her trip.

"Good. Doan bodda lookin' ad dat menu. Jus' order you a drink and leave da res' to me." With that, he managed to extricate his large body from the chair he had taken and shuffled off.

After they ordered drinks, the food began to arrive. The meal began with Crab Louis for a salad, turtle soup, a platter with fried oysters, crab claws, shrimp, soft shell crabs, and a filet of redfish. For dessert, homemade vanilla ice cream with a flamed rum sauce. All through dinner, people arriving or leaving waved at Will or stopped by to say hello. Tish commented. Will told her they had not yet heard about his bad reputation. Both laughed.

Back at the house, they wandered around through the structure, with Will giving a brief history of the reconstruction. He explained that he and his aunt used the facility the most. He and Carole Anne had apartments downstairs, while his aunt had one upstairs.

The wind picked up; outside it was a bit chilly. However, the moon was full and cutting a beautiful streak across the lake. Will got a coverlet from inside, and they sat together on a comfortable glider.

"I've told you about most of my trip," said Tish. "Tell me about yours. How was your meeting, and how was your grandmother and grandfather?"

Will turned a bit on the glider to face her directly. With a sheepish grin on his face, he told her he had had an interesting visit with his grandmother.

Tish rose quickly and exclaimed, "What did she tell you?" Will just smiled. "Damn it, what did she say to you, Will?"

Will did not understand her concern. "Why are you upset?"

Tish took a deep breath. "Just please tell me what you talked about."

"Well, she said she understood you were in town. She wanted to know if you were the same pudgy little girl with red hair and crooked teeth. I told her yes."

"Come on, Will, nothing else?"

"Oh, yeah. She said maybe you were not up to my standard of tall, skinny blonds with big tits, but she wanted to remind me that we had been friends for a long time and you were no stranger."

With that, she again said, "And that is all you talked about?"

"Well, she said she thought we were both still young, thought it would be nice if we had some kind of a relationship. She said the General would be the happiest man in the world if he thought there was a possibility that we might raise a family together and produce another MacMorogh to carry on the name. I promised her I would give it some thought."

"And you never told her that I was not still the same little pudgy redhead with the crooked teeth?" Tish asked.

"That is another thing, I think maybe I told her you were ravishingly beautiful or something like that. I don't think I told her I was smitten."

Then Tish once more, "And that is all?"

Will promised it was. "But I got to thinking about what she said." Then he took both her hands, "Tish, will you marry me?"

Her eyes got big as saucers; her hand flew to her mouth. She looked at him, and he was not smiling. He had a very serious, questioning look on his face.

"You are serious aren't you?" she said.

"As serious as I have ever been. My grandmother said there was not much better recommendation than to have been practically raised together."

Tish leaned into him and began to cry. Will stroked her head. When she rose, she looked into his face. "If you are asking me because you love me, and for no other reason, I would love to marry you. I have been in love with you for as long as I can remember. But there are some things you have to know first."

She had told him there had been other men in in her life, one in particular for a long time. There had been others, but nothing serious. He needed to know a little more about her than he knew. After she had seen him the last time and they'd had that wonderful weekend together, her life had changed. By Christmas, she was very ill. She reminded Will of what she had told him earlier.

Then she said that after the sickness had subsided, she went into a deep depression. Her wonderful mother took full charge of everything, got her back on her feet, and encouraged her to go back to school for her final semester. Her application for graduate school at Cambridge was accepted. Her mother was determined not to let her give that up.

She began to live again; she was delighted with the way things were going. As soon as she arranged with Cambridge, her mother went to England and got a suitable flat for them, and their plans were well underway. She made friends with two couples who were also going to Cambridge. They were older and had kids. They all encouraged each other.

On the day they left, they were at Midway Airport. The group was flying over together. She was standing watch over several of the children while their mothers went to the rest room or did last minute shopping. As she stood there holding a child, a lady walked by who looked familiar. The lady turned and came back to her. She asked her if she was the Mullens girl. Then Tish said that the lady was Miss Annie. Will's grandmother.

Will said, "My grandmother? What was she doing at Midway airport? She has never told me about that."

Tish told him the rest. Miss Annie asked her first what she was doing there. Tish explained that she was on her way to Cambridge. She continued to look at the child. Tish told her that she was watching over the lot while their mothers did last minute shopping.

They had been in Cambridge maybe three months. Tish settled into school; her mother, of course, made friends and was enjoying being with her. On a Saturday morning, they were getting ready to leave the flat for their regular Saturday shopping and walk in the park. Then the telly rang, and it was Miss Annie. She was in town and wanted to come by to say hello.

Again, Will was astonished. "What?"

Tish excused herself for a moment, and then came back with her handbag and some tissues. Then she continued. "She arrived at the flat about half an hour later. When the bell chimed, I went to the door; my mother went into the bedroom.

"I welcomed her and told her she was a pleasant surprise. Then I asked her what had brought her to London."

Tish pulled a brown envelope from her bag, untied the binder, and spilled out three small photographs. They were face down.

"Miss Annie took these out and told me to look. She showed me this one first; this was your grandfather when he was a toddler. Then she spilled this one out," and she showed that one to him. "This was your father about the same age. Then she spilled this one out," and she showed it to him. "Of course, that is you."

Then Tish looked at him. "Miss Annie turned to me and said she was concerned about the child I had been holding at the airport. She told me to look at the eyes in the photographs. I did. About that time, my mother came out with the child." Then the tears began to flow.

"Miss Annie's next words were, 'That is Will's son isn't it?'

We have a son, Will. His name is Charles Mullens and he was born April 30, 1951."

"Why was I not—?"

Tish would not let him finish. She touched his lips with the tips of three fingers. "No why, no if, no past to try to change. All that is important is that the last time we were together, a new life began. We have to go forward with that new life." She pulled Will close to her, and they both began to cry.

They regained their composure and Will said, "And where is he now?"

Tish looked at her watch. "It is ten here, so it is four a.m. in London. Right about now, Mother is shaking him awake and preparing to start the journey here. They will fly to New York tomorrow and then arrive here Saturday at noon. I could not bear to put my mother or our child through fourteen hours on the plane in one day. Both would have been exhausted."

"You have pictures, surely?" Will said.

"Come inside; the light is better." Lying on the coffee table was an album three inches thick. They sat together, Will in a large easy chair and Tish perched on the arm.

"Let's begin with the last page; those will be the latest pictures."

Will carefully turned to the end of the album. There, with a big grin, dimples, and new front teeth already crooked, sat his son. Will began to cry, and then sobbed as he never had before. He started over at the front. The cover page was a large photograph his grandmother had provided. It was a picture of Will standing next to a Grumman Bearcat fighter. Underneath in big print: "MY DADDY." Each time they had added pictures to the album, Charles was a part of it. Each time, they pointed to the picture and asked him who it was.

Tish had taken hundreds of pictures and had documented many. She had even kept a diary of special events in the child's life. The first time she was halfway through changing a wet diaper and he cut loose again, spraying her in the eye with warm pee. His first word, "bud," which was "bird." His first step, his first tooth, on and on. On every page or two, another note. Several pages over, Tish's mother had taken a picture of Tish and Charles, side by side, kneeling by his bed. "And take good care of my daddy," *was* the inscription underneath. Tears rolled down Will's face again. Will turned each page slowly, touched some of the pictures as if touching the boy. Then out of the clear, he said, "You know that your transition into the most beautiful girl in the world has not gone unnoticed."

Tish left Will to the book. When she came back into the room, his head was on his chest, and tears had dried on his cheeks. He was asleep. She leaned over, kissed the top of his head, and shook him awake. She stood before him in a sheer black nightgown that left nothing to the imagination. "Don't you think it is time you came to bed?"

The next day, Will wanted to know how his grandmother could have gone so long, keeping the secret. Without further questioning, Tish began, "When your grandmother, now known as Grannie Annie, came to us that day, I asked if she had expressed her suspicion to anyone else. She had not.

"I was rude to her and apologized later. I told her that outside of her, my mother, and me, no one knew anything about our son. I told her that if the news about him came back to me through anyone else's lips, I would blame her. She could be damn well sure I would hide the child, and she would never see him again. I knew at some point that I had to tell you. But it was my responsibility, and no one else's. Your grandmother came again several months later, this time to tell me that you were missing in action." Then tears came again, and they both cried a little more.

"Your grandmother was an angel; she came to see us frequently. As soon as there was news that you were in captivity, she came to England to tell us. I loved her visits and got a lot of joy seeing how much she adored Charles , but each time she came, she was bearing bad news. I was so afraid that one day she would arrive and it would be all over. The time that she came to tell us that you were free, and homeward bound was one of the greatest days of our lives."

Saturday

The Lockheed Constellation, guided by a ground crew member, taxied into position at the gate. After the engines were off and the props quit turning, an airline employee drove the air stairs to the side of the airplane. He brought the stairs flush against the cabin and directly in front of the door. The man then bounded up the stairs and slapped on the door, signaling the stewardess inside to open up and begin disembarking passengers.

The first person out of the door and down the air stairs was an airline employee. The second was a lanky little boy with a shock of red hair, his white shirttail half in, half out, with black shorts and white stockings, one halfway down his calf. His shoes were black and white oxfords, with one lace loose. He raced across the tarmac and into the terminal.

His deep-set blue eyes were wide open, and his head swiveled back and forth as he sought his mother. Once he spotted her, he ran, a big smile on his face, dimples deep in his cheeks. Tish dropped to both knees as he approached, and they hugged tightly.

Will, a little uncomfortable as to what to do, dropped to one knee next to Tish. The little boy stepped back from his mother's arms, stuck his small hand out to Will, and in a British accent said, "Sir, I'm Charles Mullens. And you must be my father?"

It was hard for Will to hold back, but he looked straight into the blue eyes, held the small hand in his, shook, and said, "Yes, I am pleased to be your father."

"My mum has told me all about you." Then he went into Will's open arms; Will held him close and felt his little heart racing as much as his own. Then the child pushed back. "What should I call you?" he asked.

Will said, "What would you like to call me?"

"My chum calls his father Papa. I like that."

Will said, "Then Papa it is. What should I call you?"

By this time, Maureen had made it off the plane with all of their belongings and was standing listening to the interchange between the two. Charles looked up at her and wrapped his small hand around two of her fingers. Then looking back at Will, with a big grin and deep dimples: "My friends call me 'Moon.'" At that moment, the three began a new life together.

50

The General's Finale

The fact that the General had the last word was not that he insisted upon it. The rest of the family had, years before, accepted that and indeed, the last word was his. He assured Jack on his last visit that he was well pleased with the manuscript and was confident that the rest of the family concurred. He accepted the final pages and said, "I will take it from here."

Jack assumed that meant he would have the book printed and bound. That was a correct assumption. It was the plans for presentation of the book to the family that took everyone by surprise, with the exception of Winston and Matilda Jackson. The General visited at length with the couple in their home and shared the purpose of the visit only with Miss Annie.

Shortly after that visit, two days to be precise, a letter went out to the immediate family; it requested that a special family meeting on a date specified in his communiqué. Once he received verification that there were no conflicts with family on that date, he sent out invitations to that meeting to include ten additional persons. That letter of invitation stressed the importance of their attendance. The event would begin with a cocktail reception at Laura's Lodge beginning at 6:00 p.m. Dinner would be at 7:30. All out of town guests had reservations at the MacMorogh-owned hotel unless advised otherwise.

Ten days prior to the date, the General, accompanied by a nurse recommended by Dr. Rubin, flew on a commercial flight to Glasgow and returned with Mollie MacMorogh, aged ninety-nine. Three days before the date, Jonathan and Winston Jackson flew to Mobile, Alabama, in Jonathan's airplane, to pick up Maudie Lee Jackson, aged eighty-five. On the day of the event, Mrs. Abernathy's son and daughter-in-law drove to Jackson to get Mrs. Abernathy, aged one hundred.

On that same day, the other out of town guests began to arrive early in the day. A special buffet luncheon was set up in a meeting room at the hotel. Miss Annie hosted that affair. Limousines rented in Memphis arrived at the hotel; the guests drove to Laura's Lodge, arriving precisely at 5:49 P.M. Dr. Rubin had an emergency and arrived forty-five minutes late. The General promptly chastised him: it was poor planning on Dr. Rubin's part.

The General arranged for a pianist from Memphis to play during the cocktail reception. The music chosen spanned one hundred years; Miss Annie had selected it with the help of Dr. Bea.

Dinner was in the men's parlor. The décor was new. The dinner tables were set in the form of a horseshoe. The General explained the seating position. The oldest members of the family, or of the company, sat at the head table. That included, from left to right, Maudie Lee Jackson, Matilda Jackson, Winston Jackson, the General, Annie MacMorogh, Mollie MacMorogh, and Mrs. Virgie Abernathy.

On one side of the horseshoe sat the next generation of family or of friends who were influential in the family or the company. That side included, Jonathan MacMorogh, June Wittenberg, Dr. Beatrice MacMorogh, Dr. Rubin Cohen, Jack Ward, Adrianna Breaux, Nelson Goodall, and Jan Plow.

On the opposite side was the next generation of family or of friends who were influential in the family or company. That included, in this order, William MacMorogh Letitia MacMorogh, Charles Mullens, Maureen Mullens, Rev. John Pope, and his wife, Lucinda Pope.

The General welcomed all and made a short presentation explaining that the event was, foremost, a family reunion. He explained also that it was an opportune time to present to the family members the finished version of **Volume 1, Book 1, The History of The MacMorogh Family and Companies.** He would be remiss, he stated, not to include the people who had played an important role both in the life of the company as well as in the lives of the family members. .

The Reverend John Pope blessed the event and the food. After his touching words, and over the period of the next hour and a half, the group enjoyed dinner. There was pleasant conversation and tales of times past including a few laughs and a few tears.

After dinner, the General again took the floor. He wanted first to thank Jack Ward, his fiancé Adrianna Breaux, Jan Plow, and Nelson Goodall, all part of the staff who had superbly developed what he considered to be a masterpiece. At which time the family members gave a standing ovation. After they took their seats, the General presented Jack with a plaque making him an honorary member of the clan MacMorogh. He then gave Jack the opportunity to say a few words. Jack proudly accepted the membership; he truly felt he was a member.

Mollie also accepted the invitation to say a few words. She briefly stated the fact that she was so very proud of the accomplishments of the family in business. She then praised Miss Annie for the accomplishment of keeping the family together despite the sometimes-difficult situations they experienced.

Miss Maudie Lee Jackson echoed those words, but also added that Winston had been a dear son. She praised him and Matilda for teaching their daughter that she could be whatever she chose to be. Last, she was pleased to no end that her grandson was taking the stand that he was in these trying times.

The General then wanted to make note of the fact that a member of the fifth generation was in attendance, and he asked Charles Mullens, also known as Moon, to stand. He stood and was obviously pleased to be recognized.

The General stood and asked Winston to stand also. "In conclusion," he said, and as he paused, he put his arm over Winston's shoulder and continued, "You have heard the kind words of my mother and Winston's mother, saying that they were proud of the two of us." He then turned his head and nodded in the direction of Old Church and the cemetery. "I think that Seamus is standing there on the hill, looking down here and saying he is real proud of his two sons also."

It took a few seconds for that to sink in.

Following is the galley sheet that crossed Jack Ward's desk that day in June 6, 1958. The information in the article and the additional information gathered by Adrianna Breaux and Jan Plow gave rise to *the story*.

Mullens-MacMorogh

Letitia Mullens and William MacMorogh were brought together in Holy Matrimony Saturday evening,in the Garden District home of Dr.Beatrice MacMorogh, aunt and former guardian of the groom. Officiating the ceremony was the Rev. John Pope, Senior pastor of the River Methodist Church (A.M.E.) in Birmingham.

Presenting the bride was her mother, Mrs. Maureen Mullens. he was attended by Mrs. Anne MacMorogh, mother of the groom and Dr. Carole Anne MacMorogh, sister of the groom.

Attending the groom as best man was his uncle, and former guardian, Jonathan MacMorogh,

Ring bearer was Charles Mullens, seven year old son of the bride and groom. Music was by Mr. Winston Jackson who sang *The Lord's Prayer.*

Also attending the private ceremony was, (USAF Gen,Ret) William MacMorogh, New Cotswold, Miss. Mr. Charles Chacherie, States Attorney General, State of Louisiana, and his wife Addie, Mrs. Matilda Jackson, New Cotswold, Miss. Mr. Nate Ludlow of North Shore, LA. Miss June Wittenberg, New Cotswold, Miss .and Dr. Rubin Cohen, New Cotswold, Miss,

The couple will reside in North Shore, La. and London, England where the bride is currently a broadcast reporter for the London News Agency BBC.

Acknowledgements

Over the three years that it has taken for this book to come to fruition, I have been fortunate to have many supporters. Among my first readers, Gerald Walton, emeritus English professor, university administrator and author, Carol McKay, author, Jon McConal, retired newspaper columnist and author, Bill McKay and Gail Joyce walked me through this minefield of self- publication. My dear friend Bob Ferguson gave counsel on legal issues. To all of them, I will be forever grateful.

Foremost, I have to acknowledge my wonderful wife Judy who has shown me the meaning of patience, supported my every effort, and proved to be adept at critique and editing. I dedicate this book to her.

Made in the USA
San Bernardino, CA
19 April 2014